THE SORCERESS

Glinda's eyes danced and she clucked her tongue. "Afraid of a little girl?"

"I'm getting there." Promethus gestured back toward the staircase. "After you."

"You don't have to be chivalrous, with *ladies first*, and all that. I can follow."

"No, that is one thing you cannot do. You blaze your own path, Glinda. And I prefer to follow after your steps. *Please*." He gestured again.

"You are afraid." Glinda danced up the stairs, laughing.

"Yes." Promethus whispered. "Unwise power corrupts like rust. Weakens and corrodes integrity, and it can only be removed through harsh cleansing. I fear your cleansing will be harsher than you know."

CROWN OF THE DREAMER

The Hidden History of Oz, Book Two

TARL TELFORD

The Hidden History of Oz, Book Two: Crown of the Dreamer

Published by Emerald Engine Studios

Cover art by Tarl Telford; images used with permission

Copyright © 2013 Tarl Telford
Guide for Parents, Copyright © 2014

All rights reserved.

ISBN: 0615880584
ISBN-13: 978-0615880587

DEDICATION

To my wife, Aimee—my reader, my always story-listener, and the engine that brings the magic of my dreams to life.

CONTENTS

	Acknowledgments	i
	Author's Note	ii
	Introduction	iii

Section One: Tears

Chapter		
1	Schemes and Things	1
2	Opening the Curtain	8
3	Golden Cage	19
4	Wizard's Waltz	26
5	Shot in the Dark	34
6	Roses Have Thorns	43
7	Amber Eyes	50
8	Standing Army	58
9	Silver Mirror Tells No Tales	66
10	Wizardly Vision	69
11	Schemes and Dreams	75
12	Secret Apprentice	81
13	Winds of Change	90

Chapter	Section Two: Pearls	99
14	Secret Spring	101
15	The Strength of an Army	110
16	Stones and Shadows	119
17	Among the Munchkins	129
18	The Road West	136
19	Emerald Spectacles	142
20	The Search for the Wizard	148
21	The Truth About Men	154
22	The Man Behind the Curtain	160
23	Glinda's Nightmare	168
24	Seeds of Destiny	175
25	Battle of Mighty Miss Gulch	181
26	Mirror, Mirror	189
27	A Voice in the Darkness	197
28	Sister Feud	204
29	Treasure and Refuse	213
30	Eye in the Sky	220
31	How the West was Lost	229

Chapter	Section Three: Battle Cry	233
32	Oath Unto Death	235
33	The Fighting Girls	241
34	Night to be Forgotten	247
35	Unremembered Treasures	255
36	Secret of the Wizard	261
37	Morning Magic	265
38	The Witch's Army	275
39	The Proud King	284
40	Human Outside	293
41	Revelation of the Kalidahs	300
42	Morn'light War	309

Appendix		319
	Timeline	321
	The Players	325
	Locations	327
	Sneak Preview	329
	Guide for Parents	333
	On the Web	339
	Credits	340
	About the Author	341

ACKNOWLEDGMENTS

Special thanks to my family, who listen to my stories and answer random questions when they are asked. The creation of a book is a solitary work surrounded by a strong support system.

This book creation is made possible by continual advances in technology which allow dreamers like me to put dreams to paper and share them.

And thanks to you, dear reader, for sharing this dream with me.

AUTHOR'S NOTE

I believe in you, the reader. This is a special trust that we share—you and I—and I want you to know that I recognize and appreciate that. I trust you enough to share my dreams and stories of these characters that fascinate me so much. I enjoy exploring the history of the Land of Oz. There are hundreds of years' worth of history and culture to explore.

The past influences the present and gives momentum to the future. By understanding the events and attitudes of the past, we can understand the present situation and see the story for what it is—a series of connected events that finds a resolution. As we understand the story, we can plan for the future. This may seem to be a lot for one book to handle, but I assure you, the journey is worth the time and the effort.

The second portion of this trust is what you, the reader, place in me as an author. You trust me with your precious time, and (in some cases) with your hard-earned money. You trust that the time you spend with me, exploring the Hidden History of Oz, will be worth it. I can only offer my assurance and my enthusiasm that this is a story that I have enjoyed both creating and reading.

These characters have become close to my heart. I care about all of their successes and failures. I cannot dissuade them, no matter how hard I try, from their actions. If you know anything about Glinda, you know that she has a mind of her own. She is going to learn from her own hard experience, no matter what happens.

The people that shaped the Land of Oz have shared their stories with me, and I have shared their stories (so far) with you. There is far more to tell, and the stories are coming.

I thank you for joining me in the journey.

INTRODUCTION

The Hidden History of Oz is a prequel series to The Wonderful Wizard of Oz, written in 1900 by L. Frank Baum. This series explores the characters and events that shaped the Land of Oz. While Baum's original stories followed Dorothy and Ozma, with some of their friends as heroes, the Hidden History stories follow Glinda, Oscar (the Wizard), their friends, and the Witches, as they follow their goals, and seek to gain and control power.

The basic premise of The Hidden History series is as follows: Oz is a magical land powered by human dreams. The dreams in our world affect what happens in the Land of Oz. Dreams are filtered through the Emerald Engine and emerge into the Land of Oz as magic. Oscar Diggs is a young ventriloquist from pre-Civil War America who is transported to Oz through magical means unknown to him. He went up in a balloon and fell asleep. When he awoke, he was in a magical land, dropping down in the middle of a battle. This experience is related in *The Hidden History of Oz, Book One: The Witch Queens*.

Oscar does not consider himself anything special. He likes telling stories and entertaining people. The people, however, esteem him a great wizard. Why? Because he is more powerful than anyone they have ever known. What makes Oscar so powerful, compared to all of the people and Witches in the Land of Oz? He dreams. Nobody in Oz dreams.

Remember, Oz is powered by human dreams, as they pass through the Emerald Engine. Oscar's dreams are unfiltered. They change the land around him. Through no effort on his part, he can change the very Land of Oz. This is why he is the Wizard.

Glinda is a young sorceress who will one day be the most powerful sorceress in the Land of Oz. But today, she is still young and impetuous. She is the only one in the Land of Oz who has red hair. Her power grows through study and experimentation. She is very curious, and she wants to establish power to prepare for future conflicts. War is coming, as it always does, and Glinda wants to be ready.

The final piece of The Hidden History series is the relationship that this story has to the original works written by L. Frank Baum. The Hidden History series sets its course by using The Wonderful Wizard of Oz as its target. By using the facts contained in that book, and only using Baum's other books as suggestions, this author is crafting a history that expands Baum's vision and gives greater roles to the characters he introduced. The history of the Land of Oz is explored—it is more than merely a faerie land. It is a place where dreams make a difference, where good things happen, and bad things happen, too. It is a place worth exploring, for in the dreams we see lived out by others, we are able to see our own dreams more clearly.

SECTION ONE: TEARS

1 SCHEMES AND THINGS

"If you all control yourselves, we will have the Wizard exactly where we want him." Glinda said. She addressed her Fighting Girls and all the maidens of her court. "The Sky Wizard's Ball is two days away. Everything will be perfect."

Glinda's definition of perfect didn't match exactly what the other girls thought, but Glinda was in charge. It was her castle, her sorcery, and her party. She controlled what happened in the South country in the Land of Oz. She had been here nearly two years, and the land had blossomed under her watchful eye. She felt confident sharing her scheme with the girls—they could be trusted.

Glinda's right-hand girl, Wickrie-Kells, the captain of the Fighting Girls, listened half-intently to Glinda's speech. Mostly she was focused on the carrot in her hand. She heard only about every third word from Glinda's mouth.

'Control…will…Wizard…exactly…Ball…days…perfect.' *Exactly. That was all she needed to know. If there was anything else, Glinda would tell her.*

"Wickrie, any thoughts you wish to share around that carrot?" Glinda asked. She tossed her red hair over her shoulder and raised an eyebrow.

"Truth? Good carrot. Good plan. I'll follow your lead." Wickrie-Kells smiled at Glinda's acceptance. That's what best friends were for. Wickrie already had her hands full with all of the new girls that had come to South Castle.

Glinda prided herself on attracting the best and brightest girls in all the Land of Oz to her court. Some of them were fine warriors, and they composed the Fighting Girls—Glinda's elite fighting force, led by Glinda's best friend, Wickrie-Kells. Some of them were singers, like Ola Griffin, who also served as Glinda's herald. Others served in research and experimentation. There were still others that stayed behind the scenes, maintaining the wondrous palace and tending the exotic gardens all around the castle. Glinda addressed them all today. Everyone was a part of this plan.

Ola Griffin closed her eyes and wrote with her bare fingers on the table. In her mind she divided her attention between Glinda's speech and the song she was composing.

> *Lost in the absence of doubt,*
> *I know there's no easy way out.*
> *Outside of this life,*
> *Romance like a knife…*

"Ola Griffin, paying attention, are we?" Glinda said. "Your lips are moving, but your eyes are not paying attention. Please share with us, if you will, what I just said?" Glinda folded her arms and narrowed her eyes at the blonde girl.

Ola Griffin ran her fingers through her hair and smiled. This was the easy part, quoting Glinda, *"We all know that Oscar Diggs, the Wonderful Wizard of Oz, arrived in our land two years ago this week. The Sky Wizard's Ball is to honor him, but more importantly, it is to bring him to me. You all have your assignments. There are those of you who are assigned to accompany the Wizard at various points during the Ball."*

It was exactly as Glinda had said it. The girls applauded.

Glinda narrowed her gaze, but then the smile drove the stubborn glare out of her eyes. It was quite a display of memory and elocution. She even paused correctly saying Oscar's name. That drew some giggles from the younger girls.

Ola Griffin had the best memory of any of them. Her talents were very nearly a match for Glinda's keen mind.

The red-haired sorceress continued, "You know your roles and I expect that you will be suitably beautiful for the occasion. The rest of you—I am warning you now—the Wizard does not like to see anyone disappointed or let down. He will do whatever it takes to make you happy and smiling. On top of that, he likes pretty faces. Do not encourage him. Be polite and smile when he tells a joke or tells a story, but do not do anything—and I mean anything—that might interfere with our little scheme.

"Some of you will be leaving right after the ball for a joint training exercise with the Emerald Guardsmen. Let me express my gratitude right now for your exemplary efforts. You make me proud to call you friends."

Near the back of the hall a young teenage girl hung on Glinda's every word. She wasn't even supposed to be in here. Her parents were most recently from Munchkin Country, having left quickly after the harsh new laws were implemented. Eyve was too young to join the Fighting Girls, but she wanted to so badly. That desire drove her to break the rules and just follow the group into the hall. There was Wickrie-Kells, the Captain of the Fighting Girls—she was even taller in person. And there was Rala, and Corabinth, and Elka and Decla—she knew them from back home; both sisters wore their hair in side braids. These were names she had only heard of before, now she was right here, breathing the same air as they were. It was good air. It was good to be here. And Glinda had a good plan. The Wizard was important—too important to not let him know how wonderful he was. It was very absolutely clear that Glinda loved the Wizard. They were meant to be together.

When Glinda spoke, it was as if she was speaking directly to Eyve. The young girl's wide brown eyes took in every detail of the hall. This moment would be sealed into her mind and heart forever.

"There will be no additional smiling at the Wizard, batting of eyes, blowing kisses, or flirting in any way. The Wizard—Oscar—is mine, and I want him to realize in no uncertain terms, just how lucky he is to have me."

Far to the east and north of Glinda's palace, Kalinya, the Wicked Witch of the East, knocked on a door on the back side of Mount Munch. For nearly two years she had been waiting for this moment. If such a creature as she could drool in anticipation, she would, but she was very sensitive to water of any type. In addition to her water aversion, every last bit of blood and spit within her dried up two years ago, during the creation of her blood-sand armies in the Battle of Munchkin Fields.

Kalinya looked down on those faraway fields from her vantage point atop the mountain. These intervening months and years had been hard. Though she was the Wicked Witch of the East, and ruled over the Munchkins completely, she was a ghastly spectre of her former self. Where she had once been beautiful, the years of magic had taken their toll. The magic lines she had drawn on her skin to remember the spells marked her as a powerful witch once. Now, after the draining loss of all her blood, her face was sunken and aged. The magic lines crossed each other now, rendering their magic useless. What she lacked, though, in magic, she made up for in power.

Just this month she had enacted a law that forbade any Munchkin in the land from being taller than she was. It was a flattering rule, but a necessary one. It kept the Munchkins in line and fearful. So long as they feared her power, they were easy to control.

Two years—the endless months did not seem so awful now, here at the threshold of success. The terrible price she paid to create her blood-sand armies two years ago had aged her. Beauty was a thing of the past. She was a hideous shadow that ruled the Munchkins with flashing golden eyes. All of that would change today.

She knocked on the door of the small house on Mount Munch. This round dwelling served as the laboratory for the alchemist, Pipton Nikidik. Few knew of him. In fact, Kalinya had only met him two years ago, when she was on her way to an appointment with death. Glinda had created a cloud and bound Kalinya with sandy vines so she could not escape. Kalinya was unceremoniously tossed on top of the cloud and sent northeast into the sky. After almost a full day, the cloud had thinned out as it approached Mount Munch. Her terrified screams had drawn the attention of a singular Munchkin high up on the mountain.

He stood up a ladder against the cloud and retrieved her from her floating prison, thereby earning the witch's gratitude. After learning her story, the Munchkin shared his. He was working on a concept that would peel back the years of time—it was one of his many projects under development. For such a promise of youth, Kalinya swore she would pay any price.

That price now rested in her pocket. Today marked the end of her journey. For two days she had traveled slowly through the forest to arrive at this point. The line-of-sight was not clear enough through the forest, so the magic of the Silver Slippers, as far as Kalinya knew, was useless.

Pipton Nikidik, the alchemist, answered the door. He stared at the Witch for several moments.

Kalinya could not be bothered with formalities. "Two years I have been waiting for this. You have finished?"

"I have finished the ointment. Remember, Witch, when you came down from the cloud, you promised to pay any price? Have you the pearl?"

Kalinya narrowed her amber eyes at the alchemist. "I have it. But I require proof before payment."

"Fair enough." He said. He opened the door and Kalinya followed him into a small laboratory.

The alchemist pulled the cloak up over his head and covered his face with a protective mask. "Stand back, please." He measured the volatile ingredients into a small vial.

"I hear you have taken the title of Professor." Kalinya forced the pleasantries as she waited.

Professor Nikidik carefully measured the liquid into a small dish. "Beware of the burning. Keep it out of your blood."

"What are you adding to the potion?"

"Ointment. It is a topical cream. You want to look younger to catch a man—a specific man, I assume, based on the price. Keep it out of your blood."

"I have no blood." Kalinya confessed.

The man paused and glanced up. His dark eyes studied the twisted magic lines etched deeply into the Witch's face. "Interesting. And yet you live. Where did it spill?"

"I spent it battling my sis—my enemies."

Professor Nikidik held out a small dish containing the ointment. "Your sample as proof."

Kalinya rubbed the ointment into her gnarled hands and gasped in pain as the magic infused her parchment skin and peeled back the years. Her clawlike hands unclenched to become young again. The skin filled out to become smooth and unwrinkled. She laughed in astonishment.

She stepped behind a privacy screen and applied the ointment to her neck and shoulders. She gasped and laughed in pain as the magic in the ointment burned back the years.

She held out the pearl over the top of the screen, and Professor Nikidik snatched it from her fingers. He passed in the vial of ointment. Kalinya applied the ointment liberally and screamed and laughed in pain as the beauty of her youth returned to her.

She pulled on her robes and shook out her dark hair. She cinched her belt around her narrow waist and laughed in glee. She stepped out, younger than she had been in half a lifetime.

Kalinya put her hands on her hips. She laughed and swiveled her hips back and forth in front of Professor Nikidik. "What would your wife say if she could see you now?"

Professor Nikidik held the pearl up to the light, examining it. He gestured back over his shoulder and turned the light on a statue behind him. It was a round-featured woman, pleasantly plump with a pretty face. The statue was carved exquisitely in marble. The likeness in stone was uncanny. Upon closer inspection, Kalinya recognized the fear in the statue's eyes. That could not be carved, no matter how skilled the artisan.

"Ask her." Nikidik said.

Kalinya stopped in shock. She gulped. Then she smiled and shook her finger at Nikidik. "You almost had me. I believed for a minute that she was real."

"Margolotte, this lovely young lady does not believe that you are real." He reached back and stroked the statue's cheek. "For a witch, you lack a great deal of understanding. How old did you say you were?"

"I'm...older than I look."

Nikidik frowned. "You look young now, but your voice sounds raspy. Do you sing?"

"I haven't in years."

"Start. It will clear your voice and help you sound young again. A spoonful of honey twice a day will help."

"How did Margolotte...?"

"She interrupted me while I was working. I am working on an Unguent of Animation. It will bring the inanimate to life. Things that are of a form, but have no life, can be brought into activity and being. I tire of cooking dinner for one."

"How much of this Unguent of Animation are you mixing?"

"I have sufficient ingredients to make a full flask."

"How much will it take to bring Margolotte back?"

"Only a single drop."

"I wish to purchase this unguent from you. I'm looking for an army."

Nikidik stuck the pearl in his pocket, and rubbed his hands together. "An army. Hmm. That is a large request, but I believe I can help you. It will cost you five pearls."

Kalinya smiled tightly. That was her last pearl that she had paid. "It will take some time."

"Fine. Margolotte isn't going anywhere. I will be here when you call again."

Kalinya turned to leave. As her young hand wrapped around the door handle, she stopped and looked back over her shoulder. Nikidik was watching her.

She tossed her hair and flashed her amber eyes at him. "Professor Nikidik, you rogue. What would your wife think?"

"Ask her."

"Next time. I am certain I will see her face-to-face. But now, I have some diabolical schemes to unleash upon an unsuspecting populace." She flashed a dazzling smile. "Wish me luck."

Professor Nikidik pulled out the pearl again and examined it. He looked over the top of the pearl at the beautiful young witch. "Tell me—this man you are spending a fortune to entice—is he worth it?"

"I have been told that he likes pretty faces. As it was long ago, so it is again today, there are none prettier than mine. I have a stop or two to make to visit my rivals in this burgeoning love triangle, and then…I'm off to see the Wizard."

In the center of the Land of Oz, the Emerald City rose as a shining beacon of protection and liberty. It was a city built on freedom and liberty. The Wonderful Wizard of Oz, Oscar Diggs—from the far away territory of Nebraska, in the western frontier of the United States of America—ruled the people kindly and fairly. He established laws based on the principles of equality, justice, and personal responsibility. He encouraged trade and welcomed all who were willing to abide by the laws of the city. Everyone knew the Wizard and loved him. He was powerful beyond their wildest imaginings, but he kept himself so approachable and affable that the people thanked him every moment they could get his attention.

In truth, the power that Oscar wielded was not of his choosing. The Land of Oz was powered by human dreams, and Oscar was a human dreamer. This close to the source of magic, his powerful dreams had an astounding effect on the city—new structures and designs appeared every night. This impressed the people greatly.

With all of the people coming into the Emerald City, a precautionary police force was established. The Emerald Guardsmen were the brave and skilled soldiers that kept the peace and patrolled the land around the Emerald City. They were led by Ombrosius Ambrosius—Omby-Amby to his friends—the Soldier with Green Whiskers. He was Oscar's best friend, and his right-hand man.

Oscar and Omby-Amby looked out over the Emerald Lands from Oscar's tower in the city. Oscar turned to look south.

"She's expecting me in two days. This is really a big deal to her."

"I know it is. Wickrie-Kells is looking forward to this. All of us together again. How long has it been?"

"Thirteen months for everybody. You've been down once. Wickrie has been up here twice. And I've gone down once. Then Glinda came partway back with me six months ago." He sighed. "Has it really been six months?" He forced a smile. "That's a long time."

"Both of you have been busy. The Emerald City is growing faster than either of us thought possible. Glinda is doing some amazing things in the South. She is becoming a powerful sorceress. You two are bringing peace to the land."

"Yes, peace, but not freedom—not liberty like I hoped." Oscar replied. He yawned and kept his eyes closed for a long second.

"How much sleep did you get?"

Oscar shrugged. "Enough."

"It's barely the middle of the morning. You should not be yawning. You've got to get more sleep. All of these dreams you dream change things—they are wearing you out."

"I have to go to my meetings. The people depend on me."

"The bureaucrats can run their own meetings. They don't need you in there to supervise."

"There is nobody else but me. I *have* to be there. And in the meetings with the architects, and the daily tours. They are doing amazing things in this city."

"It is you, the Wizard, that is doing these things. Every night you dream them. They only point them out."

Oscar shook his head and chuckled. "No, no, no. It is not me. Dreams just entertain me in the nighttime hours. They can't become real."

Now it was Omby-Amby's turn to sigh. His friend was wrong. He was powerful, and he was changing the Emerald City nightly with his dreams. Nobody in Oz dreamed, except the Wizard. The people did not know what dreams were, but they knew the Wizard had power, and that was enough.

"You have to get more sleep. Emerald City would not be happy with a dead wizard. You need sleep. You need to take a break. Let the people live their own lives for a day."

"They need me. I make them happy. You see their faces. They smile. They laugh. They like to be with me."

"You cannot make everybody happy all of the time. You can't make them so happy that they just accept liberty and freedom. Liberty is a personal choice and people have to choose it. They have to want it. Right now, many of them don't."

"I don't understand that." Oscar said, leaning his elbows down on the railing. He stared into the streets far below.

Omby-Amby joined him down on the rail. "Neither do I, Brud. Neither do I." He clapped a hand on Oscar's back and stood up. "You need to get some rest today. Glinda expects you down there bright-eyed in two days. Let the meetings go today. Let the people be happy and entertain themselves today. Take a day for you."

Oscar shook his head and smiled. "I am the Wizard. Like it or not, the humbug they believe is why I am in the tower. If they give me so much, how can I do less for them? Failure is not an option, Omby. I have to keep going."

"You are killing yourself."

"I know, but I have to keep going." He closed his eyes and leaned his head down on his arms. "I am so tired."

Kalinya admired herself in a small mirror for the fourth time since leaving the front door of Professor Nikidik. She saw all of her magic lines again. She was a beauty of probably twenty-four. Oh, those were marvelous years. The lads from miles around knew her and looked her way. Now they would again, but there was only one lad with the power to make her stay—that was the Wizard of Oz.

There still remained the matter of that red-haired brat, Glinda. The little princess was throwing a ball in honor of the Wizard. It probably meant a great deal to her to have it perfect. It certainly would be a shame to spoil such a well-planned occasion as that. A little chaos in the mix would upset the little apple's cart and maybe, just possibly, reveal the bad within. If she was anything like her mother—and Kalinya was sure that she was—Glinda would rage and destroy something. That would be a spectacle worth watching.

The question remained—how to spoil Glinda's day to the greatest possible degree? Kalinya turned west, toward the morning sun. Her sister was there, with the captive peoples of the Winkies and the Winged Monkeys. A slow smile spread on Kalinya's face. Actually, she should think of herself as Kally now. She was a younger woman, and her name Kalinya did not inspire love.

Kally looked west to search the sky for the distant Winged Monkeys that would be a wonderful addition to the Sky Wizard's Ball.

She wiggled her toes in the Silver Slippers and sighted a high point on the distant horizon. She took one, two, three steps and she was gone.

2 OPENING THE CURTAIN

Oscar paced back and forth in the garden. These past two days had passed quickly in travel and preparations. Now it was down to a matter of minutes before the Sky Wizard's Ball. They were all counting on him. He was the one that would make or break this grand celebration.

So it was that Eyve discovered the Wizard in Glinda's rose garden, muttering and pacing back and forth. She was nearly as tall as the young man with the carefully styled yet awkward hair.

"You're talking to yourself." She said.

"I expect I am, yes. It's been quite a day for me. This is quite a place. Your Lady Glinda is quite the hostess."

"Oh no, she's not my—"

"No matter." Oscar waved away the reply. "She expects really a lot of me today, but nobody will tell me a thing. They have some plan, I'm sure of it. I know how to read an audience, and they are all of the same mind. I can't even get any of them to laugh. Can you believe that? Me, the Wizard, unable to conjure up even a giggle."

So he was the Wizard. He was much different than what she expected. "So if you're the Wizard, can't you just magic something and make everything right? That's what you did for my city."

"What city is that?" Oscar cleared his throat and spoke more proudly. "I mean, I've done so much for so many cities…no?"

"Really? I'm not buying it." Eyve raised her eyebrow. "You need to be better than that."

"I'm a humbug. They are all going to hate me. I'm not who they say I am."

"You came out of the clouds, right?"

Oscar nodded.

"And you built Emerald City. I've seen it shining and sparkling in the sky. Even the sky is green above it. That isn't something that just anyone can do. Glinda loves you. You are amazing. You are the Wizard. Everybody sees it. Even if you don't see it. I can see you need some help. Here, give me your hand. When you get in to see Glinda, take her hand like this. Look into her eyes. Think about how her hair blows in the wind, how she smiles, and how she laughs. That will make your eyes smile—like that. Good. Then, when you have her all to yourself, kiss her three times. One for love. Two for luck. Three for lollipops."

"Love, luck, and lollipops?"

"This will be the most amazingly romantic night ever. You and Glinda are so cute."

"Oh. Cute. Okay."

They were interrupted by the clearing of a throat behind them. "Your Wonderfulness...sir. They are ready for you."

"Thank you Omby." Oscar turned to the girl, Eyve. "Thank you, my dear."

"Remember."

"Love, luck, and lollipops. I've got it." As Oscar turned to go, he looked at Omby-Amby, "*Your Wonderfulness?*"

"You were entertaining a lovely young lady. I felt decorum was in order."

Oscar nodded and chuckled. "She's a good kid. I'll see you inside."

Omby-Amby clapped his friend on the back and smiled. It was going to be a good day.

"I've got a sword, too. Do you want to see?" Eyve asked.

Omby turned around to see a shining blade pointed right at his face.

One hour until the ceremonial bell chimed to begin the Sky Wizard's Ball, and everything was perfect. Still, Glinda worried.

Oscar was here, but he was not himself. Omby-Amby wouldn't explain it. Oscar just shrugged and said that he had been busy. At last he showed up on the stairs. Glinda came up to take his hand. She stopped one step below him so that he was taller. Her red hair was beautifully done in ringlets that cascaded over her shoulders.

Oscar, this land lives for you—everyone loves you, and you seem to love everyone. If you weren't here, the land would not be the same. You—Oz the Great and Terrible—The Wonderful Wizard, are the Land of Oz to many of these people. They see your power and they trust, knowing that everything will be okay. Those were the words Glinda wanted to say. Those were the words that she believed and wanted desperately to share with Oscar. However, what came out of Glinda's mouth was much different. "Gold would have looked better on your emerald-green suit instead of silver."

"I like silver." Oscar mumbled. He dug into his pocket and pulled out a wrapped gift. "I hope you like this."

Glinda opened the package. It held a silver chain hung with a carved wooden pendant. In the tangled Celtic knotwork on the pendant, a blue-painted teardrop featured prominently in the center. "Oscar, it's lovely. Where did you get this? I've never seen anything like it."

"I made it. I have a workshop, you know."

"I didn't know."

"I had some time." He shrugged. "It is a reminder of what we are building. No more tears. There will be peace—no more tears."

"I love it. Help me on?" Glinda lifted her curled hair away from her neck, and Oscar reached around her neck to clasp the chain in back. He focused on hooking the small clasp on the eyelet. He did not immediately notice her eyes widening and her lips slightly pouting. When he did, he smiled awkwardly. Glinda dropped her hair over his hand and she placed her hands on his hips. "I have missed you, Oscar."

Oscar looked down and noticed that he was taller than Glinda. He stepped down to the same step that she was on. Now they were about the same height. "I have missed you, too, Glinda. Why don't you come up to the Emerald City? There are questions I want to ask you."

"You can ask me now."

Oscar smiled and dodged the question. "This is your day, not mine. This pomp and circumstance is nice. It suits you."

"I think it suits you better than me. You are the entertainer. The people love you. I like to curl up with a book or two."

"Or twelve." Oscar interjected.

Glinda laughed, agreeing. "Or twelve." She took his hands and squeezed them. "We need you here. You would be happy here."

Oscar's smile didn't make it up to his eyes. "I know you want that." He kissed her quickly on the lips. "One for love. Two for luck. Three for lollipops."

"Three? If you keep this up, the lollipop makers will be in guild status before the year is up."

"If it were up to me, I'd grant them guild status this week."

Glinda smiled and cocked her head to the side. "Why isn't it up to you?"

In the rose garden, Omby-Amby stepped back and slapped away the blade with his scabbard. "If you draw a blade, be prepared to use it."

The girl, Eyve, giggled and held her blade rock-steady at the Soldier with Green Whiskers.

Omby-Amby smiled. "You look like you know a thing or two."

"I was the best before we left."

Omby-Amby drew his sword from its scabbard. "Best in a small pond is still only small."

"Tabulo said I was going to be better than him."

"Tabulo? I've heard that name. Munchkin. He said that about you?" Omby-Amby launched into a quick attack that drew the girl's sword both high and low. She blocked his blade and drove it point-first into the ground.

"Two years ago." Eyve smiled. "I got better."

The soldier pulled his sword tip from the ground and rubbed a hand over his whiskered chin. "Apparently. How well do you know Winko's Sickle?" He launched into another attack, drawing the girl's sword wide, then stepping inside her guard and pulling her close to toss her over his hip. His sword arm kept her sword away. "Not very well."

"Do you know Crying Lion Whisker?" Eyve asked in return. Without waiting for an answer, she shot her free hand up and grabbed one of the soldier's green whiskers and plucked it out. She spun and whirled away, giggling and pointing her sword at him.

"You made that up."

Omby smiled and launched into another attack. They ranged up and down the rose corridor and through the arch into the lily circle. Then Eyve stepped back to catch her breath.

"I had fun. I'm Eyve." She sheathed her shorter sword and bowed to the Soldier with Green Whiskers.

Omby-Amby returned the respectful bow. "Well done, Eyve. Try out for the Fighting Girls. You would make a good addition. Your swordplay is excellent. Better than Wickrie-Kells, even." When he saw the girl's eyes widen into an excited scream, he waved his hands to stop the coming storm. "Don't tell her I said that. She might just prove how good with a sword she really is."

"Really? You really mean that?"

"Are you here for the ball? Stick around for a few days. I'll make sure that you get to show your stuff." The soldier flicked his wrist out, snapping his blade at a blossom. He stepped forward and caught the falling blossom as it began to slip off its severed stem. He held the flower out to the girl. "I'll be watching for you."

Eyve took the flower gently and looked up to the soldier's smiling face. She raised the blossom to her face and breathed deeply. No flower ever smelled as sweet.

Kally, the former Kalinya, raced from horizon to horizon, using the power of the Silver Slippers. In her hands she held a golden cage. In the cage was a screaming Winged Monkey. Kally stopped when she came within sight of Glinda's palace.

The South Castle shone brilliantly on the edge of the desert. It was more a city now than the castle-laboratory it had been in the days of Smith & Tinker, inventors extraordinaire. Now the buildings extended halfway down the cliffs toward the Deadly Desert below. Glinda had made this place amazing. Kally stopped in her tracks. Even the Winged Monkey stopped and oooh'ed appropriately.

"Do you want to see inside?" Kally asked the monkey. It nodded vigorously. "Then you must keep quiet until I bring you inside. Then you can make all the noise you want."

The monkey clapped its hands. Kally smiled. The devious plan danced in her golden eyes. The chaos would be extraordinary.

"This place is good at keeping time." Oscar noted to Wickrie-Kells as they stood in line to be announced.

"You have no idea." The taller girl smiled to herself. She cast her amber eyes down at the shorter Wizard. He was fidgeting slightly. "Concerns about anything?" She asked.

Oscar stopped fidgeting. "Just pre-show jitters. I know how important this extravaganza is to Glinda."

Wickrie-Kells shook her head. Her light brown ponytail swung back and forth on her back. "No, you really have no idea, Oscar. But I believe you have it in you to make it a good night. Just go to Glinda. Everyone who smiles at you doesn't need a story. Just go to Glinda."

Oscar knitted his brow. "Okay." He said hesitantly.

Wickrie-Kells took Oscar's arm and squeezed it and patted his hand. "Trust me. Glinda just wants you to see how much you mean to her."

"That's really not necessary. I thought she knew that I—"

"Liberty and justice for all, right? Glinda is free to act. In this case, however, *you* are not. Just keep your feet moving forward. The girls will guide you to Glinda."

"More than one? I must be a lucky man tonight." He straightened his jacket and stood a little taller.

Wickrie-Kells rolled her eyes as she closed them and turned her head up toward the ceiling. Now Oscar was bouncing jauntily. She shook her head and tried not to smile. Invisible whistling birds sounded all around them.

Oscar glanced off to the side as a golden-eyed girl suddenly appeared. She stepped up to the front of the line, smiled at the herald, Ola Griffin, and then proceeded into the ballroom. Oscar noticed a flash of silver as her feet walked quickly beneath her swishing skirts. He kept watching to see if the silver flashed again.

Wickrie-Kells cleared her throat. Oscar stood up quickly and smiled sheepishly at the taller girl. "Do you see something?"

"Yes. Actually, I thought I saw…" Oscar's revelation died under the withering gaze of Wickrie-Kells. "No. Not a thing."

Wickrie-Kells narrowed her eyes and watched the girl disappear toward the pile of gifts. Then it was their turn. Ola Griffin turned to them and announced in a voice as clear as it was beautiful, "From his home among the Sky Wizards, the founder of the Emerald City, and teller of stories loved and dear—The Wonderful Wizard of Oz!"

Wickrie-Kells pulled Oscar forward. They paused at the top of the stairs. The ballroom was filled with brightly costumed people from across the Land of Oz. They looked up at him and applauded and cheered. There was love and admiration in their eyes as they looked on their Wizard. Wickrie-Kells nodded to Rala, a dark-haired girl nearby, and she slowly began her approach.

Oscar smiled and raised his hand. He surveyed the crowd, sizing them up and noting which guests were the most enthusiastic in their appreciation. They would make a welcome group for his stories later.

Then he saw the girl again. She picked up a golden cage from among the piles of presents.

Ola Griffin's voice rang clear again, "Your hostess for the evening, the Ruby Sorceress, Glinda—"

The terrified screech of the Winged Monkey cut off Glinda's introduction as she rose from the Ruby Throne. Everyone turned to look at the ceiling as the screaming monkey leaped from pillar to pillar.

On her raised dais, Glinda stared in stunned horror. Then her face got red and her eyes grew stormy. In a matter of two moments Glinda's angry face was as red as her hair.

Omby-Amby leaped into action. He grabbed the nearest non-lethal item he could find as a club—a long loaf of bread—and swung at the diving monkey. He chased the monkey around the room. Several knocked over candles lit a tapestry on fire. A quick-thinking young girl ran for the punch bowl to douse the flames.

Oscar whistled at the Winged Monkey, holding out his hands and snapping his fingers. Without his noticing, Wickrie-Kells disappeared from Oscar's side.

Oscar was joined quickly by Ola Griffin. She smiled at him and reached her hands out also. She raised her voice in song—a catchy tune about a dancing star that lost its place in the sky and fell to Oz and made the first faerie magic. The orchestra quickly joined in and played the jaunty melody. The people danced and laughed. Everyone loved *The First Faerie*.

Oscar ran down the stairs after the monkey. The monkey screamed and leaped and stopped on a chandelier. Wickrie-Kells returned to the ballroom with her bow in hand. She nocked an arrow and drew back the bowstring. She took careful aim and let fire.

The Winged Monkey leaped away from the chandelier. The arrow whistled past the monkey, and the razor-sharp onyx arrowhead sliced through one of the support ropes. The chandelier creaked and the remaining ropes groaned.

Omby-Amby grabbed a heavy round loaf of bread from the banquet table and reared his arm back to launch the loaf at the monkey. Glinda saw this and screamed, "NO!"

The monkey also saw this and laughed at him. This was great fun.

Omby-Amby let it fly.

The Winged Monkey folded its wings and dropped below the trajectory of the baked projectile. The loaf flew harmlessly past the Winged Monkey. Omby-Amby's eyes grew wide as he saw the inescapable target of his unfortunate aim. He had time to gulp once before the round loaf of bread shattered against the chandelier.

Glinda watched in horror as the chandelier rocked back and forth on the remaining ropes. The added strain snapped one rope, then another, then all of them. It seemed to hang in the air for a moment before realizing the inevitability of gravity.

Glinda did not even notice the sudden weight on her shoulder as the Winged Monkey landed and watched with her.

The chandelier shattered on the marble floor. Glinda's eyes narrowed. Then she noticed the monkey on her shoulder. It was looking at her necklace.

In a flash, the monkey shot out its hand and grabbed the necklace. It looked up and made eye contact with Glinda. The monkey was a male, so it knew very well what that look on Glinda's face meant. It shot off her shoulder quick as lightning.

The orchestra was suddenly silent. So were Oscar's whistles and Ola Griffin's singing. All chatter, laughter and movement stopped, frozen in an instant. The only sound left to echo through the entire palace was Glinda's angry scream.

Oscar held the small Winged Monkey in his arms. Ola Griffin stroked the small creature's head. From the next room, Glinda's shout sounded loud and clear.

"Out! I don't care! You ruined everything. I will not be bothered with people who will not take orders. No—do not even try to explain. Get out."

Omby-Amby stormed past Oscar without a glance sideways. Oscar walked after him, and the Soldier with Green Whiskers slowed, but he did not turn his head. "If you need me, brother—my Brud—just call. I'm never far. I will be your sword and shield." He exited the large front door, letting it slam loudly behind him.

From behind a tapestry, two brown eyes watched after the Soldier with Green Whiskers. Eyve's wide eyes watched the door. He had to come back in. Everything had to be all right. It was just a misunderstanding. She heard angry footsteps and ducked behind the tapestry.

Glinda entered the hallway and spotted the Winged Monkey in Oscar's arms. She reached out her hand for the creature. "How did you get it?" she demanded.

Oscar let a small smile dance around his mouth before answering. "It was easy enough. I just made a noise like a banana."

Glinda was not amused.

As Oscar returned to Ola Griffin's side, Glinda grabbed the monkey away from Oscar and thrust it into Ola Griffin's arms. "Get rid of this thing." Then she pointed a finger at the small Winged Monkey. "Take heed, little one, any future intrusion into any noble dwelling—whether it be castle, palace, or laboratory, whatever the sacred space may be—is an unconditional declaration of war. And it will be answered accordingly." Then she waved her hand, dismissing Ola Griffin. "Get it out of my sight."

Ola Griffin curtseyed and quickly exited.

Glinda turned her angry glare on Oscar. She shook her head, but no words came out. Oscar quickly left her side and headed back into the ballroom. He saw Ola Griffin pick up the golden cage from near the pile of gifts. She slipped the small monkey into the cage and closed the cage door, smiling and whispering to the small creature.

The guests in the ballroom buzzed in curiosity and wonder about the events. Had this been planned? If so, it was a marvelous show—definitely the best they had ever seen. But if it was not, then this was a tragedy of great proportions…perfect for gossips all throughout the Land of Oz.

Oscar descended the stairs and was immediately surrounded by admirers. They all wanted to know how he managed to capture the wild monkey. "It was easy. I just made a noise like a banana."

They were amused.

Oscar looked over at Ola Griffin. She took a piece of fruit and handed it through the bars of the cage.

Glinda entered and saw Oscar surrounded by admirers—many of them females, with some of those maids from her court. She followed his gaze and turned to see Ola Griffin. Glinda narrowed her eyes and turned back to Oscar.

Ola Griffin disappeared through another door. Oscar turned to see Glinda at the top of the stairs, glaring at him. With the herald, Ola Griffin, otherwise occupied, there was no one to announce Glinda. Oscar stepped away from the adoring guests and lifted his hands and large ventriloquist voice toward Glinda, "From the Scarlet Courts of the South, our Hostess for this evening's memorable events, Glinda, the Good!"

From her hidden location on an overlooking balcony, Kally watched all of the traumatic events unfold with barely contained glee. Glinda was furious.

The Wizard was trying to patch things, but the fire in the red-haired sorceress was so very like her mother that she was bound to break something precious before the night was over.

Kally stepped from the balcony to the look over the stairs. She saw the blonde herald carrying away the golden cage with the Winged Monkey. The girl stopped when she came face to face with a tall, dark-haired man. The herald asked who he was.

"Forget you ever saw me." He answered. "I'll let myself in. I'm a friend of the original owners."

Kally saw the man's face and she paled. As the man entered the ballroom, Kally hurried to an outside window to make her quick getaway.

In the gardens overlooking the desert cliffs, Omby-Amby stared out over the desert. His back was straight and his glare unmoving. If he heard the girl silently moving behind him, he made no notice.

Eyve sat cross-legged near him and looked up at his tightly-composed face. "I put out the fire. The tapestry is stained with punch. I wasn't even supposed to be in there."

Omby-Amby sighed and let his gaze travel to the girl. If he would have had a younger sister, she would probably have been like this girl. "Did anyone see you?"

"Lady Glinda was certainly mad. Did you see how red her face was? It was almost the exact same color as her hair."

"No. I didn't see that, but I've seen it before. She has a temper like fire."

"She shouldn't have kicked you out."

"Did you see the chandelier?" Omby-Amby asked, shooting a sideways glance at the girl.

She giggled, and Omby's face cracked into a disbelieving smile. "I actually knocked it to the floor with a loaf of bread. I'm surprised she didn't kill me right there."

"If looks could kill...does she know the look of death? She is a sorceress."

"All females know the look of death. And all males know what it looks like. Did you see how quick that monkey took off? He knew."

"No. I was running with the punchbowl."

Omby-Amby turned to look at the earnest girl. "You were paying attention to the situation, that's good. You weren't distracted by the theatrics. See a need, fill a need. That's a good soldier."

"Really?"

"Really. I think you have what it takes. Try out for the Fighting Girls. I have to leave now—Emerald City beckons afar. I am no longer welcome here."

"I'm sure you could talk to Glinda. I could talk to her." Eyve offered.

"Thank you. Eyve, was it? I'll be watching for you." Omby-Amby lifted a hand to salute her.

Eyve jumped up and embraced him around the middle. "I'll be ready."

Glinda was in no mood to entertain guests, but still they came. Everything was supposed to be perfect for the Sky Wizard's Ball, but nothing was perfect. Everything was ruined. The guests all wished her well and congratulated her for a delightful evening. It was truly a memorable event. It was a fitting event to celebrate the arrival of the Wizard to the Land of Oz—destruction from the sky, chaos, and all that.

Glinda was jealous. Power came so easily to the Wizard. People clustered around him like shadows on a bright day. And like a shadow, he never cast them away—they were always with him. Such power came with a price, but Oscar didn't seem to care. He continued to direct the building of the Emerald City, and tell stories of the wonderful work going on there. And he continued to court his enemies with the easy familiarity of a stage clown. Did he not realize that they were his enemies? Was he that blind, naïve, or foolish? Or was it something else entirely—something that Glinda could not see?

It was no wonder that the powers politic were growling at his heels. The legend of Oz, the Great and Terrible was of particular consequence to the people who only respected power. They knew that they could control the power if they could just get inside his circle. It was only the crowds that constantly thronged the Wizard that kept the power-hungry leeches in the shadows. If they could ever get him alone, they would see whether or not his power truly was as legendary as the legends sang.

Glinda, too, wished that she could get Oscar alone. His continual drive for perfection in his city to the north concerned the sorceress. There was so much that he was doing that went unnoticed. It was like doing needlepoint on a dishrag, she once told him. He rejected her explanation that day. Though she argued, Oscar wanted everything to be perfect for every single person.

Her power was great, and it was increasing day by day as she learned more and more from her library in the South. What concerned her most was that Oscar's strange power to dream visions into reality was changing the Land of Oz—*her* land—into something different. That was not acceptable.

And then the Wizard was gone. He was not among the clustered knots of people. He was not at the banquet table among the delightful foods. Glinda stood up from her throne. She tossed the large bowl of half-eaten pastries on the floor. Had she really eaten that many?

She went to find the Wizard.

3 GOLDEN CAGE

In the garden, Oscar found Ola Griffin with the golden cage. She fed fruits to the chattering little monkey. The monkey turned to watch the Wizard hungrily as he approached. Oscar chuckled to himself as the monkey licked its lips.

"Hello, little monkey. You look like you are seeing something you like. Hello, Ola."

"Good evening, to you, Wizard." The blonde girl responded pleasantly.

"Oscar, please. It's what my friends call me. I'd like to consider you a friend."

The girl nodded politely, but stayed silent.

"I just wanted to see how the monkey was doing. He had quite a fright in there."

"He's doing fine now." Ola Griffin looked around, but didn't see anybody. "Wizard…Oscar, I wanted to ask you…how do you make a noise like a banana?"

Oscar smiled broadly. "You've got a good voice. You're going to love this. See, you start with the nose. Lift it high into the air, like you are holding a banana on there. Let the sound build in the back of your throat as you visualize the banana, and then you let it peal."

The girl immediately recognized the pun and laughed out loud. Her clear laughter rang through the garden. This attracted the attention of a certain red-haired sorceress.

Oscar smiled broadly. He liked to make people smile. When they laughed—true, genuine laughter—it was even better. "Do you want to see what I made for Glinda?"

Oscar held up the necklace. The polished wood caught the fading sunlight and glistened.

Ola Griffin reached out her hand to touch it and examine the fine woodwork.

From across the garden, Glinda saw the scene unfold without the sound. Hurt tears filled her eyes. *No more tears*, Oscar had promised—but he *lied*—they came anyway. Glinda turned and ran far away.

Glinda's suite overlooked the gardens. She threw herself on her bed and sobbed. Then she screamed and kicked her feet and sobbed some more. And then, when she was finished, she picked up a book and flipped through it slowly.

In the garden, Ola Griffin sang. Glinda recognized the song, *Parradime Lost*. It was one of her favorites.

As Ola Griffin sang, her voice chased away the shadows and brought the light back in to Glinda's eyes. Though the song ended with the disappearance of the City of Parradime, home of the wisest philosophers in all of Oz, the bouncy refrain cheered Glinda. She even caught herself singing along with the Chumpocles verse. By the time the song was finished, Glinda had turned toward the balcony. She walked out and overlooked the garden.

The singing stopped. Glinda looked for Oscar, but he was nowhere to be seen. Glinda smiled at her friend. "I see you down there."

"I see you up there. Are you better?" Ola asked. She lifted the golden cage to leave.

"An iota better. I like that song."

"I know."

"Where is Oscar?"

"The Wizard stepped inside. He has probably found some more friends or leeches."

"I wanted this night to be perfect. I wanted it to be special." Glinda leaned her arms down on the balcony railing, looking down at her friend.

"It was memorable."

"How can you say so much by saying so little? You are a wonder to me sometimes."

"I do my duty."

"Was there no young man here for you tonight?"

In the twilight shadows, Ola Griffin shook her head. Glinda caught the slight motion. "No."

"Tell me why you will not love."

"My duty is to you, my Lady. I will not love until you allow yourself to love."

Glinda's smile froze on her face. She stood up and knit her brows together. She puzzled on that cryptic statement. When she looked down in the garden again, Ola Griffin was gone.

"But I do love." She whispered to the wind. "He just doesn't love me back."

Glinda walked the halls, waiting and dreading. What had she seen out there? Was Oscar fading away from her? Was she fading from his heart? She would be his, but would Oscar be her Wizard still? Would he recognize her sacrifices? Would he recognize her power? This land was hers, by rights—she had been driven from her home in the North, and Smith & Tinker invited her into this castle, so she had made it her own. She was making a clear name for herself.

Her fame had grown in the land. She was not so well-known as the Wizard, but she would be. Where the Wizard was the hero of the Battle of Munchkin Fields, it was Glinda that—*no. That wasn't fair.* Mistakes had been made.

Oscar promised to help her free the Winged Monkeys. If only she had done as he had said and freed them then. But he promised to help.

She would be more inclined to believe him if he wasn't too busy building his Emerald City and spreading liberty across Oz. He had orchestrated treaties with the other lands in Oz, making Emerald City neutral in war. *No entangling alliances*, he had said. That sounded wonderful, and it was going to be. So far he had been lucky—war had not come to Oz in these last two years. Not since the Battle of Munchkin Fields, but the Wicked Witches were still out there. His luck would not hold out forever, then where would his power get him? What could his dreams do in the middle of a war?

Oscar was a dreamer. He was unique in all of Oz. People in Oz don't dream. Few even knew what a dream was. Oscar explained once that they were visions in the night when you sleep—things that once were, or are, or may be. The magic of dreams, he said, is not in what we see when we sleep, but what we carry with us into the light of day. *The magic is in the dreams we keep.*

This sounded wonderful…only Oscar didn't keep all of his dreams—he actually forgot a great many of them. Fortunately for him, the Land of Oz remembered them all to well. He dreamed an entire city into existence. The Emerald City was based on a dream he had. He would have forgotten it, too, except that Glinda had reminded him that morning, after the battle.

Even now Oscar regularly dreamed changes into the city. The Architects' Guild posted Watchers throughout the city to spot the new magical developments that appeared every night. They built the city around Oscar's dreams, for he was a mighty Wizard that changed Oz. He was the most powerful of any in the Land of Oz, yet Glinda knew that there was more to his power. What lay beneath was the greatest mystery of all. It was a mystery that she intended to solve.

If the Wizard could not control his power, he did not deserve the power. It should belong to—or at least be controlled by—someone who knew how to use it and control it. Power belonged to those who would use it responsibly.

So wrapped up in her thoughts was Glinda, that she did not stop her hall-wandering until she ran into the heavy oaken door. She came back to herself and found that she was at the heavy doorway of her Echo Chamber.

This was where Glinda spent most of her nights. It was in the lower levels of the palace, down below the surface. The stone room was large and circular, perfect for sorcery and experiments. This was also her place to think and meditate. It was her isolation from the outside world. She entered and closed the door behind her.

She sat on the edge of the large table, kicking her feet absently. It was quiet in here. She pulled on her most recent experiment—an adjustable ruby lens attached to a headpiece. She flipped down the ruby lens over one eye and stared at the floor. With only her thoughts to sort through, Glinda did not expect to see the heavy door open.

Glinda had given standing orders for the doors to be locked while she was inside. Wickrie-Kells or Ola Griffin then unlocked them at certain specified hours. However, nobody knew that she was in here tonight. The heavy oak doors kept unwanted guests out—but not this evening.

With the events of the Sky Wizard's Ball fresh in her mind, and worries about Oscar haunting her, Glinda was in no mood to entertain guests. She wanted only one guest, but to get that one guest here, she had to make room for the dozens and hundreds that were required.

She most certainly did not expect the tall, dark-haired man who arrived with no announcement. He simply walked in and closed the door behind himself. Glinda saw a flash of blonde hair through the crack in the doorway as the door closed.

Glinda slid off the table and faced the intruder. She raised the ruby lens and looked at the unwelcome visitor coldly. "I am not to be disturbed."

"I'm not here to disturb—just watching. Go right ahead. Don't let me be a bother."

Glinda narrowed her eyes and turned her back on the man. She faced her vials of powders and crystals, trying to look busy. She flipped the ruby lens back down and studied the auras of one powder, and then the next. When she glanced up again, the man was right next to her, studying the powders also. He had pulled out a monocle of emerald. He looked through his lens just like Glinda looked through hers.

"Quite a show this evening." He said.

"Is there something you want?" Glinda demanded.

The man gestured to the powders. "Interesting, isn't it? What do you see?" He asked.

"I see you."

"Ho-ho. I see you, too, lassie. But we both know that smart answers won't be clever enough for my questions." He tucked his monocle back into his vest pocket and sat on the corner of the table, waiting for the storm of questions within the red-haired sorceress' eyes.

Within the raging storm came an unexpected question. "Were you invited?"

"Ah, well…no more than you, I suppose, would be a fair answer."

Glinda's eyes narrowed, but they flicked back and forth, searching the dark man's face for some shred of an answer. He was clever. Information would not be easily obtained from this one.

"I was invited back here when I had finished my journey." The man said.

"Who invited you back? I have been here for two years. I know nothing of you."

"No. That's true. I doubt my masters would have mentioned me. By the way, I love what you've done to the place—knocking the Twisted Lighthouse into the desert below—brilliant. It had been there too long anyway. Too many bad dreams in that place."

"Wait a minute. Who are your masters?" Glinda demanded, both confused and intrigued.

"Masters Smith and Tinker, inventors extraordinaire. They built this castle, trained apprentices for numberless years, and invited me back whenever I felt my journey was complete. Imagine my surprise when I find you here instead of them."

"Imagine." Glinda muttered.

"And I'm certain that you are just as impressed to see me." The man said. "I can't say that I blame you. The first time I came into this room, I was in complete awe of the power. This chamber was home to the most powerful magicks I had ever beheld, or had ever heard of."

"This is my Echo Chamber." Glinda said. "It keeps the world out so that I can focus. Nothing out there matters when I am in here."

"So you come in here to hide."

Glinda glanced up at him but said nothing.

"That wasn't a question—it was a statement. You are Glinda, daughter of Quelala."

Glinda raised an eyebrow curiously. "Yes." She said slowly. "I am. My mother was Gayelette."

"Of course." He laughed. "Can't forget the Ruby Sorceress."

"No. We can't forget her." Glinda's eyes unfocused and she swam through the murky memories that clouded her thinking. She turned back to her crystals.

The door clicked closed, snapping her out of her silence.

The man was gone.

Glinda ordered the Ruby Throne brought down to the Echo Chamber. Wickrie-Kells arranged that project, leaving Glinda to coordinate the next phase of the experiment. It was originally supposed to happen tomorrow evening, but the events of the day rested heavily on her mind, and she could not wait. She had to ask Oscar the important questions.

She paced back and forth, anxious, as she tried to focus her thoughts on the man that Oscar was. Oscar was a good man, but she could not shake the fears she had about his power. What concerned her most was the power that the Wonderful Wizard was amassing without effort on his part.

Even without trying, Oscar was the most powerful—and the most *dangerous*—man in all of Oz. And what was worse, he didn't take it seriously. The people came to his city. They built up his name and his fame. Oh, the stories they told. And what was worse, Oscar didn't seem to pay them any great notice. Certainly he liked to be admired by the pretty faces, but he had no idea what was happening around him.

He was too busy building his city—a beacon to the world. And then he would sleep, and dream, and things would change. He was changing the world around him. He could not be trusted in his dreams, because they had no plan. He had no plan. Other than the banner of liberty for all, he did not do anything.

Oscar had obtained the name and the fame. He was the hero of Munchkin Fields. He was Oz, the Great and Terrible. He was the true power in Oz. Yet it was Glinda behind him, making these great things happen. It was said that behind every great man is a greater woman. But Glinda did not want to be behind him. She wanted him to be at her side.

Two years ago Oscar had descended from the stormy sky in a balloon. His arrival had changed the course of history in the Witch War. They won the first battle of Winkie Plains when Oscar arrived. It was thanks mostly to the storm, but stories arose that Oscar brought the storm with him. Everywhere he marched out against his enemies, the storms followed.

Glinda knew the stories, but those stories had gone on long enough. It was *her* magic that brought the storms of South Castle and Munchkin Fields. The people loved the Wizard and so all good and all power was attributed to him, the *hero*. While respect was given to the Sorceress of the South, Glinda the Good, she was not the foremost paragon of good in the minds of the people.

It was Glinda that was born to rule. As the daughter of the Ruby Sorceress, Gayelette, Glinda was heir to the North. The Witch Wars drove her out. She had finally made a place for herself in the South, in the laboratories of Smith & Tinker. She would not be second to anyone—not her mother, not Oscar, not *anyone*.

Oscar had great power, that was undeniable, but he was a strange sort of man who saw stories in shadows. He delighted more in the *appearance* of magic and the adoration of the crowd than in the power of actual magic. Why? Oscar was a mystery that Glinda would peel back, layer by layer, until she understood perfectly.

This was the purpose of throwing the Sky Wizard's Ball. She needed Oscar to come down from the Emerald City so that she could find answer to her questions.

Once the Ruby Throne had completed its transition from the Ballroom to the Echo Chamber, Glinda stopped her frantic pacing. *It was time.* The Wizard would reveal his secrets and Glinda would finally understand him.

Glinda put on her best smile and went to find the Wizard.

4 WIZARD'S WALTZ

Evening fell, and the day shattered like the chandelier in the ballroom. The moon rose, bone-white and shining. No one was happier to see the day gone than Glinda—her plans for Oscar could not begin soon enough.

When she found him in the ballroom, surrounded by an adoring crowd, Glinda expected the fawning, but she did not expect to see the shadows in Oscar's eyes. He seemed preoccupied—constantly looking around. His eyes darted everywhere, like he was following some unseen movement. Glinda watched him, but she could not see what he saw—at least, she could not see the unseen things that Oscar saw.

Glinda saw very well as Oscar glanced over every one of Glinda's maidens and Fighting Girls. They were quite pleased to entertain the Great and Wonderful Wizard, but Oscar seemed just a little bit too pleased this evening to see them. It was as if he was distracting himself from something else by making them more important.

Glinda huffed and blew a stray hair out of her face. Every last one of her maidens and Fighting Girls would be reprimanded. Despite the evening falling apart completely, Glinda had not remanded any orders—and they were breaking all the rules.

Oscar would finish with one group and they would walk away, buzzing and repeating the clever phrases the Wizard had said.

As soon as he was alone, another maiden or gentleman would approach and introduce themselves. He would quickly be surrounded again by admirers. For some unknown reason, that never seemed to happen to Glinda.

The orchestra played softly. Few people were left in the ballroom. Most had adjourned to the outside to talk and walk in the cool of the evening. Wickrie-Kells sat alone at a table. The candle was still knocked over. No one had bothered to set it upright. Glinda saw her best friend staring out the window—probably looking for Omby-Amby.

One dance, and then Glinda would bring the Soldier with Green Whiskers back inside. That would make her friend happy—it would make both of them happy. But first, she needed her dance with the Wizard. She gestured to the orchestra conductor and gave him the signal. He stopped the orchestra, and then they began to play *The Wizard's Waltz*.

Glinda swooped down and led the Wizard away from her maidens. "Begone, the lot of you. I believe you have taxed the Wizard greatly this evening. It is now my turn."

The pretty girls smiled and trailed their fingers across the Wizard's sleeve as they walked away. He waved his fingers in farewell. The dashing men repeated snippets of stories, drawing giggles from the ladies. Oscar closed his eyes and sighed.

At last the Sky Wizard's Ball ended, and Glinda could again rule her own castle. She sat down next to the Wizard. "Now you are mine."

Oscar opened his eyes, but didn't turn his head. He watched the pretty girls walk away and exit the door. "So many voices."

Glinda waited. Only when she took Oscar's hand and squeezed it did his eyes turn and focus on her. "You surround yourself with people all day, but you are walled inside."

Oscar half-smiled. "So you noticed."

"It seems anyone with half a brain could see through your charade."

"One would think so. But honesty never works on people who seem to know better."

"And what is that supposed to mean?"

"It means I am tired."

"Then look at my face and refresh yourself. You do like pretty faces."

"Of course. Why do you say it like that?"

"You are a mystery to me, Wizard, and I will unravel your tapestry until I see what you are made of."

"Humbug and stories. Memories of another life. Hopes for the future. But mostly just humbug."

Glinda laughed and took Oscar's hand. "You are priceless. You are more powerful than any in the land, and yet you think yourself so little."

"If you don't believe humbug, then believe that I am tired."

"I believe you. What's more, I believe in your unseen powers. I have seen them. I have seen the marvelous things they can do. Your builders in Emerald City see them, too. The magnificent edifices they build are from your dreams."

Oscar scoffed. "No such doing. The architects are brilliant and clever. They build faster than any I have seen. They are the ones making the Emerald City shine."

"So it has nothing to do with the Wizard and his freedom for all men? Decide your own destiny? Be the man that you dream yourself to be? I have heard these things, even here in the South. Many of my people here have visited your land, and some have stayed. They send word that you are working a great and marvelous work. The people believe in you. They love you."

Oscar shrugged, "How can they not? I'm wonderful."

Glinda hit him on the arm. "Don't be sarcastic. You are."

"I'm a humbug. Nobody can see it. The first person who does gets a prize. Get your tickets here."

Glinda frowned at him. "Wake up. You are getting grumpy."

"Would it help if the yawn echoed through the ballroom? Does it need to deafen you for you to hear and understand?"

"You can't be sleeping now. We've got too much to do. I've got a special evening planned for us. You and me."

"Lovely." Oscar raised his eyebrows in professed appreciation as he closed his eyes and leaned his head back on the chair.

"Look at me." Glinda snapped. She slapped his hand to wake him up.

Oscar's brows dropped and he set his jaw angrily. Then he closed his eyes and took a deep breath through his nose. He let it out through his mouth and forced a smile. "I'm listening."

"I want you to look at me. You are the Wizard. You are Oz, the Great and Powerful. You have what nobody else here has."

Oscar opened his eyes wide, to be sure that Glinda saw that he was looking at her. Then he settled into a stare. Glinda frowned. This was not working out like she had planned. There was one last thing to try. "Dance with me—just one—*The Wizard's Waltz*. It is written for you. The orchestra is playing it right now, just for you." She lowered her eyes and pouted her lips. That should work.

It did.

Oscar took her by the hand. "My lady."

Glinda smiled as they walked out to the middle of the ballroom. The chandelier was still there, but that would be cleaned up before morning. Right now it was her time.

"Thank you." She said.

"Every time I think I can get a moment to catch my breath, some new person asks to speak with me. They like my stories. I like telling them—I do. But there are times that…"

"It does not have to be perfect, Oscar."

"Today is anything but, isn't it?"

Glinda leaned her head forward to touch her forehead to Oscar's. "Tell me about it."

Oscar sighed. The shadows in his eyes grew deeper. Glinda was surprised to see him so tired. This was not the man she had known just six months ago when she last visited the Emerald City for a day. What happened? Then he smiled, and the moment was gone, but only for a fleeting second. The shadows crawled back in his eyes. Glinda watched them enter and settle in. They watched her back, wondering what she would do.

Oscar stopped before the second movement of The Wizard's Waltz. He pulled the necklace from his pocket. "A little monkey gave this to me. I believe it belongs to you."

Glinda lifted her hair and Oscar placed the necklace around her neck. She puckered her lips slightly and closed her eyes.

Oscar fumbled with the clasp behind her neck. It was taking too long. Glinda opened her eyes. Oscar was looking past her red hair. Glinda glanced backwards. What could be so interesting back there?

Ola Griffin.

"I'm working on it." Oscar said sheepishly. "My fingers are tired."

"Of course." Glinda said curtly. She led Oscar by the hand to a table away from everyone else. "I want you to listen to me. Everybody that's here, Oscar, has a piece of the puzzle. We're all working toward the goal of trying to figure out what everything looks like. Half of the people in this land don't even remember what happened just five years ago. And we're asking them to see a different future. We are all working on our pieces of the puzzle. Yes, *we*—you and I, and the people we love. We are creating a future that is changing Oz. We are building something that you brought with you. Your ideas have merit. You are magnificent.

"But you—you don't seem to care. You don't just have one piece of the puzzle, Oscar. You can change the entire picture any time you feel like it, and more often when you don't. You change things at every corner. Just when I think I've got something figured out, you come in with a new idea.

"I try to fit that in. Then you go off to sleep and dream, and dream something else. I can't keep track of everything that you do. Your stories don't make any sense. Who is the hero? Where is the happy ending?"

Oscar's staring eyes burned. He swallowed slowly before he spoke. "Let me tell you a story—everyone loves my stories, so you should, too. This one is about a great warrior, and the boy that hated war. The boy lived in the shadow of the warrior. Day in and day out, the stories of blood and war and laughter brought nothing but tears. If stories of war bring tears, what do stories of peace bring? No? No idea? I'll tell you. Silence. Nobody wants to hear stories of peace. You want conflict. You want dissonance. You want to have something to figure out, to conquer." He spread his hands wide to Glinda. "Here I am, Sorceress. I am your war. Figure me out. Solve me. If you want a problem—it's me. You probably had everything figured out before I fell asleep and woke up in this land. There are some days I lay awake and wonder if I ever woke up. Is this all a dream? I wonder if—"

"Do you want to leave Oz?" Glinda asked softly.

"I don't know." Oscar turned away.

"You woke up in Oz. Does that mean you were asleep up there, in the clouds?"

Oscar nodded silently.

"So maybe the key to your coming in to Oz was your dreams."

"Yeah, maybe. So?"

"If dreams were the key to your getting in, maybe they are the key to getting out." Glinda straightened her napkin on the table then she looked directly at Oscar.

"Do you want me to go?" Oscar met her unblinking gaze. "That would make your life easier. You could finish your puzzle."

"Now you seem to want to go. I don't understand you one bit, Oscar. You get all excited about new ideas, then you drop into a morose gloom just as quickly when something doesn't go together. You are building an entire city. You have the history of an entire lan—" Glinda stopped. Oscar was no longer listening to her. He was facing in her direction, but his eyes were searching behind the red-haired sorceress. Glinda turned around to see what Oscar could find so interesting.

Again. It was Ola Griffin, Glinda's herald. Ola was fair, clear of voice and eye. Her blonde hair shone in the moonlight as she laid out the crowns on the window sills. It was her nightly responsibility to recognize those kings and queens who had given all to create history. The tradition was strictly her own. Glinda allowed it because it did not distract or detract from her plans—until tonight.

Glinda turned back around and faced Oscar. She cocked an eyebrow.

"Ahem. Go on." Oscar urged. "History…"

"Yes. History. It is all you are going to be unless you keep your eyes right here, Wizard. No tricks will get you out of this trouble."

Oscar coughed, and covered his mouth with his closed hand. A bird whistled next to Glinda's ear. She turned to look. As she did, Oscar's eyes darted to the blonde girl in the next room. Then they darted back to Glinda's face, but it was too late.

"How many people do you know that have red hair?"

"In Oz? Or ever?"

Glinda threw up her hands. "Indulge me. Anywhere. Apparently one world is not enough for you. You, great and wonderful Wizard, stand astride two worlds, with your head in the clouds. You, with your all-searching eye, see everything, so one land, one face is not enough for you. Do you want my herald? She could sing to you? Perhaps lull you to sleep so you can dream?"

Foolishly, Oscar responded. "She has a nice voice."

Glinda must have learned some new magic, because the room grew as cold as ice. Oscar shifted uncomfortably. Everywhere he turned there seemed to be daggers poking in at him. He stood quickly and stepped backwards, stumbling over his chair. He knocked the chair backwards as he fell to the floor. From the next room, Ola Griffin turned her head to look.

Glinda called to her herald. "Ola, go fetch Wickrie-Kells. I have need of her bow."

Ola Griffin nodded and politely hid her smile as she quickly exited.

Oscar spread his hands on the ground to stand up, but Glinda stepped right in front of him.

"Don't even get up. You belong down there. You and your all-seeing eyes."

"Are those new shoes? They look lovely."

"Get out!" Glinda screamed.

"Should I be sorry?" Oscar asked, scrambling backwards and rising to his feet.

He scarcely had time to close the door before the goblet shattered against it.

So much for the evening plans. Glinda fumed. She wasn't even sure now that inviting the Wizard was a good idea. Who did he think he was, looking at all of Glinda's maidens, and then professing innocence? He was so frustrating. There was no excuse even near good enough to explain his actions. Tired? She yawned. That was a sham. It was a complete poppycock, or humbug, as Oscar liked to say. She yawned again and closed her eyes, just for a minute.

Wickrie-Kells shook Glinda awake. Two hours had passed. Glinda stumbled back to her room. On the way she passed by the guest suite where the Wizard was supposed to be sleeping. The lights were on and Glinda heard talking. She shuffled past the closed doorway. If he wanted to complain about being tired, then let him be tired.

The next morning, in her laboratory, Glinda held up a large ruby. She watched as the early morning sunlight glistened on its multiple facets. On the walls and table, glistening lights danced with pixie fire from the ruby. She walked with the ruby held in front of her face into the full sunlight by the open window.

Through the ruby Glinda looked out on the countryside. A blaze of churning energy drifted slowly in the distance. She lowered the ruby and saw only a dark silhouette in the field. From this distance she could not see who it was. Several times she raised the ruby. Each time she saw the magical flame surrounding the distant walker.

She quickly retrieved the multi-lensed spectacles from her table and slid the ruby lens into position. She saw the same magical fire around the silhouette. Who could it be this early in the morning? Or what could it be? That was another mystery—one that Glinda intended to solve forthwith.

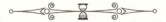

She kept a cautious distance from Oscar all day. The invitation was for two days, and he was cordial enough to stay around to say good bye when the time came. Twice, Glinda sent Wickrie-Kells out to negotiate a truce. Twice she came back and shrugged. "He's yours."

But Glinda was not quite ready to face Oscar close-up yet. She wanted to make sure that the magic was not leading her astray. She watched all of the guests, and randomly pulled out the spectacles with the ruby lens down. Some of them showed slight magic. Oscar blazed with light. It must have been some of that close proximity that made Wickrie-Kells also show up so brightly in the spectacles. She shared this thought with Ola Griffin, who seemed interested, but she had no explanation, either.

The spectacles somehow gave Glinda a glimpse of the magic of the Land of Oz. As she put them on, she saw clearly the raw magic of the land. What she had only felt before on the Ruby Throne she could now see with her eyes. There it was—the magic focused around Oscar. It was magic coming up from the Land of Oz that manifested itself around the Wizard. Was it because of his dreams? He only dreamed when he was asleep, so that couldn't be it. Or could it? Then there was the closeness to Wickrie-Kells, but the girl didn't dream. Glinda had already ruled out that possibility. So it had to be something with Oscar.

Glinda needed to explore this curiosity. Her interest in this power was not merely personal—it was also professional. She was a sorceress, after all, and she had a duty to learn and exploit this power if possible. It was her responsibility as a sorceress to protect her land, and, by extension, the entire Land of Oz.

That was quite a load to bear for a seventeen-year old girl. But she was almost eighteen. That made it more bearable, so she would just have to bear it. There was no one else able or willing to bear this task. Glinda would not let the Wicked Witches win. Wherever they were, she would be vigilant and stop them. She would do the hard work now, so that she would be ready when the inevitable war broke out. It was coming.

The war would be over power—that's what wars were always about. Whoever has the most power either wins or becomes a target for the hungrier predators.

Oscar held a greater power than any of them had ever known. He didn't control it, at least not consciously. His dreams had changed the land, and doubtless they would continue to change the land for years to come. That made him a very valuable ally, or a potentially deadly enemy. It was important to understand how the Wizard's power worked, in order to prepare herself more effectively for the future. Even Oscar understood that to fully understand something, sometimes you have to dig and cut and prod and poke. And she would, tonight.

5 SHOT IN THE DARK

"Wizard, Glinda has some questions for you." Ola Griffin declared, pronouncing the official invitation. Then she lowered her voice and whispered, glancing around to make sure that there were no errant ears overhearing her forbidden warning. "Oscar, please be true. End this charade."

The invitation was mysterious. Oscar accepted, pleased to see the enigmatic sparkle in Ola Griffin's eyes. There was something there that she was not telling him. He had stood in front of enough audiences to know when an honest response is not forthcoming. "So Glinda has some questions for me? I'm sure she does. We didn't exactly part with pleasantries."

Ola Griffin smiled politely, and glanced backward once over her shoulder as Oscar followed her down the stairs into the deeper corridors of the South Castle. Ola was cordial in her manner, and even pleasant, but there was an awkward distance that she kept between herself and Oscar. That was a barrier that Oscar recognized, but wasn't sure if he wanted to point it out, or simply go on ignoring it. Still, Ola had a sweet voice, and her hair shone in the flickering light. There was a certain mystery dancing in her eyes that she would not voice. That was, of course, flattering—what more could Oscar really ask for? But her hushed whisper begged Oscar to end the charade. *What charade?*

"Lady Glinda awaits you at the end of the corridor. Knock and the door will open. She is expecting you." Ola curtsied quickly and turned and hurried away, leaving Oscar with his own thoughts once again. She glanced back over her shoulder once, but Oscar did not look back after her.

It had been another long day. Twice Wickrie-Kells had come to talk with him, but not Glinda. Twice Oscar apologized and explained away his poor judgment by fatigue. Wickrie understood. She promised to relay the information to Glinda. Glinda kept her distance. *Strange.* That was not like her—that was more like Oscar. Glinda was the one that was usually rushing into any given conflict, bound and determined to be right. Her self-righteous conviction usually overpowered any arguments. So this was a different sort of situation. Oscar yawned. He had not slept well the night before, and mingling with people for another full day had left him exhausted again. But Glinda wanted to see him, and this would mend the bridge between them. It was a worthwhile sacrifice.

Sacrifice—how often he had given that word to himself as a reason for what he did. Sacrificing himself for the unique position of changing the course of history. It was hard, lonely work. The self-doubting voices came more and more frequently now that he was so tired. He did what he did for the better cause—letting future generations laugh and sing while he labored his days away in thankless labor.

The dark whispers came more frequently now. He had ignored them for half the day, because he had been with others and he could blame the shadowy voices on the wind. Now, though, the sputtering light refused to penetrate the shadows behind his eyes. The wind was not inside, yet the whispers came just the same. Oscar bared his teeth in a fierce snarl, and set one foot in front of the other. He had a date with Glinda, and he would make it there under his own power, no matter what came into his path.

The Wizard's shadow, high and mighty, strode down the corridor. Oscar walked more cautiously, as he noted that his bold shadow was not alone in the passage. The uninvited shadows danced around the walls with minds of their own. But Oscar intently ignored them absolutely and completely, keeping his gaze focused straight ahead on the end of the hallway. They did not go away. Why would they not go away?

In front of him was his final destination—the heavy oak door that protected Glinda's Echo Chamber. The large door with iron handles awaited him eagerly. It mockingly whispered his name. It had been a year since Oscar had been into the Echo Chamber. What secrets had Glinda uncovered in that time? What magicks had she braided into reality? The door saw all of her secrets. It had been a normal door one year ago. Why was it so different now? Why was it watching him?

Echoes splashed through the air as Oscar slowed his pace. Shades of shackles clinked up from the floor and tugged at his feet, slowing his stride. The iron-handled door breathed open a few inches, granting a slivered vision of red hair moving around. Lost in frenetic self-conversation, Glinda muttered about rubies and spectacles and crystals and shadows. In the corridor, diaphanous clouds tiptoed away from the corners and plugged the cracks in the mortar. The burnished bolts in the door creaked and blinked at Oscar as he reached out the infinite distance toward the laughing handle. His hand stretched out forever as the walls warped and bulged in their startled dance. His thick fingers closed on nothing. The door was beyond his reach. The shadows laughed. His eyes burned, but his feet would not move.

Twisting silence knotted around the door handle and gave it a shove and it ballooned out right in front of Oscar's nose. He jerked his head back to avoid the attack. The Wizard's eyes darted all around as the poetic shadow-notes fluttered all about the walls and dropped through the glimmering air to shatter on the floor. A sigh escaped the top of the opening door. In that sigh was the accusation of each and every shadow Oscar had known.

"Enter. Oscar Diggs. Wizard. Voice of the clouds. Oracle of the shadows. Defender of freedom. Grand Rubiarch of the Emerald City. Following pretender. Sunset patriot. Blind foolery. Corcorran villain. Lesser loser. Death bringer."

The whispers sliced coldly around him, each epithet pricking the goosebumps one fraction higher. In the remains of the echo, the silence crowded out his steeled gaze, and Oscar blinked.

"Oscar!" Glinda said, snapping her fingers to get his attention. "It's solid." She rapped on the wooden door three times. "Come in. It's private. I don't want anybody interrupting us—or overhearing us. I want to talk with you about us. You. Me. We'll start with you."

Oscar craned his neck and peered around the half-open door. Glinda breezed about the room, seemingly floating over the floor. She precisely positioned a candle on the thick table. Oscar looked in and saw the shadows pirouetting at the edge of the candlelight. He shuffled his iron feet into the room.

"Come in, Oscar. I wanted to talk with you about your dreams. The Emerald City is coming along well."

"You're not mad at me?"

"Of course I'm upset at you. You were looking at Ola Griffin. Your eyes are supposed to stay on me. Love, luck, and lollipops, remember?"

Oscar shrugged. This was strangely welcoming, but his eyes were distracted by the shadows. Glinda seemed to hover in the center of a spinning universe. He shook his head and pressed on his eyelids to try to clear his mind. Neither one worked.

Glinda led Oscar with a firm pressure on his back to the Ruby Throne. "Have a seat."

Oscar seated himself uneasily on the throne. "Why is the Ruby Throne here?"

"I needed to do some thinking in here. The walls are thicker here than they are elsewhere in the castle. It gives me some solitude to appreciate the mysteries of Oz."

Glinda walked back to the table set up in front of the throne. She adjusted a curved mirror behind the large candle. The light reflected through a crystal and focused in a spot in between Oscar and Glinda. The light coalesced and glistened in a scintillating ball that rotated in mid-air.

Oscar's eyes focused on the light and locked in place. Glinda smiled as she recognized the fixed gaze. Oscar had to be completely locked on the light for this to work. But she had to make sure he was not distracted by anything.

With her back to Oscar, Glinda bent partway over and then tossed her hair back. She glanced coyly over her shoulder. That was enough to grab the attention of any man. It didn't. *Good.*

"I hear you've built more on the Emerald City—some fascinating towers. Oscar. Can you hear me?"

"I hear you. Yes. I'm constructing my own room like this. Bigger. It's my Pandaemonium Chamber."

"*Pandaemonium*, that's an interesting word. Why do you call it that?" Glinda circled around behind the Ruby Throne to close the heavy door.

"Dark. Crazy. Some dreams don't belong outside."

Glinda locked the door and hung the key on a cord around her neck. Usually she entrusted it to Wickrie-Kells, but this time Glinda wanted to stay in control. She checked to make sure that the high windows were barred. There wasn't much time left now. The room was fairly trembling with power. The combination of the Ruby Throne and Oscar's hypnotic dream were allowing her to go deeper than she had seen into his mind before. "I'm listening."

Oscar started in on the storm. "I used to think that everything was spinning all around me. I was the center of everything, but I had no control. When I was young, my father told stories about the war. He would always slap me on the back and say that I would be a great warrior like him someday. A young country is doomed to plenty of wars until they get big enough and strong enough that no other countries dare attack.

"I lost two of my brothers to war. They fell somewhere far away. I don't know where they were buried. My mother always cried. My father would laugh like it was a joke, like he was proud of them. *A necessary sacrifice for the nation.* But that isn't true. The spirit of freedom, the spirit of a nation lives in the hearts of the people, not in their blood. How can war be a good thing? The monsters always came for me when I closed my eyes. My brothers—I was only little when they left. I don't know where they fell. They would come back. They were so much bigger than I was."

"How did they come back? If they were dead, weren't they gone?" Glinda watched Oscar's pale face. She leaned back on the table.

"The dead can talk to us in our dreams."

Strange forms groaned to life in the shimmering air behind Oscar. Glinda backed up a step, but the table got in her way. Giant misshapen creatures—monsters—stepped out of the swirling energy. She held up the Ruby Spectacles and saw the dream energy surging upward to surround Oscar and the Ruby Throne. The monsters glowed brightly—there was nothing physical about them, they were pure dream.

"Oscar, I wanted to talk with you about your dreams."

"Dreams are stories. They remember things that I can't remember. I thought I knew my father, but he was a strange man. He would sit and stare for hours out the window, and then he would turn to me and laugh and joke. The stories of blood and war and honor stained every history lesson. My mother would watch. Her tears were silent, but they echoed in the other rooms, away from my father. I would tell her, *'No more tears.'*"

"Why did you leave?"

"My funny stories brought light to my mother. My father frowned on them. *'Real stories have heroes.'* He said. I could not change him. I tried. He didn't want me, even though I was right there—he wanted my brothers. The dead meant more to him than me."

The monsters stepped around Oscar, and he cringed in their shadow. Even when they passed between the shimmering ball of light and Oscar, the Wizard did not blink. He knew they were there, but he didn't see them with his natural eyes. The paralysis kept him in the waking dream.

"Why do the dead frighten you?" Glinda asked, backing away from the giants.

"They took the secrets of the living with them. Now there are no lips to hide the words. The whispers echo to dreamers with listening ears. They *know*."

A shiver ran down the entire length of Oscar's spine and his fingers spasm'd uncontrollably. "They know!" He cried. Then his voice dropped to a hoarse whisper as the giants turned to look at him, as if noticing him at last. "They know."

"Piiiiissss-tilllss." The wind whispered through the sealed room.

On the table next to Glinda, two strange implements shimmered into reality. Tubes with handles and what appeared to be triggers on the bottom of the tubes.

Oscar shook his head fiercely, though he did not see Glinda, the table or the strange items. His gaze was locked firmly in the past. He shook his head to try to make the real things become unreal again. But fear is a poor weapon against memory.

"He said, *'Use them, Oscar. Use them for what they were made for. Be the man you must be. Do your father proud.'* He plied on me the weapons of war. I ran. I ran west into the storm. I ran until my story knew no more ears. On the edge of reality they don't care what the weather was at your back, only what winds you bring today. You are your mask only—your true face is yours alone to know. There are no magic mirrors in the storm. There is only me. I am not my father. I swapped the tools of war for a mess of pottage.

"The shadows on the stage became my voice. The stories blended the past with every dream and I could disappear. My voice led them through a journey away from the pain of each day and they showered me with gold. And yet every night those same shadows danced on my small walls. I lost the treasure."

Glinda backed into the table again, nudging it. The candle flame flickered, sending dancing shadows all around the room. The dreamed-up monsters noticed the red-haired girl, and took an interest in this new creature of flesh and magic. They targeted her and came at Glinda from each side. She grabbed the tube-trigger-things from the table and ducked underneath the heavy oak beams.

"Piiiiisssss-tilllss." The word came again, repeated louder this time.

Raging echoes bounced around the room as shades stepped off the walls to join the frenzied shadow dance. Oscar trembled, pale and alone in his memory.

"Oscar!" Glinda shouted. 'What did you do? What do they want? *Oscar!*"

"My story is my own. I am not bound to family, friends or history. I sold those ties. I came to the twilight at the edge of everything to find myself."

"Oscar, WAKE UP!" Glinda screamed as the giants reached under the table for her.

She leaped out to the open floor and scrambled toward the door. She lost her grip on the dreamed tubes with triggers and they clattered on the stone floor ahead of her. The giants turned their misty heads to watch the tubes slide on the stone.

"Piiiiisssss-tilllss."

Pistols. That's what the monsters called them. Glinda gathered them up and clutched them to her chest. "Oscar! You have to wake up. They are after me."

"They are looking for their birthright." Oscar murmured. "Somebody took their birthright and they are come to claim it."

"OSCAR!" Glinda screamed.

Helpless tears filled Oscar's eyes as the scene replayed again in front of his paralyzed stare.

Glinda fumbled with the pistol and pointed the open end of the tube at the closest giant and squeezed the trigger. A sound of thunder.

The booming echo nightmared off the corners of the room to meet again in the middle. The giant froze in its tracks and looked down at the hole in its chest. Then it laughed as the misty dreamstuff filled in once again.

Oscar shook like a leaf in a storm. His haunted eyes stared as the cold tears welled up and spilled over his pale cheeks. "Not again."

Glinda ran.

She yanked the key out from her bodice. It snagged it on the lace trim of her dress and fell to the floor. The terrified girl dropped to the ground after the key. Her panicked fingers searched and twisted until they felt the cold metal. She could not tear her eyes from the approaching shadow giants. Their haunted laughter became her world.

Glinda fumbled with the key and found the lock behind her.

She slammed the heavy wooden door behind her and barred it shut. Her panicked footsteps echoed in the corridors as she abandoned the Wizard to his living nightmare.

Later, Oscar awoke uncomfortably in the Ruby Throne. He stretched his stiff muscles. On the oak table in front of him, there was a curved mirror, a crystal and a stump of a large candle. He shook his head to clear it. Strange shadows moved at the corners of his vision. The shadows stood as giants. Oscar ran his hands through his hair and wrapped his arms around his head with his elbows in front, as if embracing protectively his own head.

"Go away. I don't want you here." He rocked in the throne.

After a time, the shadows disappeared. Oscar uncurled himself and put a foot down to the floor. It was solid.

"Glinda?" Oscar called, but there was no response.

He arose from the throne and stiffly walked over to the large door to try the handle. It wasn't locked, but it wouldn't budge—it was barred from the outside. He pounded his fist on the door. Again. And again.

"Glinda! Enough of this. Let me out."

Hours passed. He pushed the heavy table over to the wall and tried the windows, but they were barred shut. There was no escape.

His prison was perfect. Everyone who cared about him did nothing, because they knew the Wizard was with Glinda.

Oscar sat on the table beneath the window, with his back against the wall, wearily watching the afternoon light in its bright path on the floor. The crystal stood in the center of the light. The candle was broken into several wax pieces, marking the hours of the makeshift sundial.

The large door creaked open slightly, and Glinda stepped in, closing the door behind her. She stepped back against the door, closing it with her hip, staying as far back as she could.

"Hi."

Oscar didn't move. He lifted his eyes to meet Glinda's gaze.

"Are you okay?" She asked softly.

"What's going on? I'm not lunatic. No reason to lock me in here."

Glinda forced a smile. "I missed you."

"I've been right here the whole time."

"We have to talk about a few things. Your dreams—"

"Are mine."

"Yes, but—"

"No buts. I keep my thoughts to myself most of the time. In case you haven't noticed, Sorceress, I have a city that I need to finish building. I am building a republic. I don't have time to be a common prisoner."

"I know that, Oscar."

"How much do you know about my story?"

"What do you mean?"

Oscar stretched his legs and stood up on the table, towering over Glinda. "I don't remember much about last night. You invited me in here to talk, probably about dreams, or something. You brought the Ruby Throne in here. Now unless you are going to crown me king—and you don't seem to be the type of ruler that would abdicate—I can only guess that you conducted some sort of experiment. I woke up sitting in the throne. I felt like I hadn't moved in a few hours. Do you know what that is like? I feel like I got thrown off a tightrope without a net. Parts of me hurt inside that I didn't even know I had.

"Then this morning some shadows were out of place. Was there something in here put wrong? No. Just something that fell out of my head. Hmm. It's nearly four o'clock, Glinda, and I haven't eaten in almost a full day. My belly is empty. My head is filled with thoughts of I don't know what—just a dark void that keeps sucking away at what little trust remains. And so I will ask you again, Princess-Sorceress-Glinda, what do you know of my story?"

Glinda stepped into the center of the room, across the patch of sunlight, so that the day's light fell half on her face, leaving the other half in shadow. "Oscar, you don't understand. I can accept that this looks bad."

"Bingo." Oscar said, his eyes darkening. "I *don't* understand. And, *yes*, it looks very, *very* bad. I don't dig into your magic. I don't rifle through your drawers to find your private things. You have your country. I have my city. If you will excuse me," He dropped down to the floor. "I have an appointment with a very large sandwich."

Glinda reached out and took Oscar's hand as he walked by. He froze in place, glancing back at the girl's guilty eyes.

"Your secrets *are* safe with me, Wizard."

Oscar pulled his hand away and walked to the door, opened it, stepped through, and closed it behind him.

Glinda waited and listened closely. She wondered if Oscar would bar the door, but that sound never came. Truthfully, it would not have mattered if he did. Glinda had previously instructed Wickrie-Kells to come down in twenty minutes and unbar the door if it was locked.

Glinda picked up the crystal from the floor and silently cursed the things it had brought out of her beloved. The more she learned about Oscar, the more she loved him. And the more she understood, the more she feared him. She feared both the Wizard and the power he embodied.

If it was consciously wielded power, she could form alliances and control the use of that power through various means—not the least of which was her growing beauty. She was beautiful—even among the fine-looking girls she gathered around herself as handmaidens, bodyguards, and heralds—Glinda stood apart. What was more, she knew that she was beautiful. If it was merely a matter of making Oscar love her so he wouldn't use his power, that would be easily solved. But Oscar didn't consciously wield his power.

Oscar was a Wizard because he could change the world around him. He was more powerful than any, or all, of the Witches in Oz, but he did not control any of it. It was his dreams that shaped the raw magic of the Land of Oz. That power was beyond his control, and it was beyond the control of anyone else.

That meant Oscar was dangerous—to himself, to Glinda, and to all of Oz. And now he was upset with Glinda. *Oh, well.* As long as Glinda stayed young and beautiful, she was certain to have Oscar wrapped around her little finger. He would get over this little misunderstanding. He was a fine man, and quick to forgive.

At least that is what Glinda told herself.

She leaned her forehead on the heavy door and sighed. In the pocket of her gown, she reached in and felt the heavy shape of Oscar's nightmare—a pistol.

6 ROSES HAVE THORNS

Oscar exited the front gate of the South Castle, carrying a large sandwich. He pointed his feet toward the north and walked. He passed by a tall, dark-haired man. Oscar didn't even glance sideways as he passed by Ola Griffin at the red rose hedges. She waved a small goodbye, but returned to her pruning when the Wizard ignored her.

The dark-haired man approached the blonde herald. "Greetings, fair one. Is the mistress of the cottage home?"

Ola smiled and brushed her hair back behind her ear. "The cottage is small, but the hearth is warm, stranger. My mistress is presently indisposed. May I direct you?"

"These roses were white, the last I was here."

"It has been long, then. We have painted them all red."

"I see that—you're putting me on. That was a joke. My former masters, Smith & Tinker, would have crafted a dazzling rose of silken metal and weaved threads of ruby throughout, but it still would pale next to the true beauty here in this garden."

Ola Griffin smiled. "The roses have a certain beauty that is unmatched elsewhere in Oz. Glinda chooses to surround herself with the best and most beautiful. These scarlet roses have sharper thorns than those that were previously planted. You would be wise to watch where you place your hands."

"You, lassie, have a deft touch. I will never forget our first meeting here. The rose garden, where I was warned to keep my hands off the flowers. Lassie, I have lived many places and seen many flowers. I have learned an appreciation for their beauty in their natural environment. They bloom best on their natural stem."

"The time comes when blossoms must be cut."

"To grace the tables of the lucky."

"For a time. Then the blossoms wither and lose their bloom. They die when separated long from their home vine."

"Aye. Such is the nature of flowers. We are still talking about flowers, eh, lass?"

Ola Griffin smiled and rolled her eyes. "Of course."

"Good. I was losing track of the metaphors there. My mind isn't as keen as it once was."

"I doubt that. Few people surprise Glinda. *You* are the one Glinda saw in her Echo Chamber."

"Yes. I am. I see my reputation precedes me."

"To properly announce you to the sorceress, I require some information from you."

"Certainly. I am plum-full of information. Plenty of facts rattling around above my ears." He smiled and folded his fingers together over his front. His eyes searched around the garden, then finally found their way back to Ola Griffin.

She had her hands on her hips and an amused storm dancing in her eyes. "Ahem."

The dark-haired man raised his eyebrows innocently, but Ola Griffin wasn't buying it. "What is your name?" she asked, tapping her foot.

"I am Promethus, Chief Apprentice of Smith & Tinker. I have returned to claim what is rightfully mine."

"That is a mouthful. Are you certain you can chew all of that by yourself?"

"Quite, certain, lass. If you are not in disagreement, I wish to introduce myself to your mistress. May I? I will step inside and wait inside for the sorceress of the castle."

Glinda stubbed her toe on the top step as she entered the laboratory. She lifted her foot and pounded her fist against the stone door frame. She leaned her forehead against the cool stone as she held her foot in the air. Then she forced her eyes open and entered the laboratory. Her eyes shot wide open.

Hunched over her table, examining the prototype Ruby Spectacles was a dark-haired man. It was the stranger—Glinda had not seen him for two days. His face was familiar, but she still did not know his name.

"Out. Get out." Glinda reached into her pocket and felt the weight of the pistol. Then she thought better of it and snatched a hooked fireplace poker from the hearth. She pointed it at the man's head and crossed the room quickly. "I am in no mood for games."

The man turned his head and hooked his first finger around the curved part of the poker. He jerked his hand and pulled the poker away from Glinda, grabbing it in the middle. He set the poker point-down, leaning on the table between the two of them.

"The last time I was here at this table, you would have been termed the intruder, Glinda, daughter of Quelala."

"You have said that twice now. Yes, my father is Quelala. So what?"

"It makes a difference."

"To who? You? Not to me. They are both gone. I'm here. You are here, where you were not invited, in my laboratory, playing with my things." Glinda's nostrils flared and she glared at the dark-haired man.

He lifted the Ruby Spectacles and held them up in front of Glinda. "You entrapped the magic in wire rims. Clever. This is a very powerful weapon. Did you know that? Smith & Tinker would have been proud." He placed the spectacles on his face and looked Glinda up and down. Then again. "I must say, I'm impressed."

"Excuse me?"

"The power flows through you, like it did your mother, and your father, too. You are certainly a child of the Ruby Palace."

Glinda frowned and furrowed her brows curiously. This wasn't going properly. She walked around behind the stranger and replaced the fireplace poker next to the blower by the hearth. Then she climbed up on a tall stool and looked curiously at the man. "What do you know about the Ruby Palace?"

"Perhaps more than you. You are Glinda—your red hair fits you."

"I've had it my whole life. It should fit. Call me impressed. Anything else in your repertoire?" Glinda asked. She raised her eyebrow and steeled her blue eyes against the wry smile of the stranger who knew too much.

"The loss of the Ruby Palace was a tragedy. Certainly unexpected this early."

"It's not lost. It is just *temporarily not accessible*."

"Smith & Tinker told you that."

"Yes."

"Do *you* know what that means?"

Glinda forced a smile and studied the way the stranger's smile danced around his mouth. Her silence held for a few more seconds before the stranger broke.

He smiled as he took off the Ruby Spectacles and set them carefully back in their place on the table. "My masters were unusually cryptic, but that is as plain as the freckles on your face."

Glinda brushed her hair back over her shoulder and squinted her eyes at the stranger. "Your masters were Smith & Tinker, or so you say. Do you have a name?"

"I do."

Glinda waited.

"Will you give it to me, or should I start guessing?"

"I doubt you could. You don't even have a key to unlock the mystery."

"What keys I have, I use."

"I have no doubt of that. Tenacity fits you like a glove. My name is Promethus."

"Like the fire-bringer."

"Not quite. Pro-me-thus. Not Pro-me-thee-us. Pro-me-thus. Not like the fire-bringer. I cannot ascend to that lofty title yet. I am more the guardian type. I don't challenge the fate of mankind."

"Your loss."

The man, Promethus, barked out a laugh. "You really think that you can challenge fate?"

"If I can't, I know someone who can."

Oscar turned around after forty-five minutes and headed back to the South Castle. He had eaten the large sandwich, which made all the difference. Everything looked better on a full stomach.

He stopped to watch an athletic group of young men play a game called Hammer-head, in which they held their hands behind their backs and chased after an orb floating at shoulder height. Each young man held a position on the field. At each end of the field was a tall net, standing almost twice the height of a man. The goal appeared to be getting the orb into the net using only the head to propel it.

One of the young men saw Oscar watching and hollered at him, "Hey short-stuff, think you can play Hammer-head with the big boys?"

Oscar shook his head and held up his hands to decline.

"We'd pound you like an anvil."

The orb zipped by the shouter. He jumped and sprang up. "I need a longer neck!" He shouted as he ran after the pack.

"Then your head would sag and flop around."

"No, it would retract, see? A spring-loaded head."

"That's crazy."

"Your momma's crazy."

And so it went—young men being young men. And Oscar stood to the side and watched. After a few more minutes of watching the brutal game of smashing heads, he wondered idly if their heads might not become flat after a very short period of time. It was not a game he had ever seen before—it was more like hard-headed warfare. There were plenty of bumps, bruises and cuts on the most active of the participants. Oscar shook his head in wonder and continued on his way south.

Certainly he was still angry at Glinda, but they could work things out. As he arrived at the South Castle, he picked a scarlet rose from the hedge. He smiled at Ola Griffin, but she intentionally busied herself with other things and didn't return his welcome.

After the Wizard passed by her, Ola looked up to see if he would look back at her. He didn't. She sighed and clipped a scarlet rose from the hedge. It fell to the ground. She picked it up and carefully placed it in her blonde hair, just close enough that she could feel the threatening bite of the thorns on her scalp.

Oscar entered the castle and went down to the Echo Chamber where he had spent the better part of the day. She was not there. He twirled the rose in his fingers. His makeshift sundial was cleaned up and set on the table. The Ruby Throne was removed. Nobody was around. He decided that Glinda must be up in her laboratory.

Inside the laboratory, Glinda carefully poured the powdered ruby dust into the spectacle frames. Promethus looked on and provided step-by-step instructions.

"You must be very precise. Ruby dust is the most volatile chemical in Oz. It is essentially fuel for whatever magic can enflame it first. If an enemy were to use magic on you while you were in such a compromising position as this, you would be absolutely helpless."

"I'm never helpless." Glinda replied. The ruby lens of her adjustable spectacles slipped and fell into the swarming magic of the dust. "What happens if we—"

The explosion blew both of them backwards away from the table.

A puff of ruby smoke rose into the air and appeared for the briefest of moments to grow a face. It turned to look at them, then if focused on Glinda and opened its mouth hungrily.

Promethus pulled himself up first. He quickly crossed the floor to Glinda and pulled her to her feet.

"Glinda, wake up, lass. Please be okay." He felt her hot face and checked her quickly for burns. He looked around. "Something is here. I give you my protection."

Promethus pressed his lips to Glinda's forehead, passing the spell of protection from wickedness to the red-haired sorceress. She was the most affected by the ruby dust explosion, and so she was most susceptible to any pending attack. The vocal part of the protection spell had been cast long ago, but the physical part was only completed in this moment. To finalize the pre-cast spell, it only took the ultimate action of the kiss on the intended target's forehead—in this case, the recipient of the protection spell's kiss was Glinda.

At that precise moment, Oscar rounded the flight of stairs. He saw the tall, dark-haired man that he had seen outside holding Glinda in his arms and pressing his lips to her forehead. The silver kiss glowed for a moment on Glinda's forehead, and then it disappeared.

Oscar's fist crushed the rose in his hand. He did not even feel the thorns tearing his flesh. He cast the rose down. Blood droplets spilled to the stone steps as he walked away.

If Glinda wanted him gone, she could have just said so. It certainly did not take her long to find a replacement for him. The time spent apart must not have been so lonely after all. She was weak in the man's arms, there was no denying that. And she allowed him to kiss her forehead. It was plainly obvious that Oscar had interrupted something private—something that he should not have seen.

He passed by Wickrie-Kells on his way out the front gate. She noticed the blood on his hand. "Oscar, you're back."

"I'm leaving."

"What happened? Your hand—"

Oscar looked at his hand for the first time. The blood pooled between his fingers. He shook it off. "Serves me right, thinking I belonged here."

"I don't understand. Let me get you something for that." Wickrie-Kells headed back inside the castle, but stopped when she saw Oscar walking quickly away. "Oscar! Wait. Let me get something for your hand."

But he wasn't listening.

Upstairs, in the laboratory, Glinda came to her senses and pushed Promethus away from her. "What are you doing?"

"*Protecting* you. I am the guardian."

"I don't need your help. And I certainly do not need your arms around me."

"The ruby dust exploded. I feared that an enemy might take advantage."

"You seem to be the only one taking advantage."

Glinda straightened her hair and tried to cool the flush on her cheeks. "What happened?"

"As I was saying, ruby dust is the most dangerous powder in Oz. It reacts quickly to magic, and it usually reacts violently. It exploded, and I feared that an enemy was upon us, so I completed a protection spell to protect you from wicked magic."

"So you were not trying to take advantage of me?"

"No. A little decorum, please. I am older than your father. You are a beautiful girl, but you are still a child. If you trust nothing else that I have said, Glinda, trust this—I am come to claim what is mine, not to take what does not belong to me."

"That doesn't make much sense." Glinda said, rubbing the back of her head.

"It will. Are you okay? You hit your head on the wall."

Glinda waved away the older man's look of concern. "I'm fine. What could have caused that flare up? It was stable, but then the powder went wild."

"Maybe something passed through that excited the magic." Promethus offered. He walked over to the table and grinned. "It looks like the explosion was worth it. Come see what you have made."

Glinda looked at the glittering spectacles on the table. Her fallen lens sat off to the side of the new creation. "It worked." She picked them up and examined them. "Ruby Spectacles."

Glinda tested the surface to see if the lenses were hot. No. They were cool to the touch. She slipped the spectacles on and looked around. Auras of magic glowed in her laboratory. On the stairs, a fountain of magic energy bubbled from small spots on the stone. She took off the Ruby Spectacles and hurried down the stairs. She knelt to see the crushed rose and the spots of blood. She held out the Ruby Spectacles and looked through the lenses to make sure that the blood spots were what she was seeing before.

She ran to the window with the Ruby Spectacles on. She looked north. There it was—the blaze of magic that she knew was the Wonderful Wizard—Oscar. He was not far away, at least not as far away as he should have been. Why? Did he come back? Was it him on the stairs? Why did he leave? What could have happened? What did he see? *Oh.*

Glinda ran down the stairs. She pulled the Ruby Spectacles off and put them in her pocket. She called for Wickrie-Kells before she could see her.

The taller girl met Glinda in the entryway.

"Where is Oscar? Where is the Wizard?"

Wickrie-Kells pointed out the large door. "That way."

"What happened to him?"

"I don't know. His hand was bleeding. He said he it served him right. He didn't want a handkerchief or bandage or anything. He just left."

Glinda bit her lip and looked at the ceiling. She tapped her foot as she composed herself.

"What did you do?" Wickrie-Kells demanded.

Glinda forced a smile that didn't convince in the least. "I did this to him. Please. Go with him. Make sure that he gets to the Emerald City safely. Take all the time you need. Just go with him. Spend some time with your beaux. Give Omby-Amby my best. Come back when you are ready. Just see that Oscar is safe."

Puzzled, but pleased, Wickrie-Kells raced after the departing Wizard and caught him before he reached the first horizon.

7 AMBER EYES

Wickrie-Kells and Oscar Diggs walked along the brick road in silence. After three minutes, Oscar accepted the proffered handkerchief and wrapped it around his throbbing hand.

Oscar maintained his silence, but Wickrie-Kells could not tolerate this enforced isolation. She did the best that she could, but she could not respect Oscar's refusal to speak. "If she has forgotten about it by then, I'm sure that her birthday party is going to be a lot of fun. It's her eighteenth birthday. It's been a long time since we've been all together."

A long minute passed before Oscar spoke. To force the words out, Oscar first tried to smile, but found his face wasn't up to the chore. "A long time. Things change. Not long enough to forget completely, just to forget enough."

"Never long enough to forget completely. You always remember the ones you love. Time goes so quick. You miss your family?"

Oscar's startled look made Wickrie-Kells laugh nervously, in spite of herself. She tugged on her long braid awkwardly and then she regained her composure and tossed her braid back over her shoulder. "Don't worry about it. Forget I asked." She shrugged. "I was just trying to make some conversation that wasn't about...her."

They walked in silence for several more minutes. Wickrie-Kells kept a bounce in her step, but her hands nervously circled around her like butterflies. She just could not stay still. There were burning questions in her mind, but she was not permitted to ask them, especially of Oscar. Still, she scraped for every scrap of information that he would feed her.

"You're the Captain of Glinda's Guard, so I don't expect you to sympathize with what I say." Oscar began. "I come from a family of warriors. Me. The dreaming Wizard, imagine that. I was a black sheep—I didn't fit. This body is not exactly warrior material."

"You look fine. I think you look just fine."

"Your attempt is appreciated, but please forgive me if it is hard to believe your sincerity. Consider for yourself—there is a reason that you look at

Omby-Amby and not me. First, you're taller than I am. Secondly, handsome people tend to choose each other. And I, in case you haven't noticed, am not what you would consider handsome."

"Stop it. You look just fine. I mean, you do have a point about being short. I wanted someone who was taller than me. Do you know what it's like to be the tall girl? No, of course you don't. You're not a girl. And, you're not tall, either."

"Thank you for making my point."

"Sure. Doesn't this breeze feel nice? I love the feel of the wind on my face."

Oscar glanced over at the tall girl. She was walking with her eyes closed, her face upward in the sunlight. *So much for serious conversation from both sides.* Wickrie-Kells was a girl who did not dwell in shadows. She could not be out of the sun. Her spirit belonged in a place where she could always be free. She needed movement, freedom, and sunlight. Lofty intellectual pursuits were never a part of what Wickrie-Kells planned for her life. Her knowledge was based on her experience, not on reading. It would be hard to keep this conversation going for two more days. Still, there were some things that Oscar wanted to say, just to tell someone else. He did not want to the shadows to gain control in the broad daylight. Not today.

"My father always told stories of the war. His father was a warrior. My brothers were warriors. Even back from the Emerald Isle, my family has always been known for fighting—until me.

"Do you know what that feels like? To not fit in with the people that are bound to you by blood?"

Wickrie-Kells lifted her eyebrows hopefully. "My father was a butler. My mother was—is—a Munchkin before she came here. Even though my father was a butler, he was a baker for a little while. He had the king's belly before he had his ear. I like watching politics. The Crimson Peacocks were always fun to watch. They would spread their feathers in the sunlight to make their points. Posturing. It was a lot of fun. That's where I first met…Glinda." Her smile faded, and she put her hands behind her back again. "Go on."

"The people who I depended on for food, shelter, love and warmth did not see me as an equal. They thought I was different. I don't know what they thought I was going to do. I'm a dreamer. I like stories. I mean, sure, it's not the manly, hair-on-the-chest, stories of war that they swapped over ale, but I knew some good stories. I would be reading books while they would be drinking. I waited. It happened every time. As soon as they got to a certain point in their storytelling, when they would all get quiet, and start to get red-eyed, they would drag me in. Even as a small boy—and I was a small boy—they dragged me in to dance funny for them, make them laugh, tell jokes, tell stories, make shadow puppets. Then they would laugh and pound their fists on the table, shove each other." Oscar's face twisted in pained recollection.

"Sometimes I couldn't get out of the way fast enough." Then he shook his head violently and ran his hands through his hair. Still he continued. "Every night the same. My mother cried. So in response to your question, *No*. I do not miss my family. I chose to leave."

Wickrie-Kells studied Oscar's face for several seconds. He did not return the look. He stared off into the distance, putting his walls back in place the best he could, but the cracks would not cement very well.

"I'm sorry." Wickrie-Kells said. "Family is an important thing to me. I know that I would miss my family if I left them."

"You did leave them."

"Sure, to go with Glinda."

"Explain, if you would, the difference."

"There's a lot of difference, silly. I lived in the Emerald Valley—in Central City. My mother and I visited Munchkin Village before. I even went with Glinda to Yellow Castle. We barely spent any time there, then the Wicked Witches showed up. I met Omby. Then you showed up. We did some traveling, and then I went South with Glinda. I can go home any time that I want. They'll always be there. That's the difference. *You* can't go back."

Oscar's mouth smiled, but it did not crawl up into his eyes. "I'm the Wizard, remember, I can do anything. That's what they say."

"That's what they say." She repeated. Her darting eyes studied his face for a few seconds before shifting to something else. "But you wouldn't go back? Not ever?"

"I can't think of any reason to. I was just tired of trying to be something that I wasn't. I wasn't a warrior. My shadow puppets could not save me. They could not stop my mother from crying. They could not stop my father from pushing his bloody war stories on me. I ran. I washed my hands of the wickedness that my family did in the name of honor."

"But you kept their name."

Oscar sighed. "Wickrie, you are my friend. You are one of only a few people who know my story. I have a name and a fame in this land that people revere. Who I am is who they want me to be. They love me. When I found the stage back in my world, I became Oz, the Great. That was enough then. It has been enough here. As long as I can control my own story, I'm fine."

Oscar looked around them. There were a few people on the distant road ahead of them, and some coming up behind. He frowned and chewed on his words. "I think I'd like to walk alone for a while."

"Oh. Okay. I guess I'll go on ahead. It's a long walk. I won't be far ahead. If you need me…it's been nice talking with you. I think you're going to be okay now. You are a good man, Oscar. If I get to the Emerald City ahead of you, I'll tell them you're coming."

"Do that. They'll probably send a parade."

Wickrie-Kells walked quickly away, but she couldn't hold still any longer. Oscar watched as she stretched out her legs in longer and longer strides. Before long she was running. On the wind, Oscar heard her joyful shout as she ran toward the northern horizon.

"My name is Oz. I am Oz, the Great." He spoke quietly, as if worried that he would overhear and disbelieve himself. Then he shook his head, darkly comforted that he was once again alone with his shadows.

Oscar spent the night in a borrowed cottage. For a few powerful pronouncements, the family gladly let Oz the Great sleep in their humble home. When Oscar left the next morning, the home was anything but humble. New wings had been dreamed into reality, and the garden overflowed with amazing vegetables. As he walked away, he glanced over at the shadows peeking out of the well at him. A full shiver ran down his spine. This was a much nicer house than the family had led him to believe. It was like something he remembered once from a place he had been, but he couldn't quite put his finger on it. As the Wizard crested the hill, he heard shouts of praise and laughter from behind him. *And so grows the legend of the Wizard.* He smiled.

The open road welcomed the lonely traveler. He walked for two hours. The mist hung over the fields and gave them a dreamy, comfortable haze. He was reminded of stories of the Emerald Isle, where his family came from a generation before he was born. One of his great-grandfathers, many, many generations back composed a song about the faeries dancing with men for their dreams. It was an old song his mother taught him. How did the words go? *I dreamt of dancing tomorrow.* Yes. That was it. *Shamhlaigh mé de damhsa amárach.* From the *Mad Rymes of Orpheus O'Bannon.* That was the treasure he wanted more than anything else—that book of silly rhymes, written in the original Gaelic with hand-written English translations, but his father had other plans for Oscar—he always had other plans.

As the sun rose higher, the mists burned off, and the air grew warmer. He loosened his collar and looked up at the sky. He watched the clouds for several minutes as they twisted into strange and marvelous shapes. So lost was he in fanciful contemplation that he did not even blink when a girl appeared next to him. Out of thin air, she just appeared.

"Excuse me, do you mind if I walk a while with you?" The pretty girl asked Oscar. She gazed up from underneath heavy eyelids. Her golden amber eyes studied the young man's face as he responded.

Oscar shrugged. "It's a free country."

The girl cleared her throat. Her voice came out raspy at first and then it smoothed out. "I haven't heard that before. When did this become a free country?"

"Since I got here."

"And who are you that are so very powerful?"

Oscar stared down at the road ahead of his traveling feet. He smiled as he answered. "I am Oz, the Great."

"Oh, I see. Any relation to the great wizard?"

"Yes."

"Close?"

"Very."

The pretty girl's amber eyes danced. "How nice to meet you. Do you have another name? Or is Oz, the Great, your full and given name?" She nudged him and smiled conspiratorially. "Everyone has another name. Everyone has their shadowy secrets that they keep. Here, I'll start. I'm Kally."

Oscar looked over at her and met her smile. "Oscar."

"Oscar." Kally repeated, tasting the name. "Oz-cur? The whelp of Oz."

"No, Oss-car. Oscar. You know what? Let's just stick with Oz. I am Oz, the Great. That's what I've been for the last four years. No reason to change it now. Kally, it is an irretrievable pleasure to meet you on this fine, fine day."

"And you, Oz, are looking particularly powerful. You cast a long shadow, even at noon." Kally touched his elbow and smiled.

"So my height, or lack thereof, doesn't bother you?"

"Should it?"

"The strength of a wizard is in the words that he shares, but more importantly, those that he keeps to himself."

"One does not define himself by the mysteries he reveals, but those that remain hidden. I think everyone should keep secrets." Kally said. "I have always believed that true power is that which is *not* seen. A little bit of secret makes the magic, but a lot of cutting truth ends up being tragic."

They walked for a few moments in silence before Oscar glanced over at his new companion. "Where are you from, Kally?"

"Here and there, mostly there. My family owned some land to the East."

"Munchkin, then. That fits the blue on your dress. Makes a good look on you."

Kally laughed, a cackle at first, then she cleared her throat and laughed clearly. "Sorry, I haven't laughed in a while."

"Laughter does the soul good. Cleans out the cobwebs in the brain."

"You're not laughing."

"No."

"Does your soul not need good? Are your cobwebs so gilded that they need no rearrangement?"

"My shadows are mine to keep."

Kally smiled slowly as a plan hatched in her wicked mind. Her amber eyes danced as she studied the Wizard's carefully composed face. That sort of control was fit for the stage, but not for a long walk. "You carry a great burden, Oscar. What would you think if we lightened the mood for a while? On our way to the Emerald City let's play a game." Kally suggested. "Each of us will tell one truth and one lie, but we don't tell which one is which. The other person has to guess. You know you can learn a lot about a person by the lies that they tell."

Oscar shrugged. "Seems harmless enough. You go first. You thought of it. Though I have to warn you, I am a storyteller extraordinaire."

"Is that a challenge?" Kally said.

"I'm not a wizard, I have no magic."

"Oh? So you are starting already? I thought you said that I was to go first."

"Maybe I lied. Consider yourself warned.

"Consider me warned. Hmm. What can I tell a wizard who sees all and knows all? What could I possibly do to impress or deceive the Hero of Munchkin Fields?" She watched Oscar's face closely. His eyes brightened at the mention of the title, *hero*. That was it, then. Flattery was the key to controlling this young man's heart.

Kally sighed deeply. "You know what? I can't do this. You seem so nice. You're allowing me to walk with you. I know I said I would lie to you, but I can't do it. You would see right through me. There is no lie that I can tell to Oz, the Great and Terrible that would stand on its own. You see all and know all."

"If only." Oscar breathed wistfully.

"Hmm? Did you say something?" Kally asked innocently.

"If only it were that simple." He straightened his shoulders and looked at the girl. She was taller than he was, though not as tall as Wickrie-Kells. "Being all great and powerful, I have a responsibility to judge fairly. You're right. I would see right through you. On stage, one must learn quickly which hecklers are real and which are frauds. And when the lights go down, you are left with one thing—the memory of what once was." He paused and his shoulders stooped slightly. "What once was is all that is left inside."

"No hope for a brighter tomorrow?" Kally smirked.

"Of course." Oscar cleared his throat. "So long as the Emerald City still shines, there is always hope."

"And how long is that? All cities age and crumble."

"When they are built on solid foundations, like freedom and liberty and responsibility, cities can last forever."

The barking laugh escaped Kally's mouth before she was even aware of it. She clapped her hands over her mouth in astonishment.

Oscar looked over at her, hurt darkening his eyes. "It's a free country. I meant what I said. It has been a free country since I came here. It will continue to be a free country because the people will make it so."

"You are like no other man I have ever met, Oscar." Kally moderated her voice carefully. The scratchiness coarsened her words, but she cleared her throat and continued. "You need people around you who can see clearly the darkness in other people. You, plainly, cannot see it. If you believe that people will make freedom their binding life, you see things that nobody else can."

"I'm a dreamer."

Kally stopped in her tracks. "You're what?"

Oscar continued for a few steps before he stopped. He turned around and looked Kally squarely in the eyes. "I'm a dreamer."

The smile spread over Kally's face quicker than a heartbeat. "Is that so?" She stepped forward and took Oscar's arm, clutching him close. "Tell me, Oscar, what does a Wizard dream?"

They walked and talked all day. As sunset approached, the spires of the Emerald City came into view. A clarion call sounded out over the land.

"What is that?" Kally asked, her eyes wide in surprise.

"The Wizard is returning. The city is rejoicing. The army should be along any time now."

They heard the army before they saw it. The rolling hills hid the scores of fighting men that marched out to greet their leader and protector. As Oscar and Kally crested the hill, they saw the army, resplendent in their parade finery, marching toward them. They were led in front by the Emerald Guardsmen.

"An entire army against me?" Kally asked, nudging Oscar. "You shouldn't have. You'd think I was a wicked witch, or something."

Oscar glanced over at Kally to look at her face. Then he smiled. "For you, the world is your oyster."

Kally jumped in surprise and looked at Oscar with a strange mixture of respect and wary apprehension. She allowed a small sigh of relief when he did not notice.

In front of them, down the brick road, Omby-Amby marched at the head of the Emerald Army with Wickrie-Kells at his side. "Ho, Oscar." The Soldier with Green Whiskers raised his hand in greeting. Oscar returned the friendly gesture.

"You brought the parade to me." Oscar said, as they came within easy speaking distance.

"Everyone here came. There are some training in the South. They are here in spirit.." Omby-Amby replied. "Who is your friend?"

"This is Kally. We met along the road." Oscar turned to Kally and introduced his friends. "This is Ombrosius Ambrosius, or Omby-Amby, as we, his friends, call him. And this is Wickrie-Kells. She is the Captain of Glinda's guard."

Kally nodded politely in turn as the Wizard's friends were introduced. As she met the gaze of Wickrie-Kells, Kally's eyes flashed, silently taunting her. This was not lost on the taller girl.

"Who is she?" demanded the tall girl. She turned her back to Kally, speaking to Oscar in a harsh whisper.

"She is with me. Her name is Kally. And I happen to like her. She listens to what I have to say." Oscar said, and that was that.

The Wizard extended his arm, and Kally graciously placed her hand on his elbow. Kally pointedly shot a triumphant glance at Wickrie-Kells.

Oscar and Kally led the procession back along the brick road and to the gates of the Emerald City. The gates were open, welcome to all. There were no guards stationed there today. Indeed, Kally noticed as they walked by, that the heavy gates were still on the ground, under construction. The thick marble and emerald walls arched over their heads, free from any protective gates or gatekeepers.

Oscar and Kally walked at the head of the army through the open gates of the Emerald City, and the people cheered.

8 STANDING ARMY

The eminent people of Emerald City held a large feast that night. They wanted to prove that Glinda was not the only one who could throw a party. The City Fathers prepared a large celebration to rival Glinda's ball. After all, the Wizard was their wizard, and he had built the Emerald City, so he was eminently worthy of a feast in his honor.

While the Wizard was the Guest of Honor, other notables from the region were honored for their role in establishing the Emerald City. From across the plains, in the Emerald Valley, the King of the Emerald Lands, Pastoria, sat near to the Wizard. At his side was his advisor, the witch, Mombi.

At Oscar's side was his best friend and Captain of the Emerald Guardsmen, Omby-Amby; next to Omby-Amby was Wickrie-Kells; and then Kally. In any other situation, Oscar would have been glad to have Glinda sitting next to him, but now he was not so sure. He had his trusted friend on his right hand, and he had his chief rival, Pastoria, on his left. Spread out through the remainder of the tables in the hall were the eminent people of the Emerald City and Central City, capital city of the Emerald Lands.

These persons were naturally invited because they made the best party guests—they laughed quickly, they were beautiful, and they understood how important they were. When there was a party to be had, these people could be found either making plans for it, or scheming during the festivities.

Filling the tables of these parties was a regular exercise for the planners. Determining who sat closest to the guests of honor was a highly technical process that involved favors and gossip and subtle manipulations. It was quite a game for each one of these eminent persons to try to get closest to the seats of power. Some of them played the game very well, and they managed to get very close, indeed.

The celebration progressed with jugglers and acrobats, singers and ballads of the great battles won by the Wizard. How the greatest battles in the history of Oz had all pointed to the one man who could unite the land in power and in peace. Great cities sprung up at his feet. Fire rose from the earth to warm his toes. He was Oz, the Great and Terrible, wo, wo be unto his enemies, for they would fall beneath his great head and be swallowed in the flames of his mighty displeasure.

As the dancers danced and the celebration progressed in the center of the ballroom, the major players at the tables and on the periphery moved into position. It was clear that Mombi and Pastoria were there for some other purpose than to celebrate the Wizard. Pastoria leaned over to the Wizard and gestured to Omby-Amby, the Captain of the Guard. "You have quite a youthful Captain there. How do you find such talent?"

"To hear your soldiers tell the story, King Pastoria, it would seem that I recruited from the ranks of the demons from beneath the earth to lead my army. Or have you forgotten that my single Soldier with Green Hair chased away nearly your entire Royal Army of Oz?"

Pastoria forced a tight smile and leaned back in his seat.

Omby-Amby chuckled quietly. Loyalty among friends was one of the greatest treasures he held. He knew that Oscar felt the same, and so he trusted the Wizard in the presence of the rival kingdoms. What he didn't trust was—

Kally elbowed in between Omby-Amby and the Wizard. "I'm wondering about that Pastoria. Why does he have a witch at his side, and yet you have no one at yours?"

Omby-Amby frowned and reached his hands out to move the girl out of the way. Then he found that he could not reach around her without appearing undignified. He glanced back at Wickrie-Kells, but his hands were up by Kally's hips. So Wickrie-Kells shared her glare between Omby-Amby and Kally's prominently-positioned backside.

Kally jostled her way in even further to lean over the armrest on Oscar's chair. "You have so much power here. Why don't you tell one of your stories?"

A twinkle appeared in Oscar's eyes. "You really think so?"

Kally nodded. Her amber eyes danced. She prodded further. "You are the Wizard. See that they know that. I see Pastoria and his witch are licking their chops."

"I thought that was the sweetmeats."

"No. It is not. Prove your wizardry. Make your voice heard."

Oscar stood up and raised his hands. The musicians fell silent. The dancers stopped and their flowing skirts swished quietly to a halt.

Across the table, Mombi glared at Kally, who only smirked in return. She could feel the piercing glare from Wickrie-Kells on the back of her neck, but she didn't mind at all—she had the Wizard's ear.

The next morning in Emerald City, it was business as usual. The architects and builders went back to work, the merchants opened their shops, and the eminent persons gathered to discuss the events of last night's party. They gathered in the halls near the Wizard's chamber. Like a school of fish, they moved as one until they reached their destination, then they became like a seated flock of birds, chirping and warbling. They were very much the codfish aristocracy, though they never used those terms. They were the elite, the rulers—the upper-crust of society. Without them, the well-oiled social framework of the Emerald City would absolutely fall apart.

Of pre-eminent note was the story related by the Wizard the night before. It was quite the buzz. He called it, *The Princess with Fire inside her Head*. Each day the fire burned hotter and hotter until not even the sky could hold back the heat. She breathed, and everyone around her turned to ashes. From the ashes, she plucked the bones and the treasures. These she kept as tokens of her power. No matter how hot her fire burned, she could never burn herself—she could not feel the fire, even though it drove every waking moment of her life. In time, wars devastated the land, and the only weapon that was left was the princess with fire inside her head. As the armies arrayed against the princess, she spoke a single word…and that was where the Wizard ended the story.

Strangely, the Wizard could not be bothered with entertaining the eminent people of Emerald City today. He dispatched his advisors to accompany Pastoria and Mombi and their contingent to the back chambers of the palace. His words were that he would be with them shortly.

Fifteen minutes later Oscar entered the chambers, followed closely by Kally. Mombi stood up and pointed angrily. "She has no business here. This is a negotiation between your city and mine!"

Pastoria looked sideways at his advisor, but held his tongue.

The Wizard took his seat at the table before he replied. "She is here at my request. I have instructed her that there will be no interruptions or shenanigans, and I give you the same admonition. We are here today to discuss the costs and obligations of maintaining a standing army."

Pastoria rustled papers and tapped his fingers on the table.

He looked over at Pastoria, who studied the young wizard closely. "Your majesty has something to say?"

Pastoria scowled and then smiled. "Your tardiness has lost precious minutes in my schedule. My coachmen will need to walk fast to get home in time for the peacock procession."

"And this is an event that your majesty is unable to postpone or re-negotiate?"

"The peacocks are a rare breed. Crimson. Their feathers glow in the fading sunlight of the afternoon. Each day they hold a procession as they march back to their cribs to retire."

Kally rolled her eyes. Oscar maintained a small bit of decorum, as was his responsibility as ruler of the city. "So you are in a hurry to kiss your birds goodnight? We are discussing troop levels in our city—in the Emerald Lands. These matters have great importance to our people and to the rising generation. This is far more important than a bunch of birds, no matter how pretty they are."

"Well said." Kally breathed, patting Oscar's hand.

Mombi glared at the girl.

Pastoria waved his fingers in a circular *get-on-with-it* motion in the air. "Yes, yes. Are you finished?"

"Finished rebuking you? Or finished with what, exactly?"

"Or with the negotiations. You see, young wizard, I have very few questions, and I expect that they will be answered in short order. Is that enough for a man of your stature, such as it is, to handle?"

Oscar bristled, but he kept his composure. The barbs slung by Pastoria were a ritual in these negotiations. They had increased in frequency and in venom over the last twelve months. As soon as Oscar had put his words down on paper and signed them, Pastoria had been mocking him in private, and in every meeting they had. This was no different from the other times, except that the Wizard didn't have Glinda at his side. *That* was different.

Oscar sat down and gestured for the questions to proceed. At his side, Kally sat back and watched. She studied Pastoria's swagger, Mombi's watchful gaze, and Oscar's strained silence. Of the three, Mombi held the most advantage in this room. Pastoria was blustery, but like any storm, he would blow over quickly. Oscar would be another matter. His strained silence could only stem from frustration, which could blow up, or it could silently simmer. It would be interesting to see how each of them handled themselves in a crisis. She didn't trust the coward, Mombi—she always ran away when things got difficult. Pastoria was hard to predict, but his eyes were not hard to follow. Kally stretched and drew his gaze. Interesting how men of power could be so powerless.

Now Oscar tapped his fingers on the table. Pastoria shifted his eyes from Kally to Oscar. The Wizard glanced at Kally. "Please don't." He whispered.

"What? I was stretching." Kally protested quietly.

Pastoria stood and gestured in a wide, imposing sweep of his arm. "Little Wizard, how large is your army? You must have a great number of men to protect this fine city."

Oscar had the strength of character not to stand up and match his height to the taller king. He tapped his finger slowly on the table as he spoke. "The army grows daily. We have sufficient for now. There is not a war, so we are trying to limit the growth of our standing army. Many men have volunteered to fight at a moment's notice."

"I see." Pastoria licked his lips. "And how do you pay these standing soldiers?"

"There is a specific tax written into the code of law for maintaining what soldiers are deemed necessary by the Fathers of the City."

"In those words," Pastoria almost giggled. "those words, exactly?"

"Yes. The Fathers of the City are myself, Omby-Amby, and those whom we have chosen to help administer the day-to-day functions of the city. Does that amuse you?"

Pastoria and Mombi shared a glance. "It is just a very large job for such a small group of men. I am surprised that you have not expanded the functions of the government."

"Government is of the people."

"Of course. Of course. But it must be of the best people. Nothing less would do for this fine, fine city. Only the best people to govern and rule."

"Yes. That is what we have chosen—only the best people." Oscar stood to unroll a map on the table.

Pastoria gestured him to stop. "I will defer in my negotiations to my trusted advisor, Mombi. She will conduct the remainder of the negotiations in my stead. Her word carries great power in these Emerald Lands."

"I'm sure," murmured Kally.

Oscar unrolled the map on the table. "Don't let me keep you, then. Fly home to your chickens."

"Peacocks, Little Wizard. They are crimson peacocks."

"Oh, that's right. No bird of lesser beauty could possibly command the attention of a king."

"Exactly." Pastoria strolled to the door. He paused to wait for the doorman to open it, and turned back to the Wizard. "I leave you in the capable hands of Mombi. She bears the tedium far better than I."

The door closed. Oscar waited until the echo subsided in the chamber. He turned to Mombi and gestured to the map. "You are authorized to speak on behalf of your kingdom?"

Mombi smiled, and she glanced warily between the wizard and Kally. "I am. The king entrusts me with all matters of state."

"I would speak with you away from loose ears. I understand that you have a gift of truth-telling. I would see what the future holds between our cities."

Oscar arose and walked out the door. Mombi gathered her robes of state around her and felt the familiar weight of the Silver Mirror in her pocket. She instructed her assistants to remove themselves back to their ambassador's quarters. She whispered softly, "Memorize the map before you go. I want a replica tonight." And then she followed Oscar and Kally out of the room.

Oscar led them down the corridor and into his throne room. He closed the heavy doors behind them and locked it.

"I fear that your king does not appreciate the importance of limiting the power of a standing army. I need to know that I am dealing with an honest ambassador. I have heard, Witch, that you can discern truly. Will you prove to me that you speak the truth?"

Mombi pulled the Silver Mirror from within her robes and held it in the low light. She smiled as Kally paled. "The Silver Mirror tells no tales. It reflects the deeper truth." She leveled her stare at Kally. "It reveals all deception."

"So you deceived them?" Promethus asked Glinda. "You didn't really have the army that you said you had."

"I didn't have a choice. It was the only way to guarantee the appearance of peace between the South and the West. We have people rallying to our banner, but I would not fight the Winged Monkeys. I know how many there are. We had to have a larger army to ensure that Ondri-baba would not attack us again."

Promethus shook his head. "You have single-handedly managed to anger every witch in the entire Land of Oz. Not even your mother could do that. But then, your mother did not have the certain heritage that you have."

"The Land of Oz cannot handle another Witch War. You know what the last war did."

"Are you referring to the Second Witch War, with Queen Ozma, the Fifth? Or are you referring to your escapades on the Munchkin Fields, two years ago?"

"Two years ago. Munchkin Fields. The land..."

Promethus steepled his fingers and bowed his head in thought. When he looked up again, his eyes were dark and troubled. "You are not ready to hear most of this. All I will say right now is that there was once a great city where the Emerald City now stands. The Second Witch Wars razed it to the ground. No one really remembers the city of Parradime. There are songs, as you know, and the stories of the philosophers—Socrates, Pericles, Sophocles, and Chumpocles—"

"*Chumpocles the Wise.*" Glinda interrupted.

"Yes, *Chumpocles the Wise*. I wish that silly song had never been written. It mocks the wisest of philosophers and turns him into a buffoon."

"It's a fun song."

"Fun is relative. In any case, true history has been altered. I don't know exactly when it happened, but only fragments of independent records remain.

"What you witnessed two years ago, Glinda, was a war between witches. It was not a Witch War. The Witches were not united against the Land to conquer or perish. Pray you never witness such a thing."

"That is exactly why I am working so hard to keep the peace here and now."

"By lying to your enemies."

"By keeping an army ready to battle."

Promethus stood up from the laboratory table and crossed to the window. "Strange winds are blowing in Oz. I hope your small army will be sufficient to win the day."

"They are good girls. I trust them."

"Skilled in the sword and bow, I presume?"

"Yes."

"Any other weapons? Mass-destructors? Pity-bombs? Cyklo-kytheric gassers?"

Glinda's curious expression caught Promethus off-guard, and he turned back to the window. "Probably not. Those were just ideas. Still only ideas. Never mind. Bows and swords will have to win the day until your sorcery is ready."

"My mother said that sorceresses make things, not just toss around magic like it was dead cats."

Promethus raised his eyebrows. "She told you that? *Heh.* That was a day never to be forgotten." His gaze wandered back through memory, and Glinda saw the amusement dancing in his eyes. Glinda never knew that side of her mother that could make people smile. Then Promethus returned to the present. "She was right. Sorceresses, and sorcerers, make things. They don't just use magic—they create. The art of sorcery goes right along with the art of study and learning. You have to know before you can do. That is the only way that knowledge can be safe—learn it first, and then do it. None of this getting half-brained ideas and then running down to the spell-chambers to try it out—that is dangerous."

Glinda's sad expression bore solemn testimony to her recent experience in this area. Promethus sat slowly down at the table. "I see. Did you hurt someone?"

Glinda nodded.

"Did they die?"

Glinda shook her head. Her eyes burned with angry, accusing tears that she would not let fall to testify against her. She held them inside and held her head high. "No. No one died."

"Good. It can be fixed, then." Promethus stood to go. "If war is coming, you'd best be ready, girl. The Witches are older, meaner, and more powerful than a sprightly girl."

"If war does come, you know how to win it, don't you?" Glinda asked, trying to keep the pleading from her voice.

Silence.

"What will it take for you to trust me? I am not a Wicked Witch. I am Glinda, the Good, remember?"

"Aye. And who gave you that name? Self-bestowed, I imagine. And those can be the most dangerous names of all. Titles are not to be worn lightly, for they follow long after you sleep. Your legacy is not who you think you are, but who your actions demonstrate you to be. Others will decide if you are Glinda, the Good. For now, and for me, you are Glinda, daughter of Quelala, and that is enough for me to trust you with my word. Let that be enough for you, too."

"Very well. I hope that my youth does not bother you, Sir. It certainly gave no pause to your masters. They were rather taken with me, I believe."

"Old Smith & Tinker knew that war was good for business. A fiery lass like you was certain to stir up plenty of business." He chuckled wryly, "Plenty of business." Then he sighed. "I fear that you are both your mother's daughter *and* your father's daughter."

"And is that a bad thing?"

"That, lassie, is up to you."

9 SILVER MIRROR TELLS NO TALES

"The name that I am known by, in my present age, is Kally." The words came out forced, carefully. Kally's panicked eyes searched Oscar's face as he studied the Silver Mirror.

Oscar studied the shifting reflection in the mirror and heard the staccato whispers as they repeated back exactly what Kally said.

Mombi pressed again. "Tell him about your armies. About how you strangled your friend. About how you hate and what you really want from him. Tell the wizard you love him." Mombi let the last words hang in the air and crossed her arms, smiling.

Kally's pleading eyes begged Oscar to wave his hand and make all of this disappear, but the magic never came. Instead, Oscar waited. He lifted an eyebrow at the word *love*. Still, he had asked for a demonstration of the Silver Mirror's power. For the last ten minutes Mombi had been mercilessly grilling Kally with questions. Slowly and painfully, Kally answered each of the questions. Each excruciating pause tugged on Oscar's resolve even more. Kally's eyes sunk deeper and the shadows grew darker. Her answers to all of Mombi's questions echoed in Oscar's mind.

"I am the daughter of the keeper of knowledge in Munchkin Country. I was born to rule over all the land. I keep many secrets, especially from those closest to me. I drive away those who could care because I cannot care. I love the Wizard for the power he holds behind the shadows in his eyes."

Then Mombi asked one final question. "Are you the Wicked Witch of the East?" She smirked at Kally's exquisite discomfort. This was as pleasant as crushing the hopes and dreams of a Witch. Mombi satisfied herself with watching Kally writhe in honest agony. Then Kally stood perfectly still as she lifted her amber eyes and responded unequivocally.

Mombi did not expect the Silver Mirror to repeat clearly and purely Kally's answer.

"I am not the Wicked Witch of the East." The mirror intoned.

Mombi's mouth gaped open. She reached out for the mirror, but the Wizard held it out of her reach.

"Enough. I am satisfied that Kally is who she says she is. I wish to test the truth-revealing properties of this mirror for myself." He turned and disappeared behind a curtain.

Mombi's eyes flashed at Kally. "The Silver Mirror is unbreakable. You must tell the truth or it reveals your deception. How did you lie?"

Kally smiled and flexed her fingers. It had been quite some time since she had exercised her telekinetic magic, and she relished the thought of crushing the life out of Mombi—finishing the job that she had let go two years previous. The traitor Mombi abandoned her in the moment of triumph. Such betrayals could not long go unpunished, and now was the moment of her power.

Kally's magic reached out and grabbed Mombi by the neck and lifted her into the air. Kally stepped toward the floating witch. "In these lands, the people call Kalinya the Wicked Witch of the East. Witch, I most certainly am, but Wicked…is in the eye of the beholder. And my deeds of protecting, preserving, and expanding the power of the Munchkins—those deeds are not wicked. You failed, Mombi. You were the pretty one. Somehow you charmed your way into Pastoria's graces. Would he like your face in this shade of purple? It seems to me that he likes younger flesh—"

Footsteps approached from behind the curtain. Kally dropped Mombi to the ground. Kally folded her hands neatly in front of her. Mombi choked and sputtered as she turned away, gasping for breath.

Oscar swept aside the curtain. His face was pale as death. His shaking hands held out the mirror to Mombi. He paid no attention to her bulging eyes or her wheezing voice. He simply placed the mirror at her feet and walked quietly to his throne, where he sat and sweated.

Kally cocked her head curiously and looked down at the held reflection on the mirror. She caught the last repeated word, "—humbug." The whisper stretched out into the room.

Oscar's ragged sigh served just as well as his acceptance of the Silver Mirror's magic. "I believe you, Witch."

Mombi straightened up. Her voice was hoarse, but regal. "I prefer the title, Lady Chamberlain, if you please." She put the Silver Mirror back into her pocket. "What did your lordship see?"

"I saw myself. That is all." He whispered.

Kally stepped forward, but Mombi stepped sideways into her path, blocking her. Mombi spoke quickly, "Your majesty would do well to surround himself with such persons as would constantly show the accurate reflection of the man. I know dwarfs and minstrels that cut kings down quite nicely."

Kally stepped out from behind Mombi. "Did you see the awful words?" She cast an accusatory glare back at Mombi as she stepped onto the dais and up to the throne. "Such awful things she made you say. There is no pity in her cold heart. She truly is a Wicked Witch."

"No." Oscar shook his head, trying to clear out the clinging echoes. "I need…armies. We were talking of armies. Witches. Peace."

Mombi pulled the Silver Mirror from her pocket and held it before her face. "I have not yet demonstrated my truth, Wizard."

"NO!" Kally cried out hoarsely, thrusting out her hands. Her magic coursed around Mombi, but it only whipped her dress and hair around.

"I am the Witch, Mombi. I am the fairest of all the witches. I rule Central City with a silent fist. I—" the mirror repeated the words after she said them, causing a strange echo to reverberate in the throne room.

Shadows shook loose from the walls and crashed to the floor, twitching. Oscar trembled on his green marble throne. His pale face glistened under a sheen of cold sweat. His hands clenched and unclenched. "No." he said. "No more."

"—Wizard is most powerful—"

"OZ THE GREAT AND TERRIBLE COMMANDS SILENCE!" The voice came from all over the room and shook the floor to its very foundations. Both Kally and Mombi fell to their knees. Oscar stood on trembling legs in front of his throne.

The Silver Mirror slowly dropped from Mombi's hands and tumbled end over end to the green marble floor. It shattered, piercing the heart of the air with its crystalline purity.

"No!" Mombi screamed. She scrambled to grab the razor-sharp pieces.

Oscar slumped backwards into the throne. Kally came to sit at his feet. Mombi wrapped her bloody hands in her cloak and carried the Silver Mirror away from them, sobbing. Her tears streaked her face, leaving rivulets of paint running down her cheeks. The tears cut through the painted mask and revealed the pain of the woman beneath. She pushed her way out the door, leaving a bloody handprint on the handle.

The door slowly closed. The thud echoed like a sunken heart.

"I didn't trust her." Kally murmured.

Oscar reached out and put his hand on top of Kally's head. He scrabbled his fingers on the crown of her head to get her to turn to look at him. "Please, just look at me. What do you see?"

Kally didn't even blink, "I see the Wizard who will rule all of Oz with the power and purity of his dreams. I will help you unlock that power. I will be your Witch. I will be your heart."

An exhausted tear worked its way to the corner of the Wizard's eye and spilled onto his cheek. "I am so tired" he whispered.

10 WIZARDLY VISION

The day quickly dropped into night. The Wizard retired to his primary residence in the tallest tower in the Emerald City—the Nebraska Tower. It didn't make any sense why he called it that, and he wouldn't explain, so Kally left it alone.

Bridges connected the towers at various levels. The city existed at far more than just street level. There was the main street level, which was where the merchant shops opened every morning. The towers held apartments for eminent citizens and important city counselors. There were apartments for the leadership of the city and any visiting dignitaries. But by far, the most populous of the tower-dwellers were the Architects. They resided in, and kept their construction materials in most of the towers—they seemed to be everywhere.

In the red light of sunset, Kally walked along the Piper's Bridge from the Nebraska Tower. As birds would land on the ornamental railing, she would flick them away with her telekinetic magic. It felt good to startle the unsuspecting birds. With Oscar retiring to bed early, she had nothing to do, so she set out to explore and discover the secrets of the city.

The Architect wore an ornate yellow hat. He pulled a pair of goggles down over his eyes and sat down to watch the Nebraska Tower. Kally watched him as he watched. Her curiosity shuffled her forward.

"What are you watching?"

"The tower. I expect tonight will be pretty active."

"What do you mean by active?"

"The Wizard is under a lot of stress. When he burns off stress he dreams pretty big."

"He *dreams*?"

"Of course the Wizard *dreams*. That means that he uses his powers in sleep to create fantastic visions that translate and form the city around him into the place that he came from—up in the clouds. We are building a Wizard-city here. Every night he dreams, and we watch. When we see what he makes, we note it and draw it up in our tablets, and the builders get busy on it first thing in the morning."

"Why are you telling me this?" Kally asked, suddenly suspicious.

"Sunset. Pretty girl. Beautiful city. Brings out the best in a Winkie."

Suddenly the bridge convulsed as a wave passed through it. Kally fell forward into the Winkie Watcher. "Well, that's a welcome how-do-you-do. I'm Perilous Eddy. No one else likes to man this post—too close to danger—but I've always considered it lucky. Like right now."

Kally extricated herself from Eddy's arms. She turned to see buds forming on the bridge and pushing upward like growing seeds, until they blossomed into full-grown miniature stone trees. These lined the bridge—both top-side and bottom-side. Eddy was already scribbling away with his stick of charcoal in the tablet.

Kally leaned over the edge of the bridge to see the wave pass through the next set of towers, and then the next. She recognized the magic by its slightly reddish aura. "Did you see that?" she asked Eddy.

"I only see the results." He didn't look up from his drawing. "That's all I have time for. The first wave grew trees." He laughed hopefully. "It's going to be a busy night. He turned up the wick in his lantern and settled in to watch the Nebraska Tower.

Kally looked all around, picked a tower, and walked toward it. She looked back at Eddy. He was busy scribbling, with his nose down in the paper. No one was watching. She lifted her long skirts slightly, revealing the Silver Slippers and her striped stockings. The slippers could transport her instantly through line-of-sight. There was nobody to see. She took one, two, three steps, and she was at the other tower.

This tower had a purple color in the fading sunlight. No lights had yet been lighted inside. No voices could be heard. She stepped inside to feel the cold, stale air of a mausoleum. No construction materials were here. Stone flowers adorned the walls, accented with precious gems. The Silver Slippers glowed in the dark beneath her skirts, lighting her steps.

This *was* a mausoleum. Inside and behind the stone slabs Kally could feel the bones of the dead rattling around as she lifted her hands. She longed for a light to read the names and the inscriptions on the slabs.

Another convulsion ripped through the tower. Kally stumbled against the stone slab, bruising her cheek. She raised her hand to shatter the slab, but stopped when she heard a pained gasp.

"Who is there?" Kally crouched and crept around. "Who might I find among the bones of the dead? Do I have a visitor willing to join them?"

Kally reached out with her magic and felt a small lantern on the floor ahead of her. She picked it up. Strange popping noises sounded all around her. The bones rattled and creaked in their sarcophagi. "Who is here?" Kally felt around the lantern and found a match. She struck it to glorious light on the stone slab. The bright light dazzled her eyes for a moment.

In that moment footsteps scampered around the far side of the tower. Kally trimmed the wick in the lantern and raised it high to look around her. On the floor and also on the stone slab—that one cut through the red emblems with a match strike—were two *bloody handprints*.

"Oh, Mombi, where are you? Come out and play." Kally sang. "We can jump and sing and dance like we used to. You can tell all the boys you'll kiss them and then turn them into frogs."

"And then you'll throw them into the sky. You were a horrible best friend." The critical voice slid out of the cloaking shadows. Mombi stepped out of the darkness behind the row of sarcophagi and into the dim circle of light.

Kally frowned and shook her head vigorously. "Lest you forget, I saved you."

Mombi's eyes hardened. *That* was not a fair argument. "I have a life that I happen to prefer over your schemes of getting killed."

"You're still alive. I'm young again, and prettier than you. Everything is as it should be. Besides," Kally smiled wickedly, "You never could resist a scheme."

"For once, you're prettier, but it won't last. Your schemes never do, Kalinya. You always find a way to ruin everything you put your hands on."

"*You* turned out well. Thanks to me, you're a witch. You have the ear of the King of the Emerald Lands. You are the power behind the throne. You still have a *somewhat* pretty face."

"I only survived because I ran away from you—all of your wars and your petty rivalry with your sister. She will destroy you. You may have been cleverer than Ondri-baba, but she is mean right down to her iron-cold heart."

"Pish-posh. Ondri-baba is stupid. She has no plans, no desires. She does not compare in any way to me."

"She has the Winged Monkeys. She rules over the Winkies and the entire land of the West. And she has the Golden Cap. Wouldn't that be a perky little token to win in a game of chance?"

"I see what you're doing, and it won't work, Mombi. I see you are trying to manipulate me into challenging my sister—" Kally stopped and cleared her throat. She narrowed her eyes at Mombi, who smiled sweetly from under her dark eyes. "—from challenging Ondri-baba. I will have the Golden Cap. I deserve it. I am the eldest. And right now, I am the prettiest. I get exactly what I want."

"Ah yes, to be pretty. That was so fleeting for you, wasn't it? Then I came along, and you just couldn't make the boys look at you anymore. Is it my fault that my hips shimmy? I really need to fix that heel on my boot."

"It won't work. I won't do it. Your manipulation is so painfully obvious. You've lost your touch, Mombi. Those dark eyes and long eyelashes may work on the peacock king, but they won't work on me. See, I'm too smart for that."

Mombi sighed. "You're right. I shouldn't have even tried with you, Kalinya. You are too clever for my tricks. I guess I'll just let myself out and say goodnight. And good luck with your scheme for controlling the Emerald City. It is a fine conquest—a fine, fine conquest. You have absolutely nothing to be ashamed or jealous of. How many witches can truly say that they rule over a land? Well, *two*, actually. You and Ondri-baba. The Emerald City doesn't count as a land, since it is part of the Emerald Lands, and those are Pastoria's. You can be proud of what you have. You're the best of us all right now." Mombi backed away, a slight smile tugging at her perfect lips. She kept her injured hands tucked away in the folds of her robe. "You have won."

The lantern burned out, leaving only a glowing ember left. Kally's eyes adjusted to the darkness, but Mombi was gone.

"I should have thrown her from the tower." Kally muttered. "Right from the top of this tower. Watch her fall all the way down to the street. That would teach her. I have nothing to be ashamed of. I won. That's right—I won." Kally glowered in the darkness as she stepped on to the balcony. The bridge connecting this tower had disappeared. It was now a leaning statue extending out from the yellowish tower nearby.

Kally sighted an unpopulated bridge and stepped one, two, three steps, and she left the mausoleum tower behind. She hurried into the far tower before anyone saw her appear suddenly out of nowhere.

Behind her, in the darkness of the mausoleum tower, Mombi stepped out of the shadows and smiled. "You could have thrown me from the tower, you're right, Kalinya. But then, you are just too smart for me. My manipulations don't work on you at all. You'll be just fine without the Golden Cap. Just fine."

The wind picked up and blew Mombi's dark hair around her face. She brushed it aside with a finger and winced as the hair caught in the sticky clotting blood on her injured hands.

"I only survived your schemes because I ran away. Kalinya, do you even have a clue what destiny you are racing into? I won't be a part of your plans anymore. No matter what you say—I won't."

The next morning Oscar awoke and strolled out onto the balcony to find Kally already wide awake and busy watching the Architects.

"That wasn't there before." Oscar exclaimed, pointing out the statue on the building, and then the carved trees on the Piper's Bridge. "Neither was that. Wow. They do amazing work. Every morning I wake up and they've build something new. It is incredible how quickly—and how magnificently—this city is growing. It's like something from a dream."

"Could your dreams be creating all of this wonder?"

"No. Dreams can inspire people, but this—" he turned all the way around with his hands outstretched, "—is beyond anything I could dream. The Winkie Architects are truly master craftsmen. They deserve all of the praise for creating this great city."

"They look to you. I'm sure they feed you ideas."

"Oh, sure. They show me plenty of drawings. Every day, it's at least two hours of looking through new submissions and proposed towers or statues or walkways." He stretched and yawned. "I am so tired. You would think that I didn't get any sleep at all."

Kally noticed a shadow shudder behind Oscar as it pulled away from the wall and then collapsed into the light. She smiled as the plan began to take shape. "You have a big day today."

"I have big days everyday. It's one of the perks of being the Wizard."

"Let me plan a trip out there for you. We'll get away from the responsibility, the constant noise of construction, the stress of rulership. We'll go somewhere less busy. A place where we can watch the sun rise from close up. Maybe we'll go west."

"From up here," Oscar sighed, "I can see so much of the Emerald Lands." He turned to Kally. "Some days I would like to see not quite so much."

"Power is a burden, but power is the end result. You have obtained so much—you have a city, a name, and a fame that cannot be matched. Look at the Witches. What do they have? They have lands, but they do not have what you have. They are not legends."

"Yet."

"With any luck, at least one of them will be forgotten and never spoken of again."

"There are things unspoken that still haunt."

Kally lifted her eyes from the streets far below and watched the Wizard as he stared out into the morning sun. The wind blew his unkempt hair and watered his brown eyes. Still he kept staring. What was it out there that kept him looking beyond the clouds? What mysteries did he hold just beyond reach? In the bright light of morning, the shadows were gone. All was well. It was deep in the lower streets of the city that the shadows continued. Up in the heights, the powerful lived outside the shadows.

Oscar blinked away the moisture in his eyes and wiped them with his finger and thumb. "I've got important meetings today. I have to see what the architects created. There will be concepts they want me to review. I'm supposed to decide with Lady Chamberlain Mombi what the acceptable troop levels are going to be." He rested his elbows on the balcony railing and looked out into the marvelous city called his. "I'm tired of the meetings, the responsibilities. I want to want to spread my wings."

Kally looked at him quizzically, "You have wings?"

"No." Oscar said softly. "No, I don't."

A knock sounded, and then the bell rang, signaling visitors.

Oscar sprang up and slapped his cheeks and shook his head. He danced a jig to the door and affixed a smile to his face. "Omby, Wickrie. Come in, come in. I am happy to see you both together. Together."

Oscar clapped his hands and smiled. "You two. Together. You belong together, you know that? Come in, sit down."

Omby-Amby held up his hands to slow his friend down. "It is yet morning, and you want me off my feet? Where do you find such energy, my friend? You dream a city all night, and you rule fairly by day. When is there time for the Wizard to rest?"

"No rest for the wicked, you know that."

Omby-Amby laughed. "When did you become wicked?"

Oscar echoed the laughter. "It's just one of my many masks."

Wickrie-Kells' amber eyes darted to the girl on the balcony. "What is she doing here? Was she here all night? She has no business being anywhere close to you. Does Glinda know about any of this? You are going to be in a lot of trouble."

Oscar looked out at Kally on the balcony. She was looking out over the city. Her profile struck Oscar as being very proud and yet somehow cold and distant. "She arrived shortly before you did. I wanted her to see the view from up here. Come. Look at what the architects have created so far." Oscar pointed out the statue, and the carved trees on the Piper's Bridge. "That's just what I have seen this morning. I'm going to see the rest once you go."

"What do you mean, once we go? I'm not going anywhere." The Soldier with Green Whiskers said. "I'm the Captain of the Guard. My place is here. Oscar, you're my friend. I'm not going to abandon you."

Oscar took his friend's sleeve and pulled him away from the balcony and into the spacious apartment. "Excuse us, ladies. We have some…army business." When they were out of earshot, Oscar whispered, "You haven't seen her in a long time. Even now, you can't keep your eyes from looking at her. Go. Take a break. Get out and be a soldier again. You're not meant to be trapped inside a city, and neither is she."

"Where would we go?"

"You know what? It doesn't matter. Take a week. Take two. Be rested. If Glinda gets angry, let her be angry at me. She's got enough of that anyway. She can afford to have her Captain of the Guard spend some quality time with the Captain of my Guard. We're not at war. I do not believe we are going to be at war anytime soon. All is well."

11 SCHEMES AND DREAMS

"I don't like leaving you here alone." Omby-Amby said. His concerned eyes searched his friend's face for some hint of deception or untruth. He found none, but neither did he find any compassion toward his duty. The Wizard, Oscar, wanted some space, and he honestly wanted to be alone.

"Alone? In a city full of people? I have plenty of people all around me." Oscar replied. He forced a cheerful smile up into his eyes.

"Yes, but you still manage to stay alone. I don't like it."

Oscar gestured to Wickrie-Kells standing at the balcony. "Look at her. You would really rather stay here in the Emerald City in all these shadows than to walk in the sun with her?"

Out on the balcony, Kally kept her distance from Wickrie-Kells. It would be so easy to toss the taller girl over the edge and watch her fall to the streets far below. Indeed, that would be almost worth getting into trouble for.

There was no love lost between the two young women. Wickrie-Kells narrowed her eyes at the interloper, and Kally smiled sourly back.

"See?" said Oscar, "They're getting along just fine. I'll be here, surrounded by people. You can take a much-needed break. Stretch your legs. Go. Have fun. Be a soldier."

"There are some training exercises I could check in on. I could scout the area." Omby-Amby looked between Oscar and Wickrie-Kells twice, then smiled and walked to the tall girl. He ran his hand through his green hair and gestured over the balcony.

Kally circled the room, clinging to the shadows, and glided next to Oscar. "He's leaving."

"For a while. It'll be good for him. He's been my faithful friend, at my side, for the last two years. He and I built this place. The Emerald City is a place where a man's dreams can come true."

"Which *man's dreams*? That's an interesting turn of words."

"Life, liberty, and the pursuit of happiness. That is what each man and woman is entitled to. A person can come to Emerald City and find opportunity to follow their hopes and wishes."

"Wishes can be had by magic."

"Not the ones worth wanting." Oscar chided. "If you get something too quickly, it doesn't mean much—like you were owed it. Work is what makes a man…and a woman."

"I see." Kally said softly. "I'm impressed that you do so much alone. This is a huge city."

"It is. Lots of work. I have to have some people help me. Omby-Amby does a great job as Captain of the Guard. He keeps everything running smoothly with the Emerald Guardsmen. He says he needs more, though. I don't like it. But it is a big city. We need the City Watch. If there's one thing I've learned it's that people need to be reminded to be good."

Omby-Amby and Wickrie-Kells waved their goodbyes from the balcony and headed down the stairs to the Piper's Bridge. "I'll be back before you dream any new towers." The green-haired soldier called.

Oscar waved silently. His eyes darkened as the shadows of isolation set in. He glanced over to see Kally studying him with those intelligent amber eyes. He admitted, "The city has changed a lot over the last couple of months."

"With the things I've seen in just one night, I believe it." Kally pursed her lips. "Tell me about it."

"What sort of a present is fit for a Wizard to give to a Sorceress?" Kally asked, popping a thin curl of chocolate into her mouth. She grimaced as the confection turned to sand on her tongue. She turned away from the young wizard and wiped her tongue with a napkin. She coughed and covered her mouth with a napkin. She waved away Oscar's offer of help.

"Are you okay?"

Kally nodded, but kept the napkin over her mouth. She swabbed everything clear of her mouth and threw the crumpled napkin on the floor. "It went down wrong."

"Have some more. There's plenty of food."

"No. I'm not hungry. I'll eat later."

"Too bad. It's good." Oscar bit into a caramel. Kally watched him with hungry eyes. ""Are you sure you don't want any more?"

Kally forced her eyes down. "No. It'll just go down wrong again."

Oscar finished the caramel and licked his fingers. "Your question is a strange one. It is one that I had pondered before I met you. What would I get for Glinda on her eighteenth birthday? What should the Wonderful Wizard get for the Sorceress? That had been puzzling my mind for the last month. Then you came along. It doesn't seem so important right now."

"No. This *is* important. The Wizard has to give a gift to the Sorceress. It is political propriety. You must." Kally insisted. She tried a different tact. "What was it you said about wishes? Wishes take work. Anything impossible that you want to give the sorceress?"

"Impossible. Glinda. Now those are two words that go perfectly together." He made thinking faces and closed his eyes. He leaned backward, and then he leaned forward. Oscar shook his head slowly, visualizing impossible things. The shadows rose in his eyes and his breath caught in his throat. "No. We are thinking impossible gifts, not impossible things. It is not time to think about the things you cannot have again. Go back down. You need to control yourself. This is not your time." Oscar pressed the heels of his hands against his eyebrows and gritted his teeth. He screwed his eyes shut. "Go home." He whispered through clenched teeth.

Oscar took a deep breath. He opened his eyes wide and smiled. He breathed in through his nose. "Hmm. I've still got caramel in my teeth. It gets stuck down there sometimes. Does that ever happen to you?"

"No." Kally said slowly. "Who are you talking to?"

"You, of course. We were talking about impossible gifts."

"You were talking about impossible things."

"No, I wasn't." Oscar smiled. "Impossible gifts are different than impossible things. Here, in this land, there are plenty of impossible things: witches, magic, flying fish, talking animals...monkeys. Flying monkeys. Those are about as impossible as you can get." He rose from his seat and sucked at the caramel in his teeth. The Wizard shook his finger, at first slowly, then more rapidly. "Yes. Winged Monkey."

"Oh. A Winged Monkey." Kally's face showed a mixture of confusion, disgust, and failed surprise, "You want to give Glinda a Winged Monkey."

"No. I don't want to give her a Winged Monkey." Oscar shivered, first in his shoulders, and then all the way down to a full-body shiver. "Those things creep me out."

"Well, I suppose we can find a way to capture one. We'll need a golden cage. And it will involve traveling to the land of the West. We'll have to leave soon if we want to—"

"I don't want to give one as a present. I want to free the Winged Monkeys."

Kally shook her head and frowned, forcing her voice to sound almost pleasant. She raised her eyebrows. "How is a gift—freeing slaves?"

Oscar's face smiled, jubilant, then fell, contorted, and then finally stilled. His voice echoed from the wall behind Kally, causing her to jump in astonishment. "The Winged Monkeys are slaves to the Wicked Witch of the West. Glinda promised to free them."

"I don't understand. How did Ondri-baba—I mean, the Wicked Witch of the West—enslave the monkeys?"

Oscar's eyes shot over to Kally's face. "How did you know her name? In all the land round about here, I have only referenced the witches by their titles, not their names. What do you know about the Wicked Witches?"

Now it was Kally's turn to shift uncomfortably. She rustled her skirts, but kept her feet hidden. "I know…things."

"What things? This has to do with Mombi and the Silver Mirror, doesn't it? She knew you. Or at least she seemed like she did. How could she know you? How?"

"Mombi twisted my words, or she tried to. Remember how she made me say those awful things in the Silver Mirror. You saw. You know that the Silver Mirror reveals the truth. I saw your face—you saw something that convinced you of the truth. From me and from you. Behind your curtain with all of your secrets. You know that it reflected truth."

"I know it did. No one else knew what the mirror reflected. What is behind the curtain is mine alone. *That* man stays there, hidden. It is *this* man, here, that is asking you for truth, and I expect that I will not be disappointed.

"You, Kally, have some truth that you have hidden from me. The time has come for me to know what you know. You told me at the banquet that a Wizard should have a Witch at his side, and that you would be my Witch. Who are you? What do you know about the Witches?"

"My mother was a Witch." Kally said. Her expression showed her distaste at the admission.

"Who was she?"

"Just a Witch."

"No. There is no witch who is *just a witch*' in Oz. There are maybe a handful of witches, total. Either I've heard of them, or Glinda knows them. So who is it? It's not Locasta—she's too young. She's even younger than you, maybe. Not in the eyes, though. It is not Kalinya. She had an apprentice, and she wouldn't have taken an apprentice if she had a daughter. Ondri-baba—"

Kally snorted. Then to hide her laughter, she spit on the floor.

Oscar tilted his head at her. "You will clean that up. This is my apartment, and my city. I do not allow unauthorized spitting. Would you like to explain what that was?"

Kally fought to keep her expression controlled. She stared at the floor, not meeting the wizard's gaze. She could not lose her composure this close to the prize. She clenched her jaw and worked her hands back and forth. If things went badly here, there were always the Silver Slippers. It would only take three steps. She looked, but straight ahead was the inner wall. She would need to face outside. Kally turned and looked out past the towers of the Emerald City.

Oscar studied her profile. "Ondri-baba—the Wicked Witch of the West. You don't look much like her. Still, there could be some resemblance. Family, maybe. Is that why you spit? Ondri-baba is your mother?"

Kally shrugged, and worked her hands nervously, keeping them loose. Her eyes darted between the floor by her feet—her escape path, and the distant bridge.

"I want the truth."

Kally turned her head and raised her eyes to meet his. The fire burned in her eyes, causing Oscar to wince. "I curse this skin, this body, for its relation to her. I hate her."

Oscar laughed uncomfortably and then smiled in relief. "Now that is honesty. Thank you. I know that wasn't easy for you."

"Would you want to be related to her? No. You'd curse, too."

"I probably would. But you don't need to worry about that. You are not her. You can choose your own path in life. I'm sure you have, already. You are not with Ondri-baba. You have chosen a more difficult path than wickedness. The path of good and self-determination requires more work than evil."

"Isn't *that* the truth?" Kally muttered.

The day passed quickly. Oscar kept Kally close by during his meetings with the architects. When it came time for the troop discussions, Mombi could not be found anywhere, so they canceled those meetings. At last the sun dropped below the eastern horizon.

Oscar sat on the stairs near his balcony. "All I know is that the possessor of the Golden Cap controls the Winged Monkeys."

Kally twisted the petals off a flower and tossed them out into the space beyond the balcony. Her magic gave them a little push, but such small, frail items didn't go far. "I seriously doubt that is *all* you know."

"I don't like this idea much, not yet, anyhow. I would much rather skip the whole birthday thing for Glinda. I am not very keen on the Sorceress right now."

"It is your duty. Politics make people do things they wouldn't usually do. This is to keep the peace." Kally said.

"It would just be a lot easier for me if I didn't have to give it to her."

Kally's breath caught in her throat. It couldn't be *that* easy. "So...pretend you're getting it for someone else."

Oscar's eyes brightened.

It worked. But Kally had to make sure. "So you're sure that Glinda would not want an automaton army? We're going to look at one for the Emerald City. We can certainly get her a few. That would ease the burden on her sword-swinging vixens."

"No. She likes her Fighting Girls. Can't really say that I blame her—I mean, from a strictly wizardly perspective."

"Of course. Your eye for beautiful girls has nothing to do with appreciating their *skills*." Kally prodded Oscar.

He cleared his throat and sheepishly smiled. "Having the best guards around is definitely the best."

"I'm just making doubly sure. Your idea to go to Yellow Castle is incredibly brave. I only want to verify that you are solid in your scheme to free the Winged Monkeys."

Oscar turned to look out into the night sky. He took a deep breath and nodded his head. "Yes. For you. For me. For freedom."

"Good." Kally cooed. "Now let's figure out how we're going to get the Golden Cap from Ondri-baba."

12 SECRET APPRENTICE

Down south, in Glinda's palace, the night air did little to cool Glinda's temper. She waited for Promethus to return with the promised dinner. He had promised splatberry pie, at the very least. It was that kind of an evening, and Glinda wanted dessert first, because there was no telling what the man might say to irritate her and spoil her appetite.

She was still angry with Oscar. On top of that, she was frustrated with Promethus. How did he know what was best, anyway? He said that Glinda was both her mother's daughter and her father's daughter. Was that the best of both worlds? The way he made it sound was that she was the worst of both of them. That was an appealing thought—just when Glinda was actually making progress in securing power for the future, here comes Mister High-and-Mighty declaring her work null and void. Who gave him permission to judge?

Where was Promethus, anyway? He's been gone to the kitchen for too long. He's probably digging out something of mine...no. Not possible. Glinda's lockbox was secure, with the secret codes and symbols known only to her.

At last Promethus stepped sideways through the library door, easily carrying with one arm the heavy tray loaded with serving plates. He carried two goblets in his other hand, twirling the fragile glass stems between his fingers. He set the goblets down on the table in front of Glinda. He laid the plates on the table and sat down across from the red-haired sorceress.

"I became a student of Smith and Tinker before your father came to the South." He poured the clear water into the goblets.

"What do you know about my father?"

"He was brilliant—the cleverest child that Smith and Tinker had ever seen. He would have been the third apprentice. In fact, he was, for a time."

Glinda rested her chin on her hands. "I didn't know that."

"Few do. Quelala was in line to be the greatest apprentice. He would have easily surpassed me if he had stayed."

"Why didn't he stay?" Glinda asked. She sipped from her goblet and set it down. She traced a circle on the table with the water droplets on her finger.

"Your mother."

"She was just a girl." Glinda protested.

"No. Perhaps she *once upon a time* was a girl, but that time is lost to memory. Your mother was the Sorceress. She has always been the Sorceress. She looked as beautiful and fierce then as she did at the Abracadabra Bazaar. She never aged."

"I don't understand."

"No. Of course not. It is the secret of the Ruby Palace. She spent time in the Ruby Palace and so time became her slave. Her age was greater than what you knew."

"The Gillikin elders told me that much."

"But they did not tell you about your father. They could not, for they only knew him after the boy, Quelala, was brought to the North." Promethus took a bite of splatberry pie, then he continued. "Before Quelala was the regent prince of the North, he was the Secret Apprentice of the South."

"He never told me."

"There are far more secrets, and many more stories than you know, Glinda. You were a princess. You were destined to be your mother's apprentice."

"I know."

"But before you, there was your father."

"I knew he was a boy in the North, but—"

"The Queen of Dreams—"

Then Glinda remembered what the Flying Fish had told her. "The Queen of Dreams came to pay a visit to the Red Sorcerer and demand his daughter as a bride for her son. When the Queen of Dreams arrived at the Ruby Palace, the Sorcerer was sorry, but his daughter had gone on an extended tour of the kingdom and she was unavailable. The Queen of Dreams left. Not long after she left, the Sorcerer's daughter came back. When the Queen of Dreams came again, the daughter was already married. That daughter was my mother."

Promethus paused before letting his fork continue its journey up to his mouth. "Your knowledge is great. You have a keener insight than I was led to believe."

Glinda smiled sweetly and popped a melon ball into her mouth.

"Yes, your mother was that daughter of the Red Sorcerer. She was married to your father when the Queen of Dreams came again. But that gets ahead of the story. Before he was taken from us, your father was the Secret Apprentice."

"Gayelette came searching for the brightest and wisest man in the land. When she came to the South, she found us. Smith and Tinker were known to her, but not their apprentices. There were myself, Quelala and Ku-Klip—we were the three chosen. I was too old for her liking. Ku-Klip was short, stocky, and she found him…ugly. There was a third, Nikidik. He was to be the third apprentice, but Quelala took his place. Then Gayelette came. Nikidik was a handsome young man. He was very clever."

"She chose Quelala—my father."

"Yes."

"Nikidik was angry? But why? He…I'm sorry. Finish your story."

"Nikidik was handsome. He was strong. He was clever. But Quelala was more clever. He tricked Nikidik. The boy was a scamp and a rascal. He made Nikidik look the fool in front of the lovely maiden, er, your mother. Gayelette admired the boy. Fell in love with his spirit. He saw things that no one else saw. She took him away and left Nikidik empty-handed and empty-hearted."

"Smith and Tinker had an opening. They brought Nikidik in as an apprentice."

"Wow. So he got what he was wanting, after all."

"In a sense. He received the position of apprentice, which he wanted, but not as he wanted it. He was relegated to second-best behind a child barely half his age. Then, in the realm of romance, when the woman of his fantasies comes and smiles at him, he believes that he can become the right hand of a sorceress…and then he was relegated to second-best behind a child barely half his age. To say that he burned with anger would be understating the facts."

"Where is he now? Did he get over being angry?"

"Does anyone, really? It wasn't just that his pride was eviscerated. It was that he was beaten twice by a boy—in front of the eternally beautiful sorceress. She laughed at him, too. Where he admired Gayelette, he grew to loathe her. He styled himself a rival, not to Quelala anymore, but to Gayelette. He swore, *'where Gayelette has stopped time, I will reverse it.'*"

Glinda stopped with her goblet halfway to her mouth. Then she put the goblet down on the table. "Reverse time? Can he do that? Is that even possible?"

Promethus shrugged and ripped a crust from his bread. "Perhaps. Perhaps not. He disappeared."

"He couldn't have gone far. Oz is surrounded by desert."

"So you've see it, all the way around?"

"Well, no." Glinda admitted. "But I've seen maps. I've read books. And I can see the desert here."

"Oz is a big place—bigger than you know. There are plenty of places that you haven't been. You might think you've been all over the Land of Oz, but there are still secrets. The North holds its share."

"Like what?"

"The Ruby Palace held secrets—Gayelette stayed eternally youthful. I would imagine that the Ruby Throne holds a few, too."

"Keep imagining." Glinda smiled cryptically.

"And this castle—"

"I've explored." Glinda said, tapping fingernail on her teeth. She raised her eyebrows. "A lot."

"Oh?"

"That's right. Your secrets are now mine."

"Pretty big boasting for a girl." Promethus wiped his mouth with the napkin and set it on his plate. He got up and walked quickly across the room. He stopped in front of the Phoenix Gate mosaic and followed the eye-line down from the phoenix head and knocked three times on the painted gate of hands. The wall rearranged itself as stone hands dug away at the solid masonry and opened a portal with a stairway leading downward. "Coming? You can close your mouth."

Glinda jumped out of her seat and followed the raven-haired man down into the darkness.

"And this, my dear, is a wonder to behold." Promethus pulled the curtain from off the gold-framed painting. "*The Magic Picture*. Mr. Smith—a finer artist never was born, just ask him—painted this using fabled unguents from the Land of Ix."

"Imaginary Paint." Glinda said.

The word died on the man's lips and he deflated. He shook his finger at the girl. "You, lass, are *dangerous*."

"A little knowledge never hurt anybody."

"But a lot of knowledge did. You need time, wisdom, age, to temper your knowledge. All those thoughts and facts and information you have up in that pretty head of yours are going to twist you in ways you can't possibly prepare for. Only wisdom will guide you in your search. Otherwise you will hurt people. You know too much, and that leaves you wanting more. You push and drive and poke and prod—and then something snaps."

Promethus covered up the Magic Picture. "It's a nice painting. Very realistic. We'll come back and look at it sometime, but not now."

Glinda's eyes danced and she clucked her tongue. "Afraid of a little girl?"

"I'm getting there." Promethus gestured back toward the staircase. "After you."

"You don't have to be chivalrous, with *ladies first*, and all that. I can follow."

"No, that is one thing you cannot do. You blaze your own path, Glinda. And I prefer to follow after your steps. *Please.*" He gestured again.

"You are afraid." Glinda danced up the stairs, laughing.

"Yes." Promethus whispered. "Unwise power corrupts like rust. Weakens and corrodes integrity, and it can only be removed through harsh cleansing. I fear your cleansing will be harsher than you know."

"Smith & Tinker had three apprentices. Myself, Nikidik—"

"And my father." Glinda stepped out of the staircase and brushed a cobweb from her hair.

"For a time. There was a third, Ku-Klip."

"I think I heard that name. You did say that earlier. So what about him? My father left to become apprentice to the Sorceress. Nikidik disappeared and vowed to turn back time. You…came back here. And Ku-Klip, you brought him up for a reason."

"Yes. He was truly the apprentice of Mr. Tinker. He was a metalworker. Tin was his chosen medium. Nikidik was passion—he was emotion—but Ku-Klip was as cold as iron. Nice enough fellow when he wanted to be, but that was mostly when he found an idea that he could embrace. Always driven by ideas—always making things better. He could do it better than the faeries, or even Nature herself. See, he was the one who made the Wheelers metal. They were…not as functional before. They worked on the brick roads, but they fell apart when they went too fast. All of us worked on them, really, but Ku-Klip did the small, intricate metalwork. He was a masterworker. He was curious and he was determined. I imagine he's somewhere near a mine now. There is always call for metalsmiths—especially ones that don't limit themselves to other people's rules. Artisans."

"Think the Witches found him?"

"If he wants them, he'll move in their direction. You're not going to sway Ku-Klip with emotion. No—he's not like that at all. But when gets an idea in his head, he will move the pillars of the sky to make it happen."

"The Winkies are metalworkers." Glinda suggested.

"He is aware. Making trinkets is not his line of work. He likes bigger things—things that move. Like the Hamstrambulator—it was originally powered by Wheelers. It was supposed to have an engine that held magic, so the Wheelers could keep running inside, even off the brick roads."

"Do you trust him?"

"Yes and no. Yes, because he can be trusted. No, because I don't know what his current plans are. Mostly, though, it's yes."

"Then I won't worry about him." Glinda said.

"A lockbox is a place to keep your greatest treasures. I have one here on the castle grounds. All of the apprentices of Smith & Tinker do. Anyone who's got a secret they can't keep inside their own head has a special, impenetrable place to keep it."

Glinda's eyes darted around the room—anywhere but the dark-haired man's face. He noticed. "Including you, princess. You don't need to say anything more. I know you have one, and that is your business. What would a young princess have that I could possibly want? Not much, I assure you. I am more interested in retrieving what secrets are mine."

Promethus led Glinda out across the grounds to the river bend and the water wheel. The wheel was formed of a great ancient nautilus shell. The hypnotic spiral pattern swirled with the flow of the river. The wheel powered much of the inner workings of the South Castle. Promethus climbed up into the spiral of the water wheel and timed his steps with the hypnotic spiral, and then disappeared. He appeared two minutes later with a lockbox on top of the nautilus wheel. He tossed the box off the wheel and into the river.

"What are you doing?" Glinda cried.

"I have what I need. The rest will be claimed by the desert."

The strongbox bobbed in the river as it wound its way closer to the edge of the land. The falls roared as they leaped off the magic land to meet their everlasting demise in the Great Shifting Sands—the Deadly Desert of the South. The strongbox hung for a moment in the air, surrounded by shimmering mist, then it disappeared into the depths below.

Promethus joined Glinda on the banks of the river. He looked out at the mist separating the river from the desert. "I have completed my journey as an apprentice. It's time for a new role—a new life."

"Where are you going?" Glinda asked.

"Hear me well, Glinda, Queen Sorceress of the South, I remove my belongings from South Castle. I renounce my claim on these lands.

"I warn you, that the other Apprentices will each return one day for their strongbox. They are to be allowed, without question, to retrieve that which they have secreted away. As ruler of this castle, pass the word. See that your people know and accept this."

"I will." Glinda promised.

Wickrie-Kells led Omby-Amby down into the Emerald Valley. They walked along the sparkling river. "You're going to like my father. He's going to love you." She squeezed the soldier's hand and smiled.

They stopped at a clearing in the forest where the water pooled silvery in the afternoon light. "It feels different here." Omby-Amby said. He dipped his hand into the water. "It tingles. Like magic."

"We called it the Truth Spring when I was growing up. If you drink from it you have to tell the truth."

"How long?"

Wickrie-Kells shrugged. "We got tired of it after about an hour, and it still worked after that, so probably a few hours. This is where King Klick agreed to help Glinda return to the North—before we met you."

Omby looked down at his reflection in the silvery water. Wickrie-Kells joined him in his reflection. She wrapped her arm around his waist. "I'm wondering something. I'll tell you mine if you tell me yours."

Wickrie-Kells smiled.

They both drank deeply from the spring.

The afternoon passed quickly. The headiness of the truth water was like nothing Omby-Amby had ever experienced. "I thought I knew truth before, but this is more clear. These things—the ones I have always wanted to tell you—they are true. I could not say them if they weren't."

"I know." Wickrie-Kells smiled as she took him by the hand. "Now, there is one more thing before forever."

"I've already kissed you, what more can there be?"

"My father."

"Your father."

"My father."

"I have to kiss your father?" Omby asked.

Wickrie-Kells pushed the green-haired soldier and he stumbled good-naturedly. "No, you don't have to kiss my father. You need to talk with him. You know—ask him."

"What are your intentions with my daughter?" Tjorn Dunkle asked the soldier with green whiskers.

"I intend to marry her and bring you at least a dozen grandchildren, Sir."

"Twelve?" Wickrie-Kells exclaimed.

"Do you love her?" Donya, Wickrie's mother, asked.

"More than I have ever loved anyone."

"Really?" Wickrie smiled.

"Love means loyalty, my boy. Is there anyone or anything that would tear your loyalty from my daughter's breast?"

"Father!"

"I need to know."

The shadows grew longer as the sun set outside the valley. Time seemed to slow as Omby-Amby gauged the truth in his heart. Wickrie-Kells reached out and squeezed her mother's hand.

Omby-Amby stared into the eyes of Tjorn Dunkle. "Yes."

Wickrie-Kells stared in stunned disbelief. She opened her mouth, clenched her fist, and blinked away tears. Then she turned away.

"Who, or what, commands a greater loyalty on your heart than this beautiful young woman here?"

"Freedom. Liberty. The fate of my people, the Winkies."

Tjorn smiled. He smiled at his wife, who reached out to touch her daughter's hand. "Your father approves."

The Soldier with Green Whiskers stood up from the table and went to stare out the window. Was this a victory? To achieve the approval of his one love's father was a victory, but had it cost him too much?

"You're a fine young man, Ombrosius." Tjorn walked over and clapped a heavy hand on the young man's shoulder. "You should not be ashamed of the truth you hold most dear. As long as my daughter," he cast a pointed glance at his pouting daughter, "remembers that patriotic duty sometimes comes before family."

"Don't you love me, Omby?"

"What?" The soldier whirled around and spread his hands wide. "Didn't you hear what I just said? What your father said? Of course I do. It is this truth water, Wickrie. I thought we had an understanding when I followed Oscar. This city is more than a city of dreams—it is a place where a man can be free." He puffed out his chest and raised his head high. "I want to raise my family in liberty. Every man in my family has bowed before a king. No more. I don't have to bow down to anyone. I can live according to the dictates of my own conscience."

Wickrie-Kells shook her head. She fought the tears, but they fell anyway. "How can you say that? You…"

Omby tilted his head to try to see the girl's eyes. "Hey, can I see your amber eyes?" When Wickrie looked over to him, he smiled. "There you are. I meant what I said. I am not required to bow down to anyone." He crossed the smooth wooden floor, knelt in front of the girl, and he took her hand in his, "I don't *have to*, but I *choose to* kneel before you, Wickrie-Kells, daughter of Tjorn and Donya. I want you and no one else."

"Son, I am proud of you. I have heard your stories when Wickrie has visited, but your heart and soul is more powerful to me than any story. I think I owe you something now, too."

Tjorn pulled a sealed jar from the cupboard. He and his wife looked at each other and silently agreed. They broke the seal on the jar and poured the silvery water into two cups and drank. "Now we're all in the same happy boat, at least for a few minutes. Let me tell you about the dowry I can offer."

Donya brought a small chest into the main room. She opened it and pulled a very old parchment from beneath a dried flower and some rings. She unfolded the parchment. Most of it was blank. Donya smiled at her daughter. The tears started in her eyes. "You know this is true. We drank the water. It keeps forever in that jar." She smoothed out the paper. "Do you know what this is?"

Omby-Amby glanced from the blank paper to Tjorn, who shrugged and smiled. "It's blank." The young soldier declared. "I don't understand."

"It's not blank." Wickrie said, tracing her finger over the map. "It's a map."

"I don't see anything." Omby said.

"I don't either, Son." Tjorn admitted. "It's got to be in the eyes."

Omby looked and noticed for the first time that Wickrie-Kells and her mother, Donya, shared the same amber eyes.

13 WINDS OF CHANGE

From her balcony at the South Castle, Glinda rested on a couch and watched the sun set below the distant cliffs. The red sun shimmered on the barren horizon. Nothing lived out there. It was a sea of sand and rock. Only the ghosts of ships long forgotten would remember when the seas surged with life on these cliffs and brought travelers to Oz.

Nearby, the haunting strains of Ola Griffin's Glass Armonica began. The Armonica was a special instrument composed from a series of crystal cups aligned on a rotating central shaft. The person playing the Armonica touched each cup with moistened fingertips, similar to the way a crystal goblet sings. The Armonica functioned like a line of spinning crystal goblets. A deft player could make the haunting notes hang in the air for several seconds. A song could resonate for more than a minute.

She played every evening at this time. Glinda turned her head to one side and let her long hair fall down until it touched the balcony. She turned her ear toward the sound. What song was it tonight? A few more notes and Glinda recognized it—*The Ballad of Ozmatine Lazarus*. Then the sweet voice joined the haunting notes to dance on the air. The lyrics wove a story of betrayal and loss. Ozmatine lived during the First Witch Wars.

>   *Let your voice be kind, O' Ozmatine*
>   *For you are not forgotten in the land of your birth*
>   *The throne you one day fill*
>   *A skepter now doth seat*
>   *Return to find your heart in the people.*
>
>   *All storms be-raged the guarding sea*
>   *As shades bestrought the dreamon Queen*
>   *Armies rose beneath the rock*

> *To burst the gemstone walls*
> *O' Ozmatine restore your memory*—

The words stopped suddenly, but the music hung on the air for several seconds. Glinda smiled sadly. The ballad always brought melancholy. Footsteps sounded far away. The music did not start again. Ola Griffin must have been disturbed. But *why*? It was easy enough to figure out—she had a pretty smile and golden hair. There was a new man in the castle. It was a simple case of blind arithmetic, as in Glinda would have to be blind not to see that her herald was adding to her tally of turned heads.

Glinda had hoped for the end of the song. It was always heartening to hear the great stories of the past.

When Ozmatine returned across the seas to the land of her birth and fought against the armies from under the ground. She regained the throne of her father and became Ozma the Fourth.

How much had changed in Oz since those times? Eleven monarchs had ruled the Emerald Lands in the succeeding years. Everyone knew that the Kings Oz and Queens Ozma lived far longer than the common folk. At least seventeen generations—though probably many more—had passed in that time. The land had changed. This beautiful south land once bordered the sea. During the Second Witch Wars, the seas had been destroyed, creating the Deadly Deserts.

The hills rose from the cliffs to become the Land of Oz. Far away from the edge of the desert, the green grass and trees grew cool and tall. Glinda turned from the living green in the Land of Oz and looked out over the nearness of death in the Deadly Desert.

The Deadly Desert surrounded Oz, but this part was called on maps the *Great Sandy Waste*. It stretched on as far as the eye could see. According to the maps, the Land of Ev was across this sea of sand. On the ancient maps, it was spelled in the Old Ozzian script as *Aiobh*, pronounced *Eev*. Maybe Promethus was right. Maybe history *had* changed.

It used to be a regular sea before the First Witch Wars destroyed it. How much different it must have been then, when the Twisted Lighthouse stood as a beacon to draw people here from all across the greater land—the continent of Nonestica. What wonders passed through these ancient ports? The books knew. Someday Glinda would know, too.

At this moment, she was more concerned about the nearness of the deadly sand. It was strange—her childhood in the land of the Gillikins, up in the North, had not prepared her to be her mother's heir. Yet here she was, today, known as a sorceress. Glinda was the Sorceress to Oscar's Wizard. The wild lands of the North were untamed. The mountain regions provided protection for the hardy people that chose to live there. What mysteries were held in those north mountains?

Gayelette had been the Ruby Sorceress. She had lived in the Ruby Palace forever, or very nearly so, according to the whispers that Glinda heard in her childhood. Gayelette was Glinda's mother, only in the sense that she gave birth. In all other ways, she was just a reflection of a person—she wasn't there, available, or physical to touch. She simply *was*. So what was the difference between today and all those yesterdays past? Gayelette was still a reflection, trapped on the shard of magic mirror that Glinda kept next to her vanity. The loop of reflection played over and over. Glinda sat in front of it and watched every night. When she saw herself in the mirror, she saw her mother. Yet they were two different people. At least Glinda hoped that she would not grow into her mother.

Gayelette spent lifetimes in the wild North, inside the Ruby Palace. She never aged. Time was her slave, at least in one direction. Glinda lived now in the South. The Ruby Palace was a memory. It was 'not currently accessible,' according to Smith & Tinker.

Glinda made her home next to the cliffs in the far south—next to the sands that brought death. This was more than just a place that Smith & Tinker had once been. Glinda had made the South Castle her home. It was a place of learning for all who wished to come.

A scuff on the marble floor behind her caused Glinda to stop her reverie. "Your herald, Ola, said you were here." Promethus stepped out onto the balcony, but Glinda did not turn his way.

Glinda smiled slightly and glanced down toward the gardens that separated the castle from the walled scrapyard. The roses needed plucking. Their blooms were full. Some were beginning to wilt. "Yes. Ola Griffin would do that. She has been acting…lately."

Promethus cocked his head to the side. "She's a lovely girl."

"Oh, you noticed." Glinda said, finally turning to her guest. She spread her hands out on the carved railing. "She has that effect on men." Glinda muttered. "I will need to talk with her about interrupting what is mine."

"If it is privacy you prefer, Princess, I will certainly take my leave."

Glinda pursed her lips. "No. My thoughts are drifting on the wind right now."

"There are many winds that blow in the heart of a young woman." Promethus leaned his elbows down on the railing and looked out to the darkening sands of the desert. "Truth, fancy, anger, jealousy—each blows in its time—but the wind that blows strongest…"

"How well did you know my mother?"

Promethus shrugged. "As well as anyone could know her that wasn't in her circle of power. Which is to say, not well. My masters knew her better as an ally, or at least a non-aggressive enemy." Promethus smiled wistfully. "I heard their talk every now and then. You're asking for a reason, though. You keep staring out over that desert like it's going to give you an answer."

"There is only death out there."

"But it was not always so."

"As long as you've lived, have you ever seen a sea around Oz? Has there ever been anything but desert?"

"Nay. There has not."

"But you say that it was not always so. There is death, right there, all around us, yet we stand here and point."

Promethus narrowed his eyes and tilted his head toward the red-haired sorceress. "You are going somewhere with this?"

"I am not my mother."

"No. But you have her fire."

"And her hair, and her spells, and her Ruby Throne! I even have part of her name. Couldn't she come up with something different? Why does she need to live through me? I am not her. Look, these eyes. They are eyes like hers, right?"

"That's where you're wrong, lassie. Your eyes get stormy and dark like a slate. But that passes. They always come blue again, like the sky. Your mother...her eyes turned black when she raged. Sometimes they didn't turn blue again for a very long time. You have your father's eyes."

"Really?" Glinda didn't sound convinced.

"What proof do you need, princess? I have called you *'daughter of Quelala'* since we met. Didn't that trigger anything in your mind? You are of noble blood, true, but you have something greater than your mother ever had."

Glinda shook her head, already disbelieving. "What could I have that my mother couldn't have? She had everything."

"Your father."

"But she had—"

"No. She had Quelala—the secret apprentice, the man, the mystery. She had Quelala. You had your father."

"How is that special?"

"Quelala would have been the greatest of us all, but Gayelette took him, made him into something for her benefit. But he was, in many senses, his own man. He was a dreamer—he knew that Oz could be a better place, and he created something so powerful that not even all the combined powers of all the witches in all the lands could stop it. He created *you*."

Far north, in the Emerald City, Oscar found Kally in the Library, reading a heavy tome—The History of the Winkies. Kally traced her fingers over the architectural lines of the drawings of Yellow Castle. She looked at all the lines that the Wizard could see, and many that he could *not* see. She didn't glance up when Oscar's shadow fell over her, though she gestured with her hand to move him out of her light. When Oscar didn't move, Kally's hand tensed and she quivered as she prepared to gently nudge him out of her way.

Oscar sat down. The light flowed down onto the page. Kally clenched and unclenched her hand several times to work out the stress.

Oscar looked at the page Kally was studying and said, "That's the hall of mirrors. The Winkie kings use it to look backward into the past. Time extends both ways. We can see if we look beyond ourselves. I always wanted to see that place. When I saw the drawing in the book, it seemed very interesting. In the middle of the night, could the mirrors reflect shadows?" Oscar raised his eyebrows curiously to Kally.

"Certainly would be." Kally rolled her amber eyes, but she kept her head down in the book.

"There are places in there that haven't been seen by outsiders. King Winko gave it to me as a gift—to keep in the library here. Preserve the knowledge of Oz in one place."

Apparently Oscar wasn't going to leave. Kally lifted her eyes to look over at him. "So many books here. How do you find time to read them all?"

Oscar's eyes wandered around, searching the shelves. "Lots of stories. Lots of pictures. So much knowledge. It's always here when I need it." He smiled at Kally. "Here for you, too."

"Yes. I am certainly taking advantage of your kind nature."

Oscar laughed, but then he grew solemn. "It's just nice to have someone that isn't trying to push me into revealing secrets or ripping open my mind. It's nice to have you around."

Kally continued tracing the architectural lines, flipping through pages. Oscar watched her gold-flecked amber eyes survey the details on each page. Then she breathed deeply and closed the book. She swiveled on her chair seat to face Oscar.

"You, Wizard, have a problem. I've been listening and watching from here in the library. Your crowds of hangers-on are not as subtle as they like to fashion themselves. You are in danger, Wizard, not from the forces outside the Emerald City, not from the Witches, but from the people close to you. The rot is within your walls."

"This city is based on the foundation of a Constitutional Republic. The power is enshrined in the People—We the People. The government must fear the people. See, here in the Emerald City, the people are being empowered. There are places for them to gather and discuss the issues and make their voices heard. The rules are written. We have a code of laws. That is part of this library. The history of Oz is safe here. The people will keep it safe. The power is with the people."

Laughter exploded from Kally's mouth. "The people? You seriously trust them?"

Hurt, Oscar glared at her. "I am one of the people. You are one of the people. It's not us and them. It is *We the People*. No person is above the law. The law is equal for all."

"You really believe that?" Kally shook her head in wonder. "Where did you come from? It is always *us* and *them*. They are common people, worried about common things—food, and family, and home. They don't have the time or the sense to worry about the grander ideas that truly change the world."

"Common sense would dictate—"

"Common sense? There is a reason that I don't think like that. And if you really are honest with yourself, Wizard, you don't think like that, either. We are not like the common folk. There is a reason that common sense belongs with the common folk. I defy you to think of one advance that a common person has made that has benefited the world."

"Okay. There was the cotton gin, Morse code, the hot-air balloon."

"That ship you rode in on in the battle of Winkie Plains?"

"Yes, that one. Invented by French brothers seventy years ago. I have to say, that one certainly changed my world."

"You are a mystery, Wizard. I ask a simple question, and you give gibberish as a response. These things are not in Oz, and Oz is the world; therefore your answers simply do not fit. They must, therefore, be discarded." Kally smirked at his quizzical expression.

"Those are good answers. All of this—everything that I'm trying to do—is good answers. You are just picking and choosing what you like to believe, because that's easier for you. The people deserve the right to choose how to govern their own lives. They have the right not to be ruled by tyrants who rashly command armies to roll over them roughshod."

"Now we are getting somewhere. You want strength. Power."

"I want the people to have the power so that they don't fear rulers in high places."

"And what would you call this? The library is not on the ground floor. We can see the stars out the window. This is a high place. Should the people then fear you?"

"No."

"Why not?"

"I'm not going to hurt them. I'm not going to threaten their liberty by marching my army over the top of them."

"You have an army. Why? Why does Pastoria want to get his hands on the Emerald City and control the army?"

"Pastoria is in over his head. All his people like Emerald City better. Who can blame them? There is more work here, and the taxes are only on what is bought and sold. The people can keep the fruits of their own labors. That makes them happier. They don't have to pay to support an army they don't want."

"The big hooplah is about the army, right? You have to raise taxes to support the army."

"That wouldn't be a problem if the Witches would mind their manners. We can't allow the land to fall into war. The only way to protect the Emerald City is to keep an army. Strong arms require food, housing, training. Those things don't come free. Everyone earns what they get in the Emerald City. Nobody gets something for free. That is a common sense rule. It seems to work for everyone." Oscar set his jaw resolutely.

"You can judge the strength of a country by its health in war. If you are not going to seek out war, why have an army? Why not just keep the guards in place?"

"Isn't that what I said?"

"You are talking about an army. Fourscore is not an army. Not for a city this size."

"Then what do you suggest? To have an army, I need people. I have soldiers willing to bear arms in defense of this city. Most of them aren't paid soldiers—they are militia. They are willing to come when I call. Mostly they earn their own way."

Kally glanced around to make sure that nobody was within earshot before continuing. She kept her voice low, so that only Oscar could hear her. "To have an army, you do need people. But those do not necessarily need to be common people. I know a man who is an inventor. He is creating things—soldiers that do not eat or sleep. They follow orders perfectly. They do not hesitate in battle. They can stand as an army for a city. No enemy would dare attack when you command an army like that. These automatons never tire. An army such as this would allow your people to build, rather than destroy. Isn't that what the Emerald City is about—building?"

"I'm interested." Oscar said. "Where can I see this army?"

"Not here. We will need to go elsewhere. My family has a...there is treasure to buy this army."

"I have money—silver, gold—name your price."

"No. No. It has to be mine. That's not right. No. Yes, it is. I am going to reclaim my family fortune and purchase this army—as long as it is what it claims to be. But my family fortune is a secret. I have to swear you to absolute secrecy. If you want to see the army, you come with me, alone. Tonight."

"I swear."

Oscar led the way out of the Emerald City to the nearby stables. This was where Omby-Amby kept the Hamstrambulator. By the time the moon was up, they were out of sight of the tallest tower.

Far to the South, Glinda and Promethus stared out at the evening sky. Somewhere below them, the music from Ola Griffin's Glass Armonica started again. The music was different this time. Glinda did not recognize the song. The strange melody wrapped around Glinda and turned her thoughts to the dreams her father must have known.

> *I will watch you while you sleep, for a thousand years, or maybe more*
> *When I knock, will you awake? Will you open up your door?*

The singing stopped, though the notes continued. "No, that's not right." Glinda heard Ola Griffin say.

> *Your life has become only a spectacle.*
> *How can I love if I can't see the fire?*
> *The magic of faerie binds a lifetime as a day,*
> *Would I keep your heart holy if I had to fade away?*

"Not right." The frustrated whisper sounded among the haunting notes. The echo of crumpled paper faded as Ola Griffin played the melody again, but this time, she did not sing.

Poor girl, Glinda thought. *She wants to love, but she's waiting.*

Promethus turned and walked back and forth on the length of the balcony, leaving Glinda to puzzle over her myriad thoughts. Then it hit her. All else faded from her mind. She sat upright and looked straight and Promethus.

"Wait a minute, my father was a *dreamer*?"

Promethus grimaced. "I rather hoped you would be dazzled by your incredible legacy. I have said what I have said. Glinda, you are your father's daughter. He was bound in his duty, remember that."

"My father's duty was to my mother—that's what he said. He could not free the Winged Monkeys."

Promethus gestured out to the seemingly endless sands beyond the cliffs. "The desert was not always there. Life once flourished in the seas. Now it is a reminder that there is work to be done—healing to initiate. The desert is not death—it is a reminder that there are consequences to every action. A long life," he smiled painfully, "requires diligence and duty."

"You keep saying duty. My father was a dreamer, and you keep saying duty. What mystery are you trying to unravel?"

Promethus backed through the double-paneled doors and pulled them closed behind him as he exited, leaving Glinda's final sentence hanging unanswered. Glinda turned toward the darkening desert.

"If the deserts are a reminder; death is not the desert; healing can be initiated; why can't I see who I need to be? If this is my legacy—my father's duty was to my mother, except when it wasn't, and he, me, dreams…" Glinda crossed her arms on the railing and put her head down on her forearms. "This doesn't make any sense. Why can't the answers be easy, like in books? Why can't everything just be written out right there for me to find?"

The last notes of the Glass Armonica stopped. They hung in the air for several long seconds. Promethus had left, and suddenly Ola Griffin was finished with her song? It was not difficult to connect the circumstantial dots…or was Glinda just upset because…*no*.

The wind rustled through the garden beneath the balcony. The petals of a wilting rose fell to the ground. Glinda sighed. *It wasn't her fault.*

SECTION TWO: PEARLS

14 SECRET SPRING

The sun rose warm on their backs as Oscar and Kally raced across the fields to the southeast of the Emerald City. They covered miles before dawn, driven onward by the prospect of preserving the peace of Emerald City. The Hamstrambulator was a concession that Kally had made when Oscar pressed her.

The Hamstrambulator was a fantastic creation by Smith & Tinker, given as a gift to King Winko, of the Winkies. It was a large hollow wheel with a pair of mechanical running legs in the center to power the movement. Baskets hung on a framework over the wheel. These were lifted by a means of gears and levers. The front basket held the steering mechanism and the basket levers.

The vehicle was Omby-Amby's pride and joy. It was nothing short of miraculous that they retrieved the Hamstrambulator after the Battle of Emerald Prairie. Omby-Amby vowed that he would not let the vehicle out of his sight after that. But he wouldn't mind that Oscar borrowed it—for a noble cause, of course.

Kally was not happy with the arrangement. She suggested that they could travel more quickly on foot, but Oscar disagreed. To keep the Silver Slippers a secret, Kally was forced to accept the Wizard's way. She had one requirement—no one must know *where* they had gone, or even *that* they were going.

Though the miles went quickly, the dawn was a welcome change from the misty darkness. The light revealed a great forest ahead of them.

"I didn't know this was so close to the Emerald City. I was certain I knew the area all around."

"Time passes quickly in the presence of greatness."

"For you or me?"

"Yes." Kally replied cryptically.

Oscar maneuvered the Hamstrambulator into the forest, following the easy path through the trees. The large wheel climbed over the fallen trees better than Oscar and Kally could have managed on foot. At last, Kally directed Oscar to stop. This was as close to their secret destination as the giant running wheel could get. "Discretion is required—my family always required it. Leave this contraption and walk with me."

"We have to come back to it. Omby-Amby would never forgive me if I lost it."

"Of course. Forgiveness is our goal, isn't it?"

Oscar's silence withered the air behind Kally as she walked forward, smiling to herself. When Oscar finally joined her again, she said, "Tell me, Wizard, what is your treasure? It can be anything, but please, enough talk of liberty and freedom. It is enough to tire even my patience."

Oscar frowned. "Treasure is where a man's heart is. What he believes in becomes his treasure, and therefore his motivation. Gold and silver shine. Art is beautiful. Science is amazing. But liberty—"

Kally shot him a withering glance.

"Liberty is only a treasure to those who recognize it. I suppose the greatest treasure is stories."

"Stories?"

"Stories. You learn from stories. Sure, it may seem like the story is only an adventure or a moral, but there are always more things you can learn. Stories hold the key to controlling people. If you control the story, you control the person—the way they think and remember."

"You can buy nothing with stories. No armies or kingdoms. For most stories, you'd be hard-pressed to trade a meal."

Oscar rubbed his hands together, smiling, "On the contrary, stories are the very breath of life. People pay good money for stories. One man with a story can go forth and conquer a crown. See, the story spreads in the minds of the people. One man with a dream can change the world."

"I still don't see how a story is a treasure. Myself, I have always found a certain luster in pearls."

"I've never really liked pearls." Oscar said.

Kally stopped dead in her tracks. Oscar turned to look back at her and asked, "What?"

Kally shook her head slowly in disbelief. "Pearls are the most valuable stone in Oz. Far more than gold, emeralds or even rubies, pearls can buy and entire land. Indeed, they have." She paused, "I heard that there was one who purchased half a kingdom for a giant pearl. That was, of course, a long time ago, so I don't know if that is true."

"I'm sure it is." Oscar said, "But a pearl? Really?"

"Pearls come from the seas. I'm certain you have seen that there are no seas in Oz."

"I have seen the desert on the south. There are deserts surrounding Oz, I have been told."

"And it is important for a Wizard to know his domain—what he rules over."

"Emerald City is the only dominion I can call my own." Oscar said. "Glinda rules in the South, and the Wicked Witches rule the East and West."

"You left out the North." Kally chided.

"The North is in transition." Oscar explained. "There is no witch there right now, but we do have an ally. Locasta is the guardian of the North right now."

Kally laughed, a mocking, barking sound that reflected off the trees. "Locasta? She was an apprentice. She is barely able to feed herself, let alone rule an entire land." She stopped short, her face frozen in a strange combination of amusement and the horrible realization of self-exposure. "Or so I've been told," she offered lamely.

Oscar stopped and stared Kally in the face. "You pretend to know only a little bit about the Witches, but your scheming tongue lets slip much more than you claim. Who are you?" Oscar demanded. "Pearls, or not, you are more than you appear, Kally."

Kally lowered her amber eyes and pouted her lower lip slightly. She slowly raised her eyes, looking at Oscar from beneath heavy eyelids. "I didn't want to say anything. I thought you would hate me. My family...I hate them. I...they are—"

"You've already spoken of Ondri-baba. I believed you then, but you are beginning to stretch my willing suspension of disbelief. What are you? Who are you? Why are you pretending?"

Kally looked around. They were not too deep in the forest yet, so there was still the chance for escape.

"If you are a witch, just say so."

Kally half-smiled, and her amber eyes flashed fire. "With all the blood that runs through me, I swear to you, I am not a witch."

Oscar narrowed his eyes. "An oath by blood is a powerful thing, not to be taken or entered into lightly. Why would you say that, when a yes or no would have been sufficient?"

"Some souls are not as trusting as you are, Wizard."

"Tell me what you know. How do you know all of these things?"

"I was born to a Munchkin family who were the keepers of the old secrets. They guarded the magic of the faeries—the ancient magic that first wrote the name of Oz on the stones. We were charged with keeping this knowledge. In time, the knowledge fractured our family. The knowledge was fractured also. The thieves fled with pages of the book. They disappeared, but it is unlikely that they will ever be able to discover the secrets. Only a witch or a sorcerer can read the ancient writing. The secrets may be lost, but they are lost to time, which is better than being lost to an enemy, but no matter. No power can bring them back again."

"It's a start. So where do you come in? Your family were witches with a secret, and they had a falling out, and some pages are missing in an old book. Bringing us to today—you."

Kally walked and talked them deeper into the forest.

"Two sisters—one beautiful and one ugly—fought."

"Let me guess, you were the ugly one."

Kally shot Oscar a glare that stopped him in his tracks. "I apologize. I was making jest. You are lovely. I was being absurd."

"Do not mock me, Wizard. This beauty cost me dearly."

Oscar nodded and glanced away. "I have to do calisthenics, too."

Kally paused and furrowed her brow and cocked her head at Oscar. "What? This is not a story about me. It is the story of my family."

"Continue, please."

"The two sisters each claimed a portion of their birthright, yet it was not enough for the ugly one. She stole away in the dead of night. The family did not take kindly to the loss. They blamed my family. The burden fell to me." Her face shook with each word. "For her sin, they may as well have blamed me. I bore the shame. How could I fit after that? The people, they…"

"So you are the black sheep—you don't fit in?" Oscar asked, drawn into Kally's amber eyes. He half-smiled, resting his eyes on her sad and angry face. "It can't be as bad as my family. War heroes. Stories of blood and death every day of my childhood. And me, I despise war." He forced a laugh, and then regretted it. "Your family couldn't be that bad."

"They are dead."

"Oh."

"War came, as war always comes. The two sisters, bound by blood, began a war that destroyed their family. What keepers of knowledge were left alive turned outside the family. They polluted the legacy. The knowledge was scattered and lost. They chose their side of history—the wrong side."

"So you are alone." Oscar said softly.

Kally's eyes burned as she stared angrily at the trees. Each word stung. "Ondri-baba is all that I have left."

"Kindred spirits, you and I—my family was torn apart by war also."

"No. You are nothing like me. You have not discovered the power to crush your fear and envy beneath your heel and rule and reign over it as queen omnipotent."

Oscar stared. His mouth dropped open slightly. "You are right." He agreed quietly. "Ruling as queen omnipotent. Wow. Hmm."

"Tell me, Wizard, does your blood cry out for those it has lost? Mine stopped crying…years ago."

Oscar chewed on his words and searched the treetops for the right meaning before he spoke. "Ghosts haunt me. Whether that blood cries in my dreams, I do not know. I do not know."

Kally shook her head to clear the angry thoughts, but they would not be banished. "What use is a bloodless heart? Does it even beat? What use is belief in love, or truth, or life, if the sand just blows away?"

Oscar shrugged and smiled helpfully. "I believe you. Who would claim Ondri-baba as family?"

"Who indeed?" Kally whispered.

Kally felt burning in both of her eyes and on her cheeks. She wiped them with the tips of her fingers. Then her fingers burned. She looked down at the wet spot on her finger as it burned and blistered. She quickly wiped her fingers on her dress. Her eyes were making water. That burned as badly as the rain had. She blinked quickly and wiped her eyes with her sleeve.

She turned back to Oscar.

"Your eyes are very red. Are you all right?"

"I just need some space. I'll be back in a few minutes."

Out of sight of the Wizard, Kalinya applied the unguent to her fingers and around her eyes, restoring the youth to her skin. It should burn, yes, there it was. This familiar burning was a good thing—Kally could control this one. The burning tears were beyond her control. She did not like that. Feelings like that were dangerous and could betray her. They must be controlled.

She took a deep breath and went back to the Wizard who trusted her.

Kally peered around cautiously before she whispered to Oscar, "This is a closely guarded secret. Stay hidden here until the count of thirty. Then cross the creek and go into the cleft above the stump. It can only fit one at a time. You must comply. This is important to me."

Oscar ducked down and kept his head hidden as Kally stepped out of the shadows. She glanced back over her shoulder to ensure that Oscar was not watching, then she took one, two, three steps with the Silver Slippers, and she was on the other side of the creek. She quickly climbed the stump and slipped through the cleft in the rock.

Oscar joined her after the requisite count. "I can see why you want to keep this place hidden."

Glowing glyphs in phosphorescent moss cast a pale blue light over the cave. Kally whispered some words as she traced the symbols in the air. The wall shifted, blocking the exit and opening a deeper path into the patterned darkness below.

"Tread lightly. Do not disturb the sigils. They help the babies to grow."

Kally stopped after more than one hundred steps. The radiant pool bathed the entire cavern in blue light. "My family has held this secret for seven generations. I trust that the secret will stay in the family."

Oscar plunged into the water. He kicked and swam down to the glowing beds of oysters at the bottom of the pool. Following Kally's instructions, he chose the largest oyster first and pried it from its berth. When he felt as if his lungs were about to burst, the oyster finally came loose. Oscar broke the surface and sputtered triumphantly, holding the oyster up. It was the size of his fist.

He tossed the oyster to Kally, who recoiled in fear. The oyster clattered to the floor and skidded to a stop against the wall.

"NO! Stop it!" she screamed.

Oscar splashed some water in her direction. "Come on, what's a little water going to hurt?"

Kally glared at him as she retreated further up the corridor. "I cannot—I am forbidden to touch the water."

"So that's why you made me come in here."

"Only you can get the pearls for me—for us. Don't make me go near the water. It is my family's heritage, but I am forbidden."

"You can't swim." Oscar exclaimed. He laughed.

Kally laughed nervously. "Yes. That's it. I can't swim."

"That's nothing to be embarrassed about. I couldn't swim for a while. Then my brother threw me into the river. I swam."

"Charming. No. Not for me. No water."

"How many oysters do you want?" Oscar asked.

"I promised five to buy the army."

"Is there a pearl in each oyster?"

"If they have been fed properly, yes."

"So you don't know."

"Seven. We will judge when the shells are dry."

Oscar retrieved seven more oysters and then climbed out of the pool. The glowing water dripped from him as he dried the oysters in his shirt. Then he placed them on the ground in front of Kally.

"How are you going to open them? Tickle their tummy and make them laugh?" Oscar went over to the wall and picked up the fist-sized oyster.

Kally hummed a tune as she waved her hands over the oysters. One by one they opened their shells to reveal the treasures inside. Six held pearls, and one was empty. Kally carefully excised the pearl with forceps and a small blade. When she was finished, she dropped the pearls into a silk pouch.

"You can replace them."

"You can toss them in."

"I said YOU can *replace* them."

"Just toss them in the water." Oscar shrugged dismissively.

"These oysters are the entirety of my family wealth. I will not see them treated roughly."

"Well then maybe you had better take a dip into the pond yourself."

Oscar leaned down to scoop a single handful of water. He turned toward Kally.

"Don't!" she screamed, thrusting out her hands. The oyster in Oscar's hand shattered, and Oscar flew backwards into the pool. He sank to the bottom, wondering what he had done wrong. A single handful of water wouldn't drown her, so why was Kally worried? When he swam to the surface, Kally was gone.

Oscar set the remnants of the shattered oyster next to his rumpled clothing. Then he took the emptied oysters down at the same time and spread them among the clustered oysters still on the bottom of the pool.

He walked out of the pool and shook the glowing water off of his arms and chest. As he pulled his clothing back on, he noticed a glimmer of dark brilliance within the ruined oyster shell. Oscar pulled apart the shell and moved the tongue-like muscle aside. It was a black pearl. Oscar pulled out the large pearl and polished it on the sleeve of his shirt. "You are the most valuable stone in the land, or so I've been told. You will make a very nice present for a certain magical someone."

Ola Griffin hurried down the hallway, tears flooding from her eyes. She bumped into Promethus as he walked toward the great hall that held Glinda's Ruby Throne. Before he could lift a hand to help, Ola Griffin hid her face under her blonde hair and ran away.

Promethus entered the great hall and pointed backwards with his thumb. "I just saw."

"Yes." Glinda responded curtly.

"Why?"

"The roses were blooming too brightly and wilting on the bush. She is responsible for caring for them."

"If this has anything to do with her allowing me in last night, I profusely apologize."

"Don't even start with me. You are a man—when tears fall off a pretty face, your backbone melts. You jump in to rescue the weeping damsel. Not today. Ola Griffin no longer cares for the roses. She has a job more suited to her particular trouble-making skills."

"Is she still your herald?"

"When I need her, yes."

"She has a lovely voice. I would hate to see—"

"Stop." Glinda held up one finger to silence the older man. "She was chosen for her skills and strengths. She has not proven trustworthy."

"Where have you exiled her?"

"The junkyard. There is no trouble that she can get into out among the piles of garbage."

Promethus nodded once slowly. "Those were cast-off experiments. They are not junk—they are just not completed." Then he changed the subject. "Have you informed your…servants…that the other apprentices will be coming for their lockboxes?"

Glinda walked across the great map in the floor from the South to the far mountains of the North. She whirled around to face Promethus. "They were told. Now, I have a question for you. Where do you belong?" She pointed to the map inlaid with precious stones. "Where in Oz do you belong?"

Promethus smiled. "That is a mystery—a secret that I guard."

"So you're a guardian now?"

"Yes."

"What do you guard?"

"All mysteries have their moment in the sun. You will learn soon enough, Princess, that to approach wisdom, you must be a child."

"I am not a child!" Glinda stamped her foot.

"I know."

Several tense seconds passed. "The map is a fine legacy for the daughter of Quelala. You have made this South Castle yours. It is time that you named it truly. My masters were not exceptionally creative with the names of their domiciles—they had many castles and several laboratories. Something was here for you, and I think you have found it."

"The Ruby Throne."

"*Perhaps.*"

"The Ruby Throne, the shard, the map, the library. I have found what is here for me." Glinda was losing patience.

"Again, *perhaps.*" Promethus replied cryptically.

"I give up, then! Why don't you tell me, Guardian? What secret am I missing? What is there here for me?"

"A name."

"A name? I have a name. I have your name. I have everybody's name here."

"What is the name of this castle? What has your writing told you? The pen and paper you keep close to your throne is never blank long. You are never far from a pen, Princess. Your thoughts are collected. The name has come to you, I am certain."

Glinda studied the map on the floor. She indeed had a name for the castle, but she had breathed not a word to anyone. The name felt certain in her soul, but she feared allowing it to escape, lest it gain its freedom and race to the world beyond her grasp. She feared being wrong, and in being wrong, that the error would gain life beyond her power to correct it.

Still, the winds within Glinda's soul stirred, and she knew. "*Chronometria.*"

"A device for measuring time. It suits you, Princess. You have a long life with the tools at your disposal. See that you use them wisely."

"That doesn't sound strange to you?"

"My masters engineered wonderful clockwork engines beneath this castle to power their many experiments. *South Castle* was enough for their needs. *Chronometria* will suit yours. It is a fine name for this establishment. See that the seconds pass worthily. Your days are made of moments, and all your years are yesterday's moments built on top of one another."

Glinda pressed her fingertips together and stepped softly back to the Ruby Throne. "I have moments I regret. I wonder, *How is Oscar?*"

Promethus spread his hands wide. "Some questions I cannot answer. I am but a guardian. He is the wizard."

"Yes." Glinda agreed softly. "He is the wizard—more powerful than us all."

15 THE STRENGTH OF AN ARMY

Oscar found Kally on the other side of the stream, pacing back and forth. She muttered to herself, pounding her fist in her hand. She did not see him at first, and so Oscar watched as she vented her frustration. From his experience in front of audiences, Oscar read Kally's personality quite easily. She was used to being in charge. Anything done to upset her perceived power made her upset. That was all it was, he was sure.

"The oysters are back in place." He said.

Kally looked up and calmed her hands. "You should not have threatened me."

"The oysters are back in place."

"I heard you. Very well. I cannot touch the water."

"That's not an apology."

"No."

"Very well." Oscar echoed. He felt the black pearl in his pocket, safe and sound. "You have the pearls. Where is this grandiose army you bragged about? If it really can prevent war, I will open the whole of Emerald City to you."

Kally blinked in astonishment and then smiled. "Of course."

In the rarely-visited ruins in the underbelly of Central City, Omby-Amby and Wickrie-Kells dropped down into a musty corridor and coughed in the stale air. The young woman waved her hands back and forth to clear the dust, but the movement did not help the smell one bit. She put her bow on her back and smiled at her companion. "Nobody saw us. We're good."

"So this is it?" the Soldier with Green Whiskers asked.

"No, but this is the path to it. We'll get there. Come on."

They pushed through the cobwebs and fallen litter from the living city above. Wickrie-Kells' eyes danced with excitement. "The entire history on the walls." She teased.

Then they were there. This was it—a massive auditorium beneath the city, with walls filled with mosaics and paintings. The auditorium had been home to some of the greatest performances in history. Omby-Amby had heard of the *Battle of Named Shovels*. The reenactment used ten thousand men and a clever system of tunnels created in mounts of transported earth. That vast set had recreated the battle in the caverns. Then there was the *Opera of Vanity*, dedicated to the memory of King Oz, the Fourth, who planted the sprawling Gardens of Wonder in the middle of the wilderness. The *Lists of Boetra*, the *Congress of Phaladoon*, the *Disappointment Opera* that magnified the sounds of the chariots as they raced through the corridors. *Fae Imaginarium and the Rainbow Mist*. They had all been performed here.

The auditorium was spoken of today like an old tomb. It was dead and gone, one of the wonders of Old Oz. Yet here it was, buried under countless centuries of decay. How many other legends were likewise buried?

The light from the distant windows far above did little to light the furthest corners in shadow. Wickrie-Kells followed a sunbeam down to its resting place on an emerald and sapphire-colored mosaic. "It's the Twisted Lighthouse. I remember seeing this design as a little girl, but I didn't know what it was until I met Glinda and we went south. If you follow the progression around the wall, you'll see the Grand Tower was copied after the Twisted Lighthouse—except King Oz, the Fifth didn't want the twist in it. He wanted everything straight. It was intended to be a beacon to all of the lands to come to the center of the land—Central City—just like the Twisted Lighthouse was a beacon to all lands across the seas to come to Oz—the central land. I love the blue. I imagine that is what the sea looks like."

"If there is a sea within reach, I will carry you there." Omby-Amby promised.

Wickrie rested a hand on his muscular arm. "I know you would. The deserts block our path. Until the seas are healed, Oz is cut off from the world."

"Glinda and Oscar can fix it. They can heal the seas." Omby declared. They have magic, and Glinda is brilliant. Between the two of them—Oscar's dreams and all—I don't think there's anything they can't do."

"If they get back together."

"They will. Oscar is mad for her. And Glinda…"

"Is busy. Constantly busy." Wickrie-Kells finished.

She found the object of her search—a broken mirror. She removed it from beneath the collapsed table and propped it up in the sunbeam. "My father set this up years ago. We always hide the mirror when we leave. There is no telling who comes down here. I like for this to be my secret that I share with my father, and now I am sharing it with you."

She angled the mirror to reflect the sunbeam against the mosaic of the Twisted Lighthouse. The shimmering tiles reflected the light across the room, which reflected again and again until the whole room was lit with a pale ambience.

Omby's jaw dropped open as he looked around and up. Everywhere were mosaics and paintings. He trusted the girl's word that it was the entire history of Oz. From where he stood, it certainly looked that way. He recognized buildings from his travels with Oscar. "There's South Castle—Glinda's Palace. There is Grimmpill Graveyard. And there…is that Emerald City?"

Omby quickly crossed the broad room, jumping over tables and chairs. He walked around a fallen crystal chandelier, carefully avoiding the fractured crystals on the floor. No use breaking another chandelier. When he arrived at the far wall, he held his hands with thumb and forefinger in L-shapes to frame the image. "It looks like Emerald City."

Wickrie-Kells was only a few steps behind him. She removed the bow from her back so she could scrape away some of the dust above the art. "I think there's some writing up here. It's older Ozzian script. My father taught me to read some of it."

"Here, let me." The taller young man snatched Wickrie's bow from her hands and reached up higher to scrape away the dust and accumulated grime.

Wickrie frowned at the incursion into her space, but she let him help. He could reach higher, even though there were no words up there.

"There. All clear. What does it say?"

Wickrie-Kells stepped back and looked at the gold writing. The light was dimming quickly. She slowly sounded out the unfamiliar words. "*Smaragaid Cathair.*"

"What does it mean?"

"City of Emeralds. I'm reading the script right beside it. I never noticed it before."

"I don't see it."

"Of course not, silly. You have to stand back here."

Omby moved backwards to stand next to Wickrie. "Where is it?"

Wickrie took back her bow and pointed. Omby leaned in close to follow her arm. He put his arm around her waist. She smiled as he pressed against her. "Do you see it?"

"Still looking."

"Keep looking as long as you want."

Omby shook his head slowly. He didn't see it. He stood and furrowed his brow.

"It's right there! See, it reads, 'Smaragaid Cathair was built around the Emerald Fortress and completed in the reign of King Oz, the Third. In the

Fairy tongue, the city is called Parradime.' It says it right there. You must be blind if you can't see it."

"Blinded by your radiance."

"Good excuse. It's right there."

Wickrie-Kells looked closer at the walls. Writing appeared everywhere. In some places it was scrawled over the mosaics and art. In other cases it was in-between the art. She followed it around the wall. "There is more writing."

"Sure there is." The soldier mumbled. He moved to follow after the girl, but something drew his attention. His ears perked up and he looked around. He signaled to Wickrie to be quiet, but she was too busy reading to herself on the walls of invisible writing.

Laughter echoed from one, two, then three joining corridors. All around the room it echoed and grew.

Omby's sword was in his hand as he quickly stepped toward Wickrie-Kells.

"Well, well, well. The green-haired demon and his fair maiden. Trespassers. You don't belong in Central City, especially in the lower levels. These are the king's rules. He left us to our own particular idiom to deal with trespassers."

"That doesn't even make any sense." Omby-Amby protested, searching the several corridors for the source of the voice.

"You don't see me, do you, green soldier? Perhaps you saw more clearly in the sunlight on Emerald Prairie? Two years ago? One soldier put the entire Emerald Army to flight."

The green-whiskered soldier rubbed a hand over his chin, searching and thinking. He flexed his other hand on the hilt of his sword. "If it's a fight you want, I'm here. Face me, man to man."

"Oh, no." The voice chuckled. "One soldier who drove away the whole army? You don't fight man to man. You fight against one, you fight against all."

From all around the auditorium, green-uniformed soldiers emerged. There were at least fifteen of them. They all moved toward Omby-Amby.

"Wickrie, this could get ugly. I'm coming to you."

The girl calmly strung her bow and nocked an arrow. The emerald soldier's voice sounded familiar, like a voice from the past. "Bartleby O'Brine, is that you?" Wickrie-Kells called out. "You haven't grown any taller."

"Enough from you! Daughter of the has-been butler. Your father was a traitor."

"And you are still short. Tell me," she called out, "are you tall enough to kiss my elbow yet?" She pulled the bowstring taut.

"I am not going to fall for that one again. You knocked out two of my teeth before. I warn you, as an emissary of his royal eminence—"

"That's a lot of em's right there." Omby-Amby noticed. "Two missing teeth is probably why you don't use esses. Hissing and all."

They could hear the man's face getting redder by the second. "An assault on any one of us is an assault on the king. It will be treated as a declaration of war."

"I truly doubt that." Wickrie snarled.

Omby glanced backward over his shoulder. "No, technically, that is true. No killing any of them."

"Fine." Wickrie-Kells sighted a new target and let her arrow fly. The sound of glass shattering reached their ears just after the darkness collapsed all around them. The arrow hit the distant reflecting mirror, eliminating the ambient sunlight from the large chamber. In the absence of light, there was confusion.

"It's dark." One of the soldiers cried out.

"We're underground, of course it's dark." Bartleby grumped. "Now get them. They are the trespassers. We are obliged to treat them with incivility."

"Doesn't the declaration of war go both ways?" Wickrie-Kells asked Omby-Amby as they rushed toward the soldiers blocking the exit.

"No. 'Fraid not. We are unquestionably in a place we're not supposed to be."

"But my family lives here."

"Your family are traitors!" Bartleby snarled.

And then they were in the middle of the soldiers. Omby-Amby punched and whirled, blocking attacks with his sword. He only struck the emerald soldiers with the flat of his blade.

"Wickrie, stay behind me. We've got to get out of here without killing any of them."

"Yes, I know. I'm right here." Wickrie swung her bow, cracking a soldier in the head and knocking him down.

"Follow my lead." Omby ordered. "To the left."

"I'm going right." Wickrie flipped her bow up over a soldier's head and snapped the bowstring in his face. The man screamed as he fell to his knees.

"I'll get us out of this!" Omby shouted.

Wickrie-Kells stepped back and let the Soldier with Green Whiskers pummel his way out of the crowd. He was a good fighter—better than all of the other soldiers there, though it was anybody's guess how well any of them would do in the dark with unfamiliar footing. Omby-Amby stumbled, and the other soldiers jumped on him.

Wickrie pulled an arrow from her quiver and stabbed two of the soldiers in their backsides. The hollered and jumped away. Wickrie-Kells disappeared backwards into the deepening shadows.

Omby fought his way to his feet, shoving the soldiers down to the ground. "Wickrie!"

"I'm over here." The girl called. "Follow my voice to the Twisted Lighthouse." She worked her way to the wall and reached out her hand as she heard Omby's footsteps getting closer.

"The king will hear of this!" Bartleby cried. A heavy, fist-sized chunk hit the wall next to them, knocking loose some tiles. Then projectiles landed all around them.

"My arrow." Wickrie reached toward the mirror.

"Out. I'll make you a new one." Omby pulled the girl toward the door.

Wickrie's amber eyes saw new writing beneath the Twisted Lighthouse image. "The blood of Oz does not flow to the sea."

Omby-Amby and Wickrie-Kells raced down the dim corridor. They headed back the way they came, until Wickrie pulled them into a side passage. "This way. It will let us out near the top of the Honeycomb."

"I thought it was catacombs." Omby said.

"The catacombs are deeper. The Honeycomb is built on top of the past."

They climbed up the stairs and followed more passages. Omby followed where Wickrie led. Soon they were back in the fading evening light. They emerged from a forgotten door on the dark side of the Honeycomb—a massively crowded collection of dwellings built together on top of previous dwellings. The inner mysteries of the Honeycomb were lost in the generations, but Wickrie-Kells and her family knew enough secrets from forgotten people to learn several handfuls of mysteries.

Omby-Amby did his best to put the broken door back in place. But they didn't have time to make it perfect. Wickrie-Kells pulled him down the balcony and across the terrace. They ran away from the setting sun, getting clear of the city and avoiding all guards.

Finally they made it out to the edge of the valley. Omby-Amby looked back with his soldier's eyes. "They almost had us."

"Would it really be war?" Wickrie asked.

"It depends on the mood of the king, and if the soldiers really have his ear."

"As far as I am concerned, they can bring their war. The strength of an army comes from the heart. Numbers don't matter if a soldier has the heart, like you."

"I had to protect you."

"Yes." Wickrie-Kells averted her amber eyes and looked back toward the city of her birth.

"They will be looking for us. We should go."

"Back to Emerald City?"

Omby-Amby shook his head. "There is more I want to see before I go back into those thick walls. I need to see my home. I need to see Yellow Castle again."

"You know what Glinda said—any violation of the ruler's sanctum is a declaration of war." Wickrie said.

"So war with Central City you say, 'Bring the fight', but with the Winkies, you have cold feet? What kind of soldier are you?"

"One who loves you. I know you miss your homeland. It's not like me—I can go home any time. Well, now, maybe not. But you, you are a stranger, and your land is under control of the Wicked Witch. I just don't want you to do anything that you, me, or anyone else will regret."

Omby smiled. "Don't worry. I'm not Glinda…or Oscar. They have magic to get them out of trouble. I've only got my sword and my mind."

"And your strong right hand." Wickrie-Kells squeezed Omby's right hand. "That's me."

"That's you."

"If you won't cross the border—if we can see it from far away, I will allow it."

"I don't need to go inside. Truthfully. I just need to see it—I need to see that the Yellow Castle is still standing—to see that my people are still alive and working. I can see that from a distance. The bluffs are high. We can stay hidden."

Wickrie-Kells squeezed his hand again. "West it is. Lead the way, soldier."

Far away, Kally guided Oscar to an old road in the forest where the Hamstrambulator could drive more freely. They drove several hours under the trees before they broke free to see the sun again.

"There is Mount Munch." Kally said.

The mountain rose out of the forest, bare on one side. Oscar asked why.

"A war, a long time ago, pitted a sorcerer against a family of witches. To protect the land, and the heritage of the Munchkins from the domination of the Sorcerer and his vengeful allies, they created a weapon. It drove the enemies from the land, but it burned the mountain down to the stone—on that side. The people were safe, and the pollution was driven from the land."

"What pollution?"

"The Munchkins have always held their knowledge and their heritage as a great banner. They were brought here by the Fairies when Oz was new. Their strength…ah, their strength. They could be counted on when they were strong. None as strong as a Munchkin scorned. They crushed their unfit under their feet. Drove them out of the East."

"And that is a *strength*?"

"The Munchkins were unquestionably the masters of this land. They will be again."

"Remember liberty."

"Remember the pearl. It purchases freedom. It purchases an army that will allow the people to be truly free. They will not need to lift a finger to defend their land. Everything will be done for them. Can you put a price on that sense of security?"

"Apparently you can." Oscar breathed, furrowing his eyebrows as he stopped the Hamstrambulator and stepped down from the basket. He bent down to unhook the feet from the large wheel.

Kally stepped her feet three times and she was standing next to Oscar.

"Okay, let's get you down." Oscar turned back to the basket, but it was empty.

"How did you—?"

"I'm not one to wait. Let's go. Up."

Kally led their journey up the mountain. No path marked their way. The sun met them on the open rock face as they crossed the great scar of stone.

"How is the army going to come back down?"

"There is another way."

"An easier way?" Oscar asked, breathless.

"A more populated way."

"Then why are we..."

"My family's treasure is important to protect. We are traveling the difficult path so that we are not seen."

"We're on the open side of a stone mountain. Anyone can see us."

"Few people live on this mountain."

In the distance, they heard the echoes of an axe chopping at a tree. From this distance, against the echoing stone, it was impossible to tell where the sound came from.

"You can see the edge of the land from here." Kally pointed. "There—a brown smudge where the green ends."

"It all ends right there?"

"The land ends. The Deadly Desert begins. We need to keep moving."

"If there is a quicker way, we should go that way."

"There is not."

Oscar grumbled in silence for several minutes until they came to a deep fissure in the stone, then his silent grumbling forced its way out. "I suppose you have some magic bridge in your pocket to get us across."

"No. I do not have a magic bridge in my pocket." Kally answered tersely.

"Maybe we can braid a rope from grasses that the invisible goats have not yet eaten."

Kally stopped and turned to face the grumbling Wizard. "Humor rarely solves problems, Wizard. This is the scar. There is an invisible bridge. I am surprised that you wizardly eyes do not see it. To cross the bridge you must close your eyes. It can be a little bit nauseating. Give me your hand. Close your eyes. Step with me—stop. The bridge is two steps to your left. One, two, there."

Kally lined up her steps to a flat spot on the other side of the chasm. "The charm on the bridge allows us to cross in three steps, but it has been known to cause vertigo. Keep your eyes closed and your teeth close together. Step with me now, one, two, three."

And they were across to the other side of the chasm.

Oscar fell to his knees. He clutched his head and gritted his teeth. "Magic bridge—I hate magic bridges. Why can't they build a real bridge of good stone? Real people cross real bridges, not this imaginary, invisible hocus-pocus. Pish-posh and humbug. Are we there yet?"

Kally looked over the chasm and the vista from their location on Mount Munch. "I told you this was a scar. It is a landmark—a remembrance. Destruction has its own beauty, and its own cost. To achieve the goal, you must pay the cost. It separates the true strength from the imposters."

16 STONES AND SHADOWS

After nightfall they reached the small round laboratory of Professor Nikidik. A stone garden surrounded his house. Statues and colored stones of every shape and variety filled the garden. Kally looked carefully at the lifelike statues. Were they carved? Doubtful. This garden displayed triumphs of an alchemist that did not like to be disturbed. The statues were probably all alive at one time. She would be careful. Kally turned to Oscar and gestured grandly. "This is it."

"We are on the far side of the mountain, and it feels like we climbed halfway back down."

"It's just your imagination."

"No. Those shadows pulling off the trees and dancing are my imagination. They've been following us, singing songs and chuckling at jokes to which only they know the punch lines. I am starting to feel left out."

"I assure you, Wizard, you know what you need to know."

In the garden, a statue yawned and shifted its elbow to rest on the other leg.

"I'm tired." Oscar said.

"You've been complaining this entire time."

Stone crackled and shifted beneath them. The gravel in the garden rattled and rolled to a stop. "The mountain is moving." Oscar said.

"The door is right here. I'm knocking. You stay awake." Kally ordered.

"The shadows are smiling at me like they know the answer to a riddle I can't quite pronounce inside my head. The rocks are beating a rhythm to the stars dancing on my bed. Glamour and slammer, and flibbery jab. This broom is my joust. I'll grieve for the hag."

Kally rolled her eyes. "There's no answer. Wizard, you sit by the door—with your back against it. Keep the broom standing up straight. If I remember correctly, that is one of the tests that the Professor requires to gain access to his lair."

"Lair? Is he some predatory beast that he needs a lair?" Oscar asked, sitting down with the broom standing upright.

"He is what he is. You will find out soon enough." Kally said, seating herself on a bench. She did not need sleep, so she settled herself to watch the Wizard dream.

He did not disappoint.

The statues in the garden danced a wild waltz. The stones whirled above their heads in clattering crescendos. The avalanche of gravel rained over their heads and sparked into stone fireflies, lighting the night into a menagerie of stone philosophies, each with their own jeweled shadow. Pillars arose and arches fell. The shadows declared war on the jeweled counterfeits, shattering them into scintillating tears ground underfoot by the stone watchmakers. The granite maidens paraded solemnly beneath a flapping gravel flag and shook their fists at the night sky until the stars bade them farewell. All that had faces removed themselves and settled back into position. The actors without faces piled haphazardly like rumpled sheets on the stone floor of the garden.

Kally amused herself by magically standing the broom on the end of Oscar's toe. The sun rose at her back, casting the brooms shadow over Oscar's face. The door at his back creaked open. Oscar fell backwards into the doorway.

A tall thin man stepped over the sprawled Wizard to see the broom balancing on his toe. "Clever trick, that, but it takes more than parlor tricks to win attention, wee one."

"I have brought a gift." Kally said. "He's waking up."

Oscar yawned and rolled stiffly to his feet. He stretched and yawned again and slapped his legs to get the feeling back in them. He moved stiffly about as the pins and needles jabbed at him. He complained loudly.

"The pins and needles prove the pain is the cost. You must endure the pain to control your life again, Wizard." Kally rose to her feet and curled her fingers around the floating broomstick.

"Thinking thoughts too deep for your desolate mind." The Professor muttered to Kally.

"This is the Wizard." Kally introduced Oscar to Professor Nikidik. "This is Professor Pipton Nikidik. He offered me some assistance when I was in need."

Nikidik walked out and surveyed his stone garden. "You did this?" He asked the Wizard.

"We arrived and no one welcomed us. Not that I'm surprised. So far away from reality, you don't seem to share many manners with normal life."

"Hmm. You know, those statues have not moved since I created them. They have gotten more comfortable. I thank you, Wizard. Perhaps you can do the same for my wife."

Oscar shrugged. "I don't know what you are talking about. I barely slept last night. No dreams at all. It couldn't have been me. It's probably your inventions, Professor."

"Perhaps." Nikidik led them into the laboratory and through a swinging gate. "It keeps the cats out." He explained.

Oscar stopped cold.

In the center of the laboratory, next to a large table that served as both workbench and breakfast nook, a statue waved at him. Or, it was mostly a statue. The eyes could blink and the hand could wave, but the rest appeared to be made of marble. Those moving parts were very much flesh and bone. The statue waved and the eyes smiled at the visitors.

"Margolotte, this is the Wizard. He shook our mountain last night."

"The statue is waving at me." Oscar's eyes widened.

"Yes. This is my wife."

"She is a statue."

"Yes. *Petrefaction*. An unfortunate effect of not reading signs that warn 'Keep Out'. I very nearly have the unguent perfected. It will bring the unliving to life. Or the previously living to life, provided they have a physical form to animate. It's all quite fascinating, really. Life wants to live. As you can see with Margolotte, I have turned flesh to stone, and some stone back to flesh."

"We have come about the army." Oscar said.

"The army..." Nikidik paused, searching the Wizard's face.

"You have an army that needs no sleep or rest. They obey orders perfectly. They were part of your process of creating the unguent." Kally prompted.

"Army...yes. Yes, I have the army. Downstairs. Follow me, please. Margolotte, be good. No more cookies for you."

The fleshy finger shook at the retreating Professor, but the eyes were laughing.

Oscar shivered and turned to follow.

Behind him, the shadows melted off the walls and followed alongside. The statue's eyes widened in terror and the hand spasm'd and flailed. But nobody was there to see it. A stone mouth cannot scream. The shadow turned back to the statue and hoarsely laughed—a whispering wind in the now empty laboratory. The shadows recognized their link to the Wizard. They saw that they were seen by eyes that were once human, but now as unliving as they were, and it amused them.

Oscar and Kally followed Professor Nikidik down the deep stairs into the veined blue and red heart of Mount Munch. Winding across the walls and ceilings, veins of ruby and emerald twined and separated. They glowed with magical power at regular intervals.

"It's beating, like a heart." Oscar observed.

"T'would be a pity if the beating heart of Oz ever stopped." Nikidik glanced back at the Wizard to gauge his reaction, if there was one. "The magic never stops. It just changes forms."

"How? How does it change form?" Oscar asked.

Nikidik paused before he continued on with his explanation, pointedly ignoring the Wizard's irrelevant question. "The heart will never stop. The great weapon drained the magic from this part of the land, but the heart never stopped."

"A weapon that devastated the traitors and drowned their cities in the deserts…is what I heard." Kally said.

Oscar cleared his throat to insert himself back into the conversation. "Weapons of that magnitude should not be used. If there is to be war, let it be a war where a man sees his enemy's eyes. Let them decide with their armies who will win and who will lose."

"That is a far cry from the liberty you profess. What you are saying is the mob rules—the larger army wins power and keeps power. You are finally beginning to sound sane."

"Armies do not have to be large to be powerful." Nikidik smiled. "Which brings me to the purpose of your visit. I have an army."

"I have money." Oscar began.

"No. He's very sweet." She turned and glared at Oscar. "This is mine. I have the agreed-upon price."

"Show me." Nikidik said.

Kally poured the six pearls from the pouch into Nikidik's outstretched hand. "Yes, yes. Good. All good quality. Excellent. Six pearls. Their mass is larger than the pearl paid to Gayelette."

Kally looked at the pearls and then at Nikidik's face. She shook her head slowly as realization began to form a shivering idea in her mind. "No."

Nikidik nodded. "Yes. Where *she stopped time, I will reverse it.*"

He crossed quickly to a carved ruby pestle and placed all six pearls inside. Then he lowered a great emerald mortar down over the top to crush the pearls.

"Don't do this. Those pearls can buy—"

"An army." Professor Nikidik finished for her. "And they have. Your army is ready." He pulled a lever and the mortar crunched down on the pearls.

Kally gasped as if in pain. She cried out then quickly clapped her hands over her mouth. Her amber eyes showed the utter horror she felt.

"What are you doing? Why is this hurting her?" Oscar said, stepping past Kally.

"Pearls are very valuable in Oz." Professor Nikidik said.

"Yes. I've heard. No seas, and all that."

The mortar and pestle crunched away, grinding the pearls into powder. Kally gasped with each crunch, as if the sound caused her physical pain and made her ill. Her face showed pallid disgust.

"More than that, Wizard. The pearls have power. They take a thing and make it physical. They take a speck and make it into something precious. They can aid the magician in turning that which is *not* solid into that which *is* solid. The skilled magician can make that which is not seen real."

"Like dreams." Oscar offered.

Nikidik froze. Then he turned his head up slowly, smiling at the Wizard. "Dreams, you say? Yes. Like dreams."

The mortar and pestle stopped. Nikidik raised the lever. He leaned over the ruby pestle and grunted in approval.

Oscar watched the shadows step off the walls in the ruby light of the laboratory and walk around. They shook themselves like large dogs.

"You charlatan." Kally said sourly to Professor Nikidik.

He meticulously transferred the grains of pearl from the ruby pestle to a small crystal vial. "Gayelette was no charlatan. She understood power. She knew what this meant. You think that you got the better end of the deal when you got Munchkin Country? Did you think you were buying an alliance? Good favor? Remember before—the way your family ruled? It should have been yours already. Yet you were scheming and lusting for the power. It blinded you. How well, Kalinya, have the last thirty years turned out for you?"

In the distance, Oscar watched the shadows dance and howl. The mountain was breathing. A thrumming sounded below his feet. He was transfixed by the strange changes as the ruby flowed around the walls. He did not hear the conversation between Nikidik and Kally.

Kally glanced back at Oscar, but he wasn't paying any attention to them.

"So he doesn't know." Nikidik stated.

"He is mine, not yours."

"The army is yours. The Wizard can make his own choices. You thought you were so rich and proud because you became queen of the Munchkins? You sold your greatest treasure for what—lands, servants, a title? You wasted your treasure. But I should not expect much from a Munchkin girl who hates her own blood."

Kally threw her hand out toward machinery behind Nikidik and crumpled it.

"You hated Gayelette because she controlled power greater than yours. You hated her because she did not fear your power." Nikidik smiled. "Your power is great, Witch, but it falls beneath the magic of sorcery. You still don't know the power of dreams."

"I know the Wizard can create an entire city and change it night after night. I know that he has power beyond you—beyond all of us. He can destroy everything in his anger, and rebuild it again in his mercy."

Oscar shook his head slowly as the echoing shots sounded again and again. He clapped his hands over his ears as he heard the heavy mocking laughter. The pressure behind his eyes became too great and he screamed out, "NO!"

The boiler near the ruby lake exploded. All around the shadows, stalactites of ruby dropped from the ceiling to pierce the floor. The shadows were trapped in the jeweled cages.

Kally jumped backwards in surprise. Nikidik stood and smiled. "Fascinating."

Oscar turned to look at them. His pale face shone with sweat. He saw the crumpled machinery. "Did I do that?"

Kally took him by the arm, nodding. "I am afraid you did. Were you dreaming?"

Oscar rubbed his eyes and then rubbed his hand across the back of his neck and on the back of his head. "I'm tired. I'm not seeing straight. Are there shadows in the cages? Those cages were not there before, were they?"

"Wizard, this is a place of magic. What you see is more than what you brought with you. Worry not about the damage. I make and remake many things in this laboratory. It is constantly changing."

"Like the Emerald City—always changing."

"Yes. Like that."

Kally stepped between the Wizard and the Professor. "You have destroyed the pearls. You are not getting any more—ever. Where is my army?"

"Gayelette created the Golden Cap. She sold half of her kingdom to create it. Do you know what that half-kingdom bought, Wizard?"

Oscar shrugged. "With all this talk, I'm guessing the answer is a pearl. I think Kally told me that story."

"Oh. So she has not kept you completely ignorant."

"I'm the Wizard. I see all."

"Of course you do."

Kally glared at Nikidik. She lifted her hand to throw him against the ceiling.

"Follow me." He led them down past the bubbling ruby pool to another cavern. "Gayelette sold half of her kingdom for the price of a large pearl. It was nearly the size of her fist. Do you know what she did with it?"

Kally glared.

"She crushed it to powder. The Golden Cap is meant for far more than you can imagine."

"I can imagine a lot." Oscar replied.

"So I've heard, Wizard. So I've heard. Gayelette created the Golden Cap to give form to that which was not flesh. She halted time in her own flesh, but she could not turn back time to give flesh to that which was no longer."

Kally perked up. Her eyes showed curiosity. This did not go unnoticed by Nikidik.

"Something interesting, Witch? You didn't know that about Gayelette's experiments? She was very close to discovering the secret...but it destroyed the Ruby Palace. Pity. I wanted that red-haired monster to grovel and mew beneath my glorious triumph. But she is gone, and with her, the Golden Cap. There is no bringing either her or the Golden Cap back from beyond the night'd realms."

Kally held her tongue. She glanced at Oscar and shook her head slightly as he opened his mouth to speak.

"With the disappearance of the Golden Cap, I forever lost my chance to compare Gayelette's handiwork to my own." He stopped in front of a pedestal and pulled the velvet robe away, revealing an exquisite crown and mask. "The Crown of the Dreamer. All I lacked was the infusion of pearl to activate the power."

"And the army?" Kally asked, but her eyes were on the crown.

Professor Nikidik followed her eyes. "The army? Are you certain you want to leave so soon?" He picked up the crown from off the pedestal to display his workmanship. "How I would have enjoyed watching Gayelette squirm as I displayed the power of this *lovely*."

"How do you know it will work?"

"You wound me, deceitful maiden. I am a magician, after all. My craft is not paltry rock-tossing or deflection spells. I create. I will turn back time and give face and voice to that which cannot walk in Oz."

Oscar wandered away to look at the line of automatons standing along the wall. They were of all shapes and sizes. Some were of humanoid shape, but others were tall, stilt-legged constructs. Some had wheels. They looked like the Wheelers, but there was something different about them. None of the automatons had faces. Even though they did not move, there was nothing in them that would have given them any impression or inkling of life. A face can be a powerful thing, but these lifeless things did not haven have that. These constructs had no life as yet.

Oscar tapped on the head of one. Mostly hollow. The knocking echoed through the cavern.

"I see you have discovered the army." Nikidik approached the Wizard.

"So this is the great hope for the Emerald City. It rings hollow."

Professor Nikidik smiled sardonically. "These do not need sleep as you do, Wizard. They are suitable for their purpose. They do not question, for they have neither past nor future. They have only the present, and they obey this moment. Can you say the same of even yourself?"

"Lead them, Wizard, down the brick road. It will lead outside." Kally said. She eyed the crown and mask. A scheme and a matching hunger shone in the her golden eyes. She licked her lips and gestured for Oscar to go. He did not. Not yet.

"Are these like the Wheelers, that they can only work on the Brick Roads?" Oscar asked.

"Binding myself to such limitations would not advance the cause of knowledge. These have life of themselves. They move, they act, they obey. They are perfect." Nikidik puffed out his chest.

"Do they think?" Oscar countered.

"No. They have no need to think. They obey."

Kally walked among the rank and file of the walkers. "They are not Wheelers?"

"If you would bother to notice, Witch, there are wheels only on six of the sixteen. However, as the Wizard so cleverly observed, they are not limited to brick roads alone. They have life. Also, this composes only a small part of the army."

"Where are the rest?"

"Not here. South. At the laboratory of Smith & Tinker."

"Oh." Oscar said. He noticed the bricks on the floor leading down the cavern and disappeared around the distant bend. "You have a brick road in here."

"I find it easier to transport my materials on roads. You may lead them, Wizard. I need only awaken them, and they will follow orders."

Nikidik pulled a square green bottle. "This concoction has been passed down my family for many generations. It awakens the form and gives it life. A single drop placed on the back of the neck awakens them." His gaze darted to Kally's face, gauging her expression. "This is the opposite of the *Stilling the Dreaming Life Inside* potion."

Kally's face showed no hint of recognition. Professor Nikidik filed that tidbit away for future reference. Apparently not all of the knowledge had been passed from her ancestors down to her. She was not the adversary he had believed her to be. "Interesting."

"What is interesting?" Kally demanded.

"Everything. Everything I create is interesting." Nikidik replied.

"How have you built them if they were not awake?" Kally asked.

"A magician never reveals his secrets. There are power sources in this place to bring life to the most lowly construct. This unguent of life will awaken them and they will be alive."

"Is this what you used on Margolotte?" Kally asked cautiously.

"She aided in the development of the unguent. I required sufficient to raise the army. Once I complete the Crown of the Dreamer, I will have no more need of the unguent. I can raise them in perfection." One by one, Nikidik added a drop on the back of the automatons' necks, and they roused to animation. "These are a sampling of what will be yours, Witch. Walkers, Hoppers, Head-Throwers, and Rolling Thunderbugs are a small representation of the larger army."

He gestured to the Wizard. "Wizard, at your pleasure, you may lead them out."

At last, Oscar left. He led the line of strange automatons along the brick road and around the bend, leaving Kally and Professor Nikidik alone.

"The Wizard will not return to the South Castle. Glinda has taken residence there."

"Oh. I was not aware that Quelala's heir was in control. Has she unlocked the secrets…"

"I have not traveled south. My army—"

"Is not for the Emerald City." Nikidik deduced.

"It has a purpose."

"Of course." Professor Nikidik flipped up the mask on the Crown of the Dreamer. "Where would you like the second army?"

"The border of the Winkie lands and Quadling lands. I will meet you there. I may have an additional customer for your services, Professor. I know a king that could use such an army."

"You know my price. Have this king come to me or send his representative. If we can come to an agreement, these armies shall walk Oz and we shall have peace."

Kally looked out after Oscar. Then she looked back to Nikidik. "The Powder of Petrefaction—I want it."

"You have your army."

"The Wizard has given you shadows in cages." Kally countered.

"You broke my machine pipe, and he broke my boiler."

"He pulled ruby down from the ceiling, where none had existed before, and created cages. The cages hold trapped shadows that walked away from the walls on their own. The power in these shadows, Professor, think of it. How many can say that they have been working with things with no body of flesh? If this is what you truly meant by your experiments to rival Gayelette, the Wizard has given you all that you need. That price more than covers the Powder of Petrefaction."

Professor Nikidik looked down the cavern after Oscar, then he looked back toward his laboratory. "You drive a hard bargain, but you are correct. Again, Witch, you are ending up on the wrong side of this deal. You are handing away power for a pittance."

"Let it be my loss." Kally's golden eyes glowed with short-sighted hunger. "I will get the powder."

Kally waited impatiently for several minutes as Nikidik retrieved the powder in the small vial. She was surprised to see Professor Nikidik hurrying toward her. He pressed the small vial into her hands. "More shadows. Excellent. This is…you, Witch…I am the victor. I shall see Gayelette turn in her grave. I have all that I need. I will meet you on the plains between the lands." Then he offered a warning. "If you use the Powder of Petrefaction on the Wizard, bring him to me when you are done with him. I would like to study him further."

"I will remember that." Kally said, and she walked away. She had received the weapons she needed, but she also had a new rival for true power. She would have to watch this one carefully.

17 AMONG THE MUNCHKINS

The Wizard looked over the constructs of metal and smiled. "The army that will end war in Oz—this is a fine day, a day to be long remembered. What we do here will change Oz forever. We will end war and allow humans to do what humans do best—dream and create stories and art and be truly free." Oscar held his head up high and marched at the head of his inhuman army.

"That is what humans do best?" Kally asked, one eyebrow raised high. "That does not sound like anyone that I know."

"Maybe you need to get out and meet more people. You might be surprised at how good people can be."

"We are passing through Munchkin Country. Perhaps we can meet some of these good people there. We can amass quite an entourage."

"A crowd." Oscar frowned. "I don't see how that would help. We have an army—a small army. I thought it could just be you and me walking."

"Nikidik is welcome to walk with us. I can invite him." Kally offered.

"No." Oscar held up his hands. "I think it is better that it is just you and I. This is going to be a surprise for everyone in Emerald City. The more people we see the less chance I have of actually surprising anybody."

"I guarantee that this army will surprise, just like it is meant to." Kally assured him.

Oscar forced a tired smile. "Good. We can go, then." He walked a few steps and then stopped. "Wait a minute." Oscar protested. "We are not going through Munchkin Country. Kalinya is the enemy. She will kill us if she can. She has sworn eternal enmity against Glinda and her friends."

"Glinda is not here." Kally clarified. "Ah, but her friends also, which includes you. I see."

"How could you not see that? Of course it includes me—I'm the Wizard!"

"She's not there."

"What?"

"Kalinya is not there. I didn't want to tell you this, because I thought you'd tell Glinda. Kalinya is gone. She's gone into exile—something about searching for meaning in the forest."

"Like Thoreau."

"What?"

"Henry David Thoreau—he wanted a simpler life. Moved to the forest. Wrote books."

"Okay. Something like that. She's gone. She won't bother us if we go through. Come on, Wizard, we're just passing through the land of the East."

"With an army!" Oscar exclaimed.

"Only a small one. I promise you, the Munchkins will love it."

A small boy named Boq, who was proudly six years old, ran out of the forest as the army approached the fields. He immediately fell into step with Oscar. "Hullo."

"Hello, there. What's your name?"

"Boq. I'm six."

"That's a good age to be. Where are you from, Boq?"

"Here. My house is in the village, by the bridge."

Kally kept glancing over at the boy. He was older now than when she had seen him last. She said nothing.

"My brother is dead." Boq said after a few seconds.

"I'm sorry." Oscar glanced over at Kally. She shrugged and stayed silent. "How did he die?"

"In the rain. The monsters came. He fought them. I saw. He chopped a hand off. Stabbed the giant through the heart." Boq jumped around, swinging his imaginary sword. "Then the monster hit him."

"You have quite an imagination." Kally said.

"Then the witch came."

Kally jumped. Her face paled.

"Oh, I see. What witch was that?" Oscar asked, smiling.

"Her." Boq pointed at Kally.

"She's not a witch. Her mother is a witch." Oscar explained. "Kally isn't a witch."

"Oh." Said Boq. He kicked a rock in the road. "I thought she was."

"It's easy to fit people into the stories that we have in our heads. Sometimes the stories seem very real, but we have to know what is a story and what is real."

"But it was real." Boq insisted.

"It might have been real, but Kally is not a witch." Oscar corrected.

"Okay." Boq kicked another rock. "Hey, what are these guys you're leading? Are they your army?"

Kally sighed in relief. "We are taking them to train. Just passing through the village."

"What are their names?"

Oscar glanced at Kally. She said, "They don't have names. They're just soldiers."

"Everybody has a name. Like that guy on stilts. I think his name is Big Leebo. And the fat guy is Little Pecan."

"Why is that name even good?" Kally asked. Her face was screwed up in confusion.

"Because he is fat. And pecan pie is the best. And he likes to eat pie. Lot and lotsa pecan pie. He says, *I'll take a little pecan.'* At dinner."

"That's a good reason." Oscar agreed.

As they reached the top of the hill, Munchkin Village came into view.

"What are they doing?" Oscar asked Kally. "That framework there, what is it?"

Kally smiled triumphantly. "That is the Witch's cathedral. It is their rite of passage."

"Ever'body gots to go backwards like this." Boq walked backwards to demonstrate his skill. "Then the tall guys bump their heads and ring the bells. *Ding-dong, the Witch has said.*"

Oscar glanced over at Kally. He saw her twisted smile, but wasn't quite sure what the boy was talking about. "What has the Witch said?"

"*Tall can only stay if their children gonna pay.*" Boq rhymed.

Kally's eyes widened. "I had not heard that. Go on, child."

Boq shrugged. "*Taller than the witch, go and dig a ditch. Closer to the ground, never seen or found.* Easy."

"So the people—the Munchkins—walk backwards through that wooden passageway. If they are too tall, they bump their heads and ring bells, and then they have to leave? Who made these rules?"

"The Witch Queen rules this land absolutely. I would not question if I were you."

"I do question it. Who can control their stature—how tall they stand?"

"According to you, Wizard, any man can control how tall he stands. Or don't you remember *liberty*?"

"That is not what I meant and you know it, Kally. I meant that a man doesn't control his height."

"Listen to yourself. You are not seeing the greater picture. If a person is not raising their head to look for freedom, they don't ring the bells. So it's up to them whether they want to stand tall or not. Mostly they *don't* just to fit in. Isn't that right, child?"

Boq shrugged. "I guess. But someday I'm going to be tall enough to ring every single bell."

"Every one of them?" Kally asked, smiling sarcastically.

"Yup. All of them. I'm going to be so tall, just like Big Leebo." He pointed back to the tall automaton that he named.

"That's a good boy. Why don't you go sound the alarm? Tell the people that an army has come." Kally suggested.

"Yeah. Everyone will be so neat to see them." Boq ran ahead of them. "I'll go tell."

Boq shouted and hollered all the way down the hill. The Munchkins in the town square turned to look up the blue-green hill. They trembled as they saw the small army. The people hurried through the Witch's cathedral, until every one of them stood on the far side of the wooden framework. They stood at the base of the statue of Kalinya. Boq ran through the passageway to find his parents.

Oscar and Kally led the army through the center of town to stop in the town square.

"Why are they afraid?" Oscar whispered to Kally.

"Two years ago an army marched here. They had Kalinya to protect them then. They do not have her now."

"But there are at least twenty times as many of them. They outnumber us. *And* we don't mean them any harm."

"They don't know that."

Emeritus King Widdershins slowly waddled to the town square, where he took his place in front of the entrance to the Witch's cathedral. "You have come into our land with an army, Stranger. Who are you? And what is your intention?"

Kally began to speak, "We—"

"I am Oz, the Great. We are leading the Royal Army through your land on a tour."

A shout from back in the crowd came, "Oz is a fiery head!"

"Oz is invisible!" came another shout.

"Oz is not a man!" came another.

"Yes, but—"

Boq pushed his way through the crowd and tugged on Emeritus King Widdershins' robes of state. "Those are his soldiers. That one is Big Leebo. And that one is Little Pecan."

"Be quiet, child." Widdershins pushed the child back behind him.

Boq pushed his way back out. Widdershins held his robes in front of the boy. Boq went around the other way.

"They are real nice." The boy said.

Widdershins puffed out his chest. "We are a peaceful people, unengaged in war. We do not desire war. Additionally, and in fact, I do not believe that you are Oz. The Great Wizard would not walk among the people with such a small army. Moreover, the Wizard does not need an army. He is more powerful than us all."

Oscar stood a little taller and fought to keep the smile from his face, but it shone clearly in his eyes. Kally eyed him narrowly. Boq looked with awe up at Oscar. He believed.

Oscar said, "We are passing through. With your permission, my good king—"

"He's not king." Kally interrupted. When Oscar looked quizzically at her, she continued. "King Emeritus, sometimes called Duke. Kalinya is Queen and ruler of the Munchkins."

The rotund Munchkin frowned but nodded. "That…is correct. Our Queen and Protector shall hear of this." To his honor guard, he said, "Dispatch a runner to her Majesty and inform her of these strangers and their army. We shall see who receives their due punishment. If she is not in her dwelling, find her."

A runner immediately ran away from the square.

"We should leave." Kally took Oscar by the elbow. Quietly she said, "We don't want to be here when they discover that their Queen Protector is missing. There could be panic."

"We wouldn't want to panic them. Why would they want to be so short, anyway? I don't understand. I don't especially like it." Oscar whispered.

As they led the small army away from the city square, Kally answered the Wizard. "Their Queen Protector has spoken. No one in the land can be taller than her. We only saw the short ones. There are no more tall ones. Perhaps they are digging ditches or selling their children."

"You say that like you are proud of her accomplishment." Oscar said, casting a sideways glance at Kally. He frowned. "It's a good think you're not in charge. I'd be exiled in a heartbeat, even though I am short."

"Yes." Kally agreed.

Boq followed the army as it walked through the woods. Boq stayed close enough that he could hear some of the talk between the Wizard and the Witch.

"—fighting so no more death. Silver and gold could bring…"

"No…Emerald City…freedom…unless…"

"Liberty…destruction…"

The army followed a strange route that eventually led through the forest back to a large wheeled machine surrounded by baskets. The boy heard the Wizard say that this machine was the Hamstrambulator. That was a funny word. But it was a funny machine.

Boq hid behind a tree. The witch led her automaton army away from the setting sun. The Wizard reattached the running legs to the large wheel of the Hamstrambulator. He watched Kally lead the metal and wood soldiers further through the forest. The Wizard sighed deeply.

In the center of the clearing, the sun broke through the trees to send a beam directly down on the Wizard. Oscar stood in a fading beam of late afternoon sunlight, feeling the warm ray flow over his face. He spread out his arms. "Almost soon, Father. Almost soon I will be free from war. Then I will be free."

Kally fussed with the robots near the Hamstrambulator. She was out of earshot. Boq crept a little bit closer to the Wizard.

Boq heard a whispering voice next to him. "If you want to see change, make it happen. Dream to change the world." He jumped and looked around, but there was no body to go with the voice.

"Grow in years and in wisdom." The voice spoke again.

Boq stood very still. A small bird whistled near his ear. He could not feel it, but he could hear it. Something magical was happening.

"You will see things in your life that will be wonderful—the stories you will tell your children."

"Who are you?"

"I am the voice of freedom. If you are a friend to me, I will always be near."

"I will."

In the clearing, Oscar turned halfway and smiled.

Boq froze. Had the Wizard seen him?

"The army is ready to move. Are you finished with your little relaxation moment?" Kally entered the clearing.

Oscar glanced around. "Yes, I believe my work here is finished."

"The work is never done. There is always more power."

"Power must be controlled and used only when necessary." Oscar chided.

"Power must be gained before it can be controlled." Kally shot back. "Remember our purpose. We are going to take power from one who unrightfully gained it. As you say, Wizard, power must be used responsibly. We are going to gain power, and then we will use it responsibly."

"It is a nice afternoon. I would like to rest for a while longer."

"We have a mission. This was your idea, remember that."

"I remember, but I am tired."

"What would the world think of a wizard who is tired? What would the world think if they knew that you were not so great and wonderful as they thought?"

"I do not care what the world as a whole thinks of me."

"Then what do I think?" Kally asked. Her amber eyes pierced his heart.

"I don't know. You want me to keep pushing. I want to, but I am so tired."

"Make your mind do the work. Your mind can do what your body cannot. That is the nature of magic. You are a wizard, are you not?"

"So people say."

"You *are* a wizard. It is not rhetorical. You have power to change the world."

Boq stepped carefully around a tree to get a better view of the witch. When he saw her in profile, he was certain—she was the witch from so long ago. It was only two years, but that was nearly a lifetime to the little boy. His foot stepped carelessly, and he slipped and fell to his knees. His grunt burst out, breaking the silence.

Both Kally and Oscar turned toward the sound. Oscar knew what he would see. Kally felt with her magic, and she lashed out, shattering branches. All she knew was that she was spied on. That was unacceptable at best and a grave threat at worst. Then she spied the small boy.

"You! Child!" Kally hissed.

Boq ran.

The child ran until the echoes of the Witch's screams no longer nipped at his heels. The shadows grew long. The forest grew strange and quiet. Eyes stared out at him from behind every branch and bush. He was lost.

In the last shining remnants of sunlight, Boq saw a glint of metal through the trees. He followed the orange glints of sunset, climbing over logs and wading through a stream. He climbed up the leaf-strewn embankment and brushed off the knees of his trousers. There it was. It was covered in vines, but he knew what it was, even though he had been just little when he saw it last.

It was his brother's sword.

When the Witch threw the monster far away, the sword had been stuck in its chest. The sword was lost, but Boq knew that it would always be found. He knew that someday he would be the one to find it. He knew because he knew his brother, and his brother, Tabulo was dead now. He was with the fairies. He left his sword for Boq to find.

Boq cleaned away the vines encircling the blade and climbing up the hilt. He pulled the sword from its setting in the rotten wood. The perfect blade was free from rust and canker. No damage had come to it during its long sleep.

In the last rays of the fading red sunset, Boq lifted the sword above his head and shouted as loud as his voice could shout. "I will fight you, Witch! I'm not afraid of you!"

18 THE ROAD WEST

At the edge of the forest, Kally stopped and perked up her ears. She listened intently, but the voice of the forest faded. She peered around, searching for another echo, but none presented itself to either her eyes or her ears.

"Spooked by shadows?" Oscar asked, glancing over at her.

"I heard something. It's gone now, but for a moment I felt like everything in my life froze, and I could hear the future—like a crack in the ice. But the echo is gone."

"Behave yourself, and everything else works the way it is supposed to."

"Behave yourself? Nothing is that simple, Wizard."

"It is if you make that your one rule. If you behave yourself, you take whatever action is necessary to accomplish the goal. And the goal is, of course, being good."

"Of course." But Kally's mind was already turning. *Behave yourself*, she smiled smugly, such a rule could be quite *effective*. It would need to be implemented simply at first. The simplicity would be the key. It was a rule so simple that everyone could understand and agree to it. That would certainly make it easier to enforce. No more appealing to old law books or scrolls of the elders for rule interpretations. One rule, *behave yourself*, and one interpretation. But who would be the interpreter of the law? *Who else?* Kally smiled. It all became clear. Those cracks in the future ice just framed her perfectly.

The automaton army followed the Hamstrambulator as it rolled slowly through the fringe forest, moving toward the prairie. There were sixteen of them. Some were Walkers, others Hoppers, a few Head-Throwers, and four were Rolling Thunderbugs. The Thunderbugs could roll along for themselves, but what about the other ones? How were they supposed to travel across the Emerald Prairie?

Oscar stopped the Hamstrambulator at the edge of the tall grass. The sun dropped below the horizon. "How far is it?"

"Between the borders of the two lands? Approximately sixty-seven horizons."

Oscar turned to look at Kally. "That's a pretty specific guess. If you are just throwing numbers around to impress me, please stop. I don't know how we are going to get all of these things from one side of Oz to the other."

Kally's eye twitched. Her mouth frowned slightly, the expression dancing around, not quite settling in place. Her entire face was fighting for control. "The army can take itself. As for my *'guesses'*, Wizard, it would behoove a boy like you to believe a little more in what you are doing. This is my army, and I will get it there. You drive."

Oscar drove for hours. Once he woke up to find the Hamstrambulator cruising along of its own volition. How long had he been moving forward with his eyes closed? Too long. Where was Kally? Nowhere in sight. Quickly he spun the vehicle to a stop. His eyes frantically searched the darkness behind him, but not even the stars could brighten his tired eyes. The shadows danced and strutted in front of him. All around the corners of his gaze, the stars stepped down off their pedestals to peer curiously at this man from the world of air who dared to see into the darkness. Oscar's voice caught in his throat. He hoarsely croaked out, "Kally!"

"What? I'm right here." The voice came from the basket next to Oscar.

The startled Wizard whirled around too quickly, lost his balance, and fell from the driver's basket to the ground. "You were gone." He protested, staring up from his back.

"You are tired. The army is continuing on. I will point them in the proper direction. Are you stopping here for the night?"

"I'm not tired." Oscar protested, yawning. His eyes burned, but he didn't want to disappoint the amber-eyed girl.

"Your power comes when you sleep. We need all the power you can muster, where we are going. Sleep now, Wizard. Let your dreams of power be fully realized."

Exhausted and numb, Oscar couldn't even pull himself back up to a sitting position. He simply curled on the ground, wrapping his arms around his middle and pulled his knees up toward his chest. He stared at the tall grass all around him. Tears welled up and dropped out of his burning eyes, but he could not close them. "Stay strong. Not lose control. Not lose control. Blank slate. No memories. Blank slate. Not lose control. No more tears."

Above the shivering Wizard, Kally took one, two, three steps, and she was gone.

Three horizons later, Kally caught up with the longstrider automaton. She pointed it to travel in specific directions away from the distant lights she saw to the south. It was vital that they cross the Emerald Prairies as quickly as possible, without anyone seeing their army.

Kally returned to glance down at Oscar, still mumbling to himself. Then she raced back the way the Hamstrambulator had come. Six horizons and she found the larger automatons moving along as quickly as they could. They were close to a day's journey behind. Even if Oscar slept until morning, they would barely reach the stopping point. There was too large a risk of being seen by either the Emerald City guards or the Emerald Army from Central City. Kally had paid too dear a price for this army to risk discovery.

Kally ensured that all of the automatons were connected, then she grasped the hand of the lead automaton. One, two, three steps, and they were on their way.

Oscar's eyes burned as the stared at the tall grass. In the distance he heard strange movement, drawing swiftly closer. He rolled to his back, with his eyes to the sky. The laughing stars pointed down at him, mocking his weakness. Oscar blinked once. When he opened his eyes, he saw striped stockings and the shimmering of metal through the starlight. The sounds receded in the distance. He stared at the stars as their tails stretched out across the sky.

Far to the East, deep in the forest, a small figure clutched a sword desperately as he struggled to stay awake. All around him the forest was waking up. Crickets chirped and birds whistled their salutations to the day. The darkness gave way to a dim glow heralding the coming dawn.

"You, boy." The deep voice shattered the quiet solitude of the morning and jolted Boq awake.

Boq cried out and lunged out with the sword. His eyes were filled with frightening things, but nothing made sense when he opened them. His brother's sword met resistance and stopped cold. The clang in the heavy morning air startled him into wakefulness.

The six-year old boy looked down the blade of his brother's sword. Planted firmly in the ground, in front of a pair of heavy boots, was the head of an axe. Boq's gaze followed the axe handle upwards to see the raised eyebrows of a sturdy woodcutter, Galvan Chopper.

"There's a right lad. Always alert. But be aware that there are more fierce things in this forest than me."

"I...I fell asleep." Boq explained.

"You did at that. Your little snores could've woken the bears, but for the sun coming up. They're covering their eyes and ears for another hour or two. You're safe now, boy. Up." He extended his hand and helped Boq to his feet.

"Do you know the Witch?"

"Kalinya? Aye. I know her tall house is far from here, but it has not lit up the sky for more than two years. I know she built her strange home on the forest island in Munchkin Fields. I know she burns to control everything. Aye. I know the Witch."

"She's younger now. Her face is pretty, but her eyes are angry. She has an army."

"Oh? Is that so? And how do you know such a great thing, my young master?"

"I saw her. She chased me."

"Even with that sword, she chased you?"

Boq shook his head. He tried to clear the sleep from his eyes. "I didn't have the sword when she chased me. It's my brother's sword. He's dead. He fought the monsters and he's dead. I found his sword. It shined in the sun, just before night."

Galvan held his hands out for the sword and Boq refused. He clutched the hilt tighter. "I only want to look at it, boy. If it's your brother's blade, I've no claim to it."

Grudgingly, Boq handed the sword to the large woodcutter. Galvan examined every inch of it, from the filigree in the crosspiece to the fine workmanship in the wooden hilt. "Iron Maple and Sparkwood. That is very fine work. Your brother must have been a very fine warrior."

He handed the sword back, hilt-first, to Boq. The boy beamed with pride and nodded his head. "How did you find your way this deep into the forest? You're very nearly to Mount Munch."

Boq shrugged. "I ran. Tried to find my way home, but the forest was dark."

"Aye. The forest can be dark at night, especially for a little boy."

"I'm six."

"Oh. Not so little then."

"No."

"Are you afraid of the Witch?" Galvan asked.

Boq shook his head vigorously. "No. I have my brother's sword."

The woodcutter laughed, and the sound woke up the morning. The sun broke through the trees with his laughter. "One boy with a sword against the Witch?"

"Yes."

"There are better ways to fight than with a sword, boy."

"My name is Boq."

"Hello, Boq. I am Galvan Chopper."

"That's your name?"

"More than my name—Galvan Chopper is who I am. Take heed, Boq. When you become your name, it is more than just a name, it is who you are. When you meet someone new, say, *'I am Boq'*, instead of, *'my name is Boq.'* You'll find yourself standing straighter and taller. You will know who you are. Now, give me your name, boy."

139

"I am Boq."

"Good. How does that feel?"

"I feel strong."

"You look strong. Boq, let's get you home."

They marched a half day through the forest. Galvan Chopper pointed out trees and streams. Whenever Boq asked a question, which was all the time, the woodcutter had an answer. He was the smartest man that Boq had ever met.

They stopped at the forest at its eastern edge. Down below in the valley, smoke was rising from the chimneys of the bakery and a few other homes in Munchkin Village. Boq looked up in surprise to the woodcutter. "I know where we are!"

"You're home, Boq."

Boq took a few steps toward the village. Then he stopped and looked back at Galvan Chopper. "Aren't you coming?"

"No. I left that life a long time ago. My place is in the forest. Your place is in there."

"Wait 'till Father sees I found the sword! He'll be happy. He gave the sword to Tabulo. But when it got lost he was always sad."

"When fathers lose their sons, it is always sad, Boq. But not even a sword can bring back your brother."

"But I want to show him. Then I can fight the Witch!"

Concern clouded the woodcutter's face. "There are other ways to fight than with a sword."

"But I can fight her." Boq protested.

"I know you can, Boq. You are a smart, strong boy. To fight a Witch you need to know her weakness. You need to watch her as you grow up. You need to use your mind," Galvan tapped his finger to the side of Boq's head, "and then, when you are ready, if you choose, you can use the sword. Watch her, Boq. She will clear out the strong ones, and then she will prey on the weak that are left."

"Can I take the sword?" Boq asked quietly.

"What do you think? Do you think she will let you keep it? Do you think she will let your father keep it?"

"No. She already said that nobody can be taller than her. Some people left."

"So if you can't be taller than the Witch is tall, how can you be bigger than her?"

"I dunno." Boq mumbled, disheartened.

"By being a smarter, better, cleverer boy than she is a Witch. You will grow into a clever man, and then you will fight the Witch, and you will win."

Boq handed the sword to Galvan Chopper. The woodcutter took it and looked down at the crestfallen boy. "I will hold onto your brother's sword for you, Boq. When you have learned to fight without a sword, then you can come and claim it from me. Until then, I will protect the sword. I promise."

"You promise?"

"I swear on my father's axe that this sword will be yours when you come for it."

Boq managed a smile. "I will learn to fight without a sword."

"Your mind is far sharper than a sword can ever be. Make your mind your weapon. Now tell me, boy, who are you?"

"I am Boq." He puffed out his chest proudly.

"Yes you are. Now tell them." Galvan gestured behind the boy to Munchkin Village.

"*I AM BOQ!*" the boy shouted. The echo faded and his grin stayed plastered on his face. He turned around, but the woodcutter was gone. His grin faded more quickly than the echo of his shout.

The boy turned to walk down the hill toward his home. He heard softly on the wind, "Who are you?"

The smile jumped back onto his face. "I am Boq." He shouted as he jumped through the meadow on his way home. "I am not afraid of you, Witch. I am Boq!"

19 EMERALD SPECTACLES

The morning sunrise found Glinda in the South already awake and deep in thought. She dressed quickly and went to her laboratory. She was not surprised to find Promethus already there, working. He was hunched over a pair of Emerald Spectacles. His explanation made sense, "You have the Ruby Spectacles. To be balanced, I should have Emerald Spectacles."

"What do they do?" Glinda asked, genuinely curious.

"Explain to me first what your Ruby Spectacles do."

"I saw Oscar. I saw the magic that he is, inside him. I saw…magic."

Promethus smiled. "Now you begin to see. You have learned that rubies are of the Blood of the Land of Oz. They have powers to lengthen a person's years. They power the magic within. This was known to Smith & Tinker a long time ago. What do emeralds do?"

Glinda thought. "Red and green are opposites. Traditionally rubies are red and emeralds are green. If Ruby Spectacles can see magic…"

"Go on."

"Then green emeralds might…hide magic? Make it invisible?" Glinda guessed.

"Emeralds have power to purify and cleanse—they protect from evil or wild magic. I do not think it coincidence that your Wizard commissioned the city be built of emerald."

"He dreamed it that way." Glinda explained.

"And he told you this?"

"No. I saw it. I was sitting right there as he slept and dreamed. It was a huge city of green, with great walls and towers, and emeralds."

"And you were awake to see all of this?"

"Of course I was awake. How else would I have seen it?" Glinda snapped. "I'm not lying."

"No. You are not lying. That I can see. There are other ways to see a great city that does not exist. Think on this, daughter of Quelala, while you determine the best course to pursue with your lost Wizard."

Glinda frowned. She did not like being talked down to, and all Promethus ever seemed to speak was riddles.

The storms clouded over Glinda's eyes, and Promethus quickly changed tactics. He picked up the Emerald Spectacles and held them out to Glinda. "Try them."

Glinda put them on and everything turned green. "Everything is green. They are nice. They fit well."

"But they don't react like the Ruby Spectacles. Were you expecting a big flash of what—nothing?"

Glinda shrugged. "I thought I would see more than I see now."

Promethus held up a small mirror. "Look in here. What do you see?" He moved his fingers in front of the mirror.

"I see your fingers moving. It's a reflection in a mirror. Nothing special about the mirror."

"No. I suspect not." Promethus said. "Just a mirror. What about your lockbox? Anything special about that?"

Glinda turned around and walked to her heavy lockbox. It was bound in iron and secured to the oak island near the hearth. There was no visible lid or hinges—it was just a solid, bound box with a square of metal plating that wrapped from the front side to the top.. She reached out her finger and touched the metal plate. She pushed again and again. Nothing.

"What's wrong, princess?" Promethus asked. His mirror was pointed at Glinda's hand.

"Nothing. Nothing is wrong." Glinda traced arcane shapes in the air above the metal plate. The lockbox clicked open.

She pushed the lid down and swiped over the metal plate, clearing the magic entry code. She pressed the her finger onto the metal plate. Nothing.

"What happens when you take the spectacles off?" Promethus asked.

Glinda turned around, with her hand still on the lockbox. She faced Promethus. Half of her skirt covered the glowing magical sigils on the metal plate. "Nothing is wrong here."

"Lower the spectacles."

Glinda lowered them on her nose and looked at the plate. The runes glowed. She pushed the emerald spectacles back up, and the magic runes disappeared. She repeated this three times before she could believe her eyes. She bent over very close to the metal plate and studied it from an inch away. Still nothing.

From behind her, Promethus tried to get the mirror at a better angle. He glanced at the partial reflection of the magic runes, with the other half hidden behind Glinda's skirt.

Glinda stood up and crossed the distance to sit back at the table with Promethus. She looked through the green spectacles at the clever inventor. "I believe you."

Promethus silently slipped the magic mirror back into his pocket. "Clever little trick, isn't it?"

Glinda nodded. "It is clever. But I fail to see any benefit to hiding magic. If a person can't see magic anyway, what use would Emerald Spectacles be?"

"Ah, but to invent is not to be necessarily useful. One never knows when a pair or two of green spectacles might come in handy."

"There is something you're not telling me." Glinda accused.

Promethus slowly knocked his big knuckles on the table. "Yes." He admitted.

Glinda removed the spectacles, folded them neatly and set them on the table between them. She stared at the spectacles for several long seconds. "Promethus—*Guardian*—will you advise me? I feel as if I have lost all of my friends, and my heart needs strong words that only a friend can provide."

Promethus nodded once, very slowly. "Inasmuch as you consider me a friend, young princess, I will answer you truthfully." He reached out and rested a finger on the Emerald Spectacles. He slid them back across the table to rest by his tools.

"You have been here for a few days. What do you think of me? Am I a fair ruler? Do I give as I say, or do I demand too great a price?"

Promethus waited to answer, studying the face of the young sorceress. She was learning through sad experience the nature and disposition of almost all men—that when they get a little bit of power, as they recognize it, they immediately act out and enforce their will on others. He debated between harshly truthful and condescending. In the end he opted for tact. "Your power is great. You are beginning to be your mother's heir as a sorceress. You have a great distance to go until you are your father's equal. Your friends, as you call them, recognize your growing power. The price you pay, yourself, is great, and the cost to others is also great." He sat back in his chair and sighed.

Glinda also sat back in her chair. She switched her gaze back and forth between her fingertips swirling on the table and Promethus' face. She chewed on her words before they escaped her mouth, then she thought better of it and swallowed them again.

"Powerful people have powerful friends. It is well that you surround yourself with the best and brightest in all of the lands. You are well-armed and well-protected. Yet you find yourself alone at this moment."

"Yes."

"Then the best advice I can offer you, young sorceress, is that you must decide what is most important to you. What do you stand for? What secrets do you keep from your friends?" He paused, studying the face of the young sorceress.

Glinda glanced back and forth between the table and the man's face. She sighed.

"With your position, you cannot help but keep some secrets. That is the nature of power. You do not need to tell your friends everything, but you must find a cause in your life—something worth fighting for—and then do all you can to bring that to pass. Your mother had hers…but she kept it so close that none of us knew what it was. However, it drove her every day of her life."

"Tell me about it." Glinda muttered. "No time for family or friends or anything except her work."

"And what is your work?"

"I have to guard against the Witches. They are still out there. Kalinya is a constant threat. She's been quiet for almost two years, but I don't trust her one bit. Ondri-baba is better. She has the West, but she is satisfied there. A truce holds between her land and the others, provided there is no aggression. If she sends another Winged Monkey…"

"You will answer fire for fire."

"I must. It is my duty. I must protect the land."

"That is a great burden for a young sorceress to carry."

"It's not me alone. I have the Wizard…" she sighed. "I need the Wizard. I need Wickrie-Kells. I need Omby-Amby. I need Ola Griffin." Resolve settled in her face. "I will get the Wizard. I will apologize, make amends, show him that I'm sorry, kiss it better—whatever it takes to make him love me and want me again. I need him. I'll go up to the Emerald City and find him and make him see that I'm sorry he left." She rose from her seat. "Ola Griffin, see that my chariot is prepared!"

"You sent her to the scrapyard." Promethus reminded the red-haired sorceress.

Glinda's hand fell slowly from up by her mouth to her side. "Oh. Yes. I had forgotten."

"You can go make amends with her right now. She is still on the grounds."

"And she will be here when I get back. Right now I need the Wizard." Glinda hurried down the stairs to prepare for her trip.

Promethus pulled the small mirror from his pocket and watched the magic replay of Glinda going to her lockbox and pressing and tracing the shapes in the air. He saw the pattern her fingers made, but he could not see all of the magic glyphs. He pounded his hand on the table in frustration. He pocketed the mirror as he heard Glinda's voice echo up the staircase.

"Guardian, are you staying here?"

"Aye." He responded. Then quieter, he said, "I'll be here until I have gotten what I came for."

Before the sun cleared the horizon, Glinda was outfitted in resplendent riding leathers. She walked out to meet her chariot in front of the rose gardens. She looked up at her laboratory tower. Promethus held up a hand in farewell. Glinda snapped the reins, and the powerful horses launched forward. She would be back soon, with the Wizard. Then everything would be happily ever after—the way that it was supposed to be. Glinda turned to bid a soft farewell to her castle—her home—*Chronometria*.

Far away, on the Emerald Prairie, Omby-Amby and Wickrie-Kells walked toward the morning sun. The night had passed in Wickrie's childhood home. Omby-Amby had slept happily on the floor near the hearth. Over her protests, Wickrie was locked securely in her room to spend the night. Even with the prospect of marriage between the two children, Tjorn and Donya were not about to let them live a married life.

Despite the hospitality and the laughter, Omby-Amby was happy to get back out into the open air. He let the breeze blow over his face and short beard, savoring the smells and the sounds that only an outdoor breeze could carry.

Wickrie-Kells joined him outside when she finished her goodbyes. She hugged her mother close. Two sets of amber eyes bathed in smiling farewells.

Wickrie-Kells turned her eyes West, toward her true love, Omby-Amby. "Where to?"

They waved goodbye and walked until they were out of earshot of the family farm.

"I want to see Yellow Castle again. I know the land is occupied, but we can see it from a distance. I'm not going to do anything that jeopardizes the borders."

"You're worried about them—your people."

"Aye. Every day I think about them. Under the Witch, they won't be happy."

"Why don't they fight?"

"We haven't had war in the West for two generations. The army was old. I was the best they had. I left to find my future." He reached out and squeezed Wickrie's hand. "I found you."

"And Oscar."

"Aye. And Oscar, with all of his crazy dreams, and freedom and liberty. I found what I had been looking for. I found something that I could believe in. That, to me, was stronger than family ties."

"Is it so easy for you to walk away? You did it with your family and your people."

"I followed the path that was best for me. Sometimes seeds fly on the wind until they find the place right for them and they put down roots. I'm putting down roots here pretty quick. I have found where I want to be."

"I left my family to follow Glinda. She gave me command of her army. But I still come to visit my family. You don't."

Omby-Amby smiled sadly. "Most of my family is free and clear. I followed the soldier's path, like my father before he became an architect. He brought most of the family to build Emerald City. I have a brother somewhere in Winkie Country. He was a farmer. He didn't want to leave his orchards. Stubborn fool. He had the opportunity for a new life in Emerald City—we have good land all around. Sure he'd have to start over, but it's a good land. There are good people that could help him. Instead, he wanted to stay comfortable. Then it was too late."

They walked a while in silence.

"If you could go back in there and free him, would you?"

Omby-Amby shook his head. "The peace is too fragile. Anyone who crosses the border triggers a declaration of war. Even if I did, I don't know if he would even come. He is proud of what he built. Proud enough to stick through conquering—as long as he has his trees."

"Isn't that a little bit harsh?"

Omby shrugged. "It's his life. I tried. I really did. I don't care."

Wickrie-Kells rubbed Omby's back with her green-painted fingernails. "Sure you care. You just don't know how he can be different—"

"He's my brother."

"He is not you."

"We were raised the same."

"He is not you. You can't force him to like what you like, or believe what you believe in." She studied his whiskered face. "Are you sure this is something you want to do?"

"Yes."

"Do you want to get the Hamstrambulator? We could get it on the way back past the Emerald City?"

Omby-Amby looked at the amber-eyed beauty at his side and smiled. "Then it would all be over too soon. I'm going to walk these steps with you—every one of them. You and I together will walk in the sunlight."

"Together in the sunlight."

20 THE SEARCH FOR THE WIZARD

Glinda urged her powerful horses even faster. The northward miles turned to dust behind her chariot. She raced the sun through the morning sky.

When the sun hit its zenith, Glinda rolled through the gates of the Emerald City. The workers were in the process of attaching the large gates to the outer walls. The gatekeeper's window was open, and the workers stopped and waved as the fire-haired sorceress passed through. Glinda politely smiled in return.

Few animals were allowed in the city. Glinda's chariot was one of the few private conveyances that the city had seen. Most of the wheeled traffic was construction carts. They were primarily on the edges of the city—the central towers had all been built up to a great height. The buildings were bare—stone and brick. They were beautiful, but they were cold. They needed a loving hand to shape them. They needed another softer dream to give face to the immense potential. She smiled. It was nice to be here.

Glinda opened the door to Oscar's apartment. Silence. She quietly crossed the floor to look all around. Things had changed since the last time she had been here. She glanced out the window. There, that bridge had changed. It had different carvings on it before. Now it had trees.

Glinda tapped on the door of Oscar's private chamber. No answer. She tried the handle—it was unlocked. She slipped through the door and crossed to the bed. The room was dark. The silence was overpowering. Glinda pulled open the curtains. She noticed, with a certain flattered satisfaction that the only window in the room faced south.

The bed was empty. It had not been slept in. She felt the covers—cold. Oscar was not here, and he had not been here for some time.

Glinda stormed out. Nobody knew where Oscar and the girl had gone. They might be in the city, or they might not be.

When Glinda checked with the Emerald City Guard at their barracks, they did not know, either. They didn't seem to know much.

"You don't know where the Wizard is? How can you be a guard of the Emerald City and not know where your liege is at every moment?"

Stunned silence echoed from the guard.

"Where is your captain? Where is Omby-Amby?"

"At this moment? Or in general?"

Glinda's stare nearly pinned the hapless guard to the wall.

"At this moment, I don't know. In general, he left. He wanted to go out for a few days. He said that he was going to see the sun again. Wickrie-Kells was with him."

"So the Captain of my Guard, and the Captain of your Guard, are out frolicking in the sun? That figures. Do you know which way they went? How long have they been gone?"

"They went out the front gate, and they headed toward Central City. That was the day before yesterday. The Wizard gave them leave."

"Omby-Amby is an honest man. If he told you that, it is so. Thank you."

The guard saluted Glinda. "Your majesty."

Glinda allowed herself a small smile at the guard, but that was enough. His face split into a wide grin. This episode would be all the talk of the guardhouse at supper this evening.

Glinda mounted her chariot and headed toward the front gate. At the gates she stopped. All the workmen paused in their work and looked up at her. Glinda's fiery hair was haloed in the afternoon sunlight.

"I am looking for the Wizard. Have any of you been party to his comings or goings in the last two days?"

Nobody knew.

"Where would I find a chariot, if I wanted to leave the Emerald City?"

"You have a chariot." One of the gate-builders observed.

"Yes, I know I have a chariot, but what if I did not? What if I were the Wizard and wanted to leave the Emerald City? Where would I get a chariot, or a carriage, or even a horse?"

The gate-builder pointed to distant buildings, to the East of the Emerald City. "The stables."

"Thank you. Your work on these city walls is wonderful. You have built a beautiful city."

Again, the workers could not contain their grins.

Glinda smiled as she drove away.

The stables held all the chariots and horses. None of them had been taken. The only empty stall was near the door, and that contained only a large canvas tarpaulin folded neatly on the floor. When Glinda asked the stable-keeper what was kept in that stall, she received the answer, the *Hamstrambulator*.

"How long has it been gone?"

"I noticed it gone yester-morn. I get figured Cap'n Omby took it. No worries."

"Yes. No worries." Glinda echoed, but her eyes searched out the door to the distant horizon. "That will be all. If Captain Omby happens to return, will you tell him that I came to see him?"

"Aye. He'll be excited as a baby bounce-bug on its momma's knee. 'Tis not often we get a visit from a queen."

Glinda smiled softly. "No. I don't suppose it is. Affairs in my kingdom have kept me occupied."

"I meant no disrespect, mum. I merely was statin' that it's always a pleasure. A city deserves a king *and* a queen."

Glinda's face reddened slightly. She nodded and walked out of the stable.

She pointed the noses of her horses west, toward Central City, and snapped the reins. Her chariot sped north then wound around to the west. The single large gate of Emerald City faced south, the direction opposite Glinda's course.

She preferred driving this way because it gave her a chance to look northward. A few minutes passed, and the Emerald City lay between her and Central City

Glinda looked toward the north, her native homeland. Where once the Ruby Palace glittered in the mountains, only a crater remained. The Ruby Palace was *temporarily inaccessible*, according to Smith & Tinker. What did that mean? If it was not accessible now, when would it be accessible? Was there some predetermined time, or was it all dependent on events in Oz?

There were times that she missed the way things used to be—it was a simpler life, reading, and being angry at her mother all the time. Her father was always the peacekeeper. Somehow he managed to keep two fiery redheads from destroying each other.

The wind whipped through Glinda's hair and her eyes watered. Let them water. Let them weep. What is past is past and gone forever. She snapped the reins and urged her horses ever faster.

The chariot sped toward Emerald Valley, toward the home of Tjorn and Donya Dunkle.

At the same time Glinda drove her chariot around the north side of the Emerald City, Pastoria led a delegation in through the large gate at the south wall. He carried his ornate peacock scepter, carved to look like a peacock

feather. The gate-builders stood aside as Pastoria and his entourage passed through. When they passed, the gate-builders laughed and pointed. The head gate-builder even pantomimed Pastoria's walk, much to the amusement of the others.

The delegation clustered closely together and pushed their way through the streets of Emerald City until they arrived at the Ambassador's Ballroom, where they found their kind of people gathered.

At the north table, sitting in the Wizard's dinner throne, Mombi conversed with the chief architects. On the outer fringe of the architects, Perilous Eddy stood on tip-toes, trying to see over the hunched shoulders and fur-lined coats.

Pastoria pushed through the room, stepping outside the reach of some overly-friendly socialites. He worked his way up to the north table without actually touching anyone. He lifted his scepter above the backs of the Chief Architects. "Excuse me. Lady Chamberlain. Mombi, my dear? Excuse me."

Mombi glanced up from her conversation to see the peacock scepter dancing above the heads of the architects. She gestured with both of her hands and parted the crowd of architects down the middle. They turned to see Pastoria, King of the Emerald Lands, march up the middle.

Mombi raised an eyebrow.

"There are things you need to do, back at home." Pastoria began. "There are papers to sign, treaties to review, estelcrats to entertain—"

"Aristocrats?"

"And those." Pastoria finished. "I do not correspond as well with these people as you do. They do not paradigm with my particular idiom."

"You have been reading a book again." Mombi observed. She gestured to the architectural drawings on the table, and the architects quickly rolled them up. They hurried back through one of the back doors, buzzing and chattering about the magnificent changes planned for the Royal Palace. These improvements were faerie-inspired changes. These would join the two sister-cities in style and substance. Freedom and history would be combined in one great style that would immortalize the architects forever.

Mombi looked up. Only one architect remained nearby. Perilous Eddy took a step closer to Mombi's seat. Pastoria brandished his scepter threateningly. Mombi lifted a hand and rested a finger on the scepter. Pastoria grudgingly followed Mombi's unspoken command and lowered the scepter.

"You have a question, Architect?" Mombi asked.

Perilous Eddy stepped forward again. He opened his book of sketches and displayed tall towers with gardens and trees growing on the sides.

"Interesting. What am I looking at?" Mombi asked, gently taking the sketchbook from Eddy.

"Hanging gardens, Lady. The Wizard wanted me to find some seeds for trees. I know we have gardens down here on the streets and in the courtyards, but I thought that to truly make a magnificent feature in the Emerald City, we could put some of the gardens way up high. Then the rulers could look out and see them, instead of looking down on everything. They could look up and see some things, too."

"An interesting thought. Why have you not approached your masters about this?"

"Mombi—Lady Chamberlain—please, may we go?" Pastoria shifted his weight from foot to foot.

Mombi turned to Pastoria and held up her index finger in front of his face. "If you want me to do your job, you will have to wait until I have completed everyone else's duties, right? Here, sweetie, sit in the throne. I want to see what this young man has to offer."

Mombi vacated the throne, and Pastoria quickly slid in. He kicked his feet up over the arm and twirled his peacock scepter above his head. He issued royal commands to himself as Mombi and Perilous Eddy walked outside.

Mombi shielded her eyes from the afternoon sun as she looked up to the tall towers of Emerald City. Perilous Eddy pointed to several unfinished sections near the middle of the towers.

"Those areas are where I want to plant the trees. The hanging gardens will include trees, large flowers, and some climbing vines. And over there, in the Crypt—that's the purple tower, where the bones of the heroes of The Battle of Emerald Prairie are kept—I want to add some night blossoms. On nights of the full moon, that would be an incredible memorial to the fallen. Their bones would blaze in brilliant light, like they were coming back for one last hurrah."

Mombi knew what that tower held. That tower was where she had spent several hours, nursing her wounded hands. Her Silver Mirror was broken. It could not be put back together. About the only thing it was good for now was the magic component of Quicksilver, but there was little need for that in governing.

"Would not that be a fitting memorial, to have a spiral of night blossoms wrapping around the tower, unfolding their midnight petals in honor of the fallen?"

"Yes. Fitting. I see you have put a great deal of thought into these designs. What does the Wizard say?"

"He only told me to find trees. I searched, and I finally found the ones that he wanted."

"Make sure those are planted in a place that he can see." Mombi ordered.

"So I can build the gardens? The hanging gardens—for real?"

"The Wizard does most of the work around here, doesn't he? Always changing and updating all of the fine work designed by the Chief Architects. Perhaps it is time that a young draftsman make his impression on the monument that is the Emerald City. Build your gardens. Let the entire world see that small seeds may grow."

Mombi handed the sketchbook back to Perilous Eddy. He hopped up and down in excitement. "Thank you." He repeated over and over. "I'll let you get back to your king now."

"Yes. Thank you." Mombi forced a pleasant smile. Once the young architect was gone, her smile dropped completely off her face and left an exasperated sigh in its place. It was bad enough that she had to take over all of the day-to-day governing and ruling duties of Pastoria, but now he was following her here, to the Emerald City. If she was going to successfully upstage Kalinya, Mombi would need every last second of time to lay the groundwork for her plan. She could not be constantly entertaining the whining Peacock King. Even so, it was nice to be needed. She could work in the sunlight with Pastoria, instead of in the shadows. He might be a self-centered fool, but he was her self-centered fool.

She entered the Ambassador's Ballroom and stopped at the door. The afternoon sunlight silhouetted her inside the door frame. "Come, King Pastoria. We are going to tour the shadows and corners of the Emerald City. You will be my special escort as we discover the secrets of this great and wonderful place."

21 THE TRUTH ABOUT MEN

Glinda halted her chariot in front of a small cottage on the outskirts of Central City. The shadow of the Grand Tower fell over her. It had been a long time since she had been here. Too long, now that she thought about it. This was the closest place to a home that she had ever felt, and yet she felt like a stranger at this moment for not having come sooner.

Donya met Glinda halfway from the royal chariot. "Glinda! It is so nice when you come by to see us."

Glinda accepted the motherly embrace and the kiss on her cheek.

"Your hair is just as red as ever."

Glinda raised her eyebrows and forced a silly smile. "Yep. Still red. Hello Mama Donya."

A booming voice echoed from the house. "Is that the Ruby Sorceress I hear? Is Gayelette back from the great beyond to brighten our doorstep?"

"No, dear, it's not the Ruby Sorceress."

Tjorn Dunkle bellied up to the door and hooked his thumbs in his large belt. "You don't mean that this is the other red-head? It can't be little Glinda. This young lady is far too grown up and dazzling to be little Glinda."

Glinda nodded and smiled again. "Hi, Papa Tjorn. Yes, it's me."

"Glinda! You make me happy. Your red hair shines brighter than the sun. But you can't be Glinda. You are so grown up."

"It's only been a year" She protested. Then quietly she added, "or so."

"A year too long." Mama Donya chided. "Come in, dear. Tjorn, take care of the chariot." To his unspoken question, she answered, "Yes you can hug the horses." She took Glinda by the hand and led her into the house. "Have a chair, Glinda. It is so happy and wonderful to see you again. I wish Wickrie were here. Then we could all laugh and sing like we did."

"That was a fun week." Glinda agreed. "That's part of why I'm here. Have you seen Wickrie? I'm looking right now, actually for the Wizard. I thought he might be with Omby and Wickrie."

"What has he done?" Donya folded her hands on the table and looked down her nose at Glinda.

"It's not him…it's me."

Donya reached out and patted Glinda's hand. "There, there, dear. You're still young. You'll learn in time that it's never your fault—it's always his fault. If you want to be a truly free woman, you need to learn that men are very, very simple. See this finger? Tjorn is wrapped completely around it. He does whatever I want, and I get to do what I want, because he loves me."

Glinda dropped her eyes to look at the table. "No. This one was me. Even if he was looking…"

"Did you have your eyes and lips done up? Your hair perfect? Glinda, dear, it takes work to be the only woman in his heart. Who was he looking at? Was it Wickrie? If it was, I'll be mad, but I'll also be very, very proud. You understand, don't you? My Wickrie is a beautiful girl. I'm so glad that she has Omby—he's a fine young man."

"I tore open his secrets."

Donya pulled her hand back and sat back in her chair. She studied Glinda carefully. "What do you mean, you tore open his secrets? Secrets meaning clothing? Because young people—"

"No! No." Glinda shook her head. "Oscar is a gentleman. He is so sweet. I wanted to see what secrets he kept from me. I used magic."

Donya shook her head. "Well, if that's all it is. Glinda, I don't know what you are worrying about. Men don't have secrets. They wear their heart on their sleeve. Right there. It's out there for you to see and read and protect."

"The Wizard had secrets."

"And now you have the Wizard's secrets. Oh, my dear, you are in an enviable position. Not that you aren't anyway. You love him and he belongs to you. That is the place that every girl fancies being."

The door opened and Tjorn thundered in, only hearing the last part of the conversation. "What's the place that every girl fancies?"

"Being in love."

"Ah, yes, love. I was in love once." Tjorn began.

Donya met Glinda's gaze with a knowing smile.

"I got lost—totally, hopelessly lost in love. I could not for the life of me find my way out. Everywhere I turned, there was love right in front of me. Pretty soon I forgot what it was like before I got lost, so I gave up. I'm still hopelessly, madly, crazily lost in love." Tjorn took his little finger and hooked Donya's little finger and brought it up to his lips and kissed it.

Glinda's eyes melted. She smiled at Donya.

"But when I find my way out, let me tell you, watch out lovely ladies of the court, you've never seen such a heart as this."

Donya nodded slowly. "Of course, dear. I suppose I'll just have to build some more hedges in this labyrinth. It looks like he's trying to break out."

"Ah, it's hopeless for me. I try to find the door and she turns my world upside down. I'm lost, but you, Glinda, are not. You are here. How is your beau?"

"Lost."

"I know the feeling."

"No. He's gone, missing, lost, not where is supposed to be."

"Oh, lost." Tjorn repeated. "That's different."

Glinda shared an exasperated look with Donya.

"Has he passed by here? Have you seen Wickrie or Omby?"

"They were here yesterday, but they left. Omby had his heart full of grandchildren and liberty and the future. He is a strong young man. He might be the one strong enough to tame—even just a little bit—Wickrie's spirit."

"Which way did they go?"

"Could be different ways. Maybe east—I have relatives out there in Munchkin Country." Donya said. "Maybe west—Omby seemed like he wanted some answers. He was anxious."

"Yearning."

"Yes, yearning. That could be from wanting to see family."

"But most of his family is in the Emerald City."

"Most, but not all." Tjorn observed. "A man has to know where his priorities lie. Ombrosius Ambrosius knows well what he wants. The boy is bound to freedom. He has made it his life's desire—even more so than my wonderful daughter."

"He is a fine young man. I know that Wickrie will be very happy with him. As long as she has the wind in her hair and the sun on her face, she will forever be happy." Donya smiled and squeezed Glinda's hand.

"So you don't know which way they went?" Glinda asked.

"Nope." Tjorn shook his head. "But we have time to sing one round of Chumpocles the Wise."

"It's getting late, I really should be heading home."

"All the way south? Nonsense. You would not make it if you flew. The sun is too low. You might make Emerald City, but not your castle."

"I've named it." Glinda said. "My castle."

"Good for you." Tjorn said. "Rosybeam?"

Donya playfully slapped Tjorn's arm. "Not Rosybeam, you silly. Seriously, every time something needs a name, he tosses out Rosybeam. It was his first horse."

"Before that, a sled. We did not get much snow, but when we did, oh how that sled flew down the hills."

"So everything now has to be named Rosybeam." Donya concluded.
"I named it Chronometria."
"Oh." Donya's eyebrows raised. "That's lovely."
"Sounds like a pocketwatch."
Glinda was silent.
"So…Chumpocles the Wise?" Tjorn broke the uncomfortable silence.
Glinda looked toward the door uncertainly.
"One verse." Donya insisted.

Six verses later Glinda made it to the front door. Two more verses before she climbed into her chariot. And one final verse as the sun touched the edge of the Emerald Valley. Glinda sang as she sped her chariot back toward Emerald City.

"And this would be the Wizard's Throne Room." Mombi declared. She breezed past the Chief Architect and entered, twirling around. She walked quickly back and took Pastoria's hand. "Isn't it amazing? It is so quiet."

Pastoria looked at the throne of green marble, raised up on a pedestal above the floor. "There's no gold. No silver. There are not even any emeralds."

Perilous Eddy stepped forward and raised a finger. The Chief Architect frowned, but Mombi cut off his protest with a single glance. "Go ahead, young architect. You have something to say?"

"The green marble is a cleanser for magic. It aids in keeping the bad out. This is a very clean room."

"I can feel that. No magic at all in here—except for me, of course. Only one—wait." Mombi walked around the back of the throne. "There's something else." Her eyes grew wide and she quickly turned to the door.

Glinda stood in the doorway.

"What are you doing here?" The red-haired sorceress hissed.

Mombi quickly stepped in front of Pastoria. "We are touring the Emerald City. This is our last stop—the Wizard's Throne Room. Feel the magic? No? That's because only you and I are magic in here. The green marble cleans the magic. Feel how clean this air is."

"The Wizard is not here." Glinda said.

"No. The Wizard is out. He didn't leave a forwarding address. Was there something you wished to tell him? I'm sure one of us will be nearby when he comes back." Mombi offered.

"I would speak with you." Glinda said. The Chief Architect recognized that tone and gestured to Perilous Eddy, who quickly retreated.

"Pastoria, will you give us witches a moment? Have you walked in the Palace Gardens in the moonlight? There is supposed to be a full moon. See if you can find the ivory peacock."

"I did not know—" Pastoria perked up and quickly headed toward the door.

"Of course you didn't." Mombi waved her fingers goodbye to the King of the Emerald Lands. "Tell me when you find him."

Glinda waited until the door closed. She turned to see Mombi half-smiling at her. "You are in his throne room."

"I expect it will be mine before long." Mombi sat down in the green marble throne and brushed her fingers on the cool stone.

"He will never join you."

"He doesn't have to. The Wizard already has his hands full with another little witch. She'll lead him with a flaxen cord down the golden road to destruction. Of course, he already had a head start with you—kicking him the way you did."

"I didn't kick him anywhere."

"Of course you did. I've seen the stars in the Wizard's eyes. He had eyes only for you. All of the other fine girls here—and there are many fine girls here—in Emerald City hung on his every word. He didn't want to disappoint them—he never wants to disappoint anyone—he's been pushing himself harder and harder. He shapes the city in his image every night. I don't know if you've noticed how much things have changed since you've been here last. When were you here last, Glinda? Has it been six months? Almost a year? That is a long time for a wizard to go unloved."

Glinda brushed a stray hair out of her face. She reached her arm across her body to hold her elbow. "Almost thirteen months since I stayed. It was just for a day, six months ago. He came to see me twice." She said quietly.

"Men are like loyal dogs, you know that? They will lick the hand that feeds them. Stern discipline, smile at them, send them away, praise them when they do good. Their tails wag."

"Not Oscar—not the Wizard—he's not like that."

"What makes your Wizard so different? Is he not a man? And a young man, at that."

"He is a man. His heart is hurt. I…pushed him too hard."

Mombi swirled her robes around her and stepped up to the green marble throne. She seated herself and smiled at Glinda. "To gain power you must break some spirits."

Glinda's eyes hardened.

The change was not lost on Mombi, who quickly changed tactics. "No matter your sorrows, you did not break his spirit. The Wizard is confused right now. He found a pretty face—such as it is—that was willing to smile at him and sing for him."

"I am always willing to smile at him!"

"Really?"

Glinda backed down. "He is just so frustrating."

"What secrets did you find? Long-lost loves? Mysterious homeland? The secret to his power?"

Glinda turned all the way around, looking at the marble throne room. "He said this was his Pandaemonium Chamber. He said some things didn't belong outside." Her eyes stopped on the emerald-green curtain.

"The Wizard is more powerful than all of the Witches, combined. So it is said." Mombi probed. "That includes you."

"Yes." Glinda was halfway to the curtain. "He is powerful."

"And you know why." Mombi quickly stepped down from the throne and followed Glinda.

"Yes." Glinda pulled aside the green curtain.

22 THE MAN BEHIND THE CURTAIN

"Why did you build it—the Emerald City?" Kally asked Oscar. It was not just idle chatter. She was discovering that the Wizard was a wealth of knowledge about a great many subjects. Even if his single trumpet happened to be liberty, he could be prodded and poked and give up precious nuggets of information. But the most amazing thing was that Kally could just ask him anything, and he would answer.

They stopped the Hamstrambulator at a bend in the river and set camp. They had to wait for the remainder of their automaton army to catch up with them. They moved swiftly during the day, and they saw no one, so the plan was unfolding perfectly. Only one more night until Kally and Oscar would have the Golden Cap. *And the wizard*—she corrected herself—would have the Golden Cap. It would not do well to let slip so quickly what her true intentions were. Better to keep the Wizard thinking about himself.

Oscar stared down into a still pool of water next to the river. He tossed pebbles in, watching them disrupt his reflection. Then a tall, dark reflection wearing a witch's face appeared over him. His hand froze, and the pebble fell to the ground.

"The Emerald City, why?" Kally repeated.

So the reflection had a face in the real world. It was Kally. Still, it was better than the things Oscar had been seeing recently. Maybe tonight he would actually be able to get some sleep.

"The Emerald City was a dream. After the Battle of Emerald Prairie, I met up with the army. That night I dreamed. It was a tall city with thick walls. It rose up from beneath the ground to shine for the entire world to see."

"So the entire world could come to your feet."

"There are secrets in the Emerald City that our generation will never know."

"Such as?" Kally prodded, taking a seat on a nearby log.

"Glinda knows. I know some. The rest of the secrets are a mystery to me—I don't know the history of Oz."

"You are Oz. History is what you say it is."

"Not so." Oscar waited for the ripples in the pool to clear. "History simply is. There are people who lie and tell wrong stories about what happened in the past. There are groups that don't write their history. There are things that get lost. But for the most part, history is remembered. The great artists and writers knew that the way to preserve history was to hide it in plain sight."

"Your Emerald City is less than two years old. How could it have any history?"

"Many good men and a few good women died at the Battle of Emerald Plains. They battled against the Wicked Witches for freedom in Oz. They believed in liberty."

"You and liberty."

Oscar tossed another pebble and watched the ripples in the pool. No matter how many pebbles he tossed in, eventually the water calmed again, and his reflection was the same as before. "No matter how many rocks I throw at me, I never change." Oscar murmured.

"Where have you commissioned your secrets hidden?" Kally leaned forward, catching Oscar's eye. She raised her eyebrows and parted her lips. "It'll be our secret."

Oscar stood and stretched his legs. "Okay. Sounds fair. Look at the buildings—really look at them. Hidden in corners and ledges, on rooftops and above doorways, you will see pieces of history. Each sculpture tells a story. Each statue holds a piece of history. Every artwork remembers. Those that hold such things precious are keepers of the stories. What is history but stories of our past and where we came from?"

"History is conquest—over and over, power changes hands. To be on the right side of history, you must control the power. Only then will you control the story and the history."

"Keep throwing rocks." Oscar murmured again, tossing more pebbles.

Kally stood and walked to the Hamstrambulator. Half of the automaton army was here. The other half was coming. On the sunset horizon, the line of six robots glinted in the orange light. Excellent. They could leave within the hour. Night would be their cover.

Oscar moved from the small pool to the river. He tossed pebbles into the flow of the river. The splashes, and any ripples they might cause, were carried quickly away in the unrelenting current. "Time only flows one way." He turned to Kally. She was looking out to the horizon.

"Hmm?"

"Nikidik was wrong. Time only flows one way. You can't turn back time."

"He has the power to bring life to senseless things. Consider the army we have here—they are base metal, yet they live."

"The move. They follow simple orders. That is not living. A dog does the same—*more* with a good dog." Oscar mounted up into the driver's basket in the Hamstrambulator. He kicked off his boots and leaned back, putting his stocking feet up over the side of the basket. "Living is much more than simply moving and going through the motions."

"Do not say liberty."

Oscar smiled. "If you have to say that, then I have already said it. My work here is done." He stretched big and settled in for sleep.

"The others will arrive soon. Then we will move into Winkie Country."

"Then we can be done with this."

"Yes, then it will be finished." Kally repeated.

In the Emerald City, behind the emerald curtain, Glinda glanced over the simple room full of shelves. The boxes were filled with building materials and containers. A workbench held an assortment of tools.

"Your Wizard is a tinker." Mombi observed.

"He has more to say." Glinda moved her finger around, searching with her eyes. "I know Oscar."

"So you said."

"He's hiding something."

"Oh?"

"Why curtain off a workshop? What would he be hiding? There is more in here."

Mombi took a square green bottle off the shelf. She shook it and heard liquid sloshing around. "I knew a man when I was young who kept a bottle like this. He called it courage in a bottle. Said it was magic."

"Was it?"

"No. It was ale—intoxicating. Courage yes, wisdom no. Poor man. Kalinya threw him into the sky. If he hadn't been turned into a toad, he could have really hurt himself. At least I turned him back. I think he went on to do…something. I saw him with Ondri-baba once. Then I left—better things to do than stay in the small town." She replaced the bottle on the shelf.

"Oscar would not do that. He is a good man."

"All good men have their secrets. You can tell a man's secrets by the fine clothes he wears. Beyond a certain point, the fine clothing and robes merely cover the darkness and deceit within."

"Oscar doesn't dress in finery. I mean, he does when I see him, but not when I don't."

"Which makes perfect sense, Glinda. Why would he dress up for you ? You are just a common girl like any other, right?"

"No. That's not what I meant."

"You are still young, and you have much to learn about men. The simple truth is that men need us. Every man owes his life to a woman—not just in birth, but where he is in life, for good or ill, is the result of a woman."

Glinda looked at a pendant on a chain, hanging from one of the shelves. The chain was looped around a hook on the front of the bookcase, but the end of the chain disappeared into the back shadows of the bookcase. Glinda lifted the pendant—it was a single tear, much like the carved necklace she wore around her neck. "No more tears." She whispered.

"What's that?" Mombi asked.

"No more tears. It was what Oscar told me when he gave me this necklace. This pendant is a teardrop. It doesn't fit what he said." Glinda unwound the looped chain from the hook. She pulled on the chain to remove it from the shelf. A click betrayed a switch behind the bookcase.

Mombi looked at Glinda with surprise. "Well, well. You may know more about him than I thought."

Glinda reached into the lower shelf and her fingers quickly found the lever. She swung the bookcase aside, revealing a passage. She looked with surprise at Mombi. "Everything, for good or ill, because of a woman? I don't know if I'm ready for this." Ready or not, Glinda started walking.

She led the way down the short hallway. She turned a sharp corner and stopped in front of a rough wooden door. It was painted red. "What do you think?" She asked Mombi.

"The same as you, except I'm waiting for you to admit it."

"You're right." Glinda turned the knob and opened the door.

It was a room. The walls were painted yellow on the top half. On the bottom half, the walls were papered with strips of paper decorated with flowers and lines. It looked hand-drawn. The rough table in the center of the room was surrounded by chairs. The closest one had a very intentional gouge in the backrest. On the walls, corresponding to the chairs at the table, were images of people.

"He made this." Glinda said. "This gouge was put here for a reason. I wonder who these people are?"

Mombi searched the portraits closely. "These were not drawn by the same person. That one shows great care and skill, especially around the eyes. See how they are sad? A master artist drew that."

"It's his mother." Glinda realized.

"The same artist drew that one—probably his father. Those eyes are strong. Look at how fiercely they stare out. Strength and sadness."

"This was his home. These pictures are his family. I know those two. Oscar drew those. Those are the giants from his dream. They were his brothers. He said, *They want their birthright.*' I can't tell you want that means."

Mombi spoke quietly. "This is the Wizard's secret that is most sacred. He has hidden this away from the world. This is what he keeps from everyone—even you. Each person forced to wear a face in public has something like this."

"You speak from experience." Glinda noted.

"You are a quick study." Mombi smiled. "Yes. My special place is well-hidden. I have killed to keep it hidden. You are young, Glinda, and you have your entire life to do things right. Make your life in the sun, not in the shadows. Make friends, not playthings. When you retire to your bed at night, the shadows will watch. It is up to you how dark those shadows are."

"Why are you telling me this? You are supposed to be a Wicked Witch."

"I manipulate kings and generals and mayors. I engineer the transfer of power from one ruler to another. I have been many names, and I have been even more faces. I owe you an explanation for that night, two years ago. I believe that I can serve myself better with you as an ally than an enemy."

"Are you saying you are not wicked?"

"I have crafted my share of wickedness. I toppled kingdoms before you were born. I have been loved by many. I have been wicked. The appellation fits me. Where it does not fit me nearly as well as Kalinya, I make it look better."

There was much that she would need to think on. Mombi was asking for an alliance, but why now? Why here? It would serve Glinda best to allow some time to think this over and digest these confessions of a self-proclaimed wicked Witch before she agreed to anything. Glinda pursed her lips and silently turned away.

She studied the pictures on the wall. If this was all Oscar's family, why were there different artists that drew them? All of the pictures were drawn in the same style, except the mother and father. Glinda put her hand on the gouged chair at the foot of the table. It wobbled. She wobbled it back and forth. Then she got down on her hands and knees and looked at the front right leg. "He cut it off."

"This is where he grew up." Mombi observed. "He has surrounded himself with his family. You said those two were his brothers. Why are their faces not clear? I supposed they were older brothers—much older—and he doesn't remember what they look like. You said they want their birthright. Who received it—Oscar? He is haunted by the past. Look, his chair looks straight at his father. He was not relegated to a side position in the crowd. He might not have been the youngest. I can't tell with that girl—whether she is older or younger. But he held a chosen place in this home."

"Why is he so silent about this, do you think?" Glinda asked.

"He probably doesn't know. Most people don't see where they fit, and how things move around them. It's like a clock—I bought one from Smith & Tinker more than twenty years ago. It was a little cloud that moved around. At certain times of the day a rainbow lifted out. When it hit twelve, a Winkie soldier jumped out onto the cloud. I really love that clock. It reminds me of a simpler time. But I was saying, a person is like a clock. What does a clock do?"

"It tells time."

"Glinda, you know better than that. What does a clock itself do?"

"The hands move. Chimes. Gears."

"Exactly. There are so many parts moving at the same time—this gear connects to this gear, which moves this, which moves the hand—at any given moment you can look at a clock and only see the time. And then it's gone. That time—that moment—passes. Where do you fit? Where is the full realization of identity and belonging in the big picture? To those with eyes to see, it becomes clear."

"And you have eyes to see, is that what you are telling me?" Glinda crossed her arms.

"I have toppled kingdoms, Glinda. I have to know how each of the gears works in order to pass power successfully. One wrong move and it comes crashing down on top of me. I happen to like this beautiful skin. I prefer not dying or being strung up as an example by a vengeful tyrant."

"So Oscar built all of this to remember, but even though he has all of the pieces in place, he can't see how they fit—how he fits?"

"One more tragic twist to break your heart—that door behind you should lead to a bedroom. You'll find a small bed, probably unmade."

Glinda touched the handle with her fingers and paused. She turned back to look at Mombi's dark eyes. "Are you coming?"

Mombi shook her head. "I've seen it before—enough times that I know what will be there. It's what he remembers. I don't need to see this one."

"I have a lot to balance with my responsibilities in Central City. You may not understand this right now, Glinda—you are still very young, so young. Be *good*." Mombi hardened the momentary softness in her eyes. "I need the Wizard as a rival and a strong leader. I don't need the details of his shadows. I cannot afford to have everything crumble down around me now. I am too close."

"Will you wait for me?"

"Yes. Pastoria can wait. He's looking for the ivory peacock."

"I haven't seen that one. Where is it? I know you said the garden, but where?"

"If Pastoria finds it, I'm sure he'll tell me."

"You made it up!"

"I redirected him based on his own biases. I don't know that there is not an ivory peacock in the garden. I know that there are other peacocks. That will be enough for him. He's not going anywhere without me."

"You love him."

Mombi was silent. Then she allowed a small smile to climb into her eyes. "He is irresponsible to a fault, constantly admiring himself in the mirrors, and utterly helpless at ruling, but there is a certain dumb charm about the man. He makes me feel needed and wanted. Like I said, I am too close to my final success to have everything crumble down around me. So, you go in there, Glinda, but don't tell me what you see. I'll read enough of it in your eyes." Mombi pulled out the gouged chair and sat down. The short leg bumped on the ground. Mombi turned the chair to face away from the bedroom door.

Glinda pulled open the door and slipped inside. The room was dimly lit by the final light of the setting sun. Somehow Oscar had designed this apartment in such a way as to be completely hidden, yet still get light from outside. There were other rooms beyond this one, but they were much smaller—one was even set into the wall, more like a shelf than a room. Each small room held beds and furniture. The small alcove contained what looked to Glinda like a stretched out pistol. It was small, hanging over the bed on the wall, on tiny little hooks. It had a long tube, but it also had a long handle. Glinda looked through all of the rooms—four bedrooms—but none of them were as painstakingly detailed as the first one with the large bed. One of them held two beds, but the sheets were missing on one.

Mombi was wrong. It wasn't a small bed. It was a large bed. Oscar had a good memory. Trinkets and small items stood on shelves and on the dresser. There was even a carved compass. Glinda held it up, but it didn't move. It was only for decoration. And East and West were mixed up. When would Oscar ever learn that East was on the left and West was on the right? That's how it was in Oz, and that's how it should be everywhere. Glinda placed the compass back down on the dresser. She looked at the mirror stand in the corner. It was backwards. Glinda turned the oval mirror over slowly in its stand.

The hidden surface was paper, not glass. Instead of a reflection, there was a drawing. A sad woman, lovingly drawn, but not by the master artist. This was drawn from the memories of a devoted son. The sad woman stared into the mirror. A tear was on her cheek. A little boy with a curl in his hair clung to her side. He had a tear drawn on his face, but then it was crossed out. This was the picture that faced toward the wall.

Glinda felt wetness on her own cheeks. She felt her cheeks with her fingers and discovered that she was crying. As soon as she realized this, her heart ached, and she sat down on the bed. *Such loneliness in here.* There was everything a family could need replicated here from the memories of a young wizard, but there was not the one thing that he needed—a family.

Glinda dried her eyes. There was one more door. This one was a smaller door next to the large bed. The door wasn't large enough to be another bedroom. It was more like a closet. She steeled herself by closing her eyes and taking a deep breath. *What secrets were in Oscar's hidden closet?*

She pulled open the door and opened her eyes. Her heart collapsed within her chest. She sobbed out loud and the tears gushed from her eyes. On the floor of the closet, recently used—a crumpled and dirty pillow and blanket.

Glinda left her token on the chest next to the compass. The south arrow pointed to the teardrop pendant.

Glinda exited the bedroom silently. The gouged chair was empty. Glinda replaced it carefully at the table. She walked back through the hallway and into the workshop. She closed the secret entrance behind her and pulled the emerald curtain back into place. At the sound of the rings sliding on the curtain rod, the older witch froze at the door.

Glinda's voice was thick with emotion. "You left."

Mombi did not turn around to look at the weeping sorceress. "I have read enough faces to see entire stories. I knew that I could do the same with you when you came out. I need the Wizard to remain great and powerful. If I see his true story on your face, I cannot complete my purpose. Do not speak with me again, Glinda of the South, until you have buried this story deep. I do not want to see it."

Glinda nodded against the tears. She forced out one single plea to the Witch of many faces that had toppled kingdoms. "Don't use this against him."

Mombi opened the door. "You, either."

Glinda touched her neck. The place where Oscar's necklace had previously lain was empty. It was a promise he had made to Glinda—*no more tears*. Now Glinda was returning that promise to the Wizard. She hoped that it would be received in the spirit in which it was intended. She hoped he would realize it was a recognition of unfallen tears, not a rebuke for tears currently falling.

The booming sound of the closing door echoed off the green marble walls. As the echoes died, the sobs of a broken-hearted young sorceress slowly brought them back to life.

23 GLINDA'S NIGHTMARE

Later, in the Emerald City guardhouse, the deputy guard, Toobalott, listened to Glinda's request. "It is imperative that I find the Wizard. He is in danger. The witches are plotting against the Emerald City."

"I have heard no such rumor." The deputy said.

"The Wizard is in danger." Glinda placed a small package in the man's hands. "These are magic signals. When you find the Wizard, point one of these at the sky and pinch the end. It will shoot into the sky and give a signal that I will see."

"Most of the guardsmen are on active duty during construction. Tempers can run hot in the summer sun. We are tasked with keeping the peace. The Emerald Guardsmen are divided right now. I am sorry, Sorceress, but I do not have many available men."

"Where are the rest?"

"They are training, further south, with some of your Fighting Girls."

"Oh, yes. Of course. In the commotion, it slipped my mind. Can you spare a single soldier? Just one man down to deliver this message? I know my Fighting Girls will aid in the search."

"I can spare one."

"If you will call him, I will explain the use of the signals."

The deputy called a young guard, barely Glinda's age. The young man blushed when he saw the red-haired sorceress. Deputy Toobalott bowed quickly and stepped out the door.

"What is your name, soldier?" Glinda asked.

"Kopp, milady."

"Manners. I like that."

"My mother taught me, milady. Always be respectful."

"I have a mission for you. I need to find the Wizard." Glinda explained how the signals worked. She had the soldier repeat the instructions back to her until he had it correct. His keen mind grasped and memorized the concept after the second time, but Glinda made him repeat it back three more times, just to be certain.

Deputy Toobalott approached, holding the reins of a chestnut stallion. "The soldiers are training near the gulch. You know where that is?"

"Yes, Sir. Follow the brick road until the first hills, then west until the river, then south again until everything dries out. The gulch isn't far from there."

"You will leave tonight. Immediately."

"What about my shift, Sir?"

"I will cover it. We do not have royal disappearances, *or royal requests*, every day." He leveled his eyes at Glinda.

She gave him a small smile in return before turning to the young guardsman, Kopp. "The Wizard's safety is our utmost concern." Glinda said.

"Get this message to the soldiers at the gulch. They will be the best trained for this mission. Fly like a storm is at your back, for it very soon may be."

"Is this a secret mission, Sir?" Kopp asked.

"You may tell officers or soldiers of your mission. The mission is to find the Wizard and signal so that the Sorceress may be notified. That is all."

Kopp saluted, mounted the stallion, and kicked his heels. He was through the gate in a heartbeat, on his way south.

Glinda tried to hide her yawn, but the perceptive deputy caught her movement.

"You'd best stay in the city tonight, milady. No sense running off pell-mell into the darkness."

"Is there a room I could use?"

Deputy Toobalott gave her a bemused look. "New rooms appear every night. Of course there is a room for you. I'll make the arrangements."

High in the Nebraska Tower, Glinda looked down over the city of lights. The emerald-green towers sparkled beneath the stars. This room was taller than the highest room in her castle—Chronometria. It made sense why Oscar stayed here in the Emerald City—the view was spectacular. Did he have a special name for his city? Would he tell Glinda if he did?

Glinda closed the curtain, but not the window. The breeze felt nice this high up in the sky. It brought the sounds of the city up to her ears. Some of the city was sleeping, but there were those who refused to sleep during the night—it was so much different than her home in the South. The celebrations of the night parties rose into the sky, uncaring and seemingly heedless of the empty throne in their midst. Or maybe that was the reason for their celebrations. Glinda did not trust them. Even though they constantly surrounded Oscar, she was certain that the Wizard did not trust them, either.

She crossed the room to the mantle and took down a porcelain doll. It was a pretty princess in a lovely blue dress. She had her hands clasped up under her chin with a painted expression of amazement and wonder. She stood on her tiptoes. Everything about the porcelain doll was wonderfully exciting.

"What would you say, little princess, if you were alive? I imagine that you are excited to dance and sing and skip. You are a fine explorer of life's fun mysteries. No darkness behind your eyes. No broken fingernails or scuffed knees for you. Butterflies and moonbeams hold all of your wonders. You see the beauty of life, but none of the shadows. How could you? Inside, you are empty. Even if porcelain could live, what kind of life is that? *Empty*. Magic could make you live, but you would still be empty." Glinda smiled a sad little smile. "You belong on a shelf, looking pretty. That's what you were made for." The excited expression never changed. The hands stayed clasped up under the chin. The excited posture now looked empty to Glinda.

She set the doll back up on the mantle.

"You are expecting something wonderful. So am I." Glinda tasted her bitter words before slowly forcing them out. "He does not see how wonderful he is. And I have ruined him. I'm going to make it better. I am not going to be like my mother. I will fix what I broke. You will see. He will see. This city, amazing as it is right now, needs its wizard back, never to leave."

Glinda pulled aside the hanging curtains on the large bed. She sat down and pulled off her boots. A breeze blew into the room, ruffling the curtains and spilling moonlight over her wiggling toes. Glinda laughed and lifted up her feet as the gentle wind passed between her toes. "Moonlight on the little piglets—this little piggy went to market, but this little piggy stayed home…and this little piggy went crying all the way home." She fell backwards onto the bed, wiggling her toes in a disorganized group.

Then Glinda sat up suddenly. "What if the little piggy couldn't get home? He would be the last little pig crying all alone." Then she shook her head and pointed sternly at her toes. "That's silly. I'm tired."

Glinda changed quickly into a nightgown and then stepped out onto the balcony. In the darkness, Glinda felt her hair whipping around her face. Her eyes scanned the invisible horizon far away. This high up, the wind cut through her thin nightgown quickly. She shivered, but her eyes still searched. She even pulled out the Ruby Spectacles, but saw nothing. Oscar was somewhere out there.

How many times had she looked north from her own balcony in Chronometria? Many times, but not enough—not nearly enough to make a difference. How many times had Oscar looked south? Right now, she could not know.

She bid the wizard best wishes, wherever he might be on this night. "Sleep sweet, Oscar. Dream well."

High-pitched laughter drew Glinda from her bed. She pushed aside the curtains to see orange light pounding through the tattered remains of drapes by the balcony. The hazy sun was quickly overwhelmed by the putrid clouds twisting in formation. Noxious shadows danced through the air, winding among the discolored clouds.

Glinda covered her mouth and nose with her thin sleeve as the rancid air assaulted her. A callous wind whipped her nightgown up around her knees. The laughter continued. Glinda searched for the source. The twisting clouds linked their corners and formed a square. As the last orange cloud twisted into place, the central curtain pulled aside and a shadow puppet danced on the sky stage.

"Once was a sky wizard come into Oz. Dancing and prancing and lying romancing. Tipped his hat to the *grabled* cloud guard and distinguished the poppy knockers. Threw his voice out, now he can't walk straight."

The shadow puppet sprouted thorns from its shoulders, wrists, neck, knees, and feet. Tendrils of shadow grew from the thorns and leaped upward to a waiting hand. Yellow eyes opened on the shadow hand. The thumb grabbed on to the index finger and moved up and down like a mouth. The laughter timed itself to the movement of the thumb mouth. It was a hand puppet controlling the dancing shadow puppet.

Once the shadow hand took control of the strings, it shook the shadow puppet horribly. The crying of a small voice reached Glinda's ears. Then the shadows shook loose from the puppet and revealed Oscar—the Wizard—dressed in his green and gold finery.

Mirrors appeared all around him. Another shadow puppet appeared, but this one had no strings. A sickly green eye glowed from the shadows, revealing her location in the many mirrors. The laughing hand puppet danced Oscar around the mirror room.

A single word wrapped around a windbeam and flew through the discordant clouds to reach Glinda. "Dream."

As she caught hold of the word, she felt the string in her hand. She looked down and saw the string in her hand, connecting her to the Wizard. She pulled on the string and Oscar twitched and jerked spasmodically on the distant stage.

Glinda reached out her hand to Oscar. The farther she reached out over the edge of the balcony, the further away Oscar receded into the mirrored stage.

Lightning flashed. Dark clouds poured into the putrid twisting clouds to compose a kaleidoscopic maelstrom. Lightning swirled in the twined vines of the stage border. Oscar cried out as the thunder shook the stage.

The dark, one-eyed shadow loomed large over the dancing wizard. The shadow hand laughed and winked a yellow eye at Glinda. It jerked Oscar out of the way.

The scream of fright whispered on the wind and the laughing thunder hungrily devoured the tiny voice.

Glinda pulled her hand away from the yawning edge of the balcony. The string tightened, and Oscar came toward her. She pulled further away, and he came closer. He stepped out into the swirling maelstrom. Pools of befuddled storm rippled under his feet. The shadow hand jerked the wizard backwards. Glinda pulled harder. She reached out her other hand, but Oscar retreated. The only way she could bring him closer was if she pulled away.

Glinda's tower shook. She looked down and a shimmering cloud, crimson and iridescent green, chewed hungrily at the foundations. The tower leaned backwards, threatening to fall.

"How can I help you?" Glinda cried into the storm. Her tears blew from her eyes and froze on her cheeks.

"Dance, puppet!" the yellow eyes laughed wickedly.

Glinda shouted into the slicing wind. Oscar seemed to hear her, but he was trapped by the strings. One by one, the strings binding him fell away, until there were only two left—one binding him to Glinda, and the other binding him to the shadow hand with yellow eyes.

Oscar looked sadly across the vast gulf separating him and Glinda. "You are my friend." He said, and doves carried the parchment across a rainbow bridge to Glinda's balcony.

Glinda screamed and yanked on the string.

The shadow hand closed its eyes and screamed.

Oscar sliced through both strings at once and fell into the maelstrom. He disappeared into the swirling chaos of blue and black. The shadows coalesced in the center of the air and spewed out munching chuckles.

Lightning flashed. Thunder boomed, shaking the tower. All around, the storms blackened the sky. They grew heaviest around Glinda. The lightning poured down on the Land of Oz as quickly as the rain, fracturing and scorching the land.

Then the shadows dropped below Glinda's balcony. The clouds revealed their fluffy tops to her. Up above the storm it was so quiet and serene. The yellow sun was shining with no worries. A small cloud rose up and sat on Glinda's feet. She stepped forward onto the stairway and walked down. The storm gurgled and died. The clouds disappeared.

Glinda's feet touched the scorched remains of the Land of Oz. It was barren. Mountains fractured and rivers swelled with sick water. Then those very rivers thickened and turned to mud. The mud hardened and cracked. A dusty wind blew paper bits across Glinda's bare feet. She bent down and picked one up.

"Dream." It read. The frayed edges betrayed this word's origin from a larger volume of text. Nevertheless, it was the one word she could hold on to. Oz was gone.

Glinda felt the hot ground beneath her toes. "This little piggy went to market." She began. She took a step. "This little piggy had no more home to stay in. He went to the place where dreams come from. He said his salutations to magic, but it did not bring back his home. You are number two, little pig, and you are not forgotten."

Glinda walked across the river of dry, cracked mud. No footprints marred its surface. She walked for hours. The cities were gone. Even the great Emerald City no longer stood. The tower that she had stood on during the storm was carried away. She was alone—the daughter of the eternal sorceress had lived to see the death of Oz. Nothing remained.

Harsh wind blew dust into Glinda's face, stinging her eyes. She looked back at the source of the wind. A whirling vortex of hot air warped the brilliance and even made Glinda light-headed looking at it.

"Who are you?"

"I am the Queen of Oz. Kneel and you shall live. In your death, I will split your bones into trees and your tears will water the deserts. Mountains shall rise in your honor. Kneel and you shall be made wondrous." The vortex reached out toward Glinda with invisible tentacles, drawing her closer. The hot wind dried out whatever tears remained in Glinda's blue eyes.

"Can you promise me something?" Glinda whispered.

"All shall be yours as you become mine to command. Only kneel."

"No more tears?"

A howl pierced the air around Glinda, giving her goose-bumps. Then the vortex shook with unseen laughter. "You cry like a child. Look at your land! Look at all you worked for and built with your own hands! Look at your legacy! You have nothing! You have wasted the land to live forever."

"*With my own hands.*" Glinda murmured, looking down.

The scrap of paper was still held between her thumb and finger. The wind howled fiercely around her, but the scrap stayed firmly in her fingers. She turned it over slowly to read the single inscription. "*Dream*" Glinda read out loud.

The vortex screamed and the tentacles lashed every which way, tearing up the earth and lacerating the swollen air. All around Glinda, the disease, destruction, and red dust churned and swirled toward the vortex. As the pan-dimensional scream reached inhuman keening, a thunderclap shattered the vortex into a million shards of reflecting crystal.

The crystal vision swirled around Glinda, blocking out all light. Darkness gathered behind the millions of reflections. Glinda looked and saw red hair and accusing eyes, but they were not her eyes—they were the blue accusing eyes that she knew all too well. They belonged to her mother, Gayelette.

As she recognized the face, the shards coalesced into a humanoid shape, then refined themselves with the staccato scratching and shearing of breaking glass multiplied a thousand times. Glinda stared into the mirrored face of her mother, formed from shards of broken memories.

"Mother." Glinda whispered. She tried to scream, but silence—it would not come out. Her feet would not move.

The accusing reflections grew larger and larger as mirror-Gayelette leaned in toward Glinda. Her unblinking stare reflected Glinda silent screaming face.

A voice, hollow and distant, sounded all around Glinda as the mirror construct spoke. "Glinda, you see now, don't you? This is your purpose. This is why I gave birth to you. This is why you are my daughter. We will join and rule all of Oz."

Glinda shook her head mutely. Her screams would not come. The voice spoke and terrified her.

"I am watching."

24 SEEDS OF DESTINY

Cool morning breezes blew around Glinda, tickling her toes and turning the mirror shards to sand. They rolled around inside the rounded floor of the hourglass. Glinda watched the sands pour out the narrow neck beneath her feet. It was all that was left of Oz. She hurriedly reached down and grabbed as much sand as she could hold. She clutched the sand tight in her fists, but it slipped through her fingers. The sand inexorably moved on—it had a *purpose*. Who was Glinda to stop it?

Glinda lifted her hands out to her sides and let the sands flow from her fingers. The sands spiraled around her, circling toward the narrow vortex at her feet.

The hourglass emptied, and Glinda pressed her hands against the cool glass. She looked out into a strange and quiet new world. The glass felt soft and flexible. She pressed, and it flowed beneath her touch, melting away. She stepped out into the Land of Oz. It was without life, but it was not barren like it had been before. In the wake of the surging chaos, a calm stillness descended. Cracks appeared in the earth, but not the cracks of age. These were the cracks of new life hatching.

Porcelain hands pushed up from beneath the ground. Glinda took the hands of a pretty princess in a blue dress and helped her to step out of her muddy shell. "You are so pretty." Glinda smiled.

Glinda breathed in deeply of the cool morning air as she awoke. Her eyes opened and she saw the canopy of the bed, not the reborn Land of Oz. She blinked several times. Her mouth was dry. She looked around the tower bedroom. She brushed red hair out of her face and sat up. She looked at her fingers—they clutched only air. The written word had power, and she said it again, "Dream."

Then her eyes got wide and she shouted it, "Dream!"

Glinda spent the next hour writing down every detail she could remember. When she finished, she brushed her hair back with her fingers and lifted it off the back of her neck. She dropped her hair on her back, comforted by the weight of reality.

She looked to the ceramic princess on the mantle. "You were there, too. You were so pretty. And you've changed position." Glinda crossed the distance quickly in her bare feet, her robe swirling out behind her. "You were excited last night. Your hands were up under your chin. Now you are reaching out...toward me."

Glinda ran to the window. The air was clean and fresh. The smell of new rain greeted her as she stepped through the curtains on to the balcony. The towers were wet and shiny, though no clouds remained in the sky around the Emerald City.

An unfamiliar thumping sounded on the building below her. Glinda looked down to see the young architect, Perilous Eddy, harnessed to a bridge, swinging over to alcoves in the tower. The thumping sound came from his heavy boots hitting the building when he jumped.

"Good morning." Glinda called.

Perilous Eddy twisted in his harness as he heard the unexpected voice. He spun around and bumped his feet twice against the tower before he regained his stability. He looked up from beneath his helmet. Goggles hung around his neck. "Good morning, Sorceress. Quite the storm last night, wasn't it?"

"Storm? I didn't hear any storm." Glinda said.

"Sure—big storm, it was. Shook the towers and everything. It must have been right here on top of us. Maybe it rose out of Grimmpill Lake. In any case, the entire city is talking about the storm of dreams. The Wizard must have something really wonderful in store for the Emerald City to dream like that last night."

"What do you mean? What happened?" Glinda leaned her elbows on the balcony railing. The winds up this high blew her hair in dancing waves all around her face.

"Statues in the columns. Lovely female forms replacing balustrades and whatnot. He probably dreamed of you, Sorceress. He's never dreamed statues like these before."

"Can I see them?" Glinda asked.

"Certainly. Can you peek around the tower? Right down there, on the bridge. That lovely lady wasn't there yesterday."

"That looks like one of the statues at Chronometria." Glinda said.

"Where's that?" Perilous Eddy asked, untangling himself from the twisted harness. At last he got both legs free and his feet planted on the side of the building. "I haven't heard of that place."

"*Chronometria*—it's what I am calling my palace. It means a device to measure time."

"Interesting. You've got a time thing going on. It's neat. I just had not heard that name before."

Glinda smiled and shrugged. "It's new. I just decided on it a day or two ago. I had one of the old apprentices show up and tell me to make the castle my own. Smith & Tinker weren't going to be coming back anytime soon."

The architect's boots slipped on the wet tower surface, and he slammed face-first into the wall. He spread his arms out wide, embracing the tower, to keep himself from slipping again. He turned his head slowly and looked up at Glinda with wide eyes. "You met one of the Apprentices? Which one? Is he as amazing as the stories say?"

Glinda held up a hand to calm the excited young man. She covered her laughter as Eddy's feet scrambled against the wet surface. "I will tell you, but you have to tell me something, Architect."

"Eddy. My name is Perilous Eddy."

"Eddy. Why are you dangling down off the tower? It is a long way to the street? Don't you worry about falling?"

"I'm planting seeds. The Wizard wanted some trees—he showed me the kind that he wanted—so I found the seeds. I'm planting hanging gardens. When citizens of Oz come to the Emerald City, they will look up. They will see what no other city has—gardens in the sky."

"How long will it take you to plant the seeds?"

"Less than an hour."

"Very well. In one hour, I shall tell you of the Apprentice that came to Chronometria."

In her tower suite, Glinda told the wonderstruck Eddy all about Promethus and the last few days that he had spent at Chronometria. He had declared himself a Guardian, rather than an Apprentice. He claimed his lockbox, took what he needed—what he actually took, Glinda had no idea—and then sent the rest over the falls at the base of Chronometria, to fall into the Deadly Desert below. What he lost was gone forever.

Perilous Eddy hung on every word. When Glinda paused, the excited young architect eagerly shared his excitement. "The Apprentices are practically legendary. Their designs—all of the designs of Smith & Tinker, really, but more-so those of the three Apprentices—revolutionized the way that architecture could be built. You wouldn't know it by talking with the stuffy heads in charge here, though. '*The old ways are the best ways*'. I'm just glad they let the Wizard dream and change the city every night."

"About that," Glinda tapped her fingernails on the table, "what happened last night? You said the Wizard dreamed statues—specifically, female statues—which he had never done before."

"We've only had a couple of statues, but those were special cases. The Chief Architects wanted some statues in the garden. They gave the Wizard an entire book of statuary to look through. I wanted to show the Wizard some of my drawings. See, I had some ideas for statues, too. He didn't have much time. He just flipped through my book of sketches really quick. Didn't take more than thirty seconds for all fifty pages." Perilous Eddy puffed out his chest a little bit. "Imagine their surprise when my drawings were the statues in the garden. It's strange that he can see something just really fleeting and then it is made real by his dreaming."

"Eddy, what is a dream?"

There was no hesitation in Eddy's voice; no pause in his answer. "A dream is magic brought to life by the Wizard seeing it in his mind at night. Sometimes he sleeps and dreams. Sometimes his dreams come when he's awake—mostly when he's tired and heading for bed. Sometimes the dreams create things that we have shown him. Sometimes they are something completely different."

"Is it only the Wizard that dreams? I mean, could somebody else dream?" Glinda asked, her blue eyes studying the young architect's face. She scratched at a polished knot in the wood of the table.

"A dream is magic. In order to dream, someone would need magic. You could probably do it, if you tried, Sorceress. I'm sorry. I didn't mean to be so informal. I just have never been allowed to talk freely, especially not in a place as fine as this. But I watch—I watch every night and see all of the changes. Last night was spectacular."

Eddy leaned back in his chair and spread his fingers wide. "The lightning would flash, then the stone would shift and reshape itself. The lightning flashed again, and the statue was there. The bridges reformed themselves. Some of the towers are taller and thinner—this one has a very nice slender, almost feminine, appeal to it now. I think it looks better. When I am done here, I'm going to do some drawing before getting some sleep before tonight. It might be another amazing night in Emerald City."

"Do things change normally—I mean, like they did last night—all the time? Is it always like last night?"

"No. Sometimes nothing changes. Sometimes we get a new bridge or some stone trees, or occasionally a building changes shape. Mostly, it's controlled by the Chief Architects. They decide what the Wizard is going to dream by showing him only the designs that they want to see."

"And last night was new?"

"When you see the changes that happened, you will be in love with this city, Sorceress. The statues and the slender changes—they are subtle, but they are amazing."

"Thank you." Glinda smiled and folded her hands on the table in front of her. There were many unanswered questions about last night, but one thing was certain—she was going to look around Emerald City before she left. She had to see who left the greater mark on the city—the Wizard or the Sorceress.

Eddy got up to leave. He looked over to the mantle. "Your princess figurine is trying to climb down."

Glinda looked. He was right. The china princess was on the edge of the mantle, with one foot down, reaching for the bookcase. "She wasn't like that when I woke up."

Eddy snapped his fingers. "I almost forgot. I had some extra seeds from my planting. I figured that the trees needed some room, even high up. They need friends, but they need their own space to grow. I wanted to give you some seeds as a lesson."

Glinda raised her eyebrows. "A seed is going to teach me a lesson?"

Perilous Eddy smiled. He snapped his fingers and held up one tiny seed. "This seed will grow a tree that can stand for three, four, or five lifetimes. The tree will see and feel many changes in the Land of Oz. But that is not the real magic. The real magic is that this seed holds an entire forest."

"Not possible. One seed, one tree. That's how it works." Glinda responded.

"The tree grows. The wind howls and twists the growing branches. The rain pounds down. The floods come. The tree grows into the shape it becomes through all the storms. Each tree has its own shape—even those of the same kind of tree—each is unique and different, shaped by the forces of nature to become what it is. Then when the tree has reached the right age, it grows fruit, and fruit has seeds."

"And the seed contains another tree, and so on. I see. So an entire forest is inside this little seed."

"Seeds grow where they are planted. They grow into what they are supposed to become. A seed will always grow what it is. You don't grow a princess in a peach pit, and you don't grow trees by waving wands. The magic of life is different. Growth comes naturally, with time and turbulence. Strong trees don't grow shallow. They have to dig deep to find their footing. To really grow, a tree has to be as deep and wide in its roots as it is with its branches."

"Is that a message directed at me?" Glinda asked.

"My father told it to me. I'm still trying to figure it out. It seemed to make sense to him. The best I can see is that I can put this seed in the ground and it grows into a tree. However, the same type of magic happens in people, too. I have tried really hard to fit with the other architects and builders. They constantly push me down and tell me to grow straight—to do things their way. Their way is the only way. But I want to reach for the sun in my own way."

"So do I." Glinda whispered.

"I want to grow to see how far I can reach. These hanging gardens are part of that. People may not know my name, but they will see what I planted."

"Planting the seeds is the most important part." Glinda said.

"It is the *first* part. The seeds will grow. They will get rain and sunshine. I don't control that. I just need to have the courage to plant the trees in the hanging garden. Then they will grow. I will tend them and care for the garden. I will make it worth looking at. There will be something there that wasn't there before."

Glinda studied the small seeds. "Each seed grows how many trees?"

"Therein is the magic, sorceress. When you have planted the seed, you have planted a forest. All it takes is the courage at first to plant the seed."

"Can I hold on to these?" Glinda asked. "The seeds are a good reminder. Growth comes through turbulence. This will give my mind something else to consider on the trip home."

Perilous Eddy poured the remaining tree seeds into his hand. He closed his fingers over them and held out his hand to Glinda. Glinda cupped her hand below Eddy's hand. "Sorceress, there is one last thing you need to know about seeds."

"What is that?"

"No planted seed is ever wasted."

25 BATTLE OF MIGHTY MISS GULCH

Far to the west, where the grasslands met the rocky hills, Oscar and Kally and their automaton army sat in the shadows of a bluff. To the south and west of them, they could see Yellow Castle. A broad swath of dry sand separated the rocky land from the hills.

"This was once a mighty river." Kally said. "I visited here when it was still flowing—much smaller, but still flowing. You can see the path in the center of the gulch there."

"Back in America we had some mighty rivers, too. The mightiest I ever saw was the mighty Mississippi. I have never seen so much water moving in one direction before. The Mighty Miss cut the land in half—kind of like this here."

"Mighty Miss Gulch. That's what we shall call this. It is yours and mine. The border of the West is guarded by *Miss Gulch*."

"Sounds like a person."

"A name like *Miss Gulch* is only suitable for a perfectly horrible person."

Oscar tossed a rock out of the shade into the afternoon sun. "We crossed the Emerald Prairie. We made it here to the border, now what?"

Kally studied the distant Yellow Castle. "We get inside."

"The army won't be able to sneak in. They'll see us coming."

"They will see the army, yes, but they will not see us. The army is the frontal assault—the diversion."

"So you do have a scheme." Oscar smiled.

Kally smiled back. "I always have a scheme."

"I don't see why we had to leave the Hamstrambulator. We could have crossed the distance much more quickly by rolling." Oscar complained.

"The Witch likes shiny things—she always has. Driving a giant shining wheel up to her front door would most certainly get us noticed and probably destroyed."

Oscar peeked over the top of a large stone and watched the small automaton army march up toward the front of Yellow Castle. This field, two years ago, was where he landed in his balloon. The middle of the Battle of Winkie Plains, as they called it after that. What a storm it had been! The terror he felt then was real—this land was a wonder, but it held shadows, too.

Now Oscar was in the middle of another adventure. This adventure proved to be much more in the shadows than any of his previous outings in the Land of Oz. This one was strange and exhilarating in its own way. They were infiltrating enemy territory and recovering the stolen Golden Cap. That would free the Winged Monkeys and change the balance of power. The slaves would be freed—that was the most important thing.

Kally pulled Oscar down again behind the rock. "Keep your head down." She hissed. "We can't be seen this close."

A whip cracked. The sound sliced through the air, followed quickly by the howling of at least a dozen wolves.

Kally peeked her head up over the rock.

"I thought we did not want to be seen." Oscar muttered.

"Shh. I'm watching." Kally motioned for Oscar to be quiet.

In the distance, exiting the stables, Ondri-baba, the Witch of the West, drove her chariot onto the broad plain at the foot of the castle. Her chariot was pulled by twenty-four black wolves. Their howling cries pierced the air as they raced across the field toward the first automaton soldier.

Kally sat down and leaned back against the rock. Her shoulders slumped. "I want my chariot. But I want something better than wolves to pull it. What is better than wolves to pull a chariot?"

"I don't know, maybe horses?"

"No." Kally rolled her eyes and shook her head. "It has to be something different. Normal rulers use horses. Mine has to be different, better."

"Okay. Bears are better than wolves. They can run fast and they are stronger."

"Tigers!" Kally exclaimed. "Tigers are even faster than bears. They sound more ferocious."

"The lion is the king of beasts." Oscar suggested. "If you're dreaming it up, you can have whatever you want."

A strange, scheming gleam caught Kally's eye. "What? What was that? If you're *dreaming* it, I can have whatever I want? Do you mean that, Wizard? Do you really mean that? Are you offering me a dream?"

Oscar shrugged. "Sure. I suppose so."

"I don't like lions. They are always at the top. I want something new to be the most ferocious beast in the Land of Oz. You promised I could have whatever I want. I will hold you to it. Tigers, bears, tigers, bears." Kally debated back and forth. "Tiger-bear, tiger-bear." Then her eyes widened. "TIGER-BEARS. I want tiger-bears. Combine them. Make them into one beast. Those can pull my chariot. Then I will be the queen."

"Yes. That sounds like quite an idea."

"I will give you a pearl. Here." Kally pressed a pearl into Oscar's hand. "It's a black pearl. These are valuable even among pearls. I know you don't put the same stock in pearls that I do, but this seals our deal. I give you a pearl, and you dream tiger-bears for me."

Oscar smiled at her enthusiasm. "I have never seen someone so excited by a dream before. Okay, sure. Thanks." He stuck the black pearl in his pocket. It was an unexpected match for his other pearl. He felt his pocket—his pearl was gone! There was only one pearl in his pocket—the one that Kally had just given him. He looked at Kally with a growing suspicion, but she smiled sweetly back at him. Oscar could not bring himself to accuse her of theft.

Shouts from the Winkie guards sounded on the wind. The guards had encountered the automaton army. Metallic clashes bore witness to the beginning melee.

"The Witch and her guards are suitably distracted. Now we can enter unseen. Take my hand, Wizard. We will run."

Kally used the magic of the Silver Slippers to race them across the empty space to the stables at the side of the castle. She was careful to only move them a short distance with each step, so that the Wizard would not suspect the greater magic at work. It was all part of the scheme, and it was coming together wonderfully.

They stopped at the door of the stables, but they heard no guards inside. Kally moved to go in, but Oscar put his hand up. "Wait. I'll make sure it's safe." He disappeared through the door and around the corner.

Kally smiled softly. How long had it been since a man treated her like this? She could not remember. It was most likely that no man had ever treated her like this, yet the Wizard made it seem so easy, like he was not doing anything special. It was just who he was. And then he was back, gesturing for Kally to enter.

"I found something." Oscar took Kally by the hand and led her into the stable. He pointed to the Walking Hut that Ondri-baba used in the battles two years previous. "It is her hut. We can take her power."

"We are here for one reason. This is a very interesting discovery, but it is not why we are here."

Oscar pushed open the front door of the hut. The Sapphire Stove glowed inside.

"It's shiny." Kally said.

"I thought you might like that." Oscar smiled at her. "Still want to go after the Golden Cap?"

"Ooooh. You make this so difficult. Yes. I want the Golden Cap. But the Sapphire Stove. Do you know what this is? No, of course you don't. This is power. I can power anything with this. No matter how large or small, this stove can power it. I could make anything…"

"We can pack up and go, if you'd like. I am happy giving this to you instead of the Golden Cap."

Kally fidgeted and stamped her feet. "I want both. *Aarrghh*. I really want both of them."

Oscar nodded his head slightly and smiled. "All right. I will get you both."

Omby-Amby paced back and forth just below the crest of the hill. He waited for Wickrie-Kells to wake from her nap. Back and forth his feet traveled over the same path, always staying below the top of the hill. It was just over that hill that he would be able to see his home. Why was this so difficult? It should be easy to just take one look and be done. That's all he wanted—just one look.

He knew that wasn't true, and so did Wickrie. No. What he really wanted was for his brother to give up his roots in the West. It wasn't only about the fruit trees, either. For longer than Omby-Amby could remember, his brother wanted nothing to do with anything else in the land. His fruit trees and his farm were the most important thing to him. It didn't matter that his entire family had left to seek the greener lands near the Emerald City. The entire Winkie population could leave, and he would still stay with his trees. He just refused to change.

That is what Omby-Amby really wanted to see—the stubborn streak in his brother. He wanted to see that, pierce it through the heart, skin it, and stamp his feet on it. He wanted his brother back.

He felt a soft touch on his hand. He turned his head slightly to see Wickrie-Kells.

"You stomped up a cloud of dust."

Omby looked down to see his boots covered with the thin dust. "Oh. I was thinking."

"He won't let go of the past." Wickrie squeezed the soldier's hand tightly.

"The past won't let go of him. The trees aren't holding him back."

"The future belongs to *us*, but not if you keep your heart in the past. He was your brother, and he will always be your brother, but you need to look forward to the vistas ahead. No not beyond that rise, but here—with me."

Omby-Amby reached out and brushed a stray hair out of Wickrie's face. "The same blood runs through our veins. Why do I get it and he doesn't? The future is not there, shackling himself to the way that things have always been done. Freedom, liberty, life—these are available to anyone who is willing to accept it, live it, and defend it."

"I think you've answered your own question there, Omby."

The Soldier with Green Whiskers angrily kicked the dirt at his feet. "It doesn't have to be that way! Why can't he just see?"

"I think you are the exception, Omby, not the rule. Freedom calls to you. It does not call to him. Those who need liberty hear its call and they answer in their own way. Maybe he is answering."

"No. He doesn't know liberty. He doesn't know anything. He just chains himself deeper to the land. He doesn't have any books in his house—did you know that? Keeps his children from learning. Everything they need to know is in the land, he tells them. He hated me for being a soldier. My father was a soldier, as was his father before him. My other brothers are soldiers. Why is he the only one that doesn't fit?"

"Everyone has their own destiny to embrace or deny. In every person's life there comes a time when they recognize the moment of decision—the moment when destiny becomes so clear that you can see horizon to horizon. Both ends of your life—the beginning and the end—come into view and everything makes sense around this one point of destiny. Then you choose to embrace or deny. Either way, the vision closes up after that and you are left with your decision. Maybe some people get more than one point of destiny, I don't know. I just know two things: one, that I love you; and two, that I am supposed to be with Glinda."

"You can't have both. Not like that."

"Neither can you, with your proclamations of liberty in Emerald City." Wickrie-Kells shook her head at the sky. "It seems so simple, what Oscar and Glinda have. They are meant for each other. Everyone sees it, except them. How can two people be so blind-headed to not see that what they have right in front of them is perfect?"

"I ask that of myself often." Omby-Amby said softly.

"So do I." Wickrie-Kells admitted. "We are soldiers. You already have my father's permission to marry me. I dearly love you. I love the wind in my hair. I love my bow. I love the great work that Glinda is doing."

"And what great work is that? Certainly it doesn't compare with liberty, justice, and equality for all."

Wickrie-Kells scoffed then smiled. "If you cannot defend liberty against your enemies, what good does it do you? The powers are arraying against us,

Omby. Glinda is gathering power. She is readying against the rising storm. She is ensuring that there will be an Oz for our children."

Omby was silent for several minutes. "Where does that leave us?"

Wickrie shrugged. "Same place as always. I love walking with you in the sunshine."

They stepped the final few steps up to the top of the hill together. There was Yellow Castle—capital of Omby-Amby's ancestral homeland. Wickrie-Kells wrapped her fingers tightly around Omby's fingers.

"Together, in the moment, for all that it is worth."

Behind them, a horse whinnied. They turned to see a young Emerald Guardsman swiftly approaching on a chestnut stallion.

Omby-Amby broke the tender grip and ran down the hill to meet the soldier.

Wickrie-Kells forced a smile at the distant castle and the rising clouds of dust. "Just like that, the moment is gone."

Oscar crept to the castle door and creaked it open. No response from any guards. The diversion must be working all around. He turned back and gestured to Kally. She joined him on the stone stairs. Oscar turned back around.

A Winged Monkey was looking right at him!

Oscar screamed in surprise, but Kally clapped her hand over his mouth. "*Shhh.* You fool. You'll give us away."

Oscar stepped past the smiling monkey and into the kitchen. He kept his eyes riveted to the Winged Monkey as he closed the door behind Kally. "Why isn't it doing anything? It's smiling at me."

"Maybe it likes you."

"None of them liked me. They only liked to torment me." Oscar replied in a harsh whisper.

Kally tried to hide her smile. "Then maybe he recognizes you."

The monkey lifted a finger and pointed to the door that lead deeper into the castle. "Do we follow it?" Oscar asked.

"We reviewed the layout. The most likely place for the Golden Cap is the Hall of Mirrors. That is where the Winkies sought the future and kept their treasures. There are two ways there. We can search the rooms quickly while the Witch is out."

"Fine. We just need to find it. We don't know when the Witch will come back."

The monkey chattered in laughter. Suddenly whooping laughter echoed through the halls of the Yellow Castle.

"We woke them up."

The monkey pulled Oscar's hand and led him toward the door.

"It looks like you have your direction. I'll take the other path."

"How do I know this isn't some strange monkey trap?"

"You don't." Then Kally stuck out her lower lip and lowered her eyes at Oscar, "Unless you don't want to get me the Golden Cap."

"Stop it. I said I would get it, and I'll get it. You don't have to pull that female pouty guilt trick on me. It won't work. I said I would and that's enough for me." He turned toward the dark halls of the castle. "Lead the way, creepy little monkey."

Nikidik watched the sun moving lower in the afternoon sky. It was time. Time for him to head south and build his hidden army. Kalinya had paid him well. Not only was he able to complete his goal of completing the final stages of the Crown of the Dreamer, but he would finally be able to surpass the Ruby Sorceress in knowledge and power. Yes, the pearls were the final ingredient that would make him heir to the most powerful magic the Land of Oz could not offer—dreams.

Nikidik murmured the words of the protection spell and crushed a small emerald with a mortar and pestle. In the room beyond, the still form of Margolotte watched her husband closely.

"You'll be safe here while I'm gone. I know the shadows are still skulking about somewhere. I'm going to leave you a protection spell that I learned from my masters, back when they were still my betters. It's not usually done immediately like this, you see, but I'm in a rather perfunctory state right now and I would like to claim what is rightfully mine. I'm going south for a time, but I will return with all that I have promised you and more."

The professor emptied the emerald dust into a flask and carefully measured three drops in. "Pure water from a running river, just before the summer rain. This carries the protective power of the emeralds through all nature, on land, in air, and in the ice beneath." He boiled the water over a sprig of Sparkwood. "The Sparkwood brims with power. The earth grows fire. So you have fire, water, and emerald. Mix that with a little bit of spoken magic, and what have you got? One protection spell. I only have to cast the spoken and component part of this spell once. The final, transfigurative portion of the spell can come immediately, or it can come years later. The final part brings me into it. My kiss—the power of my heart in desire and protection of you—ignites the spell."

Margolotte's eyes followed Nikidik as he approached her statue'd form. He kissed her on the forehead, leaving a silver mark. "There, you are protected. The monsters—or anything wicked, for that matter—cannot harm you in any way."

The fingers on Margolotte's fleshy hand clapped against her palm. Nikidik squeezed the hand and kissed it. "I will be back soon. You will soon be flesh, and I will cook for you."

The statue's eyes grew sad. Nikidik responded to the unspoken question. "I don't know how long it will take to turn you back. No? How long I will be gone? Not long. I have my things to recover from my former masters' southern laboratory. I must fulfill my contract with Kalinya. Then I will come back. I have the ingredients I need to make the Powder of Life. That will bring you fully to your old self. Then we can go down the mountain and into town and buy a pie."

Nikidik pulled a jacket over his shoulders. He paused at the stairwell down into the laboratory. Margolotte's eyes followed him. "I will be back soon. Watch for me."

He pulled a hat on his head and disappeared down the stairs. Margolotte's hand waved slowly for a very long time.

When the shadows crossed out of their ruby cages and approached the statue, they were repelled by the protection spell. The silver mark on the statue's forehead kept them away. As night fell, and darkness settled heavy on the mountain laboratory, Margolotte was comforted by the faint silver light that shone from her forehead. The light was a reminder of the power that Nikidik created. It was only through the power of their love that it was activated. Such power could not be overcome by evil. So Margolotte fell asleep trusting in the magic that bound both she and her husband together. *Such magic did not fade over time.* Such magic was forged over a lifetime. And so Margolotte would wait and she would watch. All of the shadows in the world could not make her doubt.

The protection spell was a comforting reminder that darkness did not control this home. Though the enemies of craft and logic constantly made their presence felt, such would never prevail. And so Margolotte slept and waited on the morning.

Outside, Nikidik mounted a stilted interloper, a specially-created construct to carry him swiftly over the long miles to South Castle. There were stops along the way, but time was short. The army had to be ready for Kalinya—Kally—when she was ready to wage war. Then all the powers in Oz would see that Nikidik was the worthy heir of Smith & Tinker. Nikidik was the master of motion, the creator of the immortal army. Nikidik would be the one they remembered in immortality—not Gayelette—Nikidik.

26 MIRROR, MIRROR

"Wait." Kally said. "Are you sure you know the way?" She didn't mean to let that much concern slip into her voice. It was just that Oscar was walking away. Everything that she had worked so hard for was so close, and she was letting him walk away. Certainly, he was the Wizard, but she just felt better when she was around him. She didn't want anything to happen to him—for any reason.

"I'll find my way well enough." Oscar said. "I've got monkey. Unless you want to lead the way?"

Kally fought the emotions as they tried to parade across her face. "There are rules, Wizard. We have broken many of them."

"To what end? Peace? Or war? If we get the Golden Cap, we will have peace. That is enough for me—it should be enough for you, too. Be safe."

"Remember the architecture book. You wanted to see the Hall of Mirrors—it's that way." Kally pointed down the stone hallway.

"I'll need to see where my guide is taking me. Are you going to be all right? Which way are you going?" Oscar asked.

"Up. I need to see our escape."

Oscar placed his hand on the blurred wall. He shook his head but could not get the image to focus. "Can you see this? It's blurry. I can't see what it is supposed to be, but I feel it, and the wall is carved. I wouldn't see this without my fingers. It's like my eyes aren't working right on this wall."

"You're better off not trusting your eyes here. The Witch has many tricks."

"More than you?" Oscar said, half-smiling at Kally.

"No." Kally said proudly. "Not more than me."

"Then I have no need to worry."

Kally's proud smile froze as she watched the Wizard turn away and work his way up the corridor, dragging his fingertips along the wall. He really trusted her. Not just really, but really, really. How long had it been?

"Time to get moving. Be safe." The whisper next to Kally startled her and made her jump to the side. She looked in surprise down the hallway at the Wizard. He waved.

"Ventriloquism. I can throw my voice." The whisper sounded next to her again.

"Will wonders never cease?"

"Now move. Find the way out. I will find the Golden Cap." The Wizard waved once more and he was gone.

"Or am I really gone?" The whisper echoed off the walls from around the corner.

Kally shook her head and shivered. That magic he called ventriloquism was foreign to the Land of Oz. It was uncomfortable experiencing magic that she did not understand. She turned her attention down the hall—stairways went both up and down. Kally glanced back over her shoulder at the young man who trusted her to go *up* and find the way out. She sighed deeply at the weakness that came so easily, and she headed quickly *down* the stairs.

Oscar peered around the corner. It had been two years since he had been inside the castle. By his best memory, and from the architectural drawings in The History of the Winkies, he was above the throne room right now. Nothing was coming down the hall, not that it mattered to the small monkey. He was at home here. That was good, in some scenarios. The high arches in the ceiling would carry any sounds further than he wanted. With the stillness so pervasive, the impulsive thoughts in his head urged him to shout. Oh, how he wanted to shout—to hear his voice echo in the rafters and ricochet down the stone corridors. But that would reveal everything. All of the plans that he—actually, Kally—had made. Everything would be lost. But for one brief moment, everything would be absolutely, incredibly, fun.

As if they shared a single mind, the small Winged Monkey shouted and screeched. Just like Oscar anticipated, the sound echoed and rebounded through the stone and metal workings. The sound echoed very well in here. Perhaps just one little whisper.

"Monkey." The hiss sounded from right next to the monkey. It jumped up the wall and launched into the air in surprise. It chattered and screeched at the empty space on the floor. Oscar smiled. That worked very well.

Tiny shuffling sounds rebounded on the floor behind Oscar. He turned around searching in the dim light, but no one was there. All around the large room the shuffling sounded. First it was like the beginning raindrops in a downpour, but it escalated to a hail of movement all around him.

Breathy laughter echoed in the shadows. In the corners of his vision, he glimpsed movement. The prickles up and down his neck whispered in his ear that he was being watched. Yes, the small monkey had indeed led him into a trap. He looked over at the small monkey. It wagged its tail back and forth like a happy puppy. The monkey smiled broadly at him, and Oscar knew the trap had been sprung.

Slowly Oscar raised his eyes to the rafters of the tall room. Dozens of almost-human eyes stared back at him, laughing. There were all of the Winged Monkeys above his head, staring at him. They flapped their wings and swung from rafter to rafter. Yes, Oscar knew them—and they knew him.

For now they were watching, curious and full of mischief. Oscar stepped carefully and quickly from the room and closed the door behind him. To the best of his knowledge, they did not follow.

Outside the Yellow Castle, on Winkie Plains, Ondri-baba stopped her chariot and watched the battle between the strange metal soldiers and her Winkie guards. The metal soldiers appeared to be self-organizing—they were fighting as a unit, so they must have some purpose for declaring war on her land. They were few in number. They could not possibly hope to beat the Winkie guards...but perhaps that was not their purpose. Ondri-baba shot her gaze back to the castle.

She cracked her whip and the wolves howled and leaped forward. Back to the castle.

In the stables, Kally heard the howling of the wolves long before they arrived. Her mission would have to wait. She quickly slipped into the castle to wait for the inevitable confrontation with the Wicked Witch of the West, her sister.

Oscar closed the door and stood with his back against it. He heard the flapping of wings outside the door. Given the choice of the unknown darkness ahead and the flock of Winged Monkeys on the other side of the door, the darkness was much more agreeable.

He followed the stairs down. Taking steps forward he held his hands out until he found a wall. He felt his way along until he rounded a corner. Now there was no light. The air was stale and thick. But there was a slight breeze on his face. It smelled fresh. There was another way out.

Oscar whistled. The sound bounced back quickly—a wall in front of him. He reached out his hand and sure enough, there was a wall. Oscar smiled. As a ventriloquist, he knew how his voice sounded in an empty room. He knew how to throw his voice in a room full of people. It was all about the echoes. By understanding where the echoes came from, he would be able to determine the placement of the walls and the doors. Even in pitch blackness, he would be able to locate his position with echoes. *Echo-location.*

Whistling would take too long. He couldn't think of any songs that would move quickly enough. There were some fast tunes, but the words didn't fit for this situation. Vocalization would be more effective. Simple sounds generated rapidly would bounce back from the stone and help him to walk through the labyrinth to the other side. He trilled, and then lololo'd, walking confidently into the darkness with a nonsense song echoing around him.

Kally climbed to the top of the stone stairs. She trailed her fingers along the walls, feeling the unseen bas-reliefs carved into the blurred stone. What a job her sister had done, making all of the carvings invisible on the walls. It must take a tremendous toll on her to keep so many things invisible at once. That's how Kally's magic worked—she had to focus on keeping things up in the air. Ondri-baba's magic had to work the same way. If she could just turn something invisible and be done with it, that was…not fair. So it had to be the other way, that Ondri-baba was concentrating very hard to keep everything invisible. It served its purpose to keep the Winkies in the dark.

Speaking of dark, why was that stairway so dark? The other passages were lighter, at least that one down that way seemed to be lighter. What had happened to her sister? She used to be afraid of the dark. Was this castle so familiar to her now that she did not need the light?

Kally stopped. She heard her sister's voice echoing down the hall. Above her in the rafters, Kally could feel the shapes of the Winged Monkeys as they stretched their wings, noticing her. Most of them were no longer there—not like they had seemed to be when Oscar left her. She took one, two, three steps and she was at the end of the hall. She heard the startled scream of the monkey that had been watching her. This woke the several other monkeys from their apathetic slumber.

"Who is in my castle?" Ondri-baba's voice shouted through the halls. "I see you moving down there. You cannot hide from me. I know your magic. It is a presence I have not felt since…are you serious, Kalinya? You? You are the one that tossed that ridiculous army at my front gate in order to defile my home? You truly are desperate."

Kally used the Silver Slippers to lead Ondri-baba further into the castle. Somewhere there was a place where the Golden Cap would be hidden. Of course Oscar had just as much chance of finding it as her—maybe more now that she had been spotted.

The dark room full of carved pillars awaited her. She recognized this as the Cylinders of History room. This contained a pictorial history of the Winkies. She looked to the pillars, but there was nothing on them. All of the carved pillars were blurred, just like the walls.

Ondri-baba entered the room, closing the door behind her. "Why did you come, Kalinya?"

Kally hid behind a pillar. There was no line-of-sight escape presently available, but there certainly would be very soon. "I missed the sound of your voice. Now that I have heard it, I wonder why. It leaves a bad taste in my ears."

"What is it you want? Did you come to steal my power?"

"Certainly."

"Then nothing has changed. Conquer or perish. Isn't that what you always said?"

"When courting the beaus, yes. If you let them conquer you, then you most certainly perish."

Ondri-baba snorted. "It is small wonder that you never kept a man longer than five days."

"I have one now."

"I'm sure you do."

Kally's face grew red. She stepped out from behind the pillar. "You blustering pig. I may be many things, but I don't lie to you. I never have."

Ondri-baba laughed. "You are so young. Where did your beauty go?" She placed one hand over her mortal eye and focused with her glowing green magic eye. "Ah, there it is. Your magic lines become visible when I don't look with this old rattler."

"I have found someone. He is kind to me."

"You don't deserve it."

Now it was Kally's turn to laugh. "But he does it anyway."

"Who is this great and wonderful man? Shall I do as you did to me, and spirit him away and throw him into the sky?"

"What is this *tro-lo-lo* sound I hear in my sacred labyrinth?"

Oscar stopped and forced a smile. He knew that voice. But then the smile would not stay on his face. That was a voice that had terrified him when he first came into this land. He feared the Winged Monkeys, and more especially their leader. The darkness closed in around him as the laughter began. "I-I am the Wizard."

"Yes, Wizard. I know who you are. You made your choice. So did Glinda. You chose to save her. She chose to save herself. She abandoned my people to slavery. She gave her oath."

The voice came closer in the darkness. Oscar sent a burst of hissing whispers out. The echoes came back confused. The voice of the monkey was coming from the walls and the ceiling, like he was climbing around all four sides of the corridor.

"I promised to get the Golden Cap. I promised her then that I would help her free you. King Klick, I swear that is the truth."

"Then you are here with Glinda?"

"No."

"My ears hear your voice is truth, but you are threatening to lie. Why do you shake so, Wizard? What great tale do you have for my people this time? We are already slaves."

"I-I'm here with a witch. I promised to get her the Golden Cap. I…Glinda…it's complicated, and I don't really feel like talking about it right now."

From deeper within the labyrinth, a light flickered. Throughout the entire mirrored maze, the light reflected, casting a dim glow all around the Wizard. He jumped back nervously when he saw the scarred visage of King Klick right in front of him. The hideously burned monkey dropped down from the ceiling to the floor. He stood up on his back legs and walked around the Wizard, sniffing at him.

"I trust you, Wizard." King Klick cocked his head to the side. "It is the sorceress I hate. I do not trust my people with any other witch, or any other human. They all lie. You lie."

"I am not lying." Oscar declared. He turned to face the silver-furred monkey. They stood eye-to-eye. "I want to see you free. I want liberty for everyone. Freedom is the right of all thinking creatures, even if they do not look like me. That bothers me, but I have to believe it to stay true to my principles."

"Hmm. You present me with an interesting choice, Wizard. Your smell is fear, anger, and fatigue. You have not washed in several days."

Kally stared down through the pillars at her sister, Ondri-baba. These last two years had not been kind to either of them, but Kally had come out looking the better. It cost her dearly, but vanity was worth the price. The greenish tinge on Ondri-baba's skin was made more sickly by the strange light from her glowing magic eye.

"Your magic lines are strangely muted. What have you done to your skin?"

"I am young again." Kally bragged.

"You are no such thing. You have masked your age, your skin, and your spells, but you are certainly not young."

"I have a young man that thinks I am."

"How long have you had him?"

"Five days."

"Your history proves that he will be thrown into the sky before the day is done."

"No. There is no need—I like this one."

"Like you liked the other ones? Like you liked my beaus? Like you liked anything you couldn't have? The only thing you love is a scheme. Power is not even enough for you—never satisfied even with power. I want you out of my house." Ondri-baba pointed to the door. "Open it."

Kally waved her hand and opened the door.

"Go. Take your magic slippers and leave. I do not want your schemes to destroy what I have worked hard to build."

"You didn't build this—you took it by crook. You had the monkeys conquer the Winkies and then you came in as Deliverer."

"Yes." Ondri-baba smiled. "These people were desperate to cling to a strong fist—anything that would bring peace. It just happened to be me."

"Yes." Kally mimicked. "It just *happened* to be you."

"That's right."

Kally took one, two, three steps, and she was at the open door. She turned back to her sister. "What did you do to the walls? I can feel the carvings, but I can't see them."

"Today is the only day that matters. The Winkies have today. They are grateful for it. They know the horror of the Winged Monkeys. They do not have a history. All they see is blank. It is gone. They have today." She lowered her voice, "And today is what *I give them.*"

"You made their history invisible."

"A people without a history is easily drawn to stories of heroes—like those who conquered the Winged Monkeys, for a random example."

Kally thought for a minute. "By taking away their history, frightening them with the threat of terror, and promising them today, you control them. Just like that?"

"Absolutely."

"I am supposed to be the clever one. Here you are revealing all of your secrets. How clever, then, are you really?"

"It is no secret—just an uncomfortable truth that people do not bother to remember. When they lose their history, they lose their identity and their pride. They are easily molded by a strong hand. Your Munchkins could use some molding. If nothing else, it will keep you away from me."

"I will leave you now, Ondri-baba. You have done well."

"Your praise rings hollow in these walls. Only the truth resonates in this chamber. The bells ensure that."

"I am outside the chamber. And I meant it—I have never lied to you."

"Prove it. Why are you here? Why did you come to Yellow Castle? Did you come to kill me?"

"No."

"Then why?"

Kally gritted her teeth. She could not lie to her sister. Their blood bound them together—or it once did, when they had blood. Each of them had spent every last drop of blood creating their clashing blood-sand armies. All of that power, washed away in Glinda's storm. What was worse, the magic lines that held the magic spells—the lines that ornamented their faces and bodies—had collapsed into each other as the blood drained from their bodies. With the magic lines overlapping in unforeseen places, the magic short-circuited. The spells they had each taken a lifetime to perfect had been ruined. The haggard lines were a taunting reminder that power is fleeting, so grab it while you can. And Kally was here for power.

"The Golden Cap. It will be mine." Kally slammed the doors shut and took one, two, three steps and disappeared into the dark corridor.

27 A VOICE IN THE DARKNESS

"What do I need to do to prove my worthiness to you?" Oscar asked. "I came for the Golden Cap. If it will ease your mind, I will free you before I give the Golden Cap to anyone else. You should not be slaves to a piece of clothing."

King Klick circled the Wizard again. "The Golden Cap was given to the man, Quelala, by his bride on their wedding day. It has become a symbol of life and death to us. The sorceress would have slain every one of us, but the man intervened. He pleaded our cause and saved my people. The sorceress bound us with fire to the Golden Cap. All living at that time gave a hair as token of our life. She burned it and bound our tribe to the Golden Cap. We faithfully stood with the man through his life. He was sworn by the sorceress to never free my people. We had hopes for Glinda, but she was her mother's daughter."

Oscar frowned. Glinda was more than her mother's daughter. She was young, impetuous, powerful, and brutal in her curiosity. "I swore to Glinda that I would help her free you. I will make good on that oath."

"Humans lie."

"I will free you."

"What do you offer as a token?" King Klick demanded. His twitching wings showed that he was intrigued. "What is so precious to you that you would sacrifice if you fail?"

Oscar was silent for a long moment, pondering the things that meant the very most to him. There was family, which should be important, but they haunted him. There was freedom, which was fleeting. It was strong when he was with Omby-Amby. A truer patriot Oscar had never met. Omby-Amby recognized liberty for the priceless gift that it was, and he treasured and protected it. But for Oscar, liberty came with a price. To make the Emerald City free, he had to be their Wizard. He had to rule and govern every second of the day. *A republic, if you can keep it*, Benjamin Franklin, one of America's Founding Fathers, had said that when the nation of America was born. Oscar was doing all that he could to make and keep the Emerald City free, but there were many people who liked the freedoms but shirked the responsibilities. They forgot where their liberties came from, and they paraded their riches in the streets. They worked, but their freedom was an afterthought to their comfort. Yes, freedom was precious, but how could he give that up? Could he take the place of the Winged Monkeys as slaves? Was one wizard worth a tribe of Winged Monkeys? That was a question for the Wicked Witch to decide, though Oscar hoped he would not have to ask that question.

Glinda was precious. She was his friend. She had promised to keep his secrets. She received his promise, *no more tears*. Only one other woman had ever received that promise from Oscar—his mother. He had promised, but he was not able to keep the promise. He could not sacrifice Glinda. That would violate his oath of freedom.

What then, was truly his? What could he offer as a token of his integrity? He did not have magic. He was a storyteller and ventriloquist from the Western Frontier of America. He was far from home. The only thing he had that people really loved him for…his voice.

"My voice." Oscar whispered. Then his voice strengthened. "I will get the Golden Cap, and I will free you from your slavery. I pledge my voice. Without my voice, I am dead."

"It is enough. Come with me. I cannot show you where the Golden Cap is—it is forbidden by magic. However, I can show you where the Golden Cap is not." He led the way deeper into the labyrinth. "I speak for my people. We cannot help you beyond this point. We may even hinder you. I hold you to your oath, Wizard. Your voice—your life—is mine should you betray your oath."

"Where shall I look so that I will not find the Golden Cap?" Oscar asked, straightening his shoulders and smoothing his shirt.

"It is not in the labyrinth, and it is not in the reflections in history."

"The Hall of Mirrors."

"Let your voice guide you, Wizard, for my people are bound to another power. We will certainly be enemies from this point. May all your powers smile upon you—may you stay free, and your voice forever be heard."

Oscar turned and let his voice lead the way into the darkness.

Oscar slowly opened the door into the dark room. He crept inside and closed the door. He felt for a handle on the inside, but there was none—only smooth glass. The door clicked closed. He could not feel the seams. His choice was made, and he was here.

The room was dark, but there was still some small light entering from somewhere. Oscar saw across the room a shadow moving. He froze. The shadow across the room froze also. Had it seen him? It must have. Oscar crept slowly and watched as the shadow started moving. Then the voice came and chilled Oscar to the core.

"Come in. It is so rare that I have visitors anymore. I see you glowing in the dark. There is only one person in all of Oz that glows with such power. I know it is you, Wizard. You have come to steal my Golden Cap. You entered my kingdom to violate that peace we enjoy. You came to see me destroyed."

Oscar steeled his nerves and threw his voice across the dark hall. It echoed nicely across all of the many mirrors, "I am come to see peace *restored*. Oz, the Great and Terrible, has no need for trinkets. All magic is mine to command."

Ondri-baba paused. She stepped into the room. "Your magic betrays you. You cannot hide in the dark from me—I have the magic eye."

"Your magic eye, what does it see?" Oscar shifted his position.

"I see whatever I want to see. Your magic glows. I have not figured out how you glow so brightly, when the most powerful witches spend their lives carving the magic lines into their bodies. You radiate magic."

"I was born under a favorable star."

"Which one was that?" Ondri-baba asked, curious. This was not going the way she had planned. The Wizard did not back down quickly like the Winkies had done.

"The Water Bearer. Crossing me brings ill tidings for you."

"I will not give up the Golden Cap. It has created peace in this land."

"You conquered the Winkies and you keep the Winged Monkeys in slavery. That is not peace." Oscar's thrown voice bounced around the room.

"It is peace—it is what I say it is. You move around, but your flame glows and reflects in the mirrors. There is no place you can hide."

"You see a flame, but the voice does not come from the flame." Oscar's voice sounded behind Ondri-baba. "Does it? Am I really the burning flame? Or am I invisible? Or have I abandoned my physical body altogether?"

Ondri-baba took a step back and looked around. "It is a trick, Wizard. You can't fool me with your tricks. I hear you behind me. I know you are there." She whirled around and swung her arms out violently, but she found nothing but air.

"Your magic eye is failing you."

"No. It will never fail. It sees horrible things, but it never fails. The things that come at night—the moving things when I sleep. The night brings the monsters."

"The nightmares." Oscar's whispering voice sounded. "The nightmares haunt you. I know that story."

Ondri-baba shook her head. "The Queen of Dreams promised."

Oscar stopped in his tracks. *Who was the Queen of Dreams?* "Is she trustworthy? Can you, a Witch Queen, trust another queen?"

Ondri-baba raged. "Smith and Tinker swore it was all on the table. The Queen wanted to silence the dreaming inside—she wanted to see as she walked among the mortals in Oz. 'An eye for an eye,' they said. They promised me it would give me power."

"You lost your eye to them. Was it worth it? Are the nightmares you see worth the power?" Oscar asked, moving again. He felt along the mirrored walls, but there were no doors that he could find. There were mirrored pillars also. All around, his voice refracted and reflected into dozens of echoes.

"I don't know what nightmares are, Wizard. I only know that I see horrible things when the shadows grow long."

"Yet you keep your castle dark."

"The day is not when the shadows appear—only at night."

"Nightmares are dreams. If you have heard the word—nobody in Oz dreams."

"Except for you."

"Except for me." Oscar agreed. "Let's talk about your dreams."

"That Queen of Dreams will not rule over me. She gave me some of her power to see. She lied to me!"

"The Queen of Dreams cannot enter the Land of Oz, is what I have read. Your eye is not old."

"Two years. Two years without sleep."

"I can understand that." Oscar muttered under his breath.

"They cut out my eye. The lighthouse. The island is not part of Oz." Her voice echoed off the mirrors as she wailed. "They promised me I would see."

"And what do you see?"

"I see fire. I see monsters each night. I see the dark winds that blow from the desert. They sear the clouds and push through the minds of the dreamless sleepers. They stop at me. Do you understand, Wizard—they stop at me because I see!"

"So close your eyes."

"This eye does not close. It watches awake, constantly. I cannot rest. I SEE!"

"To make up for your constant-seeing eye, you make invisible the walls around you? Makes little sense, O Wicked Witch." Oscar maneuvered into position to see the far door. "You, frankly, are misguided. Back in my land, they would say that you were sold a bill of goods. You got snookered, hornswaggled, bamboozled."

"I fail to see what these things mean."

Oscar found the door he was looking for. He worked his hands into the difficult puzzle latch. "What good is a single seeing eye when your magic eye does all the work?"

"This old eye is the one giving me the troubles. After the blood-sand war, it dried up. Now it just rattles around in my skull. I don't usually see straight. The lights are dim. I keep the palace dark because I can't see with that eye anyway. At least with the walls magically invisible, I can find my way through."

"You have a solution for everything. But perhaps I am a step ahead of you." Oscar threw open the door. It was a Winged Monkey. He quickly shut the door.

"You will not find the Golden Cap, Wizard. I have it too well hidden."

"I don't need to find it, Witch. All I need to do is run out of places where it is not."

"Wha-? That doesn't even make sense."

"That is why I am the Wizard, and you are merely a witch. Granted, I understand you conquered two people, keeping them both in slavery, but that didn't really take a lot of magic. You use your magic eye as a crutch. You are old and nearly blind. Where is your magic?"

That did it. Ondri-baba huffed and stomped her feet. "Monkeys!" she shouted. "Step inside."

All around the Wizard the Winged Monkeys stepped in through hidden doors.

"You will not silence me. I will obtain the Golden Cap, and I will free the Winged Monkeys."

"You think you are so smart." Ondri-baba sneered, tossing strands of hair away from her magic eye. "The only thing keeping the Winged Monkeys alive is slavery. Have you not heard their story? They were to be executed. The only thing staying the execution was a willingness to be enslaved. You really think a king that would sell his own people into slavery deserves to be free? He enslaved them to save his sorry silver hide."

That was unexpected. Oscar paused before moving. He did not know much about monkeys, but he remembered that they did not do much in the dark. He sent his hissing snake sound ahead of him, startling several monkeys and launching them into the air. "There must be another reason."

A mirror shattered behind Oscar. A silver fist slowly withdrew from the mirror. A scream of betrayal and anger followed the fist, reflecting on the splintered mirror. King Klick had answered Oscar's question. So it was true—he *did* enslave his people to save himself.

At the far end of the room, another door quietly opened. Kally stepped inside. Her Silver Slippers glowed softly in the darkness. Oscar smiled. Now he had an ally in here. There was still hope.

"You see—or rather, you feel—the monkeys all around you, Wizard. You want to know my magic? You rightly said it is invisibility. The Winkies used this Hall of Mirrors as training for their rulers. The labyrinth was training for the warriors. This was training for their kings. I was told by King Winko himself that a warrior must see what cannot be seen and feel what cannot be felt. The stone labyrinth trained them. I assume you had help getting through. The Hall of Mirrors is much more difficult—the kings-to-be must navigate the constantly shifting maze of mirrors, all the while staring at himself. Tell me, Wizard, can you look past yourself to help these people? They will change the maze. You will be hopelessly lost—trapped by the very people you claim you want to liberate."

One, two, three steps and Kally was at the Wizard's side. She pulled his head close and whispered in his ear. "Do not do this. Come with me now and be free. We can come after the Golden Cap another time."

"Do you understand me, Wizard?"

Oscar stepped away from Kally. She took one, two, three steps and disappeared into the darkness.

Ondri-baba pulled a lever. Gears grated together and stones shifted beneath their feet. Up from the floor rose mirrored walls. Oscar stepped back. He put his hand out on the first mirrored wall that rose up. He pushed on it, and it swiveled. The walls turned. Above him, the Winged Monkeys chattered as they flew about. They must have more light up there, because Oscar could not see much in the middle of the labyrinth.

"A single light, Wizard, to light you in the darkness." Ondri-baba lit a candle and set it on a sconce in the wall. The flickering light reflected through the shifting mirrors. Oscar looked up. The Winged Monkeys were no longer above him.

Oscar pressed on the wall in front of him. It did not swivel. A monkey must be holding it still. He threw out his voice. "Is this what you have, sassafrass?" He held his esses long to hear the hissing whisper echo around the corners.

"Where is the Golden Cap? Find it, if you can."

"I know the Golden Cap is not found in the reflections in the Hall of Mirrors. So it is plainly a ruse to admire my reflection. Not that I blame you, I have been called by some a very—albeit somewhat—handsome man. And what is more," Oscar smiled, "I have an excellent voice."

Omby-Amby mounted the chestnut stallion and held his hand out to Wickrie-Kells. She leaped up behind him. The young Emerald Guardsman, Kopp, handed the magic signals to Wickrie-Kells.

"You point it at the sky and squeeze. The sorceress will see it."

"You have done well, soldier. I am sorry to leave you like this, but we can travel more quickly by horse."

"The exercises are near the gulch." Kopp said.

"I know where they are. Thank you. Dismissed."

"Good luck, soldier." Wickrie-Kells waved as the horse raced toward the distant gulch.

Kopp held his hand up until they were out of sight behind the hills. He smiled. *A job well done.* Then he squared his shoulders and headed home.

28 SISTER FEUD

Oscar's excellent voice bounced and reflected all around the mirrored labyrinth of the kings. Behind him, a dim golden glow escaped from the cracked mirror, fractured by the hand of King Klick.

"What is this *tro-lo-lo* spell you cast, Wizard?" Ondri-baba demanded. The Wizard was not behaving according to the rules—he did not get lost in his reflection, he was not disturbed by the twisting walls, and he was not bothered by the hundreds of reflections that surrounded him in the labyrinth. In short, he made a very good king, but right now he was rapidly becoming an adversary of legendary proportions. "You will not get away from me so easily." She trundled off her stool and entered the mirror maze.

At the far door, Kally looked back. The mirrored walls were constantly shifting. She could feel with her magic the movement of each mirror turned by a gleeful monkey. She stepped into the maze to find Oscar.

"You did not come here alone, Wizard." Ondri-baba accused. "You have an ally nearby. I can feel her presence."

Oscar paused in his graceful dance among the moving mirrors. He let the echoes off the walls die down. He put his fingers to his forehead. The echo-location was helpful, but it took a lot of concentration. And, unfortunately, this much concentration was giving him a monstrous headache. He had no choice, though. He had sworn to free the Winged Monkeys. His voice was all that he had left. But he was so tired.

The Wizard closed his eyes for a few seconds and hid his face in his hands. Behind him in the mirror, his reflection shimmered, and two large shadows stepped out. Behind them, additional shadowy giants stepped into the reflection. Oscar opened his hands and wiped the sweat from his forehead. He shivered, but he did not turn around—he knew what he would see.

Ondri-baba was in the maze. So was Kally. Oscar had to protect Kally. He shook his head and vocalized again, sending his echo-location out to lead him to safe passage through the maze.

Kally felt with her magic as the Wizard started to move. She saw his reflection in the shadows look around. He was looking for *her*.

"Wizard, don't worry about me. Find the object of your desire." Kally called out. The power of the Silver Slippers was useless in the maze of mirrors. Line of sight was only as good as her vision. With reflection upon reflection, it was not safe to use the magic. She was as lost as Ondri-baba in here.

"She is my prisoner, Witch." Oscar declared. "You know who she is, I assume. If you do not give me what I came for, I will carry her away to the clouds, and you will never see her again."

"Yes." Ondri-baba answered. "What has it been, five days? I predict clouds are very much in your future, Wizard."

On the plains beyond the forest, Nikidik stopped his long-legged mechanical interloper. He was now far enough away from Margolotte and from home to conduct one of his more dangerous experiments. This far away from Mount Munch, the experiment would not endanger either his wife or his laboratory. He set up a handkerchief on the ground and set up mirrors on every side of the handkerchief, with the reflective side inward, and the backs of each mirror oriented toward each point of the compass.

Then Nikidik pulled a vial in the shape of a twisted hourglass from his bag. He held it up in the afternoon light to see the dark grains of shadow alternatively flowing up and down in the hourglass. He unscrewed the top of the twisted vial and poured a shadow out onto the center of the handkerchief. The shadow stood—it was small, this one. That was the intention. There was little use conducting an experiment on a full-sized shadow until he knew that the power would work.

This misty entity was one of the shadows brought into reality by the Wizard. Nikidik pulled the Crown of the Dreamer from his bag and placed it on his head. He ensured that the mask was firmly secured in the upright position. The shadow walked toward the edge of the handkerchief. It saw the mirror and backed away. It turned around and saw the other mirror, and then the other two. The tiny wailing pierced the air from the center of the handkerchief.

"Now, little shadow, step into the real world." Nikidik focused his thoughts through the Crown of the Dreamer. The tiny wail gained stronger hold on the air, creating an echo. The shadow shuddered and writhed as the mists solidified and became real. Then it was still.

The shadow looked at the mirror and leaped at it, attacking its reflection. No longer was it repulsed by the strange energy flowing back to it—the solid shadow saw its reflection as an aggressive adversary, and it leaped to battle.

"Excellent. The pearls made it solid. I have given life to the unlived. I have made a shade into a beast. Gayelette, I have beaten you. I am the true sorcerer in Oz." Then he slammed his open hand down on the tiny shade beast, smashing it into its component grains of shade. For good measure, Nikidik ground the thing to powder beneath his heel.

"I have the power to give life. I take it away. How long, Gayelette, did I labor? Thirty years? How long did you labor? Three hundred? I won. You spent your life laboring for the one thing you could never achieve, only to be destroyed at the hand of a two-bit witch. Now the name of Nikidik will be forever associated with power, bringing the dead to life, and giving life to those that had none. You are dead, and I will live forever."

In the maze of mirrors, Oscar took a deep breath to steady his nerves. It was time to play his one final card. "I have your daughter here. She's in the castle." Oscar declared.

Ondri-baba stopped short. *Could it be? After all these years, that someone—even a young Wizard such as this—had discovered her secret?* "I don't believe you." Ondri-baba challenged. But her voice caught. She was not confident. This single faltering note was not lost on the Wizard.

"She is here with me."

"Prove it. You have nothing, Wizard. Just a pretender, full of tricks."

"The witch that accompanied me is your daughter."

"My daughter?" Ondri-baba laughed. She snorted in surprise. "You think...you think that she is my daughter?"

Oscar paled. A cold sweat broke out on his forehead. "I did."

"I'll tell you who she is. I suppose she's lied to you about everything. She probably brought you here under false pretenses. One of her schemes, no doubt. What was it? Gain power over the entire land, one Witch at a time?"

"If I controlled the power, then the land could be at peace." Oscar admitted.

"Oh, I see." Ondri-baba sneered. "And who controls you?"

Oscar glared into the darkness. There was no sign of the Witch's glowing green eye. She had done something clever at last. "No one controls me. I control my own fate—my own destiny."

"We are all stringed-up, Wizard. There is always someone that pulls the strings. The key is knowing what powers come with which strings. Take your little Witch friend, for example. You claim that she is my daughter. She is not. She is my—*oof!*" Ondri-baba fell forward onto her face on the ground near Oscar.

Kally's voice sounded out of the nearby darkness. "Lies. All lies. Do not believe her, Wizard. I will teach her a history written in stone. I have just the magic powder to freeze you forever, Ondri-baba."

"You don't have the strength to best me!" Ondri-baba growled, rising to her feet. "I'll—grunnkh." She pitched forward as Oscar threw his shoulder into the Witch, dropping her to the floor.

At the same instant, Kally threw the Powder of Petrefaction at Ondri-baba's location, only now she wasn't there. Yet the Powder of Petrefaction fulfilled the purpose of its creation as Ondri-baba's mortal eye, shriveled and sunken, flew from its socket into the magic cloud of petrefaction. It hit the ground and rolled like a marble.

Ondri-baba screamed, "My eye! My eye! *You*...actually that's a lot better. I don't have to worry about the double-vision any more. I see both of you and the magic you embody. The dark is all around, but I don't see it any more. It certainly must be a pity to be you who cannot hide in the dark—especially you, Wizard. The magic flows around you brighter than anyone I have seen since the Queen of Dreams."

Sweat dripped down Oscar's face. He could no longer hide. When he tried to help Kally, he only made things worse. This war he started with Kally's urging had just slipped out of his fingers. War. Again. It followed him. Why could he never escape its bloody clutches? Why did these pangs always growl hungrily after him? What could he do?

The Wizard's feet slipped out from beneath him and he fell to a seated position against the wall. Goose-pimples prickled his skin as he felt them step out of the wall behind him—the giants were back, and this time they brought their friends. Burning tears stung Oscar's eyes as he felt their accusing whispers against him.

Ondri-baba gasped in horror. "What are those *things*? Wizard, what have you done? Where did you go? *Wizard!*" the Witch scrambled backwards, pushing open a mirrored door into a room that Oscar had not seen before. Dim golden light glowed out of the open doorway, silhouetting the witch.

Kally picked up the stone eyeball and put it in her pocket. "I'd prefer eye of newt, but this might become useful someday." But nobody heard her.

Ondri-baba's ornaments clanked and clattered on her as she hurried through the doorway into the hallway behind the mirrored chamber.

Oscar followed after Ondri-baba into the mirrored hallway. At the end of the hallway, a soft golden glow radiated just out of sight.

He could not catch up to her, and he could not stop her, so he might as well try to scare her. Oscar took a deep breath, leaned his head back, and let his voice peal.

Behind him, all of the Winged Monkeys froze and looked toward the sound. Then they all went crazy, shouting, "Banana! Banana!"

Ondri-baba jumped, but she still trundled quickly forward. Oscar stumbled down the corridor after the loudly clanking witch. They rounded a corner. To the right and up ahead was the cracked and broken mirror. The dim light from the Hall of Mirrors shone through the cracked mirror, casting prism'd rainbows on the floor and walls.

On the other side of the wall, the monkeys chattered and flew around the dimly-lit room. Some of them twirled the mirrors around. King Klick shoved mirrors aside, searching for the Wizard. Oscar glanced briefly through one of the mirrors—he could see through the back of it into the Hall of Mirrors. Yet the mirror opposite him did not show his reflection. What strange technology was this that could let him see through back side the mirror?

Ondri-baba gasped for breath as she approached the alcove. In the center of the alcove, the Golden Cap rested on a pedestal. She waved her hand and turned the pedestal invisible.

Oscar slowed down and approached slowly. He had only seen a little bit, but there were some sharp corners on that pedestal and he didn't want to injure himself so close to his goal. The Golden Cap was unaffected by the invisibility. It glowed in mid-air, about ten feet above their heads.

"Here it is, the great treasure that drove the great wizard to war." Ondri-baba slowly spoke, catching her breath. "So close, yet just out of reach."

"Freedom is not a cheap prize to be won and put on a shelf. It is a duty and a constant responsibility."

"Do you ever give up?" Ondri-baba wheezed. "Really? You are like a one-trick asparagus. Is freedom all you've got?"

"If you understood what you were asking, you would never ask if freedom is *all*...freedom is *everything*. And no, I don't give up. Not when another depends on me. Never." Oscar replied. He studied the shadows on the floor. The pedestal was three levels. There were sharp corners, and there were probably stairs, but the Witch was in the way. This confrontation must be handled very carefully.

"Like the Silver-furred freak depends on you. I told you, Wizard, he sold his people to save his skin."

"That is not the fault of his people."

"Do you think they chose him to be king? Or did he just assume the throne? Where is the justice in that?"

"Says the Witch who conquered a people by guile. You have no ground to stand on. You are a hypocrite and a tyrant. Your life will melt away like the snows in winter. These people will not long tolerate your tyranny."

Ondri-baba laughed. She actually laughed. "They will tolerate. They always do. Humans have adapted a remarkable capacity to tolerate tyrants. Your world may be different, Wizard, but here in Oz, that is all we have—tyrant after tyrant."

"*Eternal enmity against tyrants.* Thomas Jefferson swore to fight against tyranny in all of its forms. That is a battle worth waging."

"You will lose."

"Perhaps I will. But someone will come after me. And then someone will come after them. And so on and so on, until freedom rings in the hearts of every surviving person. There will be freedom, and there will be peace."

"No. There will war. There will be tears. There will be some blood. And there will be submission. When no one raises their head against my hand, then—and only then—will there be peace."

Oscar stepped toward the invisible pedestal. He had a good idea where the stairs were. He was faster than the Witch. He could get there first.

"It is there waiting, Wizard. Once you get it, what are you going to do? Are you going to free them? It is not so easy."

Oscar jumped onto the pedestal and scrambled over the pointed corners, and clambered to the top. Ondri-baba swiped her hands after him. Atop the pedestal, Oscar grasped the Golden Cap and shouted in triumph. "I have it. I have the Golden Cap."

His voice echoed in the alcove, but little escaped into the Hall of Mirrors.

Ondri-baba forced a wide smile. "Your shadows, Wizard, where are they? I see them with you. They are not interested in *my* monkeys—or shall I say, *your* monkeys—anymore. You've stolen something from them. I hear their whispers. Do you hear them?"

Yes. Oscar did hear them. In the moment of exultation, he blocked them out, but there they were again, as insidious as ever. They wanted their inheritance. He didn't have it—not anymore. He had the Golden Cap. That was power, but that would not bring them back. Nothing could bring his brothers back, no matter how hard he wished.

The Golden Cap glowed in his hands. The shadows stepped through the mirrors and looked eye to eye at Oscar. The mists curled around them and solidified. "Ossss-currrrr." The shadow giants said.

Oscar's head shook slowly back and forth. "You are not real. You are dead."

Ondri-baba watched the Wizard closely. The magic still burned around him, but tendrils of shadow were penetrating the light. She forced her voice to sound piteous, "This is the power of the Golden Cap, Wizard. You have made your...*nightmares*...real. They haunt you now. This is the responsibility of the Golden Cap. Are the Winged Monkeys and their devious silver king worth this fear?"

Oscar stepped backwards. His heel hit the edge of the pedestal and he tottered for balance. He reached out and grabbed the top of the pedestal. He clutched the invisible pillar with one hand and the Golden Cap in the other. His eyes never left the shadow giants, now solid in front of him. His nightmares had come to life.

"This is the Golden Cap." He clutched it tighter, as if the physical sensation of feeling it in his fingers would give him the power to banish his past.

"Power, responsibility, vigilance, fear, nightmare—they are all tied up in a neat little bow on top of the Golden Cap. It is yours. Free the traitor. Free the entire traitorous tribe. They will not live long. They betrayed the Winkies. I do not think that that the Winkies will be so forgiving of betrayal as I would be. Blood for blood, I assume. Free them, and they will die."

"What a people does with freedom is their destiny." Oscar forced the words out through clenched teeth. His eyes were wide in terror. They flashed back and forth between the giants.

"Oh, Wizard, how right you are. And what will you do with *your* freedom? You have the Golden Cap, and all power is yours. What will you do with this freedom? You have brought liberty to the Winged Monkeys and life to your dreams. They are yours. They will go with the possessor of the Golden Cap."

Oscar's fingers loosened on the cap. Ondri-baba noticed and pushed her advantage. "It is only one tribe. Their blood is not so precious. They are not so important. No one will even remember them. You may as well forget them right now. Wouldn't that be easier?"

"No." Oscar whispered. "No more tears." A single teardrop rolled down Oscar's cheek. His fingers let go of the Golden Cap. It fell to the invisible pedestal and slowly tumbled toward the floor.

Ondri-baba's magic eye followed it. Her smile grew wider as the Golden Cap fell to the floor. It sat there for two infinitely long seconds. Then she turned to look up at Oscar. His head dropped in defeat.

"You have won, Wizard. You are the hero. You have achieved the greatest success any politician can hope to achieve—that nothing changes. You have saved a tribe of inhuman monkeys from death, and at the same time doomed them to slavery. You have sacrificed yourself to bring your dreams into this reality. They are flesh. They know you, and they will destroy you." She smiled wickedly. "There is no escape now, Wizard. You have failed. Whatever it means to you—right here, right now, Wizard—your dreams die with you."

"Freedom always finds a way." Oscar stumbled down the invisible stairs and jumped through the cracked mirror, shielding his face with his arms. He rolled on the ground and scrambled to his feet. The shadow giants pushed through the broken glass and surrounded him. They formed a guard against the magic of the Witch. That was small comfort, as Oscar had to now navigate the mirror maze filled with Winged Monkeys.

"Wizard! Follow my voice!" Kally called from far away. She threw out her hands toward the maze and all of the mirrors turned parallel to each other, opening up a path for Oscar to run.

Oscar ran. He grabbed Kally's hand as he reached the door. His momentum threw him into the far wall, where he hit his shoulder and spun.

Kally ran ahead of him, dragging him behind. She was a fast runner. Then she let go of his hand. The sound of glass shattering reached Oscar's ears, chilling him even further. His heart was cold within his chest. He knew the shadow giants were angry. It sounded like they were destroying everything back there. They would come after him. All was lost.

"Keep running. I'll lead them away." Kally's voice faded as Oscar ran deeper into the castle.

Omby-Amby and Wickrie-Kells arrived at the training camp. The Soldier with Green Whiskers immediately called his troops. "Status, Guardsmen. Is the border secure?"

"Aye, Sir. Nothing has crossed in our sight. There is a commotion toward the Yellow Castle, but it is beyond our sight." The head Emerald Guardsman, Toro Plantain said. His voice was crisp and certain. Toro had light green hair, not quite as dark as Omby-Amby's, but he kept it cropped short.

"Any sign of the Wizard, or of any Witches?"

Toro shook his head. "We have seen nothing."

"Do we have any scopes? I want to see the castle."

"No scopes, Sir. We have single glasses."

"Bring them. We'll improvise."

While Omby-Amby gathered the lenses and fashioned a telescope, Wickrie-Kells met with her Fighting Girls. It had only been a few days, but much had happened. She embraced each one and pulled them away from the males in the group.

"Gather close, girls. Glinda lost the Wizard. Some of you were at the Sky Wizard's Ball—you know the mess they made. It turns out the Wizard is lost. Glinda is looking for him. I've got some magic here that will signal Glinda when we find him. And *we* will find him. These boys aren't going to be the heroes today. They'll see that it is Glinda's Fighting Girls that are the best in the Land of Oz." The girls cheered. But Wickrie-Kells wasn't done. "I've seen the Emerald Guardsmen—I fancy one myself. But let us have an agreement here and now. None of us will bat an eye or blow a kiss to any of these fine gentlemen until the Wizard is found and he is back where he belong—with Glinda. We will not love until Glinda loves."

Wickrie-Kells sauntered back to Omby-Amby. He glanced over at her sly smile. "You look proud. What did you do?"

Wickrie-Kells smiled. "I'm just happy to be back with my girls. We are looking forward to finding the Wizard before you or any of your boys."

"Good. Competition never hurt anybody." Omby-Amby lifted the telescope to his eye and looked out toward the distant castle. "There is something out there in Winkie Fields. It looks like metal soldiers." He turned to the girl. "Do any armies have metal soldiers? I don't know of any."

"Not that I have seen. Glinda showed me some broken things in the scrapyard once. They looked like a person, but they were made out of metal. They weren't alive. Those are the only ones I've seen." Wickrie-Kells reached out to touch the soldier's arm, but then she remembered her promise to the Fighting Girls. She pulled her hand away without touching him.

"These ones are broken. It looks like they were fighting with the Winkie Guards; maybe with the monkeys. They are scattered. No sign of the Wizard. That is strange, though, so I am going to believe that Oscar is somewhere down there."

"Girls, spread out—three groups of five—along the gulch. Fan out and keep your eyes open for the Wizard. Remember, eyes for the Wizard before anyone else." The girls spread out along the length of the gulch, watching and searching for any activity in the direction of the Yellow Castle.

"Guardsmen, follow suit. Remember—nobody crosses the border. We don't want a war triggered by our calisthenics." The Emerald Guardsmen spread out, each one following after a particular Fighting Girl. Each one was told in no uncertain terms that the Wizard was more important today than anything else. Thirty-two pairs of eyes searched across the miles of the West for anything that resembled trouble.

Omby-Amby and Wickrie-Kells stood on the hill above the training camp. "When one of the Guardsmen gives the word, we'll send up the signal for Glinda."

"What do you mean *one of the Guardsmen?* It's going to be one of my Fighting Girls."

Omby-Amby raised the telescope to his eye again and scanned the valley. "We shall see."

"It's that girl. You know that. She is the one behind all of this."

"Most likely. But it's not just the girl I worry about—though you would think that is quite enough. Oscar's dreams have been getting more hazardous. The architects wear harnesses now when they watch at night. A bridge went out. We found the poor fellow hanging by a gargoyle on the wall forty feet above the ground. So if Oscar's dreams are getting more powerful, and he is with a pretty girl, I think that is cause for worry."

"There are prettier girls than that one—me, for example; Ola Griffin; Rala; Corabinth; LeeAnya; and we can't forget Glinda."

Omby-Amby knew better than to answer to any of those other names. "I'll accept your first example, but that's all. Glinda is a friend. The other girls—I trust you know them well enough to decide for me." He glanced over and met Wickrie-Kells' playful glare. "I know you, Wickrie—testing me. But this telescope is watching for the Wizard. I already have you saying yes."

"Yes, but not yet. *After* the Wizard."

"After the Wizard. I'm worry about him. He has a fondness for pretty faces. He can never say no. I fear it will get him into trouble."

29 TREASURE AND REFUSE

The afternoon sun shone down on the southern country and glistened on the piles of discarded experiments in the scrapyard near Chronometria. Promethus followed the haunting strains of golden song through the piles of scrap. He paused behind a stack of empty picture frames, watching Ola Griffin as she stepped slowly around the mirrored platter she had set on the ground.

> *Lost in the absence of doubt,*
> *I know there's no easy way out.*
> *Outside of this life,*
> *Romance like a knife,*
> *You are now only mine through a spectacle.*

She finished her song and stared down into the reflected blue expanse.

"That is a very sad song." Promethus said.

"I am a very sad vessel." Ola Griffin responded. She picked up the platter and folded her arms across it on her chest. "Did you want something?"

"Yes. I wanted to talk to you."

"Glinda sent me out here. I'm supposed to guard. I'm not supposed to talk to anybody—especially men. Glinda doesn't want me turning any more heads away from her."

"It's that clear to you, then?"

"Isn't it to you? Here, let me explain, because you're new here. There are three groups of girls here. There are the groundskeepers and servants who mostly stay out of the way. Then there are the Smile and Thinkers—this is Smith & Tinker's old castle. It's a play on..." The girl continued as she saw that Promethus grasped the humor. "The Smile and Thinkers are Glinda's Brain Trust. They do with brains what the Fighting Girls do with swords.

Then there is Glinda's inner circle. Nobody gets to the inner circle without going through all of the obstacles first…unless there is a weak link. You got through twice. I'm the weak link."

"I should think that an exception should be made for me. I am a very knowledgeable and powerful person, prone to finding ways to get through just about anything. That's why I'm the Guardian."

"So knowledgeable are you then? Just how many of Glinda's Fighting Girls do you know?"

Promethus knitted his eyebrows and counted on his fingers. His silence was deafening. The whole time he fiddled with his fingertips, Ola watched him and nodded self-righteously. Promethus looked up and met her knowing gaze.

"Let me guess—Glinda is one, Wickrie-Kells is two—"

"I haven't met her."

"Consider yourself introduced by proxy. She's Glinda's right hand, the Captain of the Fighting Girls. And me, Ola Griffin, makes three. Is there anyone else I might have missed?"

Promethus smiled sheepishly. He half shrugged, surrendering any sort of witty reply.

Ola Griffin sighed. She tossed her head and flipped her blonde hair out of her face. "I apologize. My temper is a bit out of sorts since I've been out here."

"For what it's worth, I am going to speak with Glinda about this punishment. It is not commensurate with your supposed crime, especially for someone of your…" He paused, seeing her curious eyes studying him.

"My…what? Beauty?"

"Talent." Promethus declared. "Your voice should not be spent out here, singing sad songs."

"Forty-six, as of last week."

"Forty-six sad songs?"

"Forty-six Fighting Girls. We received a new recruit from Emerald City last week. There was an issue with the Emerald Guardsmen. She distracted one of them. To keep the team solid, Captain Ombrosius sent her down here to join us. Her name is Cornyss Waters. She's the oldest of five girls. Her father is an important councilman facilitating the architecture study committee."

"Bureaucrat." Promethus muttered.

"She wears her hair in three braids, tied together in the back. She is good with a bow, but she prefers the spear. Her preference is the one with the fishhook carved in the base—it has a ring at the base to tie a rope around it. This week she has read two books—"

"I get the point. As I said, you have talent."

"I have a good memory. I'm almost as good as Glinda. That's why she chose me to be her herald."

"Not for your voice?"

"You can find many girls with good voices. We have some amazing singers among the Fighting Girls. The best and brightest are coming here. It really is an amazing thing to see. Among those, I *hold...held* a certain position of esteem." She forced a sad, resigned smile. "I knew everyone that came through that door. You were the second stranger that day. I didn't know the golden-eyed girl. She just appeared. Then she was gone before I could get her name."

"What girl?"

"She had golden eyes—a little bit lighter color of amber than Wickrie-Kells, but you don't know her yet." Ola Griffin set the platter back on a pile of scrap. There is nothing for me to do out here. I am bored. I could be in there, reading, studying, doing what I am good at, but I'm stuck out here by sorceress decree."

Promethus awkwardly changed the subject. "Glinda told you about the three apprentices of Smith & Tinker?"

Ola Griffin nodded. Her hair fell into her face again, and she brushed it back behind her ear. "I remember everything. When they come for their inheritance, let them into whatever part of the estate they request, and let them out with what they can carry. Notify Glinda and keep an inventory of the good silver."

Promethus shot her a quizzical look.

"Okay, I added that last part. I got you, though." She laughed—a clear, joyful sound. "Oh, that's the first time I've laughed since the Winged Monkey was loose in the ballroom. Thank you."

"For what?"

"Being such a stick-tighty that I could make a joke on you."

Promethus chewed on his reply and then thought better of it. *No; best to let pretty girls smile.* "Certainly." He turned to walk away. He stopped when he heard the girl start to hum a new tune. "I know that tune—*Odyssey of Wrenwraith*. Oh, the monsters that man faced...I'd like to hear your version of the *Dance in the Desert Fjords*, if you are willing."

Ola Griffin curtseyed. "I would be glad of the company."

"And when you finish the song, perhaps you could demonstrate just how finely tuned a memory you have. I don't know that I quite believe—"

"Is that a challenge?" Ola smiled.

"Well, I believe it is." Promethus seemed surprised by his own words. "Consider it so. I do need to be back to the castle to watch for Glinda."

"Climb up this pile here. I stacked the frames so you can step on them and see the road south. Just don't fall into the frames. They go different places—just one way, though. Some of them are cold." She shivered. "But I put those ones down deep. You can climb up and sit there. That way you can see the road and you can see me."

"Lass, I'm older than your parents."

"You issued a challenge. I want to be looking right here," she pointed her two fingers at her eyes, "so I can prove just how finely tuned this pretty little head can be."

Ola Griffin sang the *Odyssey of Wrenwraith*. The song told of the man who tried to heal the seas, but became angry with the faeries when the wind whispered their deeds. He was both blessed and cursed by the faeries to fly as a wren on the winds during the daylight hours and to walk as a shade on the cliffs overlooking the desert at night. Ever he sought his true love, but never could they meet, for she had joined the sand of the Deadly Desert below.

The winsome song left an emptiness more powerful than the voice of the dragon by the Emerald Sea. The odyssey was only half of the story. As with all ballads of this type there was adventure, but the rest of the story was painfully tragic. Ola Griffin scarcely completed the *Odyssey of Wrenwraith*, when she slowed her voice to a whisper and began her melancholy version of the *Dance in the Desert Fjords*.

The song told of how the poor girl joined the tribe of sand men in the desert in return for her love's safe passage home. But he was beyond their power. The shade walked high above on the forbidden silent cliffs. The bird flew down into the shadows of the fjords and saw the strange writing by the solitary sand-girl. Every day they would dance for the last few minutes of sunlight—the bird who would not remember and the girl made of sand who had nothing but time.

Ola's perfect voice tugged on the older man's heartstrings. He cleared his throat a number of times as he sat on top of the scrap pile. After the song concluded, Promethus leaned back and laid his head back on his arm. He closed his eyes and stared back into his memory. He was silent for more than a minute.

"Are you dead? Did your poor heart break within you?" Ola asked, looking up at his unmoving body.

Promethus was slow to answer. "I'm not dead—just pining for the fjords."

"Did you like it?"

"Aye, Lass. You have a gift." He sat up and breathed in deeply. "Your voice is easily among the three best I've heard. I group you with the finest voices in Oz."

"Thank you, kind Sir. I count it a rare privilege to be complimented by someone of your great…venerability."

"Someone of my great age, you mean. Wisdom is a virtue."

"*Not wholly reserved to the old.* You know who said that? Solomon Sessefress, a poet who lived in the reign of King Oz the Sixth. *'Wisdom is a virtue not wholly reserved to the old, but found sometimes unawares, like flowers in the causeway.'* It was in his poem, *Song of Smaragaid Cathair.*" She smiled proudly at her knowledge.

"*City of Emeralds*, in the old tongue—original Ozzian. But that's quite enough stalling from you, young lady. *Forty-three*, you say?"

"*Forty-six.*"

In the Yellow Castle, Oscar ran as fast as his legs could carry him. Kally was somewhere nearby—he heard her shouting once—but it was difficult to hear with the monstrous flapping of wings echoing through all the corridors. The chattering laughter of the monkeys as they raced along the walls was all the more infuriating because they enjoyed chasing him. Why wouldn't they just capture him and be done with it? Half of Oscar's panicked brain wanted him to stop running and just give up. Unfortunately, that part wasn't in direct communication with either of his feet. They just kept running.

In the ballroom, the hooting and laughter resounded even harsher. The monkeys were driving him to a certain destination, Oscar could feel that. Whenever he tried to deviate to the right or left, they swooped in and pinched him. The panic nearly drove him to rage at the darkness. He clenched his fists to strike out at the next hand that approached him.

He felt something on his elbow and tensed to swing, but he was jerked off his feet as Kally appeared next to him and stepped one, two, three times and slipped them through the door of the ballroom. She magically slammed the door shut behind them. She raised her eyebrows excitedly at Oscar. "Some fun, yes?"

"No."

They looked around. There wasn't much left in the way of escape routes. The large hearth rested in the corner. Kally pulled Oscar's elbow, and then pulled him into a twirling waltz. They danced and whirled their way across the empty ballroom. Behind them, the monkeys screamed and pounded on the door. Monkeys pounded on the windows at the far side of the room.

The room whirled around Oscar as they danced to their uncertain demise. "We are trapped. We can give ourselves up. I'm the Wizard. I can protect you. I can negotiate a truce—a cease-fire between me and Ondri-baba. You don't have to live this life. I'm sorry that I pulled you into this. It was never my intention to drive you to darkness like this." Oscar sighed deeply and looked back at the shaking doors, trembling under the barrage of monkey fists.

Kally laughed, "This is not darkness. I have not had so much fun in years. She is such a wart. I don't know why I ever let her do anything. She is completely and absolutely devoid of fun—no imagination at all."

Oscar stopped and stepped away from the dancing girl. He stared Kally squarely in the face. "We are trapped! You need to understand that. I am the Wizard. Only I can get us out of this."

"Wrong. You are the Wizard, but you are not the only one with plans. Here, into the hearth." The tone of her voice gave Oscar a glimmer of confidence in the gloom presently chilling his bones. He obeyed without question.

Oscar ducked under the mantle and stepped into the cold hearth. Kally pointed up.

"Up?" Oscar asked, his frown racing his worried eyebrows around his face.

Kally nodded, her amber eyes dancing with excitement. "Up and out."

In the darkness a faint silver marking glowed on Kally's forehead.

The doors cracked and splintered behind them. Oscar climbed. Kally cheered him on from below. The flood of monkeys pressed around Kally as they passed by her and up into the chimney. The chattering simians swelled the narrow space with their long arms and beating wings. They would catch the Wizard and trap him in the narrow place.

Not to be outdone, the monkeys at the windows disappeared into the sky to cut off the Wizard from his escape.

Kally looked up the hearth to the distant point of light far up at the top of the chimney. It was hard to see among all the writhing shadows in there. She could feel Oscar's panicked climb, even feel the pounding of his heart as he reached for the next hand-hold. He would not last much longer. The climbing monkeys were almost upon him. There was only one thing to do.

Oscar would hate her for this—he definitely would—but she was used to being hated. "Close your eyes, Wizard! Up and out!" she called, thrusting her hands upward, catching both Oscar and the monkeys in her magic and propelling the entire bunch upward with her force of magic. Faster and faster Oscar shot through the chimney. His scream was lost behind him. He ran out of breath just as he burst into the sky. It was just as well, because the waiting Winged Monkeys completely missed him as he shot right by. Up and up and up even further Oscar went into the sky.

Oscar kept his eyes pointed upward. He could handle the sky. It was actually a rather beautiful blue up this high. How high was he? It didn't matter, he was still moving upward. Maybe there was a safe place on the moon that he could sit and wait and put his feet up and relax. That would be very nice—to have a comfortable chair on the moon, to curl up and have a nap. That is exactly what Oscar needed right now. He needed to slow down and relax.

Slowing down is exactly what happened—Oscar ran out of upward momentum. He felt himself stop high in the sky. For an instant he was the sky wizard, up above the entire world. The magnificent feeling of power surpassed any other that he had felt. He was up over the entire world. He felt powerful. Then, in another instant, the moment of omnipotence was gone, and he felt very much like Oscar again. Oscar didn't *fly* very well, but he had *falling* down to a science. And so he fell.

His scream trailed behind him. *Oh, that's how high he was.* The world was a very small place from way up here. The Yellow Castle looked very nice—he could hold it between his thumb and forefinger. The Winged Monkeys were tiny dots, but they were getting larger by the second. Oscar's eyes widened and he flailed his arms, but it was no use—he still could not fly.

The Winged Monkeys grabbed him and raced him around the sky, tossing him screaming from monkey to monkey.

In the Yellow Castle below, Ondri-baba placed the Golden Cap on her head and recited the incantation.

Standing on her left foot, she said slowly, *"Ep-pe, pep-pe, kak-ke!"*

Then she stood on her right foot and said, *"Hil-lo, hol-lo, hel-lo!"*

Then she stood on both feet and cried in a loud voice, *"Ziz-zy, zuz-zy, zik!"*

The Winged Monkeys stopped their screaming and chattering and turned where they were in the castle to face toward the possessor of the Golden Cap. King Klick, scarred and twisted from the transforming flame two years earlier stepped in front of the Witch of the West.

"This is the second time you have used the Golden Cap to summon us. What is your bidding?"

"Drive the Wizard and his armies from the lands of the West!"

30 EYE IN THE SKY

On the hilltop, Omby-Amby looked through the telescope. Smoke billowed up from the upper windows of the Yellow Castle. He squinted and adjusted the telescope. No, it was not behaving like smoke. It was acting like birds. Monkeys. It had to be the Winged Monkeys.

And there, up in the air, the Winged Monkeys were flying up high after something. If Omby-Amby knew anything, it was that the Winged Monkeys would not act without direction. If they were flocking out of the castle, then they were ordered to do so. There could be only one reason that the Wicked Witch would order the Winged Monkeys—the Wizard.

"He's out there, Wickrie. We have to save him."

"We can't cross the border." Wickrie-Kells protested. "This is not our war. Glinda forbade anyone to cross into other lands, remember the ballroom?"

"I was kicked out, remember?"

"If the monkeys catch him, they will kill him, or worse. I don't want to see the dreams the Wizard makes when he is terrified."

Omby-Amby leaped onto the chestnut stallion. "No they won't. We will be there to protect him."

Wickrie-Kells followed after him on another horse. They raced toward the border of the lands. Like or not, the Wizard was over there. The orders were to protect the Wizard at all costs. And they would. Omby-Amby urged the horse to greater speeds. He would be there when Oscar needed him. He had promised his friend that, and he would fulfill—he was a man of his word.

The Winged Monkeys flooded out of the Yellow Castle and streamed into the sky. Those within the sound of the Witch's voice had their orders. Those who had not heard would shortly be given their orders. Smaller monkeys scurried to the window and opened it wide. The once-majestic silver-furred King Klick, galloped across the floor and hurled his scarred body out the open window into the sky.

Below the monkeys, on the Winkie Plains, the remnants of the automaton army pulled themselves toward the Winkie guardsmen. At the sound of angry wingbeats above, the Winkies retreated to the safety of the castle. This battle was out of their hands.

Inside the palace, farewells were said and old wounds were broken open once again. Ondri-baba glared at her sister through her single magic eye. The other empty eye socket collapsed into a grimace of its own. "You did this." She accused.

"Yes. I had fun. We'll have to do this again sometime soon. One monkey wish left, sister."

"You cannot come into my land and insult me and just walk out! You may have the Silver Slippers, but I control the exits." She cast a blanket of invisibility over the entire wall, rendering it transparent. "Where will your precious slippers take you now? Where is the window? Do you magic little shoes walk through walls? I didn't think so."

Kally took one, two, three quick steps and she was at the transparent wall. She reached out and felt it with her hands. She idly glanced down to see the automaton army being torn apart by the Winged Monkeys. She glanced up in the sky to see the screaming Wizard doing sky acrobatics between monkeys. Kally smiled and looked back at Ondri-baba's smirking face. "You look so old. I remember so long ago you had pretty green eyes. What happened to them?"

"You know what happened. The Wizard isn't the first young man in my grasp that you have thrown into the sky."

Kally laughed out loud. "You're not still mad about what's-his-name, are you? That was a hundred years ago."

"It was forty-three years ago, and you never wanted him. He wanted you, but you would not even lower your eyes to look at him—he was beneath you. He was wonderful. But you couldn't bear to see me happy where you so obviously failed. You threw him into the sky to get rid of him."

"And—?"

"He died."

Kally cocked her head. "Sad story. Those always tug the heartstrings the hardest." She touched her heart. "I think you broke that day."

"No. *He* broke. I got angry. Do you remember? Do you remember the hailstorm that Sonadia cast over you? You were trapped in that cage I made invisible. So many things going on around you that you couldn't tell where the bars of the cage were. So much for your rock-tossing powers extraordinaire."

Kally nodded in agreement and patted her hand on the invisible stone wall. "See…that's the thing about rock-tossing—I'm good at tossing rocks."

Kally pushed her hand against the invisible wall and the magic exploded out from her, decimating the entire invisible wall.

Ondri-baba's smirk fell right off her face.

"This has been fun, but I really have to run. I've got a Wizard to catch." One, two, three steps and Kally was gone.

Ondri-baba stood a long time on the ruined wall, watching her sister dart around the field with the Silver Slippers. Just one wish is all it would take to be rid of her. But then the Golden Cap would be useless to her.

Far away, on the valley floor, Kally watched as King Klick winged rapidly toward the screaming Wizard. Kally had heard the orders. She had seen the look in the silver monkey's eyes. Driving the Wizard out was not an option—he meant to kill him. Kally reached out with her magic. It was a very long reach. He was at the edge of her range. Actually, she didn't know that she could reach this far. She nudged him to the right. Okay, that was good. But she needed to be closer. She stepped three times and she was directly under the Wizard. There, much better. She could feel him like a warm wind against her hands. He enjoyed acting, or so he said, *let's give that golden voice another workout*.

Kally yanked the Wizard down out of the sky, just as the monkeys were about to grab him again. He plummeted toward the earth. The monkeys dove after him, folding their wings tightly against their bodies to go faster. As fast as they dove, Kally pulled the Wizard still faster. She threw him through the sky toward the distant border. *This was fun*. And there was his scream.

One, two, three steps, and she was underneath him again. Another hop and they would be temporarily out of reach of the Winged Monkeys. She pulled him on a trajectory closer to the ground. Three steps and she was beneath the screaming wizard as he hurtled toward certain doom. Three, two, one. Kally grabbed Oscar's hand just before he hit the ground. Her feet were already on step three. The Silver Slippers blinked them away.

Kally kept Oscar afloat for six more hops all around the Winkie Plains before letting him down to the ground. As he fell to the ground, he dragged her down with him. They tumbled, his remaining momentum spinning them head over heels onto the ground.

Kally wound up on top of the gasping Wizard. She smiled and touched him on the nose. "I told you I would get us out."

"You call that an escape plan?" Oscar gasped. His eyes shot back toward the distant Yellow Castle, where the circling Winged Monkeys searched for the escaped fugitives.

"I call it a marvelous performance."

Oscar alternately gasped and laughed. He squeezed the tears away from his windblown eyes and wiped his thumb and forefinger on his trousers.

"Step with me three times. Exhale on the third step." Kally took Oscar's hand. "One, two, three." Oscar's hand clutched tightly to Kally's as they repeated their magical leaps toward the border of the land.

Suddenly Kally stopped, and Oscar stumbled into a bush. He grumbled as he pulled the stickers from his sleeves.

"The border shouldn't be far now."

"It's not. Not far at all." Kally responded, glancing back toward Yellow Castle.

"I know the gulch is wide, but we can make it before they see us. We have to hurry. The dots are getting bigger." Oscar pulled Kally toward the East.

Kally resisted. "I need to go back. She has magic…that can help us. If the Wicked Witch loses some of her power, she will not be able to hurt people. I need to try to stop her, at least for your sake. You have been so *transparent* this whole time. I feel like I have been looking right through you. I owe you this."

Oscar leaned in to kiss Kally.

The young-looking witch turned her face away. "Please don't. Kisses are for good-byes and I-do's, and this is neither. I *will* see you again." She stepped away, but Oscar held her hand. He squeezed it.

"Be careful." Oscar's fingers squeezed again, but Kally's smaller hand slipped away as she took one, two, three steps, and she was gone.

On the rising wind, Oscar heard the screech of the Winged Monkeys. He looked at the shimmering in the sky—it was alternatively real and not. That was in the direction that he needed to go. Maybe that was a sign to him to get moving. Maybe it was his overactive imagination. He wasn't sure if he could trust his eyes anymore. He was so tired.

In any case, if the Winged Monkeys found him, there is no telling what they would do. A shiver passed through Oscar's entire body. He took one step backwards, away from Yellow Castle.

Oscar turned toward the setting sun and the distant border of the lands of the West, and he ran.

On the bluffs overlooking the gulch that marked the border, Omby-Amby dropped off the horse and pulled out one of the magic signals. He raised it to the sky and squeezed, just like Guardsman Kopp instructed. The magic shot into the sky and exploded in a puff of red dust. Omby-Amby saw the puff of red smoke. What he did not see was the magic cloud sending its tendrils toward every horizon, scintillating and sparkling in the orange sunlight.

"Only one signal?" Wickrie-Kells frowned.

"If Glinda said she would watch, she will be watching. I trust that she will see the signal." Omby-Amby said.

"What if she doesn't? Give me another."

"This is not a wise idea. This is to signal Glinda, not to light the sky on fire. You don't know what that many signals will do. Look at the signal up there right now." The tendrils stretched to the clouds in the sky, joining them together in a magic shining web. The web was invisible to Omby-Amby's otherwise keen eyes.

"Trust me. Glinda will see this." Wickrie-Kells held the remaining signal launchers to the sky and squeezed.

The road south was dusty. Glinda's chariot kicked up clouds of dust as she raced back to her home. She watched the sky anxiously for the signal that someone—anyone—had found Oscar. There was a group of youth playing Hammer-head. She lifted a hand in greeting. They stopped to watch the fire-haired sorceress drive by. The most obvious gawker turned his head almost all the way around watching her go past. The ball-handler launched the ball at the gawker's head, knocking him face-first to the ground. Laughter echoed across the field.

Glinda pulled her horses up suddenly. The sudden pressure on the reins caused the horses to rear back. Glinda turned to the western sky. She felt it—the signal.

An insistent pulling in her throat and chest tugged toward the west. Glinda stepped off the chariot and shielded her eyes against the bright sky. An explosion tore a great rift in the blue sky, revealing purple and black behind it. Thousands of glittering gems shone through the astral laceration.

"What are you doing?" Glinda cried out as one explosion after another widened the rift and revealed a watching face, haughty and beautiful, surrounded by flowing green hair.

The tugging pulled Glinda toward the rift, but she dug in her feet and clung to the side of the chariot for support. Somebody had found Oscar—probably several guards. It was an accident that they launched all of the signals. It had to be. Nobody would be that foolish to launch all of that ruby dust in the same area at once. Glinda gasped in pain as the tugging on her heart grew more insistent. She glared back and shouted at the sky as the ethereal face turned to look at her. The sky-woman's face smirked, and then it turned to look at something else.

"I can't...can't breathe. It's pulling me." Wickrie-Kells gasped and fell to the ground. She stared up at the sky. Where red explosions had been just a moment ago, a face appeared and looked her way.

Omby-Amby dropped to her side and pressed his hand on her collarbone. "Breathe. Just keep breathing. Wickrie, there's nothing there." He turned around to the sky to look, but he saw nothing.

Wickrie-Kells stared over his shoulder, her eyes wide and unblinking. "She sees me. I can feel my heart, it wants to jump out of my chest. Omby," she clutched his hand tightly, her frightened fingers twisting the soldier's knuckles into knots, "Something inside me is trying to get out, to fly into the sky, into the darkness beyond the desert. *An dleacht mar a shainltear thuas sa spear,*" her terrified voice cried out in an unknown tongue. "Oh faeries, please don't let me say any more out loud. *'The duty, as defined in the sky above.'* Where are these voices coming from?"

Omby-Amby shook the girl's shoulders roughly. "Wickrie, look at me. *At me.* There is nothing there. The sky is blue with some clouds. That is all. There is nothing behind me, nothing in the sky. Wickrie, look at me!"

Wickrie-Kells clapped two hands over her mouth. Her amber eyes dropped frightened tears onto her cheeks as she screamed into her trembling fingers.

At the Yellow Castle, Ondri-baba felt the familiar tugging at her heart. This was what always happened when she learned a new spell and tattooed the lines on her skin. She turned toward the source of the power. Her magic eye saw through the vortex and saw its matching eye. The owner saw her and nodded politely, then pointed to her other mortal eye and winked once.

Ondri-baba smiled tightly. She was coming, but it was not the comfort that Smith and Tinker had promised. Every eye would see and every knee that would not bow would be swept away in the dark winds that blew across the desert every night. Ondri-baba saw those winds and knew what they carried. From what the Wizard said, she could only define the coming war as a nightmare that lasted through both day and night.

In the stable of Yellow Castle, Kally also felt the familiar tugging. She walked to the door of the stable and looked up at the sky. She felt a sickening sinking in her breast. That was the one who would come. That was the face that had promised her grandmothers power, but then required flesh to pay the price. That was a face not real, yet at the same time as real as her empty beating heart. She could ignore it, but the power was always there, just waiting for the right moment to make its presence felt.

"Go away. You don't belong in this land. This is my land."

Then Kally heard a strange whisper from across the deserts. It was a dark whisper of dreams. How could this be? Power could be hers, for a simple exchange. Kally licked her lips. "I'm listening." She whispered to the sky.

From the window of her tower in Central City, Mombi saw the face in the sky. She witnessed the great ripping gash in the expanse of infinity. What power was this? The face turned to look at her. The deadly sparkle of gallows humor flickered in the haughty face.

Mombi gasped and rushed down the stairs of her tower. She threw open the doors of every room, searching frantically. She stopped at the kitchen. There he was.

Pastoria froze in the middle of dumping cake seeds in his mouth. Several fell onto his neatly trimmed beard. He was caught—again. He looked over at Mombi's breathless smile. Her chest heaved with panicked exertion. "You have found me, Lady."

"There you are." Mombi laughed. "You are okay."

"Full of cake seeds and proud as any peacock, but more-so than most."

"You are well? Your head, clear? Thinking clearly?" Mombi quickly crossed the kitchen and picked the cake seeds from Pastoria's beard. She threw them to the side. Pastoria tried to catch them before they fell to the ground, but he missed. "You are well?" She put her hand on his forehead to feel his temperature then felt his cheeks.

"I am moderately disturbed. Cake seeds are not a trivial commodity to be tossed around like gold coins."

Mombi laughed, breathless and relieved. She wiped her fingers across her brow and felt her own burning cheeks. She bowed her head before the king and took his hand, touching each of his knuckles with her thumb. Then she looked up into his eyes. "I need you to be clear-thinking—to be honest and truthful and forthright with me right now. You are what is important in this moment. Will you trust me enough to do that?"

Confusion danced elegantly through Pastoria's eyes, but he managed to nod.

Mombi smiled broadly and wrapped his fingers around hers. She brought them to her lips and kissed them. "Madness comes with that face." She looked up, searching for the words. "I have witnessed an omen of ill tidings. I feared for the king." Then her official veneer cracked. "I feared for your safety."

"I assure you, I am well. My mind is brimming full of things right now. You do not need…" his brows knitted as he thought, "I think…an omen, you say? Did you see me?" He puffed out his chest and turned his chin slightly.

"All I see is you. There are foul magicks afoot, Pastoria. I need you to simply be wise. Be the king you are meant to be."

"I am that king—every moment."

"All right. Good. Wonderful." Mombi squeezed his hand and then caressed his cheeks. She turned and walked to the kitchen doorway. She stopped and looked back at him. Her dark eyes sparkled. She smiled back at Pastoria. "Be safe." Then she disappeared around the corner.

Pastoria smiled long after she left. What a fine queen she would make. That would be a fine party, with plenty of dancing and cake—cake seeds. He bent over to pick up the fallen cake seeds and popped them in his mouth.

Mombi returned to the window of her tower. The gash in the sky now revealed to her armies and strange things—humanoid and other strange figures made of metal and wood—an army. The creatures with the army were dark and short things that did not see the light of day. Their squat bodies were accustomed to the hard rock of their world. They clustered around the gash, trying to see what the haughty queen saw. That was the one that commanded the armies. A strange chittering sound accompanied the creatures. Their laughter? Or was it anticipation? Glee from the strange things, *Nomes*, they were called. Yes, *Nomes*. She remembered reading that word long ago from within the heavy book on her shelf, *Galen's Grimoire*. The voice of madness that described them as *'from beneath the earth, that never see the sky. Their gold and gems—twelve kingdoms' worth; grinding stones their battle cry.'*

The haughty face smirked. Mombi was not certain if that was directed at her, or at some other passing thought. She watched, and she knew the haughty face of the queen knew that she was watching.

They would not take her king. They would not drive Pastoria to madness. The face always preceded madness, so the scholars said. That would not play out this time. Mombi would protect him—with her life, if necessary. She…it was her duty.

Promethus felt the awakened energy. He turned to the sky, even though he could not see clearly, he witnessed a strange vortex stealing color from the sky. "Glinda, where are you? What have you done? That ruby magic is dangerous. It has awakened enemies outside the Land of Oz. You are whetting their appetite of forgotten things long forbidden them. You bring their wrath upon our generation."

Nikidik stopped his landstrider and looked up at the strange display in the sky. He shook his head in bemused wonder. "Wizard, what have you done?"

In the East forest, in the Country of the Munchkins, a short, squat man with thick goggles, looked up from his tin construct. The tinsmith was Ku-Klip, the third apprentice of Smith & Tinker. He looked out at the distant sky and mumbled, "A storm is come to Oz. Business will be good." He chuckled once and then he went back to his tinsmithing.

Far across the Deadly Desert, another powerful being felt the magic of the ruby dust signal in the sky. From her dominions within the Kingdom of Dreams, the Queen of Dreams peered out from the magic tear in the protective shielding around the Land of Oz. She felt the rifts beginning in the strength of the blood of Oz, and she smiled.

She called to the Nomes to unlock the orrery—the massive computational device to calculate the movement of the stars in the heavens and the other spheres in the dreamlands—and to gather her scrying devices. She would be prepared for the next disaster in Oz.

She greedily gathered her remaining children around her feet, and the Nome leaders at her throne. She reveled in the coming power and laughed.

"Soon, the Land of Oz will belong to the Nomes. And I shall have the work of my hands once again. The Emerald Engine will again know its true master. You have kept me out too long, Sister. I will own the land I discovered and enchanted. Your reign, Lurline, has come to an end. The dark dream is upon Oz."

31 HOW THE WEST WAS LOST

The young soldier, Kopp, having completed his mission, came within sight of Lake Grimmpill. He was almost home. A few more hours and he would be back to the Emerald City. Then he was spotted by a patrol of emerald soldiers from Central City.

Kopp hailed them warmly and approached them. The leader of the patrol, Bartleby O'Brine, sneered his bruised face at the young Emerald City soldier. "You're a long way from home. Spying, no doubt." Then he cuffed Kopp upside the head.

Two soldiers grabbed Kopp's arms. He struggled, but he could not escape their grasp.

"Bind him and bring him to the king." Bartleby ordered.

Several hours later, in King Pastoria's throne room, Kopp was forced to kneel before the throne of the great Kings Oz. Mombi stood next to Pastoria. She glared at Bartleby as she saw the rough treatment he had given this young soldier from Emerald City.

"We found a spy on the borders of our lands. He is from Emerald City. This is only the latest spy that we have discovered trying to learn all of our secrets and gauge our strength." Bartleby announced.

"Only the latest, you say?" Pastoria asked, circling his hand in the air. "Where are the others?"

Bartleby bowed his head. "They escaped. After rudely beating me and my men in the undercity, their troop escaped. There were at least twenty of them, Sire."

Mombi stepped in front of Pastoria. "How many were you?"

"Twelve, Lady Chamberlain. We were twelve."

"And they let you live? After you had discovered their spying activities?"

"We surprised them. They fought and ran like the cowards they are."

"But not before bruising your proud face."

"No, Lady Chamberlain."

"Which is why you bruised this young soldier's face."

"He tried to escape."

"Is this true?" Mombi turned her dark eyes to Kopp. "Please, stand. You look uncomfortable on your knees."

Kopp slowly and painfully rose from the tile-inlaid floor. "I tried to escape, after he hit me. I was happy to see them. Our cities are friends, or at least I thought they were. But I'm no spy. I was sent on a mission. I completed the mission—no, that's not true, either. I was stopped from completing my mission by my commanding officer. He sent me home." Kopp used his bound hands to rub at his sore knees. "I just want to go back to the Emerald City, ma'am."

"What was your mission?" Bartleby demanded. "He wouldn't talk earlier."

Mombi's eyes flashed anger at the arrogant soldier. "He is talking now. What is your name?"

"Kopp."

"What was your mission?"

Kopp sighed. "The Wizard is gone. Glinda wants to find him, but so do the Witches. If the soldiers find him first, they signal in the sky. Then the Wizard is safe."

"The signals in the sky? Did you understand them?"

"The Sorceress told me that they were signals that she could see. I was to pinch the end and point it at the sky and it signaled her somehow."

"That explains my feelings earlier—in the..." When she saw the blank stares, Mombi stopped. "Continue. Is there anything else?"

"I would like to return to the Emerald City."

"What is your rank, young Kopp? In the event that you are needed once again."

Kopp smiled politely. "If you need me again, your guards are not doing their duty. They are not engraving honor on their swords. If you need me—a guard from the Emerald City—you have bigger problems than you know."

"Bold words from a guard." Mombi smiled, intrigued.

"I am a guard. That is all I will ever be. I have chosen to guard the Emerald City as a place where a child can grow up free, and live free until the ground reclaims them again. I owe you a debt of gratitude, Lady, but I am not for sale. Central City does not offer what the Wizard has offered."

"If it is money—gold or gems—I will pay." Pastoria leaned forward in his throne. "You can buy anything with money."

"I am happy with my call." Kopp said. "I would prefer to return to my city in peace, but if my release comes with shackles, I would just as soon wear them here."

"An honest man." Mombi smiled. "How utterly quaint."

"Quaint is my mother's maiden name." Kopp replied.

Mombi stepped down to the floor and circled around the young soldier. Bartleby looked on eagerly, like a hungry dog. It was clear he wanted to slap the iron shackles on the enemy soldier to replace the bonds of rope.

"Are you uncommon as a soldier?" Mombi asked. "Do all soldiers speak like you?"

"Anyone that is worth their salt speaks rightly. Those that aren't, don't speak much. They don't last long inside the walls. There are other places they find work." He leveled a glance over to Bartleby O'Brine, who bristled and gritted his teeth.

"Let him leave without incident." Mombi ordered.

Bartleby reluctantly removed the ropes binding Kopp. As the soldier exited the throne room, Bartleby turned to follow him.

"One moment, Captain O'Brine."

Bartleby froze and clicked his heels together. He turned back to the throne. "Yes, your majesty?"

"There is the matter of the armies." Pastoria waved his finger around in the air, then tapped his fingertip hard against the arm of his throne. He winced and shook his finger in pain.

"Which armies, Sire?"

"Mombi mentioned armies. She glimpsed them through a rip in the sky. Great armies fighting. You see, war is the art of kings."

"Of course. War makes men."

Mombi slipped around to the back of the throne. She needed to see the sky again. If the faces were still there, she needed to bind them somehow to her memory. Just as certain as *she* was watching the sky, *something* from the sky was watching the Land of Oz. Mombi hurried to her tower and watched the sky with paper and charcoal in her hand to draw the faces. The armies, she knew, were coming, if they were not already here. *Alas, Glinda, what chaos have you unleashed?*

Below her tower she saw the king's Peacock Chariot race from the stables with Bartleby at the reins. *Just dandy*, she thought. With unknown wars on the horizon, it would quite certainly be the spectators that wound up hurt. He was a fool for rushing off in search of adventure. Still, it hadn't been very exciting or interesting here with Mombi. Securing power took a great deal of effort. Pastoria knew that, which is why he trusted Mombi to keep everything well-oiled and running while he raced off to be a king and a man and make war.

Far away, walking simply, with his head held high, the young soldier, Kopp, headed home toward the Emerald City. Mombi watched him as he walked out of the valley. When he was gone, she turned to look after Pastoria, but his chariot was too far away now to see. She turned back toward the soldier's path. He was honest and proud of it. He was a guard who could be trusted. Mombi tucked his name away for future reference. Trustworthy men made excellent levers when shifting the gears of power.

In the lands of the West, Oscar huffed and puffed as he ran toward the wide gulch that marked the border of the land. He heard the screeching and hooting of the monkeys behind him. They were close enough that he could hear the beating of their individual wings. Why were they waiting? They had him dead to rights. Why did they not grab him up and launch him into the sky again? *What were they waiting for?*

The large and disfigured monkey dropped to the ground right in front of Oscar. The Wizard leaped to the side, narrowly dodging the swinging monkey fists. He rolled down the embankment and into the dry riverbed.

"What are you doing? We're friends." Oscar cried.

King Klick casually flipped pebbles down the embankment. "We were friends when your queen had the Golden Cap. She earned her black heart. And you, Wizard, lied."

"I had the Golden Cap. I was trying to help you." Oscar protested. He backed away. Large boulders blocked his path and he scooted sideways around them, always keeping his face pointed at the scarred monkey king.

"It matters not *why* you did. It truly matters not *what* you did—only that you did *not*. The possessor of the Golden Cap has demanded, and we obey."

"What did Ondri-baba order? The Witch of the West, what did she order you to do?"

By this time, the flock of Winged Monkeys had gathered around Oscar. The smaller ones landed on the boulders in the riverbed. The larger ones held back, leaving this hunt for their king. They hooted and screeched. They hopped up and down as King Klick threw dirt at his enemy.

"The Witch Queen ordered us to *drive you from the Land of the West*. I interpret that to mean, if possible, to kill the Wizard."

Oscar threw his voice—a screaming roar from the boulders near him. That sent the smaller monkeys screeching into the air. That confusion startled all of the monkeys. King Klick watched quickly to ensure that none of his people were in danger, then he turned his eyes back to the hunt.

Oscar ran.

King Klick saw the wizard crawling up the opposite embankment. His frantic hands scrabbled for purchase in the rocky dirt. He was halfway up when the scarred monkey caught up to him.

King Klick's breath burned hot on Oscar's neck as the monkey taunted the Wizard. "You have not left the Land of the West. You broke your oath. You swore to me, and you failed. Now, Wizard, as we agreed, I will kill you."

SECTION THREE: BATTLE CRY

32 OATH UNTO DEATH

Oscar scrabbled his feet, trying to get up the loose dirt of the riverbank. King Klick caught up with him easily, and grabbed his foot. He pulled Oscar down to the bottom of the dry riverbed.

The disfigured monkey leered in the Wizard's terrified face. "Your death, Wizard, my honor. I will obey. By so doing, my people are one wish closer to freedom."

"If you don't kill me, I will get the Golden Cap again. I will fight the Witch and give you your freedom. I promise."

"Again? You failed. You failed my people. What good is the promise of a dead human? It is as good as the promise of a living human. The only *good* a dead human can do is not lie. Humans lie. You lie right now."

"No. I am not. I will get the Golden Cap for you."

"My honor, Wizard—I will have your voice. It will not sound anymore in ringing lies. My honor will not allow me to disobey. That would make me a liar, like you."

"I am not asking you to disobey. Just let me go. I am close to the border. You can say that you drove me from the Land of the West."

"No. You betray. I will not betray my honor. This is your voice, your life, and your lie." King Klick raised his fists at screamed at Oscar. At the apex of his swing, his scream changed from anger to pain. An arrow sliced through his wing.

All of the Winged Monkeys screamed in anger as their king dropped backwards, grasping his wounded wing. He screamed at the riverbank.

Oscar scrambled backwards. He felt rocks falling from above. He ducked as a shadow passed over the top of him.

Omby-Amby leaped down into the riverbank with drawn sword, placing himself between the Wizard and the Winged Monkeys. "Get him out of here!"

Oscar felt hands grabbing at him from above and behind. He kicked his feet to try to help as he was pulled up the riverbank. Soldiers hanging by ropes pulled up the Wizard suspended between them.

"Is he safe?" The Soldier with Green Whiskers shouted.

"Aye. He's safe—for now." Wickrie-Kells answered.

King Klick paced back and forth just outside the reach of the soldier's sword. "My quarrel is not with you."

"Quarrel with the Wizard and you quarrel with me." The soldier retorted.

King Klick growled and Omby-Amby growled.

"Omby, get up here. I will cover you." Wickrie-Kells shouted.

"Get Oscar back."

"Take him back." Wickrie-Kells ordered the soldiers.

They took Oscar by the arms, but he shook free of their grasp. Oscar gasped in the girl's ear. "What are you doing?"

"What are YOU doing?" Wickrie-Kells snapped back. "I'll tell you what you are doing. You are starting a war."

"He is trying to kill me, but he doesn't have to. If we get the Golden Cap—"

"No! You betrayed the truce. You started this war. I should throw you back down there and save Glinda the trouble."

In the gulch, King Klick launched into the air over top of the Soldier with Green Whiskers. Omby-Amby swung his sword an instant too slow. The Winged Monkey landed on the top of the riverbank.

Oscar and Wickrie-Kells jumped backward. The Monkey growled and bared his teeth. He advanced slowly.

"I am owed a life—the life of a betrayer and a liar. His throat is mine."

"Or just drive him from the Lands of the West." Oscar offered as an alternative. "That is what I was told. I wasn't there to hear it—I was otherwise engaged, but I am certain that driving me out was the better option."

"The riverbed is the border. He is driven." Wickrie-Kells nocked another arrow and drew her bowstring back.

"The Witch is appeased in her wish. I, however, am not. I have liberty to choose." Rage filled the monkey's eyes. "I know you know liberty, Wizard. Your words have even reached the ears of a slave. So for you, I choose the liberty of death."

"You choose your own death."

"My people will be free. My honor will be satisfied." King Klick advanced.

"Don't do this." Oscar begged. "Wickrie, not you, either. We can solve this. We just need to get the Golden Cap again. We can free him and his people."

Wickrie-Kells' arm trembled as she held the bowstring taut. "Stop. King Klick, stop. I beg you. Stop."

"His throat or mine."

A tear rolled down Wickrie-Kells' cheek.

The disfigured Winged Monkey leaped into the air. The archer moved her bow to follow. The Wizard lunged into the girl as her fingers released the arrow. The monkey screamed as the arrow missed his heart and passed completely through his throat. He grabbed the Wizard. Then King Klick gurgled through his pierced throat as a sword buried itself in his back.

The Winged Monkey twitched and wriggled atop the fallen wizard. He grinned a morbid death's grin into the Wizard's horrified face. His shattered voice breathed one final word, "Freedom."

Omby-Amby grasped the hilt of his sword and twisted.

The king of the Winged Monkeys writhed in the unmerciful throes of death. The awful grin froze on his face as the life drained from his eyes.

Oscar coughed and tried to choke back the tears. He glared up from the ground at Wickrie-Kells. He tried to lunge out at her, but his coat was pinned to the ground by the impaling sword. "WHY? He wasn't going to hurt me badly. He was just doing what he was commanded to do."

Omby-Amby pulled the monkey off of Oscar and roughly hoisted his friend to his feet. "So were we. Look at my sword, Mate—it nearly ran you through, too. Wickrie's arrow could have hit you just as easily with that blamed-fool stunt."

The soldier pulled his sword from the corpse. Oscar paled even more as he stood and saw the hole that Omby-Amby's sword had sliced through his shirt.

Omby-Amby issued orders to the soldiers with ropes. "Lower the body down to the bottom. Be careful. No desecration."

The soldiers quickly carried out the orders. The Winged Monkeys screamed and growled and circled around overhead. The largest of them swooped down to the body of their king. They lifted it into the air and flew away, leaving half of their army to keep watch over the humans.

Glinda whipped her chariot to a stop in front of the castle Chronometria. She jumped from the chariot as one of her Fighting Girls came to take the panicked horses.

"Guardian! Guardian! I have great need of you!" Glinda shouted in the front door and up the stairs as she hurried to her laboratory.

Promethus met her at the top of the stairs.

"I need to talk to you."

"And I, Princess, need to speak with you. Your treatment of Ola Griffin is profoundly unjust."

Glinda pointed toward the window. "There is a face in the sky!"

"You were protected. Remember the face in the ruby dust explosion in here? I gave you my kiss—the final component in the protection spell. You were protected. Did you look through the Ruby Spectacles?"

"I saw it with my own eyes. Didn't you see it? She was right there. She looked at me. She dared to pull at my heart."

"Did you say anything?" Promethus asked. His fingers stretched out to take Glinda's hand. "Did you make any signs with your hands?"

"No. Why would I say anything?"

"The powers that rip open the sky can pull from some unwilling vessels the words to bring them through. Willing vessels are even more dangerous. If they make the signs and say the words…"

"I did not say anything. I shouted. I was mad. Who was she?"

"I saw a vortex."

Glinda stared at the Guardian. "There was a vortex in my dream, I—"

Promethus raised a finger and slowly shook it at Glinda. "I…you. Danger. Much, much danger. You have awakened the enemies of this land. Look through your Ruby Spectacles. What do you see?"

"I see the sky is knitting together. The storms are growing behind the scar. There! Far away. I see Oscar. His magic is still alive."

"We may yet have time." Promethus sighed in relief.

"The Wizard must be brought here. He is too powerful to leave alone any longer. Emerald City may finish without his hand. I will bring him here."

"You're about to lose him." Promethus observed.

"I have said no such thing"

"Your power is threatened. You need me to provide your story."

Glinda removed the Ruby Spectacles and put them in her pocket. She sat down at her desk and looked at her lockbox.

Promethus watched Glinda warily. "You are frightened and you don't know how this is going to end. You want him by your side, but you are afraid of him. He is the monster in your fairy tale."

"Fairy tales are entertaining for children."

"Yes. But remember, Glinda, fairy tales happen in fairy lands, of which we are a part. Who wins in the end? That is the question we must ask."

"This is not a fairy tale." Glinda said sternly. "I would thank you to remember that, *Apprentice*."

"My Masters sent us into the world to become Masters ourselves. I have not been an apprentice for seven years, and certainly not to you. One would be wise to remember her station, *Princess* Glinda, daughter of Quelala and the Ruby Sorceress. You need me, and I expect to be respected according to my station."

Glinda fumed. Her eyes grew stormy.

Promethus did not relent—he pressed his point further. "I was Chief Apprentice to Master Smith, and a confidante where the others were not. Do not displease me, Glinda. I expect that our mutual purpose will be accomplished with a minimum of argument."

"Fine."

"Can you assure me that your plan is the correct one?"

Glinda crossed the floor to her lockbox. She turned the dials and traced a symbol on the lock-plate. She glanced quickly back over her shoulder to see if Promethus was watching. He had his hand up on the wall and was staring out the window.

Glinda opened the lockbox and removed one of the pistols. She closed up the lockbox and spun her fingers over the magic locking plate, scrambling the glyphs. "I will return with the Wizard."

"Undoubtedly."

"He will stay here with me. I will protect him and control him. He must be kept safe."

"He must be returned to the Emerald City to complete construction."

"The plans are set. The architects are wise. He can be brought here." Glinda stated.

"Without the Wizard, the Witches will not fear to attack the center of the land."

"What is at the center of the land?"

The Emerald City grows where the Emerald Fortress once guarded. The city of Parradime held in its heart the source of magic. The Witches do not yet realize, but the enemies beyond this land know well what lies beneath the Emerald City. If they again ally with the Witches, and they conquer and wrest control over the magic, the Land of Oz will see only darkness, forever. It is imperative that the Wizard stay in Emerald City. That close to the source, his magic will protect the land."

"You mean his dreams."

"Which make the magic."

"I had not considered that." Glinda looked out the window toward the northwest, where she had seen the flames of Oscar's magic.

"You should go. There is much work to be done."

"I will bring the Wizard here, then I will return him to Emerald City." Glinda turned quickly to leave. "We are understood, then?"

Promethus listened to her quick footsteps down the stairs. He waited in the same position for several minutes until he saw her leave out the front gate with a score of her fighting girls. They headed toward the walled scrapyard. Soon a cloud arose with the group seated on top. Glinda's long red hair whipped in the wind as the cloud headed northward.

Promethus waved with his free hand. When Glinda was far enough away from the castle, the dark-haired man lifted his other hand from the wall to reveal a mirror with Glinda's moving reflection on it.

In the reflection, Glinda turned the dials and traced the magic glyph on her strongbox. Promethus crossed the floor to Glinda's strongbox and traced the magical glyphs, following Glinda's moving pattern in the mirror. He clicked the box open and looked at the greatest treasures of the Sorceress. On top of them all was Glinda's most recent acquisition—the weapon from Oscar's dream, a pistol.

"Yes, Glinda, we are understood. I fear the power you wield. As you said so well, the power must be protected and controlled." Promethus slipped the pistol into his pocket and closed the magic lockbox.

33 THE FIGHTING GIRLS

Evening fell heavy on the border land. Neither side of the river was still. The humans set up defensive positions that could be protected against aerial attack. In the rocky bluffs, there were few trees that they could harvest and use as spears. The defensive locations were quickly scouted, and the soldiers watched constantly and waited for the inevitable attack.

On the other side, the Winged Monkeys were agitated and angrily shouted at the enemy humans. Some of the smaller ones hurled pebbles at the opposite riverbank. One of the smaller monkeys picked up an arm from one of the automatons and hurled it down into the dry riverbed. This set off all of the monkeys.

The Winged Monkeys screamed as they flew back to the battlefield and gathered the pieces of the humanoid automatons. These they threw down into the dry riverbed. Every single piece was gathered and piled up. Arms and legs stuck out at unfortunate and painful angles. This bizarre sculpture was a grim monument to the work of death. It was a fitting tribute that the Monkeys made—empty men piled in war. Yet it did not bring back their king.

The Winged Monkeys saw the cloud first. It started out small and grew larger as it came closer. They flew upwards, but they did not cross the border between the lands. Screeches of "Glinda, Glinda" echoed through the air.

The cloud chariot slowed as it approached the border zone. It descended over the camp. The heavy mist surrounded all of the soldiers and clung to their skin. As the mist became so heavy that it threatened to push them to the ground, it thinned and evaporated, leaving the group far larger than it was before.

Glinda and her Fighting Girls had arrived.

"I witnessed the sign in the sky. It bore ill omens." Glinda said. "I have come for the Wizard. Where is he?"

A soldier pointed toward the dry riverbank. There was Oscar, sitting by himself, staring into the lengthening shadows.

Glinda looked to the chaos on the other side of the riverbank. "What happened?"

Glinda's face tightened as the soldiers told the story. They were specific in the details of the rescue, but vague enough in the ensuing violence to only mention that a Winged Monkey died. Glinda's eyes darkened. Then she called Wickrie-Kells. "You saw this?"

Wickrie-Kells nodded.

"Is there anything you can add? The Wizard has done a very bad thing."

"He tried to stop me, Glinda, I swear. Don't—"

Omby-Amby pulled Wickrie-Kells aside and stepped in front of Glinda. "It was me. My sword. See? The blood of an old ally stains my blade."

Glinda paled. Then her face turned red with anger. Her stormy eyes locked on the green-whiskered soldier. "Show me your hands."

Glinda turned the soldier's hands over and narrowly examined them. Dried blood crusted in the dirt in his knuckles. She threw his hands down and glared.

"Who are you protecting?"

A tear slipped down Wickrie-Kells' cheek as she stepped backwards, behind Omby-Amby.

"The Wizard." The Soldier with Green Whiskers replied.

"Why?"

"Because you ordered it. He must be protected at *all costs*. This was the cost."

Angry tears shone out of Glinda's eyes, battling her steely will to see which would fall first.

"Stay here." Glinda strode past Omby-Amby and stormed toward the distant Wizard.

Oscar did not look up when the Sorceress approached. He knew she was here, and that was enough.

"What have you done?" She demanded.

Oscar was silent for a long minute before he spoke. His voice was a hoarse whisper. "I did it for you."

"What?"

"He's dead." Oscar stood up and faced Glinda. "I have to live with it. So do you."

Glinda shook her head slowly at him. Her jaw clenched. No words came out.

"You lost control. Someone died. Welcome to my world, Princess."

"I h-hate you r-right now." Glinda sobbed. She clenched her fists and growled hoarsely, keeping her screams inside.

"Me too."

Glinda pointed her finger at him. The unspoken message that she could not force out, was *stay here*.

Oscar shrugged and sat down again on his rock. He watched the Winged Monkeys throwing stones at the remains of Kally's automaton army. As the hurled stones shattered the fingers off the lifeless inhuman hands, the echoes sounded up and down the riverbank, but the Wizard didn't even wince.

As the evening descended, Professor Nikidik paused his landstrider several times. Each time he pressed his palm gently to the ground. The tremors were getting stronger the further south he traveled. Something had happened, wondrous and amazing. He only hoped that he could witness some of the glorious changes that this power would lay bare.

He stopped at a fine cottage as night fell. For more than two hours he glanced out the window as the family told their story of giving refuge to a short stranger who turned out to be the Wonderful Wizard of Oz.

After the meal, and sharing some stories of his own to break even the burden, Nikidik excused himself. He needed to tend to his iron horse before the night was much deeper. They waited for his return inside—they waited a long time.

Miles to the south, Nikidik sped his landstrider under the glaring stars. His eyes were on the treasures and the unborn armies waiting for him in the scrapyard of Smith & Tinker.

Glinda returned to the camp and organized her Fighting Girls as the front line near the riverbed. This gave the Emerald Soldiers some time to come back to camp and eat and rest. The Sorceress joined Wickrie-Kells near the fire and leaned over to her. Desperation hoarsened her voice. "I need your counsel. Come with me."

Glinda led the way deeper into the wilderness, out of earshot of the furthest guard. She desperately looked into the sky and on the ground—everywhere but the face of her friend. "How can I do this? How could he do this? At least one of the Winged Monkeys is dead. Oscar told me that much, but he doesn't care. And Omby is taking the blame for it."

Wickrie-Kells looked down at her own hands. She studied her words, tasting their bitterness before she spoke. "*They* have to carry that burden."

"Oscar threw it right back in my face. It's like he's numb and this is just falling off him like rain. What should I do? I have to do something. A friend is dead."

"Whose hands are the bloodiest?" Wickrie-Kells asked softly. She knew the answer even more truly than Glinda.

"I know. But I don't want to do that to you."

Wickrie looked up sharply, but Glinda was looking back toward the camp.

The taller girl tried to stifle a sob, "Glinda."

But Glinda wasn't listening. She stepped quickly past Wickrie-Kells and walked around the camp toward the Wizard.

Wickrie-Kells followed a few steps behind her friend. She kept her confession ready on her tongue. The bitterness choked her, but she clenched her jaw and held it inside.

"You're back." Oscar observed. He saw Wickrie-Kells approaching and turned to Glinda to draw her attention to him.

"I love you, Oscar, but I am very angry with you." Glinda said. "Your irresponsibility has started this war."

Oscar shrugged. "Power losing control." The shadows around his feet shimmered and danced.

"I would remind you, Wizard, that it is I who was born to rule, not you. The responsibility to act rests with me."

"So that makes you better than me?"

"It makes me more responsible."

"Doesn't make you better. Doesn't mean that people like you better."

Glinda's eyes grew stormy. She held her tongue and said nothing.

"I don't know why you are so upset. I did what I did for you."

"For me? You think I want a war? You think that I want to fight the Wicked Witch and her monkey slaves? I want them free."

Oscar leveled his gaze at Glinda. She threw up her hands and turned away. "You have no idea what you are doing, Wizard. You are playing with magic that you can't control."

"I'm still alive."

"For now, you're alive. There is no telling what the night will bring."

Wickrie-Kells motioned to Glinda to request permission. "Come." Glinda said. "Find out why King Klick has not responded to my request for a meeting?"

Oscar's eyes met Wickrie-Kells'. She shook her head almost imperceptibly.

"I see down in the camp that another has come in his place." Wickrie-Kells responded. "He is down there."

Glinda narrowed her eyes and pushed past her friend. "I am the Sorceress and Queen of this land. No one does that to me. I demand to see King Klick. I demand—"

Glinda stopped short. There was King Klick's body. Behind the corpse stood his son and heir—Docket—the new king of the Winged Monkeys.

"Princess, I had hoped to meet under more favorable circumstances. I come to you as a representative of my people. We do not desire this war, but it has been thrust upon us. With the death of our King, we are obliged to wage a retaliatory war until the aggressor has been subdued. Satisfaction is demanded."

Glinda looked back at Oscar. He said not a word. Behind him was Wickrie-Kells, her anguished face half-hidden by the tired Wizard.

Glinda motioned to the attendant Winged Monkeys. "You may remove the body of your king." To the new ruler, she said, "I would speak with you in private." She turned to glare at Oscar, speaking volumes with her stormy blue eyes.

They walked away into the darkness. It was a long time before Glinda returned to the camp.

"Wizard, I would speak with you." Glinda gestured to her Fighting Girls. "Bring the shackles."

Glinda led Oscar through the camp, followed by several of the Fighting Girls. Wickrie-Kells was conspicuously absent.

Glinda led the small group out of sight of the group. When they could no longer hear the fire crackling in the darkness, Glinda stopped. "Shackles." She put the shackles around Oscar's wrists and locked them. "I hope the cold iron wakes you up to a sense of your dire predicament."

"What do you want to hear from me?"

"An apology would be in order."

"Oh. I see."

Glinda waited.

Oscar stared at the ground. Then he looked up and met Glinda's stare.

"Well?" she said.

"I'm thinking."

"You don't care what you did. A king is dead because of you. King Klick—"

Oscar cut off Glinda and plowed forward in his thoughts. "Two years ago King Klick told me that I had already chosen. I just needed to see that I had chosen you above him. I did. I have. And I do."

"—betrayed and stabbed in the back. And you have the gall to say this was a test?"

"Maybe it is." Oscar pulled his wrists apart, clanking the shackles.

"No. You don't get to pick and choose what *means* and what *doesn't* mean. You killed him."

"No. I didn't."

"He is dead. You violated every truce you made as Wizard of the Emerald City. Your actions took away his rights to be free. Isn't that what you stand for, Wizard? Every person has inalienable rights, isn't that what you say? Your actions killed him. I had a plan!"

"And what was that, Sorceress? Wait until the witches die? Wait until one, two, or three generations of Winged Monkeys die in slavery? You have youth on your side, Princess, but even for you, that plan is cold and callous. How many must die for you to keep your hands clean? Inaction has never been—nor will it ever be—your strength. You are one to act, even if foolishly."

Glinda's hand flew swiftly. The stinging slap echoed across the entire camp, freezing every soldier in their tracks. They pretended not to hear, but the silence was deafening.

It was broken by the slow, wheezing laughter of the Wizard. His slow laughter cracked like ice on a frozen pond.

Madness danced in his eyes as his face burned. "Whose inaction killed him? Whose action killed him? Who is the accused? And who is the accuser?"

34 NIGHT TO BE FORGOTTEN

Glinda leaned back against a rock, closing her eyes. She lay away from the rest of the group, trying to calm her anger and hurt. Everything that Oscar had done destroyed the trust she had in him. Why was he doing these things? It made no sense. His pathetic excuse of *I'm tired* was no excuse at all. The power was bursting out of him, the Ruby Spectacles showed that clearly, and it was up to the Wizard to control it. That's what witches and wizards and sorcerers did. It was their responsibility and right to control the power. Why couldn't Oscar see that?

Nearby, Wickrie-Kells shifted back and forth on her feet, watching Glinda try to force sleep.

Wickrie turned around and walked to the edge of the riverbed. The Winged Monkeys were still anxious. Their smell—sweat, fear, and anger—floated on the breeze. Some of them still tossed rocks at the pile of automaton parts. *The doomed army. Why had they come? What was the purpose of the war against the Witch of the West? Such a small army for such a grand plan. They had no chance of winning, so why would Oscar even try?*

The death of King Klick was on Oscar's hands. Yes—*his* hands. It was *his* declaration of war that made this horrible night happen. Wickrie's first arrow didn't do more than tear through the monkey's wing. That *one* arrow. That didn't kill him. The other…it would have missed. She would not have shot him. It was Oscar that made her do it. What actually killed King Klick—Omby's sword. Yes, it may have been Omby's sword, but this was Oscar's war.

Wickrie-Kells wiped her hands on her hips, but they still didn't feel clean. She looked at them again and again in the darkness, but she still felt the blood. Her hands stank.

Glinda stirred. Beneath her, the ground shifted and rumbled slightly. She blinked open her eyes and looked around. Everything was normal—at least as normal as it could be in a military camp after a night of declared war. She laid back down.

The rumbling started again. Then the earth shook. The monkeys across the river launched into the air, hooting and screaming. All of the soldiers jumped to their feet, brandishing their weapons. Glinda sat up and looked up toward the seated Wizard. His head nodded and strange shapes surrounded him. Glinda quickly rolled to her feet and shouted.

A pillar of solid emerald burst up from the ground next to Glinda, throwing her backwards. All over the soldier's camp, pillars of emerald pushed up from beneath the ground. The primary emerald pillars ringed the camp. Smaller emerald shafts thrust upward between the major ones.

"Wake him up!" Glinda shouted.

Omby-Amby raced toward Oscar. An emerald shaft shot up in front of him, but he leaped over it and rolled toward Oscar. He drew his sword and shattered an emerald shaft that sprung up next to the Wizard.

The soldier with green whiskers shook Oscar. The he slapped his face on both sides. "Come on Brud, wake up. You can't be seeing these things again. Wake up."

The dark shadows took form and stepped out to surround Oscar. Emerald pillars launched from the ground and pierced the shadow giants. Horrible breathless screams echoed on the back of Glinda's neck as the shadows writhed in agony. Under the magic of the pure emeralds, they withered and dissolved.

Omby-Amby jerked Oscar to his feet and pulled him toward a gap in the large emerald pillars.

"Everybody out!" Glinda ordered.

Oscar woke up with his feet pounding the ground, racing toward a tall emerald wall. "What's going on?" Next to him, Omby-Amby held his arm and pulled him roughly forward. The ground convulsed and shook. Emerald shoots were growing up all around his feet. Suddenly on the other side there was a tug on his arm. Wickrie-Kells joined Omby-Amby dragging the Wizard to safety. Emerald strands grew up out of the ground like clutching grass, tangling the Wizard's feet. Then there were others—more soldiers—pulling and hacking at the emerald tangles.

The shadows howled in agony, their demise coming quickly. Their echoes lasted longer than their bodies did against the purifying emeralds.

Glinda raced toward the exit. She had to make sure that Oscar got out. He was a few steps ahead of her, being dragged by soldiers. His fist clutched tightly around something. A spear of emerald shot up in front of the Wizard and knocked his arm loose of Wickrie-Kells' grip. His clutched fist opened, and a small round object flew from his hand. A pearl—*a black pearl*. It disappeared into the clutching emerald tangle of growing grass.

One of the Fighting Girls saw the glint of the item against the starlight and turned to find it. She swatted away at the stalks of emerald that clutched after the Wizard. Whatever he had held was important, and it must be recovered. She dug her spear into the tangle and shattered the crystal strands. She thrust her hand down into the broken tangle and found it. Her fingers closed around the pearl. The shattered crystal edges sliced into her hand and then grew new stalks. Her hand was stuck. She kicked her boot at her hand. Two kicks. The emerald stakes broke. Her fingers broke. But her hand was free from the entangling emeralds. Then she ran toward the exit.

All around her the emerald spears thrust upward. The power seemed to center around the pearl. She held it out in front of her in her emerald and blood-encrusted hand. In her other hand she gripped her spear tightly. A ring in the hilt of her spear caught on an upthrust emerald, holding it fast, and yanking it out of her hand. The girl stumbled. Three more steps. Glinda was just beyond the large emerald pillars. She was screaming something. Then Glinda's eyes grew wide. The girl leaped forward. She heard the great roaring at the same instant that she felt the wave of liquid emerald wash over her. Her eyes caught Glinda's horrified look. She forced a smile as she pushed her hand with the pearl beyond the barrier of the emerald pillars. Then the emerald froze around her, trapping her like an insect in amber. It was done. Then the roaring stopped, and there was only silence.

In the scrapyard, Ola Griffin gazed up at the twinkling stars. The fading moonlight made her tawny hair shine silver. A strange *whumphing* sound drew her attention to the road south. It approached her location. She stood up on top of the stacked frames and peered over the scrap pile. Suddenly the sound stopped. *Voices.*

There was Promethus. His large voice was unmistakable. But there was another voice, thinner, more arrogant. The cutting of syllables so precisely bothered Ola. She did not like the other man, even though she could not see him. She missed the first part of the conversation, but she quietly climbed to the top of the scrap heap and turned her ear toward the voices.

"You cannot hinder my return. I am owed complete liberty with respect to my creations."

"I am not stopping you, only warning you. This estate is under my protection. You may take your belongings and what you can carry, but you do not have free reign. You did not then, and you do not now."

"Still the Guardian. Very well, your watchful eye would do best to watch the good silver with my dancing fingers creeping around."

Promethus chuckled. "Nothing. Just a thought." He said.

Ola Griffin smiled. She knew the joke. The other man must have made a face.

"Will you be here in the morning?"

"My client has requested product before tomorrow night. I don't believe that I am welcome here, so I will take my creations and leave."

"Renounce your claim."

"*After* I have obtained what is mine."

"Excellent. Now, Nikidik, my brother in mind, what is this grand experiment you must complete before moonrise tomorrow?"

"An army."

"Quite the feat. How did you dig up that contract? There aren't any wars right now. Not like there used to be. Building weapons does not provide job security any longer."

"You've been too long in your idealistic travels. There is always war. It is a glowing coal, just waiting to burst into flame."

"So you are fanning the flame."

"I am the tongs that carries the coal to the highest bidder. Five pearls."

Promethus coughed, choking on his words.

The other man cackled, an unpleasant sound. "Five. I have succeeded where Gayelette failed. I have become the *magician*. I am powerful beyond all other magicks in Oz."

"You destroyed the pearls?"

"I infused their power into my creation."

"May I see it? You have it with you—I know you do."

"You *will* see it, but not now. Not in the dark night, where no eyes, save two, watch us."

Ola Griffin gasped, then she clapped her hand over her mouth. She flattened herself down and scooted backwards on the scrap heap. The metal and wood scraped her belly as she went backwards. Her feet hung over the edge and kicked out, feeling for the stack of frames. She knocked several of them over.

"It sounds like our spy has been caught." The unpleasant voice observed.

"She is under my protection." Promethus warned.

"I am here for what is mine." The other voice snapped.

Ola Griffin pushed backwards. Her shirt snagged on an errant corner and held her fast. She pulled harder against the caught fabric. She felt it rip, and then she fell backwards. The ground was not far away, but she kept falling. Her hand slapped out and hit the side of a frame as she fell through.

Her echoing scream sounded hollow in the empty scrapyard.

The voices continued, unaware of the hidden girl's plight.

"Nikidik, it is clarifying to see you again. My warnings stand."

"We were taught to innovate and overcome. That is *my* warning."

On the ground, half in shadow, Ola Griffin's hand pushed out of the empty frame and grasped the side. She forced her elbows up onto the corner of the frame. She constantly glanced back down the length of her unseen body. She could feel them down there. The strange chittering and shivering fingers. Now they were on her legs. She whimpered as she kicked and worked her body out of the frame. She pulled herself up to her waist and bowed out over the ground. A relieved laugh forced itself out of her mouth.

It was strangled by a surprised gasp as something pulled her back down. She caught herself by the elbows on the corner. They were pulling on her legs. Their fingers dug into her ankles and cut the skin. Tears fought out of her eyes as she grimaced in pain. She kicked, but they held her legs fast.

Then a shadow fell over her. An unpleasant, clipped voice, asked, "Are you having a problem, little one?"

The tall, thin man pulled her out of the frame and stood Ola Griffin on her feet. She trembled violently as she wrapped her arms around herself.

Professor Nikidik flipped the frame over with his foot. "There. Let them sniff dirt for a time." Then he turned his attention to the shivering girl. "Such things as that are not meant to be explored in the night. That is when they are most active." He took his jacket off and wrapped it around her shoulders. He looked the girl up and down and stopped his visual examination by focusing on her legs.

"W-w-what?" She forced through chattering teeth.

"Your legs are bruised. They are bleeding."

Ola looked down in horror, but the damage was not nearly what she had feared. "What were those things?"

"Nomes, or some of their ilk, I imagine. I did not see what you saw."

The blonde girl shook her head and sat down on a broken half-barrel. "They were everywhere. Laughing. Like crickets, they laughed."

"Interesting."

"How can I make it stop?" Ola Griffin clapped her hand over her ears and shook her head violently. "I don't want to hear them."

Nikidik's eyes softened. "You are a lovely girl, much like my Margolotte in her younger years. I will help you, but I have a pressing duty to perform."

The trembling girl sat still as Nikidik gathered all of the frames and placed them next to his strider. He stepped to the flagpole and turned north. He walked forty-six steps, then took seventeen steps to the right. In the middle of a pathway between two large piles, he stopped and pulled out a sharpened stake. He drew on the ground. When he had completed the symbols, he traced a boundary box around them. Then he stuck the sharpened stake in one corner of the bounding box and pressed down, lifting the lid up out of the ground.

He worked the lid off the box and slid it to the side. "There you are my little precious ones. Ah, how I have missed you." He gathered all of the treasures from his lockbox and placed the lid back in place. He scuffed out the symbols and bounding box with his foot.

Nearby sobs drew Nikidik's attention. The girl was still traumatized. This night would haunt her every moment unless she could forget. Nikidik took a deep breath and sighed. She was so lovely. She didn't deserve such heavy thoughts as those she currently bore. He disappeared around a scrap pile and was gone for several minutes.

Nikidik placed a cup of water into Ola Griffin's trembling hands. "Drink this. Your worries and terrors this night will be forgotten."

Ola Griffin looked up into the eyes of the tall man. "What is it?"

"Drink."

"Where did you get this?"

"Drink. The monsters have frightened you. Their laughing, even now, sounds from the distant night'd realm."

Ola's hands trembled more.

"Let the horrors of this night be forgotten."

Ola Griffin lifted the cup of water to her mouth and drank two sips. She licked her lips and lowered the cup. Her hands no longer trembled. She returned the cup and smiled. "Thank you."

Ola Griffin sat and watched for a time as Nikidik unearthed great machines buried under the piles of scrap. He linked these together in a long train of wheeled cars. She nodded off and fell asleep as the moon dipped below the horizon.

In the stables at Yellow Castle, Kally worked the bolts free on the bottom of Ondri-baba's Walking Hut. The hut was covered with cobwebs and dust, built up over two years of disuse. The entire hut slumped down like a depressed hound. Inside the hut the Sapphire Stove glowed softly. It brightened when Kally stepped into the hut.

"I'm certain the Wizard is captured or killed by now. That means you," she tapped on the top of the stove, "are coming with me. I'll need to find a way to get you back home."

The Walking Hut rose up part way, waiting for instructions. The Sapphire Stove slid from its berth. The hut shook and fell to its resting place, the legs awkwardly bending sideways. It shuddered one last time. The bolts in the floor glowed once, and then they darkened. "As I thought—the hearth is your heart. Rip it out and you are mine. Perhaps you were faithful to my sister, but I have no need of loyalty. I'll take the heart of power and bend it to my own will. I'll cook my kingdom on a Sapphire Stove." She laughed, and magically pulled the stove into the air and out the door.

"You powered a walking hut and took orders like an animal. What else can you do? We shall see, won't we?" She rested one hand on the softly glowing hearth and stepped out of the stables.

It was still night, but the stars were retiring to their resting places in the brightening sky. Morning was coming, and Kally was still in violation of every truce threatened by every ruler in the Land of Oz. Let them come and enforce war. She welcomed the opportunity to destroy all who came against her. There would be blood again, just like in the days of her grandmother.

Where was Oscar? Not *Oscar*, she corrected herself, the *Wizard*. He was the *Wizard*. He had to be the Wizard. If he was Oscar, then he was in trouble, probably. A believing, trusting soul like his was always in the market for trouble. The problem was that he was a target—a naïve, trusting, wonderful target. And he was in trouble.

Kally gave a frustrated sigh and turned her sights east. That was the direction that Oscar had run. It would be slow going in the dark, but morning would be here soon. Then she could see.

Beside her the Sapphire Stove glowed happily. She levitated it in the air and kept one hand firmly around its leg so that it would travel with her as she flitted from spot to spot using the magic of the Silver Slippers.

Far above Kally, in the highest tower of Yellow Castle, a glowing green eye watched her movements. Ondri-baba watched the glowing blue stove as it jumped around on the land below. Soon it was out of sight on the horizon. That was the direction that the Winged Monkeys had chased the Wizard. They had not yet reported back, so they must be grimly enjoying the fulfillment of their duty.

Beyond the horizon, Kally turned north. She would approach the Wizard from the northern wilderness. *She had run away when the monkeys came after him. She ran and hid. When morning came, she came out and followed the sounds.* That was her story. Oscar would believe it. He would vouch for her—she was certain of it. And if trouble came, and it usually did, there was always the escape route with the Silver Slippers.

She jumped across the dry riverbed and tripped on some brush. The Sapphire Stove hung in the air.

"Halt! Who is there?" A stern voice barked from the darkness.

Kally panicked and threw the Sapphire Stove into the eastern sky. She would have to find it later. To the casual observer, the streak of blue light into the dark sky would be contributed to faerie magic. That was her explanation, too. *Will o' the Wisp.* They should believe that.

Kally climbed to her feet and brushed off her dress. The Silver Slippers were carefully hidden beneath the long folds of her dress, so they gave off no light to betray her position.

"Hello?" Kally called. "Is somebody there?"

Two soldiers from the Emerald City pushed through the brush. They pointed spears at her. Kally opened her eyes very wide in mock surprise. "Oh, my goodness." She said. "I hope you are not hunters."

"We are soldiers from the Emerald City. The Wizard sent us down here to train. We are securing the border."

"Oh, good. I'm lost. I was out there. The Wizard. The flying monkeys. I ran. Hid. And you found me." Kally stepped close to the soldiers and looked up at them with her amber eyes. It worked.

"We'll take you back to Glinda."

Kally's triumphant smirk froze. She followed after the soldiers, hesitant to walk as a prisoner into their stronghold, but curious to see if Oscar was still alive and breathing. The two voices warred inside her over which direction the Silver Slippers would carry her—would her sense of greed and self-preservation win out and carry her far away from here in three steps? Or would her heart win out, and keep moving forward? Step by step she debated. Step by step the answer seemed ever more apparent. She was going to leave. All it would take is three steps. She just had to sight a place on the horizon. *Three steps.* That's all it would take.

The crested a small hill and Kally saw the emerald cocoon that rose up out of the earth. Her breath caught in her throat. *What was that? Had some terrible magic occurred here? Or had Glinda learned how to harness the power of emeralds?* Kally's step slowed. The soldier's stopped and waited for her.

"We lost one in there. You're lucky you didn't follow the Wizard. At least *you're* safe."

Kally followed the soldiers into the camp, her curiosity blazing in her eyes. It was a good day to be a witch.

35 UNREMEMBERED TREASURES

"Her name was Cornyss. She joined us last week." Wickrie-Kells said. "It was just before the ball, so I never really got to talk to her. She was assigned to the training—to see if she had what it takes to be a Fighting Girl."

Omby-Amby looked at the frozen wall of emerald. The green and red crusted hand stuck from the smooth wall as a grim reminder of the cost. It could have been any of them. It could have been the Wizard. Omby studied the hand and stuck his finger up into the fist. "There is something in there."

"Leave it." Glinda said. "I don't want to know."

Omby-Amby forced the hand open, shattering crusted emeralds and twisting even further the broken fingers. The other soldiers winced as the bones and emeralds crackled under Omby-Amby's grasp. A black pearl fell into his open hand. He presented it to Glinda.

"I don't want it."

"It's yours." The Wizard's voice came heavy from behind Glinda. "I was saving it for the right time as a gift to you. Pearls are precious in Oz, or so I've been told. I wanted you to have it, but I never dreamed this would be the cost."

"*Dreamed?* You never *dreamed* this would happen? All you do is dream!" Glinda exploded. "This was all because of you!"

"It is yours." Oscar said softly, and turned away. He walked a few paces beyond Omby-Amby at the edge of the group, and he sighed deeply and sat down on the ground with his back to Glinda. His shoulders slumped almost to the ground. Everyone turned to look at Glinda. Behind her, the morning sun broke above the western horizon, lighting the sky and sending golden beams through the emerald prison behind her. Among the dancing emerald lights, Glinda swallowed hard and stuck the black pearl into her pocket.

That girl was gone because of the Wizard. It was his dreams that made this happen. For some unknown reason, the Land of Oz was reacting to the shadow dreams. Could this be something like the Guardian's Emerald Spectacles? Those blocked the view of magic. Perhaps…maybe the emerald pillars were a way of containing or blocking the dark dreams. With Oscar awake now, there were no more dreams. That was the reason that the emerald shafts stopped. It was an escape, but it was only a temporary one. The emerald shafts would be back when Oscar fell asleep again.

She hardened her face. There was only one thing to do. She could not trust the Wizard to control his thoughts or his actions right now, so she would—

"We found someone." The soldier called as he came into the camp, leading an amber-eyed young woman.

Glinda turned and looked. The girl was older than her, but not nearly as pretty. There was a fierceness in her eyes that was tempered only slightly by a strange sardonic curiosity. Glinda disliked her immediately. "Who is she?"

The soldier responded before Kally could answer. "We found her up north of here. She says she was with the Wizard. The monkeys came and she ran away."

Glinda cocked her head at the newcomer. "She ran away. Very nice—you ran away from the slaughter of a king, from the declaration of war, the near destruction of the Wizard, and my fragile negotiations to keep the peace on this border. You ran away."

Kally nodded, but the mocking laughter behind her eyes cut clear through to Glinda. "Yes." And the unspoken words were, *What of it? I had the Wizard and you did not. He's mine.*

"Who are you?" Glinda demanded. "I have had a very long night, and this sunrise only serves to make your face more clear and even more displeasing to me."

The amber-eyed girl smiled, keeping her secret quiet from the shorter sorceress.

Wickrie-Kells appeared behind Kally. Glinda glanced over at her then did a double-take. She looked from Wickrie-Kells to the new girl. "You look similar. Wickrie, who is she?"

"She was with Oscar." Wickrie-Kells offered.

Then Kally's eyes dropped into the poor waif expression. "Yes. Oscar. I was with him. Until the monkeys—they came from everywhere. I ran. They went after him. I ran until I couldn't hear anything anymore. Then I found a place to hide. When I thought it was safe I came out, then I got lost."

"I don't think so. I think you know exactly where you are and why you are here. He is not yours to have." Glinda snarled.

Oscar laughed. "Kally, do you really want to be here right now? Glinda seems more than kind of upset."

"You be silent! You and your dreams are destroying everything that I have built." Glinda snapped over her shoulder. She gestured back to the heavy rising sun in the West. "It's war, Oscar! Because of *you*. Even if I had my army coming, it might not be enough if they strike. I have secured a temporary peace with the Winged Monkeys, but they cannot honor that truce if they are ordered to attack. They cannot assist me with faith alone in my promise. This isn't like Munchkin Fields."

Kally cocked an eyebrow. "How is it not like that?"

Wickrie-Kells stepped in between Kally and Glinda. "Stay out of this. Haven't you done enough?" Wickrie glared down at Kally. There was only a couple of inches difference in their height, but that small increase in physical presence was not nearly enough to make Kally back down.

"I'm sorry. I'm only starting—"

"No. I'm sorry. Did you say something?" Glinda demanded, turning her attention to the new girl.

"—to understand you." Kally finished, smiling. "I'm only beginning to understand you."

"She knows a lot. You'd like her, Glinda." Oscar yawned and chuckled as his head rolled around on his shoulders.

"I don't like *you* right now, Wizard. I don't think your recommendation speaks very highly of anyone."

Several miles to the north of Glinda's argument, King Pastoria's chariot slowed to a stop. Bartleby O'Brine stepped from the chariot and calmed the blowing horses. "They need a rest, Majesty. It will be at least three or four hours before we should press on. We can stop here. There is good grass. There are some trees. The dawn is heralded. We should rest before the battle."

"Where would such a fashionable battle be held? Not here. Not anywhere that I can see." Pastoria hopped down off the chariot and kicked at the dirt in the dim road. "We have come so far only to sleep as the sun rises."

"The horses need rest." Bartleby removed the harnesses and slapped the horses' rumps to move them away from the chariot. They happily trotted down into the grassy glen and found breakfast.

"We have some time to rest, Majesty. May I suggest that you sleep? You want your eyes to be clear for the battle."

"Yes. My eyes. All the better to see it with. Where shall I..?"

"In the chariot, Sire. That will be the safest and most comfortable. I will watch here."

"Of course."

As soon as Pastoria's snores shattered the morning stillness, Bartleby O'Brine pulled off his boots and fell asleep next to the wheel of the chariot.

They would find the battle on the border of the West and South. It would be wondrous and great—a battle worthy of a king's attention. Bartleby smiled as he drifted off to sleep. A happy king would handsomely reward his charioteer. No doubt he would be a general before too many more hours had passed. That would show all of them. General Bartleby O'Brine, commander of all of the Emerald Armies. Yes. That would show them.

In the scrapyard, after Nikidik finished loading the rolling platforms, he shook the sleeping girl awake and pointed to the sky brightening with the coming sunrise.

Nikidik led Ola Griffin to the front door of the castle and turned to go. The door opened. Promethus stepped out.

"You're still here."

"I have my treasures, and I am leaving."

"Ola, are you all right?" No response. "Ola, are you all right?" Promethus repeated. He went and put a hand on her shoulder. "Are you all right?"

The blonde girl jumped in surprise. "Oh. Me? Yes. I'm fine, thank you."

"Why didn't you answer?"

She smiled, and she forced the uncomfortable smile longer than she needed to, and then she shrugged.

"What did you do to her?" Promethus asked, but Nikidik had already walked into the castle through the open door. Promethus followed after him and repeated his question.

"*Chronometria.*" Nikidik said, reading the coat of arms hanging above the doorway. "It fits. I like it. Your choice?"

Promethus shook his head. "No. Glinda's."

"It suits what this place is now—a temple to measure time. That is not what it used to be. This was the place where we made weapons that changed the world. This is where wars were fought—on these drawing boards. This was the holiest place in this bloody land. This is where we proved once and for all that the Witches could not be trusted. If you're born with the power, it means nothing to you. But if you earn it—if you build your destiny from sweat and metal and fire—the power is yours forever."

"The land is different now. The blood and fire isn't what it once was. Now go."

"This is a place out of time. It feels different, like the lands outside the Ruby Palace. Remember that day? All time stood still. That is how this place feels. It is not home anymore."

"It never was your home. You always returned to your lair in Mount Munch."

"Yes. There is something to be said for the familiar shadows. Perhaps that is why you haunt this place."

Ola Griffin smiled uncomfortably as she slipped in the door. "May I come in?"

Promethus looked at Nikidik and narrowed his eyes. "What did you do to her?"

"I fished her out of a cast-off frame from one of Master Smith's dark paintings. The poor girl fell through. If you'll look at her ankles, she's been grabbed. And before you point those accusing eyes at me, I have Margolotte at home. This one is sweet to look on, but I am happy with my statue, thank you."

"You keep asking what is wrong with me." Ola Griffin said. "There's nothing wrong with me. Look. I'm fine."

"Think back to last night. Yesterday. What were we talking about? How many Fighting Girls are here? Forty-three?"

Ola looked to the left, then studied the floor. She pursed her lips and rocked back and forth between her heels and toes. Then she shrugged. "I know you think I'm supposed to know that. I'm sorry—I don't. I feel like I need to be somewhere, maybe here. I'm not thinking very clearly right now. I don't know you. I'm pretty good with names. Tell me once and I never forget. I woke up outside and this man was there, but I don't think you told me your name, did you?"

"Of course not, my dear. It is mine, and I do not share well." Nikidik said.

"Her memory is gone. You gave her some of that water to drink."

"Such creatures as these are not meant for the darkness beneath the frames. They had her."

"It is no reason to—she was brilliant. She was as good as I ever was. Her mind—she knew people. How could you?" Promethus glared and clenched his jaw. His face turned an angry beet red.

Nikidik smiled wanly. "I was only thinking of the girl."

"She is more than a girl!"

"Sentimental. Females are pretty things that cook and dance and sing. You and I are the thinkers."

"*HA!*" Promethus' breath exploded out of him in a blast of indignant frustration.

"I'm still right here. I can hear you." Ola Griffin said, raising her hands questioningly. "What is the problem?"

Promethus takes a deep breath and forces a smile. "Ola Griffin. That is your name. Will you do something for me? Step outside the door and knock four times."

"That's not going to prove anything." She said, stepping outside the door.

Knock. Knock. Knock.

Promethus waited for the fourth knock. He cracked his knuckles and glared at Nikidik. The candle on the distant table flickered, casting dancing shadows on the door in front of them.

Finally Nikidik smiled. "Would you like to, or should I?" Without waiting for the answer, he opened the door.

Ola Griffin stood there, bewildered and embarrassed. Tears streamed down her cheeks. "I'm sorry. I don't know where I am. I think I was supposed to do something, but I don't remember."

Promethus sighed deeply and offered his open hand to the girl. "Come in, lass. We'll figure it out."

Nikidik fished a wrapped bundle out of his jacket pocket. He handed it to Promethus. "You know what this is. Give it to her. Time can be her friend until then."

Promethus took the small bundle and slipped it into his pocket. Nikidik touched Ola Griffin on the arm. She tried to smile, but she didn't recognize him enough to force one to her distraught face. Her eyes searched the thin man's face for any sign of truth, recognition, or meaning—anything would have helped. She found nothing for her in those hard eyes.

Nikidik said, "You sipped only *twice* of the Water of Oblivion. Your memory is not gone forever. The ruby pendant will give you a long life. May you stay forever young as your mind heals and prepares you for the coming night."

36 SECRET OF THE WIZARD

Before the sun cleared the horizon, Promethus had harnessed Glinda's horses again and hitched them to the chariot. He carried two precious treasures with him—neither of which would make Glinda trust him ever again. The one was the secret from her lockbox that she worked so hard to keep hidden. The other was Ola Griffin, who sat beside him in the chariot.

Promethus took the reins in his hands and stepped into the chariot. As he lifted the reins to snap them, he saw a small shadow out of the corner of his eye. He paused and turned his head.

A young teenage girl, Eyve, looked up at him. "I saw Lady Glinda leave last night with the Fighting Girls. Now you are leaving. When are you coming back?"

"Child, what business is that of yours?"

"I want to join the Fighting Girls. I have what it takes. The soldier told me so."

"Is that so?" Promethus turned impatiently toward the dark horizon ahead. "I suppose he gave you that flower on your ear, too?"

Eyve reached up and touched the blossom on her ear. Her eyes searched the older man's face for some hint of compassion or reason. It was not found there.

Then Ola Griffin reached out and placed her hand on his arm. He looked down at her earnest, innocent gaze. Promethus sighed and looked back at Eyve. "Child, there are very difficult circumstances right now. I do not know when the sorceress will return. I hope that all of them will return, but I cannot say for certain. War is a hungry beast that does not stop eating until it is satisfied."

"Can I come with you? I have a sword."

"If you can swing a sword, your place will be here. No land will be spared. I cannot take you, child. I have my responsibility. I wish you well, but I cannot help you." Promethus snapped the reins and headed northwest to find Glinda and her army.

Eyve watched them go. They were headed north and west, toward the border. If Glinda and her Fighting Girls were facing war, they would need all the help they could get. She rattled her sword in its scabbard on her back and then reached up and touched the flower tucked into her hair by her ear. They needed another soldier. They needed her.

Morning came as the sun rose heavy and glared down with disappointment at the borderlands. The sun had no reason to smile, and neither did Glinda. She dismissed the soldiers and ordered them privily to watch Kally—she was not to be trusted. Then Glinda stepped away to talk with the Wizard.

"Oscar, do you know what you have done? You have destroyed my faith in others. After I met you, everyone else, is just, plainly, everyone else. No matter how you protest, and how you decry, you are no excuse for ordinary. I'm sorry, but you couldn't be ordinary if your life depended on it.

"You embrace the shadows and spin your yarns to make people imagine that you are invisible, but you are not invisible. You are the thread that winds through the stories. Your light is what makes the shadows dance. Your stories reassure the people that the great shadows they see are merely puppets.

"Your majesty dwarfs any pretense of evil. You light up the world in a way that any single other person cannot. You have thrived and built and created where there was nothing before. Every time you sleep, you wake up with something new to do. You are unique in all the world."

Oscar listened with disbelieving ears. "I'm not. I'm really not. I'm a scared kid running from shadows. You know that. You've ripped out my nightmares. You're the one person in all the world who knows how deplorable and flat I really am. My tricks are just tricks. Stories are how I cope."

Glinda shook her head and rolled her eyes in angry disbelief. "You are full of madness and wonder. How can something so magnificent not see itself?"

"So you're not mad?"

"I am absolutely furious. You are the greatest danger to yourself. Death followed you from the West. War trails in your wake. Without your antagonism, we would have a stern ally still living, even though he was more of an unwilling enemy. Now we have many enemies who know your face. Oscar, I know your face."

"I know yours, Sorceress. You are not alone in your disgust of this Wizard." He laughed and yawned. He blinked his red eyes heavily. "Or maybe you are. Do you disgust me? Do I disgust me? Oh, how you will never know the depths to which the disgust of my reflected life has sunk. I defy you, Princess, to discover within yourself a greater source of darkness than that which you see before you. You have seen my nightmares, but have you known them? Have you discovered that thread which winds through every breath I take? Have you rattled the bones in my skeleton's closet? When you see more than puppets, you might be getting through to the meat of this man."

"Your closet bears no skeletons, Oscar, only shadows of the sorrows you left behind. You are the one that gives them life, Oscar. Stand up and be the Wizard you were born to be." Glinda demanded. The hot, angry tears forced themselves through her walls and dropped off her cheeks.

"Born to be a wizard? No, Sorceress, unlike you, I was not born to this. I was born to be a warrior, but I chose to be a coward. I failed in everything. And now…I have failed again." Shadows arose from the dewy brush and walked to surround Oscar in a circle. Standing above them all were two giant shadows. Glinda knew them—they were the shadows she had seen in her Echo Chamber. These were the giants that hunted for Oscar's pistols. She reached into the pocket of her dress and felt the powerful weight of the pistol there.

"Now you have what you have always wanted. Sorceress, behold my secrets."

Glinda looked from Oscar's face to the circle of shadows that surrounded him in the morning sunlight. She shook her head. "Oscar, you don't have to do this. Don't let this happen. It is a dream. It is not real."

"Being a dream does not make it any less real. See, being haunted by a dream is worse than being hunted by a predator. In sleep there is no rest. There is no escape, because I carry this haunting with me."

"Is that, then, what a dream has become—a haunting? What happened to the dream of liberty, freedom, and responsibility for all?"

Oscar's once cheery voice was silent. His bloodshot eyes gazed on Glinda's tear-streaked face. Her anger burned through the tears, so that none of the teardrops traversed in their journey even as far as her chin. She was angry at him. The Wizard turned away from Glinda and hung his head. "I am tired," he whispered.

"Are you tired of living up to expectations? Are you tired of all that you promised and filled the people's heads with? Remember this, Wizard, it was you who set the bar so high. It was you that carried forth the standard of individual liberty. You are the one who changed this land."

Oscar's shoulders slumped even further. The Sorceress softened her tone. She stepped forward, crossing the distance between them, and put her hand on his shoulder. Her eyes followed the sad Wizard's gaze down to the shackles on his wrists—the shackles that Glinda had personally placed on him. "Oscar…it is for your own protection."

"Sorceress, your attention is required." Glinda heard Omby-Amby's gruff voice call to her from behind the brush.

"I will return momentarily, Wizard. Oscar, please look at me." When Oscar refused to meet her earnest gaze, Glinda turned to walk down into the bushes toward the sound of the voice.

Oscar stared down at the ground and smiled bitterly to himself. Glinda would be angry, but throwing his voice was a trick he did not perform often enough. With everything falling apart, what more was there to do? He could at least have a little bit of fun before she marched him to the guillotine to ceremoniously remove his head.

Kally appeared next to the Wizard. His eyes followed the skirt up to Kally's dancing amber eyes. "Walk with me, handsome?"

Kally took the Wizard by the elbow. One, two, three steps, and they were gone.

Glinda came back around the brush, gritting her teeth and fighting back a grimace of embarrassment—Omby-Amby was nowhere near; he had not called her. Glinda stopped short when she saw the empty stone.

The Wizard was gone.

37 MORNING MAGIC

Glinda yanked the Ruby Spectacles out of her pocket and quickly held them up in front of her eyes. Far in the distance, away from the rising sun, she saw the burning magic of the Wizard. He was traveling extremely fast. Glinda ran to the top of the rise, but then she lost the Wizard's aura over the horizon. "Omby! Wickrie! He's gone!"

Across the dry gulch, the Winged Monkeys howled in anger. The strongest among them took off into the air, spiraling higher and higher. Their distant screams echoed on the wind, raising the hair on the back of Glinda's neck.

Omby-Amby made it to the top of the rise only a step ahead of Wickrie-Kells.

"He's gone." Glinda snapped. "You called me, and I turned away. When I turned back, he was gone."

"I did not call you, Glinda. I was with Wickrie at the edge of the riverbed." Omby-Amby answered.

Wickrie-Kells nodded her head in agreement. There was still a hollowness in her eyes that she hoped Glinda would not see.

"If you didn't..." She narrowed her eyes and looked out to the horizon. "Oscar. He tricked me."

Omby-Amby and Wickrie-Kells exchanged a quick glance. "Glinda—" Wickrie-Kells began.

"How did he escape? I had him shackled."

"You had him shackled." The soldier with green whiskers repeated.

"I just said that." Glinda snapped. "It was for his own protection."

"His protection?" Omby-Amby asked, "Or your satisfaction?"

"One of my friends is dead. The Winged Monkeys are ready for war. Their king was killed because of the Wizard."

"I showed you my hands." Omby-Amby clenched his fists. "I showed you the blood."

"It is on *his* head!"

"It is on *my* hands." Omby firmly declared.

Wickrie-Kells shifted back and forth. She pulled her long ponytail up over her shoulder, and her fingers nervously twisted the hairs at the end. "Glinda."

"What?" Glinda snarled.

"It wasn't just Oscar. Last night…"

"Then who? That girl? Who was she?"

"Glinda we need to talk about last night. You need to know what happened."

"I know what happened. I know more than you do. I talked with Docket, the new king of the Winged Monkeys. He told me what happened to his father. He saw it all."

"Glinda, don't blame Oscar. We saved him."

"You saved him from his own bone-headed monstrousness. You should have left him to pay for his sins. He very nearly ignited a war between the South and the West. We can ill-afford a war right now. You know that—you're the captain of my guard. And you," Glinda pointed a finger at Omby-Amby, "Are the captain of the Emerald City Guard. Why were you not protecting the Wizard?"

"I did protect the Wizard."

"You stuck your sword through the heart of a king!"

"He was going to kill my best friend." Omby declared, crossing his arms over his chest. "I did what any friend would do. I reached out my hand to him. I didn't shackle and bind him for his own protection. I did what I do best."

Glinda's eyes crashed from stormy into full-blown maelstrom. "*SILENCE!* I will not be talked to in this way."

"Glinda, it was all of us." Wickrie-Kells said quietly.

Omby-Amby shook his head at the taller girl. Tears spilled over her cheeks. She held her chin high, but Glinda turned away from her.

"Who is she?" Glinda asked. Her eyes flashed and stormed. All around her feet, pebbles and dirt shook with the fury of Glinda's anger. The Ruby Spectacles showed red all around Wickrie-Kells, but that was probably just the residual effects of the Wizard being here. "Who is she? They went that way. You have one minute. Then send your soldiers after him."

"Glinda, about last night—"

"WHO IS SHE?" Glinda demanded. She pulled the Ruby Spectacles from her face. "I am done with last night. Do you want your hands to be as bloody as his?"

"My hands are as bloody as his." Wickrie-Kells said softly.

"Don't lie to me. I want the truth. Tell me! Who is the little witch hanging on the Wizard's arm? Why does she look like you?"

Omby-Amby and Wickrie-Kells exchanged a surprised look. "You know, now that you mention it, she does kind of look like you." Omby-Amby said.

"She does not."

"Who is she?"

"Her name is Kally. Oscar met her a few days ago when he went up to Emerald City."

"I told you to stay with him."

"He told me to go. I needed the sun, and he was a big puddle of glum."

Glinda turned to Omby-Amby. "Soldier, what can *you* tell me about this witch?"

The formal address was not lost on Omby-Amby. He stood up a little straighter, though his eyes hardened against his friend. "I don't know if she's a witch. Oscar likes her. She's a pretty face that keeps him from dreaming bad things. If you are not going to be at his side, at least he's not storming up Emerald City with dark clouds."

"Where is she from? How did they meet? Why does she look like Wickrie-Kells?"

"I don't know. Wickrie already told you. And I don't know. Maybe she is a long-lost cousin."

Glinda put the Ruby Spectacles back on and looked out to the horizon. Nothing. "He's gone." Glinda forced her voice to moderate. "Omby-Amby, order your soldiers to spread out and find him. I want the Wizard within two days."

"How many?"

"We hold this border. Send who you can spare. Wickrie, order the girls the same. Give your orders and return. I will be watching."

Far away, Glinda was not the only one who was watching. From her tower in Yellow Castle, Ondri-baba watched with her magic eye. The eye gave her powers to see far distances. She watched Glinda and her friends as they gathered on the border. Then several soldiers left to head east. Her Winged Monkeys flew high into the sky all along the border, but they didn't cross it. The Wizard had been driven from the lands of the West. The Monkeys had fulfilled her command.

The cost was acceptable.

She saw the body of King Klick. His death was a certain reminder that this war was not over. There would be many more casualties before power was settled. It was a shame—his ugliness was a helpful illustration of the power of the Golden Cap. The vicious burns served to remind the other monkeys of the price of rebellion. He had received them during the Battle of Munchkin Fields as he tried to retrieve the Golden Cap from the flaming ruins of Kalinya's house. His gruesome appearance had kept the other monkeys aware of the power the Golden Cap held over them, and, by extension, the power that Ondri-baba held over the Golden Cap.

Two commands. Twice now she had used the Golden Cap. Once to conquer the Winkies. That had won her this marvelous land of the West, with the Winkies as her faithful subjects, and all of their metalworking skill at her beck and call. And the second command was nearly as gratifying as the first. Yes. *Drive the Wizard from the lands of the West.*

So much for Oz, the Great and Terrible. The coward had run. The Winged Monkeys had driven him out. He was not so great and powerful after all. It required the betrayal of her sister to get him out of Yellow Castle. Given Kalinya's history of destruction, Ondri-baba was pleased that the damage to the castle was not more extensive.

Ondri-baba descended from the tower. The events on the border could wait. There were at least a score of enemy soldiers left on the border. They would be there for a while, and so would the Winged Monkeys.

The Wicked Witch of the West pulled the Golden Cap out of her pocket. Such power, but such a hideously unfashionable accessory. How could Gayelette create such a thing of ugliness? It was no matter, the Golden Cap belonged to the West now, with Ondri-baba as the head.

The Wizard had quickly found the resting place of the Golden Cap. It could not be kept in a place where it would easily be found. That would risk its theft again. No. It had to be someplace where it could be easily accessed, but not easily found.

The Witch crossed the kitchen. She had no use for the kitchen. All food turned to sand in her mouth. The cupboards were very nearly bare. She had no need to eat, so she did not bother to command the servants to keep the cupboards filled. They were empty all the time now, and they were never used. She stopped in her tracks.

The cupboards were bare, and they were never used. It was simple, easy to remember, but no thief would ever think to search the kitchen for one of the most powerful magical items in all the land. She cackled at her own brilliance. She opened the cupboard door and placed the cap inside, smoothing out the dents and wrinkles. "Await my last and final command, my little ugly thing." She grimaced and closed the door. "Such a hideous thing."

Slowly Ondri-baba crossed the kitchen and entered the throne room. She seated herself on the throne and looked up at the ceiling. It was blurred and indistinct. She waved her hand and removed the invisibility spell from it. All around her, the carvings that detailed the history of the Winkies emerged into full focus. There was a giant pig, and a rainbow, and clouds, and a strange, snakelike witch on a cloud. It looked like the rainbow shackled her.

It was better that these things were not remembered. Let the history begin two years ago with the liberation of the Winkies from their conquerors—the

Winged Monkeys. The Winkies had accepted Ondri-baba as their queen. They were free.

Even though it was morning, the shadows grew long in the throne room. Ondri-baba had searched for her natural eye, but she had not found it anywhere. All she had now was her magic eye, which saw strange things in the shadows. She waved her hands again, and all of the carvings on the walls and ceilings blurred and grew indistinct. The invisibility could not make them disappear completely, but it could make them blurry enough to blend with the shadows that lay over the land. It was better this way. *Forget all the past and live in today only.*

With no past, there were no hurts, hates, or heartaches. There was only this moment, lived in shadows, unworried by the darkness of former actions. Unfettered by the concerns of past failings, fears, or friendships, Ondri-baba could live her life fully free.

She frowned and slouched in the throne. She drummed her fingers on the arm of the ornate metal throne and scratched her empty eye socket.

"Tomorrow." She said. "Tomorrow I will see the border lands for myself."

Kally and Oscar sped across the landscape, zipping from horizon to horizon in three steps. Kally only stopped to allow Oscar to catch his breath at the edge of a forest. The silence all around them was punctuated by Oscar's gasping and gulping in air.

Kally peered down at the flopping wizard and smiled at him. "We escaped."

"How did you do that?"

Kally studied the horizon behind them, "My family knows secrets to travel quickly."

"Where are we?"

"The forest."

"Which forest?"

"Doesn't matter—the forest. We are safe from their prying eyes and binding hands." Kally crouched down to touch the shackles binding Oscar's wrists. "You are hurt."

Oscar twisted his wrists in the shackles. "My wrists are raw. I would like to get out of these cuffs."

"I think we can figure out something." Kally wrapped her fingers around the bars and chains binding the wrist shackles together. "Up," she commanded.

Oscar rose unsteadily to his feet. He tried to stifle a yawn, but his hands couldn't help to hide it. His mouth opened wide.

Kally flicked her finger, and a tiny pebble on the ground flew backwards and into Oscar's yawning mouth.

He choked.

"Close your mouth. You're not trying to catch flies."

Oscar choked and spit. He stared at the ground in bewilderment. Then he laughed. "What are the odds? I open my mouth and a fly goes right in."

"What odds indeed?" Kally repeated.

The young-looking witch led Oscar into the forest. They jumped over streams and zipped through open spaces with Kally's secret quick travel. At last they found what Kally was looking for. "There. Now we can get these shackles off your poor wrists."

"It's a stump."

"Yes. We can break the shackles."

"With a stump?" Oscar's tired mind was earnestly trying to catch up, but the shadows danced wildly behind every tree, distracting him from any rational thought.

"I'll find a rock or a stick to pry the chains apart. Simple." She looked around and found a suitable wedge-shaped rock. "A-ha. I can put this in between the ring there. Then I can pound it in and it will pry the ring apart."

"Okay." Oscar agreed hesitantly.

"Put your wrists on the stump."

Oscar knelt and clenched his fists. He set them down in front of him on the stump. Kally set the point of the wedge in the metal ring. She raised the wedge high above her head like a dagger. Oscar flinched and closed his eyes.

Kally slammed the rock wedge down, using her telekinetic magic to drive the stone deep into the stump.

Oscar pried open an eye and wiggled his fingers. "All there." Then he pulled up on the shackles. They didn't budge. The stone wedge was embedded in the stump.

"Oops. I thought that would work."

"I'm stuck."

"I'll fix this."

"You'd better."

"What are you going to do?"

Oscar yawned again. "Right now, probably nothing. I can't even keep my eyes open. Fine. You figure out a way to break these bonds, and I'll stay here and sleep."

Kally walked around the stump that imprisoned Oscar. It was a good prison—no chance of him getting away. Now, there was just the matter of his promise. There were certainly wild animals somewhere in the forest that she could use to her advantage.

"Wizard, you owe me a dream. You promised, remember? And a Wizard's promise is better than gold."

"I will dream for you later—another time. Just fix this, please. I don't want to be chained to this stump for long."

"I'll get you out."

Oscar's head drooped and he yawned widely.

"Oh. Are you tired? Didn't they let you sleep? That wicked, wicked girl. Here, I'll give you my jacket as a pillow. Just lay down your head and sleep." She rolled her jacket and placed it on the stump. She put her hand on the top of Oscar's head and guided his head to the makeshift pillow.

Oscar laid his head down, but he didn't close his eyes yet. "You have striped stockings."

Kally looked down and lifted her long skirts slightly. "Yes, I do. Now sleep. You have been roughly treated, and your strength is depleted, Wizard. You are going to need all the strength you can get for the coming days. Big things are ahead for you."

"I'll sleep, but I don't know if I'll dream. I'll try because I promised." Oscar yawned again. "Kiss me good night?"

Kally swished her skirts uncomfortably. "Why?"

"So I can have sweet dreams."

Kally leaned down and kissed Oscar on top of the head. "There. Now dream. Tigers and bears."

"Oh my." Oscar smiled. Then he closed his eyes. "That's one for luck. Now for love." Oscar puckered his lips. "Then for lollipops."

Love, luck, and lollipops. Kally froze. That was an old Munchkin phrase used by youth back when...when she was young. It meant that two people were falling in love. Could it be? The Wizard and a Witch? With all that had happened, it just might be worth a try.

Kally leaned in close to the Wizard's face. He was so *young*. She watched the furrow of his brow as thoughts went through his head. Comparing her to Glinda, no doubt. But his eyes didn't open. For a man who held nearly the whole of Oz in his power, this Wizard was so naïve and trusting. Kally pressed her lips to Oscar's. A wave of strange warmth flooded through Kally, and she pulled away. That couldn't be right. *Love*. She leaned in for one more quick kiss. That was *luck*. Her entire body felt warm. Did she dare? *Lollipops*.

"Dream now, Oscar." She said, stepping backwards. Then she turned, and took one, two, three steps and disappeared.

When Kally looked back from the top of the hill, the Wizard had not moved. She felt the flush on her cheeks. It burned all the way to the back of her neck. The sun was certainly warm this morning. It filled her entire body with warmth. Then she forced herself to stand straight, and turn back to the forest. There was work to do, and only a Wizard's dream-time to get it done in.

Kally's amber eyes softened as she looked down on Oscar. "You make me feel like I could be loved. But one does not become powerful by being loved." Three steps, and she was gone.

On the stump below, Oscar licked his lips as he drifted off to sleep. He mumbled, "Yuck. Tastes like sand."

Kally flitted around the forest, listening and reaching out with her magic. The dream would start soon. She had to make it possible. She had to be there when it happened. Oscar was many things, but he was not a liar—he would dream for her. And oh, what a dream it would be.

"You, Wizard, are the best thing that has ever happened to me. You and your…" Kally's voice grew hoarse and gravelly. She coughed, but it would not clear. Then she looked at her hands. They were starting to age, also. She applied the unguent to her skin and face. She felt the burning as it penetrated deep, searing away the years of age to leave only youth behind. What was it Nikidik had said about her voice? Oh yes, singing. Singing would help to make the voice sound younger.

Kally sighted a nearby sunny hilltop and stepped one, two, three steps, and she was in the sun. She looked around and found the Wizard's dreaming stump down below. She could make her voice heard from here—just enough to remind him. Kally closed her eyes and let the familiar melody fill her until it floated from her throat in gravelly notes that worked off their rough edges. Before the end of the first few lyrics, Kally's voice was clear and strong again. She sang, and the melody filled the wood.

> *Twinkle, twinkle while you sleep*
> *Powr's of dream are mine to keep*
> *While you slumber over there*
> *Dream for me a tiger-bear.*
>
> *In the forest deep and dark*
> *Fearsome beasts will make their mark*
> *Hungry tiger, angry bear*
> *Monster pulled from world of air*
>
> *Then my chariot shall pull*
> *The beasts for all my golden rule.*
> *That, my Wizard, is my dream*
> *To conquer Oz a Witchy Queen.*
> *Twinkle, twinkle while you sleep*
> *Powr's of dream are mine to keep.*

When the last notes ended, Kally listened closely for the expected echo. Growling and snuffling sounded from the shadows of the forest. Kally clapped her hands and peered through the trees. There they were! Huge shadowy beasts, sniffing and pawing at the ground and trees. *It worked!* The song and the dream of the Wizard worked! The beasts were real. They were as wonderful as she imagined they would be.

The beasts boasted the fearsome heads of tigers with the strong paws and bodies of a bear. Yes. They were far better than wolves to pull a chariot. That would show her sister—that would show everyone. Nobody was ever going to have a chariot more powerful than Kalinya, the one true Witch Queen.

The strange beasts emerged into the light. Their round pupils resized as they looked at Kally. She clasped her hands in front of her and bounced up and down in excitement. Then she could bear it no more.

"You are wonderful!" She rushed to the beasts and hugged them around the neck. She kissed every one of them on the top of the head. The growled and snarled in their throats, but they recognized her as their master. "You are mine. Come. We have a wizard to awaken."

Kally skipped through the forest using the Silver Slippers. She only skipped about thirty yards at a time, allowing the hulking beasts to see her each step of the way. They crashed through the forest, snarling and roaring their excitement. The entire forest held its breath as these newly-dreamed monsters made their presence felt in the Land of Oz.

Oscar slowly rose through the levels of dream to waking. He didn't want to open his eyes. This was the first sleep he had in a while, even if...was that growling? Oscar's eyes popped open. His head was laying sideways on the stump. Where were the shackles? There they were—still pounded securely into the stump, but they were no longer around his wrists. How did the shackles get off him? They were securely locked, but they were not locked on him. Oscar looked at his wrists, red and sore. They he looked up at Kally.

"You probably dreamed them off. But you're awake now? Good. I have a surprise for you." Kally smiled at him.

It was a nice smile—strangely nice. Oscar wrinkled his nose. What was that smell? And that sound...sniffing? That sound must be coming from a very large nose. He felt the heavy, insistent pressure on his back. His eyes widened and darted up to see Kally's smile again. She nodded excitedly.

Oscar turned his head slowly as he sat up. Several panting tiger faces stared back at him with yellow eyes. He slowly turned back to read Kally's face.

"They have my eyes. Aren't they wonderful?"

"I'm not dreaming?" Oscar whispered.

"Not anymore." Kally smiled broadly. "Yes, they're real. And they're absolutely amazing."

"Oh." Oscar nodded numbly.

Oscar's scream echoed over the entire forest for a full minute.

38 THE WITCH'S ARMY

Oscar glumly followed Kally from the trees into the prairie where a caravan of junk awaited. "Are you quite satisfied with yourself, Wizard? You frightened them away. Now I shall have to find them."

"It was a rotten thing you did, waking me up with tigers in my face."

"Tiger-bears. They are Tiger-bears." Kally corrected. "Ah, Nikidik, such a pleasure, as always." She surveyed the caravan with a frozen smile on her face. "This is it?"

Nikidik nodded.

"For this, I paid pearls?"

"Yes. When the army rises, you will see the future."

"Very well, then, make them rise."

Oscar looked back behind them to the dark forest and wondered what dreams he had unleashed on an unsuspecting people with his scream.

The startled beasts raced through the forest. Once the initial fear was gone, they ran for the sheer joy of running. The forest ended all too soon, and the Tiger-bears burst out into the fields of Munchkin Country. They stopped and sniffed the air. It smelled different than the forest—strange grass and smoke. All but one of the creatures turned and shuffled back into the shady coolness of the trees.

The Tiger-bear crossed the field to a wooded hillock. The dark house of the witch was here, but it was not the house that interested the creature. It was the strange smell of the small two-legged man in blue. He smelled of delicious fear. The creature crouched and crept around the side of the dark house. The Munchkin knocked on the door. The beast growled in its throat. The man screamed.

The boy, Boq, pushed through the legs of the assembled crowd. They were all worried. A monster was in their lands. Even after three days, the Witch did not answer their summons. This was the more worrisome of the two facts—if they had no Queen Protector, then the monster was a greater threat.

Boq pushed his way to the inner ring of the circle. A man, Boq recognized him as the runner for Duke Widdershins, lay on the ground. His jaw looked funny, kind of crooked. His fingers spasm'd as he tried to sit up.

Duke Widdershins appeared, and the crowd parted for him. "What is the meaning of this? Mukluck, what happened, my good man?"

The injured runner, Mukluck, raised himself up on an elbow and gestured with his hands back the way he came. "Monster." He slurred.

"A monster?" Duke Widdershins exclaimed. "What monster? Where?"

"Kal...i...ah." Mukluck painfully forced the syllables through his crooked jaw.

"Ka...lee...dah?" Duke Widdershins repeated.

Boq ran forward. "He said, *Kalinya*. The monster was made by Kalinya."

"Quiet, boy. I know what I heard. He said *Kalidah*. That's what he said." Then Duke Widdershins turned to the assembled crowd. "This man, my friend, was mauled by a Kalidah. Be on your best guard, good people. We have fierce monsters in our land. They are called Kalidahs."

Boq frowned and pushed his way through the crowed to run out into the fields. If there were any monsters, it was the witch who brought them. Boq was not afraid of her, and he was not afraid of any monsters she brought, either.

Someday they would listen to him. Boq stopped and sat down in the tall grass outside the field. They would know he was right, and they would listen to him. On that day, he would have a sword. Then he could fight all of the monsters and all of the wickedness in the land.

One by one, Professor Nikidik raised the automaton soldiers from the scraps he brought with him. Not one piece was wasted as he stood them up in a line. There were prototype wheelers, sickle-hands, hammer-tails, and more. As he finished each soldier, he crowned it with the Crown of the Dreamer and slid the mask over its face.

Kally watched in growing wonder as the automaton shuddered and moved of its own volition. Nikidik pointed each soldier toward Kally and whispered some words. Then he removed the Crown of the Dreamer, and he moved on to the next soldier.

Kally joined Nikidik at the scrap cart. The animated soldiers assisted in removing all of the scraps and placing them in separate piles for animation.

More than two dozen automatons of various sizes were assembled and moving on their own. "That is amazing—better work than the first batch."

"What did you do with those?" Nikidik asked.

Kally averted her eyes and looked over toward Oscar. "They were destroyed in the siege of Ondri-baba's castle."

"Pity. They cost you a fortune."

"How are you raising these ones? I have the unguent. You cannot animate the unliving without the unguent."

"The prototype unguent which you have is to give life to the thing which has a semblance of life. It animates, certainly, but it does not do anything but obey." Professor Nikidik smiled silently, daring the next question.

Kally withstood the dare as long as she could, but her burning need for knowledge would not allow her to let the question go unasked. "Then what does the Crown of the Dreamer do?"

"It does exactly what the Golden Cap does. It gives form and solid existence to that which is no longer solid, or that which has never been solid."

Kally looked around in surprise. "What have you done?"

"Oh, you recognize this place? Good. I picked this location for its historical significance. On this spot your ancestors slaughtered all who opposed their standard of power. They marched from here north to Parradime and utterly destroyed it. There was not an emerald block atop another. The shining walls were forgotten until your Wizard ordered them built again. Yes, Kalinya, the ghosts of the past remember this place. I have shown them that you are their leader. I have given them hands to fight once again. They burn in their desire for battle."

"Those generations-ago ghosts now live in these metal soldiers?" Kally asked, unsure of their loyalty. "Whose army are they?"

"They are your army."

"Will they turn?"

"You are afraid they will turn and rend you. No, they will not. The ghosts of this place only remember the battle. They do not remember faces or names. Show them their new face and they would probably disconnect from material reality. They suit you, do they not?"

"Yes." Kally answered cautiously. "What do you get from this? The soldiers far exceed the price paid."

"Exceed, yes. Far exceed? No. In a word, my reward is *vindication*. With this army, and the resulting demonstration of its *shade'd* power, I will prove that my masters and my fellow apprentices were wrong—*war is the surest path to relevance*. It is not a dying art, nor is it a passing fancy. *War is life*. And I," Nikidik stuck his chin proudly to the sky, "bring life."

Oscar wandered over to Kally and Nikidik. He watched the ceremonial placement of the Crown of the Dreamer on the unliving automaton and its subsequent shuddering animation. "Why don't you just wind it up?"

Nikidik forced a cold smile. "My dear Wizard, wind-up toys are for my masters. I have moved beyond such trinkets. These are life incarnate. They are the ghosts of battles past reborn in new bodies. They are in every sense the perfect creation."

"They don't have faces—well, a few do, almost."

"They have no need of faces. They act, they do not think. All they are built for is present in their form. The function fits the form. They are an army to serve the needs of the greatest good."

"And what good is that?" Oscar asked.

Kally quickly stepped between Oscar and Nikidik. "What does it matter? These soldiers will stand as a sleepless adversary to all those who would control others."

Oscar walked up to one of the faceless automatons. It stopped and turned its head toward the shorter man.

"Don't hurt him." Kally ordered.

"I am going to try something." Oscar replied. "I won't hurt him."

"I wasn't talking to you." Kally muttered.

Oscar dug in his pocket and pulled out a red wax crayon. He drew eyes and a smiling mouth on the faceless surface of the head. Then he turned around to show Kally. "He has a face. He looks more like a person now."

Nikidik was not amused. "They have no need of faces." To the smiling automaton, he ordered, "Finish unloading those pieces."

Kally took Oscar by the elbow and pulled him away from the soldiers. "Oscar, darling, you need to let the Professor do his work. He doesn't need your criticisms right now."

"I know his type. He is like my brother Conroy—older than me but not the oldest. He always had to prove himself against my oldest brothers. Never found my jokes very funny. When he found out that they...he didn't cry. He was angry. I don't know what he wanted—after them, he was the oldest."

"That's nice. This used to be a great battleground. Do you think you could find a wall or something that we might be able to do some demonstrations around?"

"Sure." Oscar said slowly. "I can do that." He turned away. "You don't have to like him, Kally. You hired him to do this. It's his job."

"It's my army. I need that wall. Go."

"You know the strength of Glinda's army? It is less than these, I presume?" Nikidik asked the Witch.

"I will crush her and be rid of that red-haired scourge forever. And I will test my army. So I win both ways."

"Where is the Wizard?"

"I cannot have him underfoot right now. I need these soldiers to rise up and do exactly as they are told."

Behind them, on the scrap cart, the smiley-face soldier picked up a piece of reflective metal. He stopped as he saw something. The automaton slowly reached up and touched its face plate. In the reflection it traced the crayon-drawn eyes and mouth. Another automaton returned to the cart to collect parts. The smiley-face held out the shining metal in front of the other's face plate. No response. No recognition. The second automaton took the metal and turned and walked away.

"They will be your perfect army." Nikidik rubbed his hands together. "There is more. When you are ready to crush them, release the thunder colossus."

"Sounds terrifying."

"For *them*. I have entrapped the essence of true power inside this construct. When it is released, the colossus will rise up. Lightning is his eyes and thunder his shout. He will rain destruction on your enemies."

"To what do I owe this unexpected surprise?" Kally asked, suddenly suspicious.

"Victory. Vigilance. Vendetta. I expect that this will be the beginning of a fortuitous business relationship. Life will come again to Oz."

"By life, you mean war."

Nikidik answered, "War is life."

Oscar walked through the trees at the edge of the forest. He had not found any wall yet. It was probably just a ruse to get him to leave the Professor alone. Kally seemed much more distant today. She had her soldiers—that was what she really wanted. She had her monsters. Those were a nightmare, thanks to him. Nothing about this day had gone right. Considering the few winks of sleep that he had gotten in the last five or six days, it all seemed like one horrible, terrible waking nightmare. There was no way that this could get worse.

The Fighting Girl saw the Wizard from across the broad valley. Her keen eyesight spotted him as he went into the trees. She made her way from cover to cover, always keeping her eyes open for the enemy. Then she saw the soldiers—constructs like the ones that the Winged Monkeys had destroyed. There was an entire army of them. She raced across the final open space to the forest. She searched quickly and quietly for the Wizard.

There he was—his feet twitched once as he slumped down at the base of a tree. Was he dead? She looked around and silently dropped to the ground beside him. She felt his neck for a pulse and put her ear close to his mouth to listen for breathing.

Oscar opened his eyes to feel a hand on his throat. He screamed, halfway. The Fighting Girl's grip tightened and cut of the scream before it reached the edge of the forest.

"You're alive. Praise be to the faeries." The girl said.

Oscar pulled the hand away from his throat. "Who are you? You're one of Glinda's girls, aren't you? I'm not going back to her."

"They have an army down there. I was sent to find you."

"Everybody was sent to find me—I'm the Wizard. Don't you know? Everyone wants me."

"Yes, everyone."

"If only that was true." Oscar murmured. "If you please, I'm trying to sleep. There is going to be a demonstration soon, and I want to be awake for it."

"I am going to bring you back."

"I am not going back. I made my choice—long ago. The die has been cast. This is the life I have. With all of its shadows and terrors, I deserve nothing else. You have a better chance of forgetting and moving on than I do. My best wishes with you."

"I thank you, Wizard, but I need you to come with me to the edge of the valley. You need to see what I see."

"What is your name?" Oscar asked, blinking his eyes sleepily.

"Rala. You very nearly asked me to dance at the Sky Wizard's Ball."

"Did I?"

"Lady Glinda had the perfect evening planned. I was to take your hand from Ola Griffin and dance with you. Then she would feign jealousy and snatch you up and carry you into a cloud. That was very nearly my role. Then the monkey happened."

"Yes. That was not exactly a splendid evening." Oscar whistled a bird call under his breath.

Rala glanced over to her shoulder, but saw nothing. "Was that you?"

"The birds favor you with their song. Thank you, Rala. I dearly appreciate your effort, but I choose not to go back."

Rala stood up and looked back toward the valley. "Not even to see the metal army that I see?"

Oscar closed his eyes again. That was all.

"You may not believe in us, Wizard, but we still believe in you. I will see you again, soon."

Kally dragged the groggy wizard out of the forest. Her hurried steps nearly caused Oscar to stumble twice between the forest and the army. "Hurry." She kept insisting.

"Can we see this demonstration quickly? I am very tired." Oscar tried to stifle a yawn. "We have been all over the land, and I just want to crawl into a bed and sleep. Kally, why do we have to do this now? Isn't there a better time and place to demonstrate these...whatever they are?"

"You saw what the Winged Monkeys did to the original army. This is a new army. This can be your army, too, Wizard. Think of it—soldiers that never falter in battle. They eat nothing, they never sleep, they never tire, like you so easily do. They are strong, where meat-soldiers can be weak. They follow orders perfectly. The protect and they conquer."

"We had the demonstration of the soldiers outside the Witch's castle. Why do we need another demonstration?" Oscar persisted. "That battle is over. Miss Gulch, the Wicked Witch, the West is lost to us. We don't have an enemy to fight. Fine, I'll take the soldiers. Just march them up to Emerald City and we'll be done. I can go back to my room and sleep for a week, a month, or even a year."

"Oh, no, Wizard, you don't want to sleep through this. You see, while I was rescuing you from the wicked sorceress, I realized that there is another army that threatens the peace in the land. The Winged Monkeys are bound by the confines of their orders. They pose no threat to us while we are beyond the Land of the West. But there is another army on this side of the border that will disrupt the peace that you and I have worked so hard to build. If this threat is not stopped, there will be chaos. There will be blood on your hands."

Oscar's yawn disappeared, and a cold chill passed through is body. His eyes froze on Kally's face. He saw her earnest smile, and it chilled him to the core.

"You don't want blood on your hands, do you?"

Oscar knew what was coming. He saw the trap far too late—he had been caged and imprisoned this whole time, but he only now realized it. He shook his head slowly. "No."

"Yes. We move now. We will see who has the best interests of the Wizard in mind at the end of the battle. We will see who will rule Oz. Will it be Oscar, the Wizard, or Glinda, the pretender?"

In Central City, at a table in the kitchen, Mombi shuffled through papers until she found the proper document. She sat across the table from a pretty girl who cared for the king's Crimson Peacocks.

"I have always been partial to the name Tippetarius—for a boy. It is a clever name. Tippetarius was the hero of *Positus Pax*—*Searching for Peace*. What do you think?"

Leina Le'Mo, the Peacock Girl, made little reply. Her pretty face searched Mombi's face for some sign of consternation or anger—anything that would give away some deceit. There was none. She cleared her throat and spoke. "It's a nice name, Tippy-tare-ee-usss."

Mombi's eyebrows rose and she tried to feign a smile, but the girl's nasally voice and awkward pronunciation made it difficult to take her seriously. Mombi realized that she had never heard the girl speak. Such a pretty face. It was a pity that she looked so much prettier when she did not speak. "Yes, Tippetarius. To be clever is better than being strong. The strongest man may fall if his shoes are tied together."

"But if he was so strong, wouldn't he...*not* tie his shoes together?"

"No, my dear, you see, a clever man can tie a strong man's shoes together, which weakens and limits the strength of the stronger man."

Leina Le'Mo lifted her head halfway in a nod, then stopped with her eyebrows furrowed. She brought her head down and smiled. "Oh."

"That's all right, my dear. You can help me plan this wedding feast. Pastoria and I are going to be married." Mombi reached her hand out toward the girl, but Leina pulled her hands away and folded them in her lap.

"Oh." She said, looking down at her hands.

Mombi searched the girl's face. She wasn't hiding anything—darting eyes looking everywhere but at Mombi, and hands clutched tightly in her lap—she was surprised. "Does that surprise you, girl?"

"Yes, I guess so. I thought that Pastee was never going to marry—he likes his peacocks, you know."

"I am aware. You didn't actually think that you...?"

"I'm pretty. He likes my face. He told me so, once."

"As did I, Leina. As did I. But there is one thing I have that you do not have—power. And power, coupled with a pretty face—like the one that I have—changes everything. He loves me because he wants to keep power, but he cannot keep the power without me. Therefore, to keep the power in his hands, he must take my hand. It's simple enough, even for a girl of your dazzling abilities."

"What'd'ya think I am, stupid or something? I know what you're doing, Mombi. You're not going to take him away from me. I see him every night when he marches the peacocks to sleep. Where do you see him, hmm? He smiles at me. Does he smile at you?"

"I make this kingdom work. Night and day, I ensure that the gears of this city keep moving. Were it not for my efforts, you, my dear, would be out slopping pigs, instead of sweeping the feathers of a king."

"Tippetarius is a dumb name. Who ever heard of a Tippetarius? You said it's from some book. Who reads books? Nobody, that's who. It's not about how you read or how smart you are, it's about how you look. A girl can't get anything in this world if she doesn't look the part. I look the part. My mama told me to keep my mouth quiet and smile like the moon is mine and the boys would come calling. I did and he came. Then you and your books and your meetings, always bringing him to things he doesn't want to do. Why can't you just let him alone? Why do you have to be so always in the way? Let him be with his peacocks. They love him."

"Fancy is a fickle fly on the wall. One that will be swatted, forthwith." Mombi growled.

"The thunder colossus," Nikidik proudly told Kally, "is a magnificent weapon to overcome your enemy. He is too large to build standing up. For greatest effect and surprise, when you are ready, use your magic to stand him upright. He will stand taller than the trees here."

"How does he work? Did you use the Crown of the Dreamer?" Kally asked.

"This one is an experiment in harnessing the power of storms. This fellow was once mighty, but he has forgotten all—just like the rest of this army. His power comes from what he once was, and the inborn need to storm and thunder. I know your issues with water. You would not want to touch this water. There are those better than you that have forgotten its taste."

"There are none better than me." Kally glared.

"Of course."

39 THE PROUD KING

The Fighting Girl, Rala, raced from the valley back the way she had come. Along the way, at the highest points of her trail, she shouted the signal to each direction, letting the other soldiers know that the Wizard had been discovered.

Rala arrived at the camp late afternoon. She quickly related her journey and discovery of the Wizard to Glinda. The red-haired sorceress listened and commanded her small army. "We go to retrieve the Wizard. An army of metal soldiers is our enemy. Give them no quarter. Show them no mercy. Protect and retrieve the Wizard, whatever the cost. We march now."

Promethus arrived at the camp in the borrowed chariot. He approached Glinda with Ola Griffin in tow. "Sorceress, I must speak with you. It is urgent."

"My attention right now, Guardian, is on the missing Wizard. I find you and my herald a distasteful match. You need not flaunt your conquests. She has chosen you—take her."

Ola Griffin recognized the spite in Glinda's voice. "I'm right here. I can hear you. He has done nothing wrong."

"Glinda, she is not the same person. Her memory—"

"That's all she is to me—a memory. If you please, I have an army to command, and an errant Wizard to recover. The future of the Land of Oz is in my hands alone. Do not waste any more of my time."

Glinda mounted a white horse and followed after the soldiers. Two of the Fighting Girls took the reins of the chariot and followed after Glinda, leaving the Guardian and the herald behind.

Promethus looked at the blonde girl that held his hand. "What do you remember, lassie?"

"About what?" Ola Griffin asked innocently.

"Anything, my dear. Anything at all."

"The sky is blue. The grass is green. I know you have kind eyes. I think I remember that I like to sing. Yes, I'm certain of it. I like to sing."

"What is your favorite song? Do you remember what you sang to me in the scrapyard yesterday?"

Ola Griffin smiled awkwardly. Her face reddened and she dropped her gaze. She shook her head.

Promethus patted her hand. "It's okay, lassie. I'll start, and you just pick up where you remember."

> *On meadows dark, o'er cold frosted hill*
> *The nameless wren e'er flutters still*
> *His love is glacien, turning cold*
> *For her his footsteps ever roam.*

Ola Griffin's face brightened as the music struck a familiar chord in her soul. She joined her golden voice to the Guardian's as they filled the sky with the *Odyssey of the Wrenwraith*.

> *He flies the skies, a marcant shield*
> *To Deadly Desert, fjord, and field*
> *And nightly walks him as a man*
> *Still ever-calling Marujan.*

> *The wren-wraith cries, ah Marujan.*
> *I'll find you someday, Marujan.*

They walked side-by-side in the footsteps of the army. Their clear voices filled the air with song. When the song was over, they walked in silence for a few minutes.

Ola Griffin asked, "Where are we going?"

"To find the Wizard."

"Oh. Is he a good man?"

Promethus sighed. "He is a man that needs us to be good for him. He needs our help far more than we need his."

"He sounds sad." Ola Griffin said. "Do you know him?"

"No."

"What's your name?" the blonde girl asked.

"I am the Guardian." Promethus smiled sadly at her. "Do you like to sing?"

"I think so. Yes, I'm sure that I do." She started to hum, then she stopped. "I can't remember how it goes."

"I'll start, and you can join in when you remember."

"There it is, your majesty." Bartleby O'Brine pulled the chariot to a stop.

Pastoria looked over the valley at the assembled soldiers. "They are metal. They shine in the sun. What a fine sight. Fine, fine sight."

"Would you like to get closer?" the soldier asked.

"Take me there."

The chariot leaped into the valley toward the automaton army.

The soldiers from Emerald City and the Fighting Girls gathered to the marching army from all directions. The call had gone out and echoed among the hills. Everyone had heard the echoes. From her position above her army, Kally heard the shouts and she smiled. The red brat was coming.

Glinda placed the Ruby Spectacles on her face. She saw the familiar blaze of the Wizard in the distance. He was still alive. He would be safe before morning.

Glinda's army crested the valley as the sun touched the eastern horizon. It would be a night battle. That was not a good option after a day of marching, but they had no choice.

"Their army stands before you. See their ranks. They are more than us. Look closely—see as I see. They are not living. The heart of a warrior does not beat in their chest. They are cold metal scraplings. Omby-Amby, Wickrie-Kells, you know your soldiers. Cut down the enemy and bring me the Wizard!"

The Captain of the Guard and the Captain of Glinda's Fighting Girls shouted to their soldiers and formed ranks. This was the sole purpose of their training for the past two years. It had been long since the land hand known war—they each knew that they held the fate of Oz in their hands.

"Some of you were with me in the Battle of Emerald Prairie when we fought the bloody sand armies of the Wicked Witches. We have learned much since then. Our arms are strong. We fight for freedom and liberty. We seek not for power, but to pull it down. Our hearts and our voices we raise to the cause of liberty. We conquer this night!" Omby-Amby shouted. His men echoed the shout. The Fighting Girls shouted their agreement.

"Beauty, brains, and belligerence!" Wickrie-Kells shouted. "Are you going to let a bunch of smelly boys win this day? There are the metal men. Crush their heads and capture the Wizard."

The Fighting Girls shouted louder.

"You hear that, men? We have a challenge brewing. They say crush their heads, I say throw their heads into the sky. Hack their arms and let them, disarmed, dance with death."

The Emerald Guard and the Fighting Girls charged the field of battle. They were few against the larger metal army, but they were fierce.

This was not like other battles. Glinda had watched her girls train before—she had even trained with them a few times. Her skill with weapons was nowhere near that of Wickrie-Kells, or really any of the Fighting Girls, but she could swing a sword and stab a scarecrow better than most girls her age. She sat back in her saddle and watched her Fighting Girls attack the unfeeling enemy. They fought for her, and they fought for the Wizard. She hoped that was enough to keep them alive.

The battle turned sour. The swords were not as effective against the metal soldiers as they had anticipated. For every automaton soldier that fell, at least five serious blows rained down on the human soldiers. They were strong, but their flesh was subject to bruising and crushing, where the metal skin of the enemy was not. With every life on the field resting in her hands, Glinda could not sit back any longer. She needed to be part of her Fighting Girls. If they were to conquer, she would bleed with them. If they were to perish, she would be one with them.

Glinda spurred her horse down the hill. Another girl fell under the crushing blows of a hammer-handed automaton. The metal soldier was over seven feet tall with large blocks on the end of its arms. It may have once been used for pounding rocks, but now it put them to use smashing much softer human soldiers. Glinda knew her short sword would be of little use against the giant metal body.

She felt a weight in her skirt pocket, pounding against her leg with every galloping stride the horse took. She reached into her pocket and pulled out the pistol. The hammer-hand lifted both hands for the killing blow. Glinda raced her horse between the fallen girl and the automaton and jerked back on the reins, rearing the horse up on its back legs. She extended the pistol out toward the giant's chest and pulled the trigger.

The sound of thunder.

The entire battlefield froze. Each soldier—flesh and metal alike—turned to look toward Glinda and her unknown weapon.

The hammer-hand soldier slowly toppled backwards. A gaping hole in its chest spat out small gears and springs. It hit the ground and collapsed inward. The body gave up its ghost and lost all movement.

Glinda reared her horse back again and shouted angrily at the inhuman armies. She pointed her pistol and fired again. Another metal man fell, its shattered head slowly rolling off its shoulders, while its body fell the other way.

Fighting Girls and Emerald Guard alike raised a deafening shout.

"I have the Wizard!" Omby-Amby shouted.

Glinda set her sights on the commander of the metal armies. She recognized the girl across the field. Based on the descriptions she had received, there was no doubt that this was the witch that had seduced Oscar.

Glinda shouted to her and to her alone. "You want the Wizard? Come and take him!"

The thunderous echo of the pistol shot sounded throughout the corridors of the unseen realm. From her dominions far away, the Queen of Dreams looked up in surprise as she heard the pistol shots. She smiled in gleeful triumph.

"The chaos has begun—chaos that will bring the Land of Oz under my control. Very soon will come the day when I will enter Oz and rule over your land completely, *Sister*. I will rule Oz completely, Lurline. Then I will be the one *true* Queen of the Faeries."

The battle raged beyond the setting of the sun. As the shadow lengthened, and the thunderous blasts rang out, more and more Emerald Guardsmen and Fighting Girls swung slower and slower. Several more fell.

Up on the edge of the valley, Promethus and Ola Griffin came into view. Promethus visually scanned the valley to find who was living and who was dead. Thankfully, there did not appear to be anyone truly dead yet. And there, across the valley, was the Witch. She commanded the metal armies. There was the Wizard, moved away from the metal armies, but still not completely safe. And there was Glinda, her red hair raging in the last moments of light. Across the valley, watching from a different perspective, was a greater danger—*Professor Nikidik*. That was one adversary that Promethus could face.

As they circled around the perimeter of the valley, Promethus kept himself between Ola Griffin and his former colleague, Professor Nikidik. "What are you doing here?" He asked.

"She is fiery, isn't she?" Professor Nikidik observed, gesturing to Glinda.

"This war is on your hands."

"Yes—the work of and the triumph of my hands and mine alone. This is what we were trained for. All those decades in the shadows of Smith & Tinker, our masters, for this. We were trained to bring life once again to Oz."

"This is not life, this is death. You have brought the strange work of death again to the peaceful land. Your lifeless constructs only know how to destroy."

"Not entirely true. There is one that strangely will not participate. But he is missing out on the fun. Look at her. That weapon she wields—I have never seen its like, have you?"

Glinda leaped off the horse and screamed angrily as she fired another shot from the pistol. It shattered the chest of another automaton. The metal soldier shuddered and collapsed to the ground. The smiley-face automaton watched and waited for the tide to shift, and then crouched beside his fallen compatriot. He dipped his finger in the leaking fluids from the shattered chest and drew a crude face on the blank face plate. An metallic scream arose from the shattered body. The smiley-face held the other until it stopped shaking. The metallic screeching stopped.

"She is truly a power to be reckoned with. I must study that weapon. How can it destroy from far away? This will change the balance of power utterly and completely." Nikidik watched closely through a spyglass.

"Why are they doing this?" Ola Griffin wrapped her hand around Promethus' elbow. "I don't understand."

"With all my years, I don't understand it, either, lass. It must end. All things must end—even war." Promethus pulled out the stolen pistol and raised it up in the last rays of daylight. He extended his arm and pointed the pistol.

One squeeze of the trigger is all it would take. That would end it. But which player on the field of battle was the most important? Which *death* would halt the work of destruction most quickly?

He pointed at Kally, the fraudulent witch. She who had beguiled the Wizard and spirited him away. She was in command of the inhuman army. To destroy her would be to end the immediate battle. Then the Wizard would be scooped up by Glinda and taken back to a prison and poked and prodded and studied. Kally's death would mean one less Wicked Witch in the Land of Oz. That would shift the balance of power strongly the other direction. With great power comes the urge to use the power. And power, once used, does not retire quietly. The vacuum of power with the death of Kally would shift all of the power to Glinda.

He shifted the pistol to the fire-haired sorceress. What if she died? What then? The metal army would roll over the scattered soldiers and onward to Emerald City. The Wizard would remain with Kally. He would most likely be used, abused, and then cast off when his usefulness was ended. That was not a good ending for the Wizard.

Glinda was young and impetuous. She was dangerous because of the power she wielded and the wisdom she lacked. Her knowledge was great, but her power was greater. The curiosity that drove her endangered everybody. She needed to be tempered with wisdom, but that wisdom would only come at a great cost. What cost could be so great as to stop the heir of Quelala in her destructive course and turn her to a greater good?

He turned the pistol to the wandering Wizard. Poor young man. He was lost, trapped between two sides that both declared themselves good. But pride never recognizes itself. They both wanted the wizard for power. Whoever controls the Wizard will control the Land of Oz. Perhaps it was better to pull the trigger and end it for him. With the Wizard gone, the fight would go back to being petty and small. It would end tonight. *Yes.*

"No."

Promethus felt the soft hands on his arm. He allowed the girl to pull his arm down. He looked at the tears in her eyes and felt the shame of his self-appointed role of judge and executioner.

He nodded his agreement to Ola Griffin. She smiled appreciation and understanding—even in her own small way—at him.

Nikidik stepped closer to Promethus. "May I see it?"

"No."

Pastoria slunk through the trees at the edge of the forest. He motioned Bartleby O'Brine to stay back. There it was, glowing softly in the dim twilight—a crown. Three people were just past the crown. Two of them were talking—both of them older men. The other one was a pretty blonde girl. Her hair shone in the darkness. She would be a lovely thing to have around the Family Palace. Pastoria smiled and licked his lips. She would be almost as good as that glowing crown. It had something to do with the army—that much he was sure of. He had never seen a metal army like this one. They had the bodies of men, but no faces. It was easier that way. They were all pawns and knights. They could be whatever they needed to be, without concern. Yes, war was the sport of kings.

There, the dark-haired man and the beautiful blonde girl were moving away. They quickly moved toward a crying noise further out in the valley. It was probably a soldier. They tended to fall and get wounded in battle. Such was the nature of the sport. That left only one thin man, but he was not near the glowing crown.

Pastoria strode out of the shadows of the forest and grasped the Crown of the Dreamer. He raised it high over his head and set it down on his brow. "Let this coronation be over the king of war. Let my name be known and my fame be great. Let all shudder who whisper my name unworthily."

The mask fell over Pastoria's face. The cold metal glowed within. His breath grew hot and clammy. The mask reached out and grasped his face. Swirling and rushing, forward and reeling, the mask pulled him through darkness and twilight, through stars and across rainbow conflagrations scattered in the screaming emptiness. He opened his mouth to cry out, but the mask blocked all sounds.

Like fingernails on a slate, the mask tore open holes at his eyes to reveal the phantom soldiers. Great glowing blue and green specters, weakly clad in thin mortal trappings, charged the battlefield. Their howling cries rent the air with lacerating ferocity. They screamed and pounded and pushed, but the bodies moved slowly and methodically.

"What are those things? By all that is decent and good, what are those things?" Pastoria shouted.

As one, each of the specters turned to face the crowned king. Smoky tendrils rose up from the earth all around him to wrap him like twining vines over a statue—for truly a monument he was in this realm of ghosts.

Then the chittering laughter started. It began beneath his feet, then it echoed into the air all around him. Then the mask itself laughed at him. Across the field of battle, mounds of earth shuddered and pushed upward. Dark squat creatures emerged and shook the dirt into the air. They jumped and laughed and mocked as the statue-bound king screamed within his mask.

> *Did you think to ask, trapped within the mask,*
> *Can you even think to cry aloud?*
> *Wondering afar, lost in who you are,*
> *Was it you who made the peacock proud?*
> *Listen once again, tiny little man*
> *Can you capture respite in your sleep?*
> *Underneath the ground, is where we can be found,*
> *Crawling up to conquer from the deep.*

The song whispered and shouted in the whirling wind around him. The vortex rose with the voices and shattered the mirrored sky to reveal a laughing queen above him. Her green hair swirled in the chittering chaos.

"The dream begins with a man of Oz—one that prides himself of the seed of Lurline. Ecstasy, little king. Ecstasy and terror."

The queen disappeared, and in the place of her visage appeared hundreds and thousands of little holes—burrows in a vast subterranean city. Each one sang the song, "*Crawling up to conquer from the deep.*"

Pastoria felt the world tilt beneath his feet. He tried to scream, but the stinging needles had already sewn his lips together. He crashed to the ground and the Crown of the Dreamer flew from his head. He curled in on himself and shook uncontrollably.

Nikidik glared down at the trembling king. "You are a waste. You know it and I know it. Your fathers would spit out of their graves on you. Coward and weakling, sniveling worm. You are soft. The men before you knew war."

"War is the sport of kings." Pastoria whimpered, staring with wide eyes up at Professor Nikidik.

"Where is your army, Pastoria-King?" He reached down and picked up the glowing Crown of the Dreamer. "You have seen my army, on the field and in your mind. It shall haunt your eyes as long as you live. Such ill-prepared eyes such as yours are not meant to glimpse true power. To command and to be commanded—that is not power. To give life to the unliving; to give the ghosts a mortal face; that is power. That is mine."

Pastoria scrambled to his feet. Nikidik swiftly kicked him in the rear end, driving him face-first back onto the ground. Pastoria sobbed and lay still.

Without warning, Omby-Amby shouted a retreat. The Emerald Guard and the Fighting Girls dropped back and ran toward the protection of the trees. Alone on the battlefield, Glinda fired shot after shot.

Kally disappeared into the forest shadows. Rather than giving chase to the fleeing humans, the automaton army clustered around their fallen and gathered the usable parts. The metal soldiers closest to the forest melted into the shadows between the trees.

Glinda raced after the automatons. She was the only human soldier that did not slow down. Some of the pistol shots missed. Other shots only buried the metal ball in the metal body but did not stop them. Surrounded by clouds of acrid smoke from broken and damaged metal soldiers, Glinda suddenly stopped. The battle was over.

40 HUMAN OUTSIDE

Kally appeared at Nikidik's side. "Glinda has fled. Her army is broken. Unleash your colossus and crush them all. We can finish this war right now." She glanced down at Pastoria on the ground. "Oh, you have a king. Another casualty of science?"

"I will have no part in this war beyond that which my masters trained me for. I will convey the king up to the Emerald lands. Then I will return to my home. When you wish to call upon me again, Witch, you know my price."

"I know you like pearls and I know you like pretty girls. I should have no problem paying your price."

"I have a pretty girl waiting for me at home, Witch. Do not tempt my anger with your ill-bought charms. I humored your original purchases. I will not be so lightly bought again. The charms of youth are fleeting. Remember that, Kalinya. I remember my brother was a suitor of yours back before the lines of knowledge marked your face. Back then your skin was smooth, but your temper was, even-then, legendary. You and your dark-eyed friend threw him into the sky. When he fell down, she changed him into a frog."

Kally smiled, remembering. "Whatever happened to him? That was fun."

"He was my brother."

"So you said. What happened to him?"

"He found another love. Someone less haughty, more dedicated. Someone less likely to break his heart or his body. But she broke his heart anyway. He's dead."

"Oh. Anyone I know?"

"You share her blood."

Kally laughed. "Your brother could not dance with the best, so he settled for my cast-off sister? That is rich."

"Beware, Kalinya, daughter of Eliyana and Korsovich, your family were not the only keepers of knowledge among the Munch-kin."

"Are you threatening me?"

"My family had more than enough reason to hate you, even before his death. I am all that is left."

Kally draped one hand over her hip and lowered her eyes at Professor Nikidik. "Do you regret not feasting your eyes on my youthful charms?"

"I saw how you treated my brother. Your friend was little better. At least her transformations could be changed back. His violent expulsion into the great yonder at your hands left the predictable result of grave injury. I was young, but I remember. When I grew older, I found my place. After I laid eyes on your better, I could never be turned by you again."

"My *better*? There is no one better."

"She had many things that you do not have—charms that you have never had. Before she turned her blue eyes away from me, I was certain her red hair would be mine forever."

Kally paled. Her jaw clenched. Her hands shook. The ground all around them trembled. To get her mind off of her one-time rival, she changed the subject, and she ordered, "Fix the army."

Nikidik forced a tight smile, and gave a half-nod. "I swore I would crush her in all her power. But she is gone now. My brother is not the only one who could not dance with the best. It appears that you, Kalinya, could not rightly follow her steps, and so you throw yourself at the daughter of the Eternal Sorceress."

Cracks appeared in the ground around them. Pebbles danced back and forth as the ground shook.

"I accomplished my purpose." Nikidik said. "What have you to say for yourself?"

"Fix the army." Kally growled.

"As you wish, princess. They will be living soldiers again before first light."

Glinda screamed her battle cry again at the retreating silhouettes. She took aim with her pistol and slowly squeezed her finger, relishing the anticipation of the recoil against her hand. Then she froze, her eyes squinting at the barrel of the gun. She stopped. She stared at the pistol. Her eyes grew wide. She smelled the smoke and looked at the battlefield littered with shattered parts of inhuman soldiers. She heard the echo of shots past. Her face twisted in a horrified grimace and she threw the pistol from her hand. She shook her hands and wiped both hands frantically on her dress to clean them from the filth of battle. They would not come clean.

Tears poured down her dirty face as she sobbed and tried to catch her breath. It could not be—she was *fighting* the monsters. *They* were the monsters. *They* were the destroyers.

Then the smoke parted and she saw Oscar. His haggard face was deep in the shadows. He stepped forward into the flickering light of a sparking automaton head.

"Oscar, I'm glad you're safe." Glinda's voice came out giddy and exhausted.

Oscar shook his head. His horrified stare penetrated through Glinda's façade of relief. "No. I will never be safe." Then he turned and walked back into the shadows.

Guilt burned her face. Glinda gathered up the hated weapon in her skirts so that she would not have to touch her hands to it again, and she ran into the forest. Time was of the essence. The quicker she got rid of this horrid weapon, the quicker she could put her mind to rest. Such terrible things should not exist either in dreams or in reality. It was little wonder that Oscar was deathly afraid of these pistols. Such violence these weapons made possible from a distance...the horrors that war could bring. It was no longer face-to-face. It was a single finger against a life. *It changed everything.* The ramifications for war that this single pistol presented boggled her mind.

Glinda ran until her heart nearly burst through her chest. She found a clearing beneath the open sky. She pulled the pistol from her skirts and then pulled a small knife from the other pocket. She dug at the earth. The soil flew as her panicked jabs into the earth dug deeper and deeper. For hours she dug and chopped and scooped dirt out of the hole.

The field of battle was empty once again. The wounded had been gathered to safety, and the enemy had retreated into the darkness of the forest. Glinda was gone. She was not among those fallen from their injuries, nor was she among those walking and wondering. She simply was not there.

As the eldest in the group, Promethus took control and saw to the care of the wounded. He arranged fires and stood guards as sentries to ensure that they would be safe that night. When all was settled, he gathered the Emerald Guardsmen and the Fighting Girls around the fire. After the horrors of the evening's battle, the rivalries of boys versus girls no longer mattered. They were simply soldiers, and they were tired.

"The battle tonight was only the most recent of many battles on this field. Do any of you know the history of this place?"

When nobody answered, Promethus shook his head in astonishment. "What are they teaching you in schools? Is there no memory preserved of the history of this land? If you do not know where a civilization has been, you will make the same mistakes as previous generations! It always happens. Look to history as your guide. Five different peoples met their fate on these grounds. How can an event such as that be forgotten? It was scarcely five generations ago that the Munch and Gilly clans nearly destroyed each other.

This valley was their bitterest battle. The blood soaked the ground for thirty years—nothing would grow. It was a place of sadness. That is why they called it Cairn.

"The Munches were the keepers of knowledge. They preserved the knowledge and it gave them power. They were quite content to exert their control over the workers by virtue of their greater knowledge. Keep in mind that this was not the actions of all, but the actions of a powerful few that colored the attitudes of the rest. The Gillys were industrious—they were builders and inventors. My kin came from among them before the dark times. They would no longer be treated as slaves. They built the great cities of the East and powered them with their inventions. Yet they were relegated to the lower levels of the cities.

"The records are not clear how it began, but there was a rising up by the Gillys. They separated themselves in all aspects from the Munches. The Gillys enthroned their own king. They would no longer be subject to the witch-kin who guarded their knowledge. The unthinkable happened. The Munches and their kin used the knowledge given them by the faeries to destroy. They betrayed their oath of protection and used their power and stature against the Gillys and their kin.

"The Munch-kin Civil War lasted for months. The Gilly city, Rokkamoorah, fell into the desert. The refugees ran. They fled to what they thought was safety. The Winkies would not help. In this valley the witches and their Munch allies unfurled the banners of destruction and slaughtered hundreds. If not for the timely protection of the Red Sorcerer, they would have been destroyed. He provided refuge for them in the wild North."

Omby-Amby studied the fire for a few seconds. "What was the knowledge of the Munch witches? I know we have some Munchkin soldiers among us, and Wickrie-Kells has relatives in the East. That does not make them bad."

"No. A child is not held responsible for the sins of the parents. The ancestors of certain persons alive today were the perpetrators of the great tragedies. The Gillikin people remember. The Munchkin people have forgotten. Two people now who once were one. The tragedy is that the lessons of history have been forgotten."

"But my question—"

"Yes. The knowledge. About that…it is not meet for soldiers to know everything. However, I will say that it has long been the practice of wicked people and rulers to dehumanize their people and soldiers to the point where it is rarely human against human. They make the enemy to be less than human, and the standards of decency and caring that once were present in all hearts is nearly eaten away through corruption. Thus, an angry Munchkin may kill a Gillikin without remorse for two reasons: one, the Gillikin is seen as less than human—an animal, or worse; and two, the Munchkin cares little for the resemblance between them, because he knows that he is superior. When the morals of the past are rejected, the wars of the present grow bitter and ugly. They are fought with the amoral creations of ill-used minds."

"That says a lot, but I am asking for things specifically to watch for from the Witch. I don't want the past to repeat itself." Omby-Amby said.

"Then *repeat* what I said!" Promethus exploded. "Morality, decency, and mutual tolerance—these things prevent war. Without them, societies crumble, people are dehumanized, and the result is always extermination. *Always*. The outcasts are never righteous enough, or blue enough, or tall enough, or pure enough—we are all the same shape. Our minds work. Our hands can be productive. These things are important."

Wickrie-Kells picked up a fallen arm from one of the automaton warriors. "This metal arm has hands. It was human in shape—head, two arms, two legs—should we not fight them?"

"They are not alive. They can never be alive. They are creatures of metal and stone and wood. They are not natural, yet they move and live like we do. They are of inanimate stuff made living. We are of meat." Promethus urged the soldiers to think. "Each one of them is a body, but look at each one of you—you are body, brain, heart, filled with courage and hope. These are the things worth living. Those things can never feel what you feel. Certainly, they do not feel tired, but that only means that they cannot know the peace that comes when the war is over."

He turned his gaze on the battered soldiers around the fire. "You fought well. There are none dead among us yet. We cannot say the same for our enemies. Many fell, thanks to the efforts of Glinda."

At the mention of Glinda's name, Oscar turned away from the fire. He was back among friends, so they said, but it was clear that he was destined for shackles again.

"Wizard, you traveled with the witch, how came her army? What magic was used to graft life into the metal bodies?" The Guardian asked.

Oscar shrugged. He glanced back over his shoulder to see Promethus watching him.

Omby-Amby nudged Oscar. "C'mon, Brud. What made the metal soldiers?"

"The Professor. He had magic. The Witch—I don't even want to say her name—she paid for the army. It was supposed to be a good idea. I wanted peace. If an army does not require sleep, they can watch always against war. People—people like you and me, made of flesh, not metal—can do what we do without worrying about always training and preparing for war. We can live."

"I was born to be a soldier. I know that as well as I know my whiskers." Omby-Amby said. "I can speak for my men the same. We are soldiers because we choose to be. War was forced on us, but we were not unprepared.

This is what we do—we maintain the peace because it is who we are." The Emerald Guardsmen murmured their agreement. "We protect life."

"What is life?" Oscar asked. "The Professor said that war brings life. I have only seen it bring death. It's nothing short of a miracle that none of you died today. But if you were doing it for me, I'm sorry, but I'm not interested in being the spoils of war."

Wickrie-Kells finished wrapping a bandage around Rala's head. "You don't have a choice in that matter, Wizard. You left. You started the war with the West. You brought this war because you abandoned us. You ran away. You came back with monsters."

Oscar's gaze turned away from the fire. His head slumped and his shoulders fell further down. He listened as the conversation turned to the possibility of thinking, acting life that was not of flesh.

"What say you, Wizard?" Promethus pulled the Wizard back in to the conversation. "If a porcelain doll or a ten-foot tall soldier of metal can move or talk, are they then alive?"

Omby-Amby nudged Wickrie-Kells and whispered, "He's going to say *liberty*."

"No. There's no way. This is life, not politics."

Oscar turned back to the fire. He lifted his eyes to meet the Guardian's gaze. He noticed, but did not lose his concentration as he saw the blonde girl, Ola Griffin, silently rise and walk away. Let them discover her disappearance when it was all over. It would serve them right losing their friends, having them walk away, especially that man. *First Glinda, and now Ola Griffin. The man knew no shame.*

"Liberty." Oscar said. "I have the right to live, to breathe—to pursue my own happiness."

Omby-Amby and Wickrie-Kells shared an amused glance. "Told you." The soldier whispered.

"Can a being created of these non-breathing things understand what it means to breathe free air? To chase a purpose so much greater and nobler than self? To work for the betterment of another, with no thought of self-reward or aggrandizement? Were these things possible, life in other forms might be possible, even probable in such a land as this. But I fear that liberty is a cause too few of us *meat-people*—as you so adequately put it—truly appreciate. If only few humans understand the cause of liberty, how can a non-human do so?"

"Are you saying that they don't deserve liberty?" Omby-Amby asked.

Oscar shook his head slowly. "No. The Winged Monkeys deserve to be free, even though they…" he trailed off, remembering the events of the last twenty-four hours. "They deserve freedom. I just don't think that they recognize liberty as more than freedom—not being enslaved. Liberty is empowerment. And it is work—responsibility. To make a people free, you must be tireless."

Promethus looked down at the shorter young man. "And you, Wizard? Are you tireless?"

Oscar continued shaking his head. "No. No. I am afraid...I am tired."

41 REVELATION OF THE KALIDAHS

The Munchkin city was quiet when the Witch returned. She walked out of the forest ahead of two great beasts. The beasts roared their call, and the other beasts answered the call from the fields and from within the village.

The frightened Munchkins peered out from behind cracked shutters or barely-parted curtains to see the black-swathed witch leading the great beasts—the Kalidahs. She led them down the main thoroughfare to the stables.

From the window of the house near the bridge, Boq opened the curtains and threw open the window. He watched the Witch lead the Kalidahs into the stable. Their massive bear-like bodies and paws shifted impatiently. The growls and guttural roars from their tiger heads caused the entire village to shiver behind their locked doors.

The last two Kalidahs entered the darkness of the stable. From within the darkness, a jangling of harnesses sounded. Then a whip cracked. The Kalidahs roared as one, shaking the doors on every house. Even Boq jumped backwards from the window in surprise.

The harnessed Kalidahs lurched forward, straining and clawing deep furrows in the hardened ground outside the stable. They pulled Kalinya's onyx and sapphire chariot behind them as they clawed onto the brick road. Each step left gouges in the bricks. The beasts roared and the Witch laughed.

She cracked the whip again and the great tiger-bears ran toward the West. Boq watched them as they drove out of sight into the darkening forest.

In the village a great wailing went up, both of terror and of triumph. The Witch, their Queen Protector, had tamed the beasts. But what fierce enemy was she going to battle? That enemy was worse by far than the evil they knew, and it worried them and left them knowing only one very familiar feeling—fear.

Kally stopped the chariot when the forest shadows obscured them from sight of the village. She smiled in cold satisfaction. The Munchkins saw her, or rather, they saw the Witch. They saw the creatures. What were their whispers? *Kalidahs?* That was a fine word—it sounded like her name. It was fitting, considering that the creatures were birthed from her idea. She stepped out of the chariot and walked to the front of her harnessed beasts. Six pairs of fierce yellow eyes watched her closely. She trailed her fingers along their orange backs as she walked. At the front, she held the tiger faces of the two lead Kalidahs and stroked their fur.

"Come, my babies, let us roar into battle. Let us be the most feared creatures in all of Oz."

With the harnesses firmly attached, and the chariot in place behind the Kalidahs, Kally took hold of the harness on the back of the lead beasts.

"This won't hurt one bit. Walk with me, babies. The prize is the Wizard, forever." One, two, three steps, and they were gone.

Ola Griffin walked through the strange forest, an undeniable compulsion pulling her forward. She did not know where she was going, and she certainly could not find her way back even if she wanted to turn around. All she knew is that there was something forward that she needed to find, and so she kept putting one foot in front of the other. She traveled the dark forest for more than an hour before she heard the angry sobbing.

In a clearing in the center of the forest, Ola saw a red-haired girl hacking away at the earth. She was down on her knees, hacking at the ground and scooping out dirt from the hole. It didn't make any sense, but this is where she needed to be. Ola felt on the ground to find a suitably-sized stick. She silently approached Glinda and knelt down next to her and started digging.

Glinda looked up through tear-soaked eyes to see her friend silently helping her. Ola asked no questions, and only offered a small smile to Glinda's questioning gaze.

They dug in the earth for more than an hour.

Only when she was certain that the horrid construct of death would not be found by casual hunting did Glinda climb out. The hole was nearly as deep as her shoulders. She jumped up and pulled herself out, then rolled onto her back, staring at the sky. The stars shone brightly, unaware of her sin. She knew that dawn was coming, so she could not rest. Ola Griffin pulled herself out of the hole and stood across from Glinda. The work was almost finished.

Glinda took a deep breath and pulled herself to her feet. She thrust the hated weapon from her, deep into the hole. She screamed at the pistol—screamed and threw clods of dirt down on it. Grief and rage seized Glinda and she buried the weapon. Ola Griffin silently pushed dirt into the hole, letting Glinda pour out all of her hurt and anger as she entombed the dark weapon of dreams.

When the dirt filled the grave completely, Glinda pounded her fists against the packed earth, screaming in soul-wrenching guilt. At last she collapsed, wailing, onto the flattened grave.

Ola Griffin said nothing. She knelt beside Glinda and put her dirt-crusted hand on the red-haired girl's back. It was finished.

In the camp at the edge of the battlefield, Oscar wiped his burning eyes. He tried to sleep, but he could not. The sharp tang of melted metal pierced his nose and brought tears to his eyes. This was not the way that it was supposed to happen. Power was not supposed to shift. It was like a dream, where he was watching, but he could not control anything. For all of the power displayed on this field of battle, none of it was his. The Wonderful Wizard was completely powerless.

Kally had lied. This power was never supposed to be used against the people of Oz. The power of the automaton army was a power to help, not to hurt. Now it raged in the hands of an unwise steward. How could Kally do this? She had known good. Was the lure of power too great for one so young?

Oscar staggered to his feet. *The only thing that would protect this land is to ensure that all of these armies—both sides—are stopped completely.* He was trapped in the middle. *He* was the only one seeing things clearly. Neither Kally nor Glinda would make the necessary sacrifices—they were too shackled to their own schemes of power. If the Land of Oz was to be saved, it would be on *this* field of battle.

Oscar moved toward the only moving shapes that he could see through the smoke. *No matter how much you want the power, you must destroy it.* Oscar heard laughter in the smoke. What was that? He had not made any jokes. Faces twisted around in the smoke, leering and laughing at him, but not at him, actually, at the others who could not see as clearly as he could. *Yes, it was very clear now.* Even though the power exists, and where does the power exist? In the *unguent*. Kally used the unguent to bring life to the soldiers, or rather, Professor Nikidik brought them to life in the mountain. Here on the battlefield, the crown was of secondary importance. The unguent was the true power. The crown was a trick. *To prevent the power from being used incorrectly, Oscar, you must destroy it.* The unguent is power. It brought the armies to life. In order to prevent the creation of more armies, he must destroy the unguent. Yes, he would destroy the unguent.

On the other side of the valley from the weary wizard, Professor Nikidik completed the demanded repairs on the automaton army. Kally had not yet returned. She was getting to be more trouble than the price she had paid. Even with all of the pearls she had given him, there was a sneaking, horrible sickening feeling that the future would be decided in the next few hours. Such decisions as this revolted him terribly, and so he withdrew, as he always did.

Nikidik was a scientist, and a builder of fantastical things. He was a kingmaker in many ways. More than that, he invented the technology that brought kings to power. It was something that he had done again this time. However, this time it was not merely a king or a kingdom at stake—all of the most fashionable powers in the Land of Oz were on this battlefield. He had created an army and turned it over to a mad witch. He had let down his guard for just a few seconds and made the sitting king mad. Oh, it may not manifest itself just yet, but such minds as these were not meant to glimpse the greater madness of the unseen world, let alone consider the cosmos. His mind was fractured. King Pastoria did not realize it yet, but he was finished. He would never be the same again.

"Up." Nikidik demanded. The prone king would not move. He only whimpered. "It is time to return to your home, little king." Nikidik reached down to tug on Pastoria's jacket, to turn the king over.

Pastoria roared in pain as he saw the piercing stars above him. "They are coming! They have their own horrible constellations in the earth beneath. They have made the stars right. They are coming to lay waste to Oz and her treasures. They know my head, they have seen my face. I will be the first to fall in their invasion." He crawled up on his knees and clutched at the thin man. "Ghastly things that laughed and sang. They sang to me—a strange lullaby that echoes, echoes in my ears. I cannot make it stop, but I do not want it to stop. I have no flowers to write the words."

"Interesting." Nikidik removed the kneeling king's hands from his lapels and stood up straight.

Nikidik looked up to see the smiley automaton slowly approach him. "Where is the other Emerald Soldier? The king did not carry himself here."

Smiley pointed north. He hopped in that direction and pushed his hand toward the sky.

"You went to invite him here and the horse ran away. *Fantastic.*" Nikidik growled. To Pastoria, he ordered again, "Up."

Smiley helped Pastoria rise to his feet.

"Thank you, my good man. Do you have a tailor? I can recommend a fine craftsman—he has warm hands and he tells the most marvelous jokes."

Professor Nikidik turned his back on Kally's automaton army. What the Witch did now was on her own head. Nikidik had met the terms of the payment. He learned what he needed from the Crown of the Dreamer. In addition, he now had an unfortunate passenger in this leg of his journey, but there were perhaps unique observations that could be forthcoming as a conclusion to the human testing of the Crown of the Dreamer's effects. Nikidik spit on the ground where Kalinya's army waited, and he turned his cart north.

<hr />

In the forest, Ola Griffin helped the red-haired girl rise to her feet. Glinda smiled and brushed away the final remnants of her tears, smearing mud on her face.

"Thank you."

Ola Griffin smiled warmly. "What is your name? I feel like I should know you, but we have never met. I am sure that I would remember."

"I am Glinda. I am your friend."

"Yes, of that I am sure. You feel like my friend."

"What happened to you? I saw you just two days ago. I was very angry. I sent you out to the scrapyard." Then realization struck Glinda with the force of lightning. "Did you drink from the pool in the Boneyard of the Clouds? From the Fountain of Oblivion?"

Ola smiled politely, not quite comprehending. "You have dirt on your face."

"Yes, I know. You do, too."

"Oh." Ola Griffin took a dirty corner of her sleeve and wiped her cheek. "Is that better?"

"I cannot really see in the dark, but I'm sure we're both a mess." She reached out and took her friend's hand, "Ola, did you drink any water while you were in the scrapyard?"

"I don't remember any scrapyard. I was here, with you, digging. It was the right thing to do."

"Yes, it was. And I thank you. How much beyond that do you remember?"

Ola smiled silently. That was all she could offer her new friend.

"Okay." Glinda sighed deeply. "How can you not have your memory? You were the one I counted on the most. You were always there with an answer, and now you are not."

"I'm right here."

"Yes, you are right here. We need to get back to Oscar—do you remember him?"

Thunder boomed in the distance. The wind picked up, rushing past them to find the storm.

"We have to go. Do you remember the way back?"

"Back where?" Ola answered innocently. Her sweet voice cracked slightly as she recognized Glinda's disappointment in her. "I'm sorry. I can't remember. All I know is that I am here right now."

"Let's find the army before the storm hits. I'd rather not be caught in the rain."

The storm raced in far more quickly than anyone expected. Omby-Amby woke to raindrops hitting his face. Everyone around him grumbled exactly the same as him. He looked out to the sentries. Even they were raising their heads as if they were surprised. *Sleeping.* That would be punished accordingly. Guards must not sleep.

The Soldier with Green Whiskers stretched his muscles and worked his arms and legs and then strapped on his sword. He crossed the camp to the nodding sentry.

"You fell asleep."

The sentry pointed silently to a distant short figure standing in the rain.

The young wizard stared out against the rain in the brightening pre-dawn minutes. He stared out at the far side of the valley. *They were coming. Kally would not hesitate to destroy every last one of them with her unguent. She would make all of them into soulless automatons. She would slaughter their bodies and pour unguent on their necks and raise them up to do her bidding. They would all be her unthinking army.*

Oscar blinked as a heavy raindrop rolled down his forehead and tangled itself in his eyelashes. He blinked twice and saw his taller friend next to him. "Omby. They are coming."

"I don't see or hear anything."

"I know they are coming."

"Did you sleep?"

Oscar shook his head. "I tried. I keep seeing screams, hearing shadows. Glinda shot those things. She murdered them."

"They were not alive. You said so yourself last night. Liberty is what you said. Liberty means responsibility. It is not just the freedom to move, it is the responsibility to act and to protect. Those do neither. They obey orders, but they do not protect."

"If I die, will you lie to Glinda? I don't want her to know any more of the truth."

"What are you talking about? You are not dying, Brud. You need sleep. You need to—"

"I made monsters—in my dream. The shadows want me back. I have no more stories. I cannot...up here, my brain is twisting and shaking. I feel like an egg in a pan. I can feel the hissing and bubbling and popping. It's like I can't think anymore. I only feel, and it hurts. The shadows—I feel them pulling at my face—pulling me backwards into my head. Do you hear the screams?"

"Brud, I'm a soldier. I have heard screams. I have known fear. I have known *liberty*, thanks to you."

"Glinda!" came the shout from the camp.

Lightning flashed, illuminating the entire valley for a brief moment. Oscar blinked his eyes against the glare. When he turned again, Omby-Amby was gone. Oscar set his jaw against the rain and looked back over the valley.

In the forest near the camp of the Fighting Girls, Glinda stopped and looked at Ola Griffin. The early light of morning helped her see more clearly. She embraced the blonde girl and squeezed her hands. "We were friends once, and we still are, and we forever will be. I promise you, Ola Griffin, if you are ever in trouble, sing. Sing as loud and as fine as you can. I will find you, and I will help you."

"You're nice." Ola smiled at Glinda.

Glinda smiled back. "Thank you. They're coming. Remember as best you can—sing. It is what you do best."

Then the soldiers—both Fighting Girls and Emerald Guardsmen—were around them, bringing them back to the rain-soaked camp.

"Why didn't you put up shelters? I thought that's what you soldiers did." Glinda asked, laughing.

"We thought this rainstorm was from you." Wickrie-Kells answered.

"Ola, you are safe." Promethus smiled thankfully at both girls.

Glinda looked at the Guardian and saw his eyes in a different light. He really was concerned. He brought Ola Griffin here. *Why?* Why not just wait at Chronometria for Glinda to return? They had the Wizard back now, so the quest was finished. It would have been much safer for both of them if they had stayed there.

Glinda looked past the group of guards and saw Omby-Amby standing in the back. Her heart tightened and her jaw clenched. He met her gaze and nodded. He recognized the hurt and hatred that burned within the sorceress. Not enough time had passed for the hatred to find a face, so it took on the appearance of the Soldier with Green Whiskers.

Promethus noticed the sudden change in Glinda. He turned around to follow her gaze. He saw the back of Omby-Amby as he walked back into the valley.

Glinda took a deep breath and asked, "Where is Oscar?"

The storm passed over them, expending all its energy pouring down rain on the weary soldiers. With the passing of the clouds, the sun's rays peeked over the horizon, shouting their morning cries to the waking world. Yet there was one that straddled the line between the waking and dreaming worlds—he had not slept, really, in days. He was not certain what was real and what was not. All he knew is that war was coming, and it was up to him alone to end it.

Oscar slumped down, his energy spent. He sat all alone on the edge of the sodden battlefield. His breath came ragged and sad. His cold fingers brushed over the raw wounds on his wrists where the shackles bound him. There was nothing but cold pain. It was a clammy, white, numb feeling.

Glinda approached the Wizard. She stepped a wide path around the puddles, hoping to catch his eye with her red hair, but Oscar only stared down at the ground. She cocked her head to the side. Even standing right in front of him, Oscar did not raise his eyes. She stepped closer.

Oscar slowly raised his hands up, displaying his wrists to her. His eyes never left the ground. His wrists were bloody and raw. The heavy rain had wrinkled Oscar's fingers and left his hands pale and frigid. The shackles cut in deep. Those scars would not soon heal.

Glinda's breath caught in her throat as she recognized that Oscar was raising his wrists to her, not as a sign of rebellion, but in token of his broken spirit. He raised his hands up again for the shackles.

The tears disappeared quickly on Glinda's wet face. Her hair dripped from the rain, hiding her burning sorrow. She turned in shame from the Wizard and retreated to the strength of her army—her Fighting Girls. She walked past the outstretched hand of Omby-Amby, instead reaching for the strength of her most loyal friend. Wickrie-Kells took Glinda's hand and squeezed it tightly. It was small comfort.

The sorceress turned back to look at the solitary Wizard, with his back to the army, and his eyes locked on the land. He slowly lowered his hands back to his sides.

Glinda turned her glance to Omby-Amby, but the Soldier with Green Whiskers was already moving. His jaw tightened as he walked past Glinda. She held up her hand, but he brushed right by it.

Omby-Amby disregarded the angry glare from Glinda and the dangerous look from Wickrie-Kells. He turned his eye away from the fair-weather friends and focused on his true friend. He splashed through the puddles, taking the most direct way to get to Oscar.

The soldier knelt on one knee next to his friend. He placed his sword point-down in the ground, with hilt pointing toward the sky. He clapped his hand on Oscar's shoulder. "It's time to rest. You have beaten them."

Oscar refused to sleep. "Kally is coming back and she is going to end this war. I have to stop her. I have to stop Glinda. I have to stop this war so that we can all be free. I have to stop the continuous circle of killing. If the killing continues, the death never ends, no matter who lives. The death will always haunt. It will destroy lives. It will destroy all who see the shadows of what once was, and what will never again be."

"The killing has stopped."

Oscar shook his head slowly. His haunted eyes searched the shadows of the forest, where Kally's army waited and watched. "The shadows come. They always know where to find me. They feast on my fear. I cannot quench their thirst when they share my blood."

"Is that what happened to you, Brud?"

"My father...he was a warrior. My brothers—all of them—were warriors. I was not. I *am* not. I fell into their shadows and I cannot climb out."

Omby-Amby clenched his callused fingers on his best friend's shoulder. "We'll get you out. Even if it takes a lifetime, we'll get you out into the sun."

Beyond them, the morning storm finished its last rumblings and floated away. The clouds in the new sky bore no ill will toward the small army far below them, but the angry clouds still heavy in Glinda's eyes were not quite sure where they belonged.

42 MORN'LIGHT WAR

The golden sun rose brilliant over the valley. The Wizard kept his distance, always watching the far forest. The sun rose warm on his back, but he did not turn to face it—his duty was to end this. He could not spare a single moment to bask in the glorious rays of morning. Not a single solitary ounce of strength could be spared from his lonely watch. He was the only one that could stop them—he was the only one who could save them. Without him, they would destroy each other.

There—movement in the forest across the valley. The Eastern forest was still in shadow. The dawn had not yet conquered the final remnants of night yet clinging to the trees.

Roaring sounded behind him, accompanied by the creaking of metal warriors. The sun pierced the far shadows and revealed the army standing in ranks between the trees. The sunlight glinted off their metal bodies—they were whole once again.

Oscar turned slowly around to view his waking nightmare. Six of the hideous tiger-bears roared as they pulled an onyx and sapphire chariot toward the valley from the opposite direction.

"Here they come." Oscar whispered. He gave no warning to either side, for he believed in neither of them anymore. It was only him—he was the sole vision of liberty for the Land of Oz. Everything rested on his weary shoulders now. *Everything.*

"Look lively! Across the valley, they are coming!" Omby-Amby shouted drawing his sword.

A scream from one of the Fighting Girls pierced the forest behind them. "They're coming!"

Half of the automaton army raced from the forest behind the camp, attacking the unprepared soldiers. Soldiers and automatons alike ran out of the forest and onto the field of battle.

They were joined by the other automatons marching from the shadows of the eastern forest.

Glinda searched for the horses. There they were, panicking. What would spook the horses so badly?

Then she heard the roars. Kally roared into the valley with her chariot pulled by six of the most fearsome beasts Glinda had ever seen—they had the bodies of massive bears and the snarling heads of tigers. Six of them pulled the wicked chariot. *So that was the amber-eyed witch that beguiled Oscar. She was the one that caused all of this mess.*

Glinda drew her sword and strode out to the field of battle.

"Wickrie, with me!" Omby-Amby shouted as he raced into the heart of the battle. The tall girl leaped atop a four-legged automaton and shot an arrow directly into the back of its head. The construct shuddered and staggered, throwing the warrior girl off. She leaped off and pulled another arrow. She took careful aim and pierced the neck of a metal soldier near Omby-Amby. Then she raced to join him in the heart of the action.

Promethus held back as the army scattered the human soldiers. The automatons ignored him as he backed into the trees. "Ola, come here, lass. They won't hurt you if you don't fight them. Come with me."

Ola Griffin looked to Promethus in the trees then she looked to Glinda, striding down onto the field of battle. She turned and ran toward the sorceress with red hair.

"Don't—" but his warning fell on deaf ears. Ola Griffin had made her choice.

Kally watched in amazement as the Emerald Guardsmen and the Fighting Girls—even the wounded among them—stood to fight her army. Did they not learn their lesson last night? Apparently not. "Let's make the lesson more personal, shall we, my lovelies?"

Kally pulled the chariot to a stop in the middle of the field. She waved her hand and unlatched the harnesses of the six Kalidahs. "Pick your pretty and go play." The beasts roared and surged free from their harnesses, charging the field of battle.

Oscar watched the unfolding chaos. There a metal soldier fell. Here a human soldier dropped to the ground and stopped moving. There was no more time. He gathered his breath and stood up straight. They were out there, chattering and yelling. Were those monkeys? They didn't belong here. Was a third army now involved? All had to be stopped. No matter what face they wore, they must be stopped. He leaned his head back and let his voice peal across the battlefield.

The soldiers stopped and looked in the direction of the Wizard. That noise was very loud, but it didn't make any sense. Of course it wouldn't, none of them were bananas.

A single smaller automaton teetered and fell over. The Kalidahs roared in the Wizard's direction, then they continued their hunt for the soft soldiers.

Kally turned to face the Wizard. "You are sorely welcome, Wizard. I have waited for this moment. Reveal your true power. Rise up and strike down your enemies."

At Oscar's feet the grass burst into flames. The earth trembled as he walked. Shadows rose up from the ground to walk beside him. His path would lead him to the back of the chariot. Up ahead of the chariot, Glinda rapidly approached with drawn sword.

Kally stepped down from the chariot. She mocked Glinda, "Such crude weapons. We are Witches. We have no need of such brutish thuggery."

"We end this now."

Kally saw the look in Glinda's eyes. The storm raged in them—she got that from her mother. Even from this distance, Glinda's eyes were dark to behold. Kally pulled the bottle of unguent from her pocket and set it inside the chariot. Glinda slammed her sword against the chariot wheel.

"Face me, witch!" Glinda swung her sword again, this time at the black-cloaked body in the back of the chariot. Her sword met steel as Kally parried and pushed back.

"You drive the chariot of the Witch of the East." Glinda stepped back and studied the other witch.

"So I do. Fancy that." Kally smirked. "How is your darling Wizard?"

"He's on his way." Glinda snarled.

"To do what? To help you? Or to help me? You see, I am his latest love. He has a penchant for pretty faces." It stung like a slap in the face. Glinda face reddened.

"He is mine."

"No, he is mine." Kally smiled. "Here he comes. Let's ask him, shall we?"

Ola Griffin ran toward the battle. She watched as Glinda fought against the dark-clothed witch. Ola remembered the one thing Glinda said to her—she could not remember much, but she remembered that Glinda told her to sing.

Nearby, Omby-Amby and Wickrie-Kells fought two Kalidahs who set their sights on Rala. The Fighting Girl had fallen again in battle against the metal automatons. The Kalidahs thought it an easy meal, but Wickrie-Kells would not hear of it. She fired arrow after arrow into the beasts' thick hides.

The Soldier with Green Whiskers struck out as the beasts got close enough. The sting of his sword preached caution to the ferocious beasts. Blood stained the blade five times before they heard the song.

The Kalidahs raised their heads and looked toward the source of the beautiful music. They all turned from their hunt to face the blonde girl with the magical voice. One by one they growled softly and padded quickly to her.

Ola Griffin saw the beasts turn in her direction. What was the second thing that Glinda said? The first thing was to sing, but Ola could not remember the second one. Was it that she should find Glinda? Or was it that Glinda would find her? That was probably it, but the monsters were coming. They were getting so close. *Oh, faeries, they were big!* What was that second thing? Ola could not remember, so she closed her eyes and kept singing.

The Kalidahs were born of dream and song, and so they were influenced by the pure voice that flowed like moonlight from Ola Griffin. They surrounded the blonde girl and nudged her with their muzzles and rubbed against her. Ola raised her hands, and two of the beasts pressed their foreheads into her palms.

Ola slowly opened her eyes. She laughed in relief as she saw the beasts bowing to her. She softened her voice and caressed the beasts. She looked toward Glinda for direction.

Kally frowned. "That was not supposed to happen. This is my victory." She stretched her hand and reached out toward the singing girl. She threw her into the sky.

In an instant the song was gone. The Kalidahs growled and snarled. They turned to look around in confusion. They swatted at each other and then turned again to find a nice soft plaything to bite into.

"NO!" Glinda screamed. She swung her sword again at Kally. "I know you now, Kalinya. Your wickedness knows no bounds. She was not hurting anything. She was my friend."

"You have terrible luck with your friends. But then what else can we expect from a spoiled child of promise born to a life of plenty. You don't believe in liberty, at least not like Oscar preaches it. Did you ever get tired of him going on and on? That boy doesn't know when to stop. He is a one-note whistle. *Liberty, liberty, liberty.* Everything is about liberty. I tried to tell him, really I did, Glinda, but he would not listen. It is about power—you and I know that. It has always been about power. That is what drove him away from you. You took something from him."

"You know nothing of Oscar." Glinda swung her sword again, harder this time.

"Kisses—one for luck, two for love, three for lollipops."

"He doesn't love you!"

"I would say that he doesn't much love you. See, Glinda, you don't believe in freedom. You were born to power. You have never known fear. You have never known the terror brought on by tyrants and bullies."

"I ran from you and your sister. You tried to kill me."

"Yes, well, beside the point. I am lecturing you." Kally thrust her hand out and threw Glinda backwards thirty feet. That gave them some breathing room. Kally stepped away from the chariot and looked toward the eastern forest. There was a wonderful surprise waiting there for Glinda and her army. Professor Nikidik had activated the thunder colossus. It only remained for Kally to stand the giant on its feet. It truly was a marvel. That would be the final blow that would destroy Glinda's precocious little army. Then they would all bow to Kally—Kalinya—she needed to refer to herself by her proper name, not the one that Oscar had called her—Kalinya.

"Daughter of Gayelette, you have never been small. You were born great. You have never had to hide; never had to embrace the shadows and filth to stay hidden from the monsters in the real world. Glinda, you are empty of everything that it means to be alive. Perhaps fear will make you feel more humble."

Kally raised her hands and reached out magically to the distant colossus. She closed her eyes and lifted it from the ground. *Great faeries, it was heavy.* She realized in a moment how tired she was. This younger body was wonderful, but it, apparently, also had its limits. Tree branches snapped and thunder shook the valley as the colossus rose to stand above the trees. It stepped forward, snapping trees beneath its massive metal limbs.

"How do you like that, Glinda? Just a little thunder colossus to rain on your little army. Care to surrender? There is no way that your army can defeat my man-sized soldiers, let alone my Kalidahs, or my giant. You have lost."

Oscar stumbled into the flames at his feet. He tumbled headlong, and lay face-down for one eternal breath. The flames roared all around him, leaving a broad trail of scorched earth, but they did not burn the Wizard. The fire vines snaked out, marking his path to the chariot.

"Oscar, stay there!" Glinda ordered. "This is not your fight."

"Yes, Oscar, she doesn't want to lose you. First she drives you out by making you dream, then she wants you back."

"You stop this! I did what I did for him. I had to know."

"Wearing your nerves on your sleeves, are you? I didn't have to go far to find your pain." Kally cackled. "You do not own him. I scarcely think you even love him."

"More than you, Witch."

Oscar pushed himself up to his hands and knees. "I am Oz, the Great and Terrible." He gasped. "I will stop you, Glinda, Kally, both of you. I will stop you. I am...only one who can. No more. It goes no further."

"Oscar, you are killing yourself. Stop!"

"Yes, Oscar, stop. The *suspense* is killing me. What are you going to do?" Then Kally turned from them to face to the thunder colossus and ordered, "Destroy them all!"

The colossus ripped a tree from the ground and swung at the nearest soldiers, flattening both human and automaton.

Glinda saw her soldiers—all those that followed her and fought by her side—they fought valiantly. They fought with courage and honor. They were losing. None of their small weapons could hope to win against the thunder colossus. Her mind flashed back to the events of the night before. Just a few hours previous, Glinda had nearly single-handedly decimated the entire automaton army. Her hand went to her pocket, but the deadly weight of the pistol was gone. Her sword was her only weapon against the giant metal warrior.

No. That was not true, at all. She was Glinda, the daughter of Quelala and Gayelette. The secret apprentice who could have been the greatest of all of the inventors instead became joined to the greatest sorceress. From their union he created his greatest invention, the one that would change the future of the Land of Oz forever. He created an invention so powerful that no witches, sorcerers or any other power in Oz would be able to stand against it. What was that invention? What was it that Quelala and Gayelette created that was so powerful? *Me—Glinda. I am the one.*

She looked at her sword and threw it on the ground. She walked out to face the thunder colossus alone.

"What are you doing? You blasted fool! You are supposed to *surrender to me!*" Kally shouted at Glinda's back. Kally also threw her sword down and followed after Glinda.

Behind them, Oscar forced his foot to stand. His head was still bowed, and the flames crackled all around him, but he was moving. The flames turned from orange to white as the intensity of Oscar's concentration grew stronger.

Glinda passed through the fighting warriors. They were not her worry. Only the giant mattered. That was Kalinya's big scheme. If Glinda would only bow down, then everything would be satisfactory. A little liberty sacrificed for safety. Shackles in return for a bed to sleep in. A cage of iron in return for no more war. If Glinda backed down now, it would all end.

Nothing of the sort even appealed to Glinda. She adored a challenge, and this was one of her greatest. To save Oscar and her friends, she had to destroy the invincible metal giant. Would that stop the smaller soldiers? Probably not, but she trusted her soldiers to do their duty.

Glinda studied the colossus as she approached. It was large. Gaps between the metal plates showed blue lightning as it moved. That was interesting. Thunder colossus, the Witch had called it.

How had Kalinya created this army? Surely it was beyond her magic ability. She was a powerful witch, but she was not an inventor. Promethus mentioned other inventors besides Smith & Tinker—the apprentices Nikidik and Ku-Klip. Either one of them could have built it. Did it matter? Only if…wheelers. There was a wheeler broken on the ground. That was one of the automatons. At least it was like a wheeler. The only wheelers were in the scrapyard at Chronometria. Ola Griffin lost her memory, probably from the Fountain of Oblivion in the Boneyard of the Clouds. What if it wasn't Ola that drank? What if somebody gave it to her? What if that same somebody had somehow used the essence of the deceased clouds to power their appropriately named Thunder Colossus?

Glinda smiled. *And what if I just happen to know a spell to make clouds?*

"Hey!" Glinda shouted at the metal giant. "I have just one question for you!"

The colossus stopped and raised the tree to smash down on the red-haired sorceress.

"Do you want to be free?" Glinda asked.

She shouted the words the cloud-making spell. The essence of the storm, trapped inside the colossus, awakened to a remembrance of its former life. It was not meant to be entrapped in this metal tomb. It was meant to float free in the wide sky.

The colossus shuddered, then spasm'd, and then roared pain from its abdomen up to its head. The tree fell from its lifeless fingers. The clouds formed and issued from every joint and opening on the giant body. Lighting flashed and thunder shook the ground as the clouds formed up outside the body.

The giant body teetered, lifeless, at the edge of the battlefield. The sun glinted on its metal carapace. It was now an empty sarcophagus—the cloud that brought it life had been given a new life. The colossus was defeated.

A single arrow flew straight and true and plunked into the back of the giant body. That tiny *tink* sound was the only warning given as the empty titan fell toward the battlefield. The human soldiers saw the danger and ran. The automaton army was less responsive.

Glinda quickly removed herself from the path of the falling colossus. It slammed to the earth, knocking everyone off their feet. The shockwave threw Glinda down on her face, but she was free. A weak cheer arose from the few remaining Emerald Guardsmen and Fighting Girls.

"NO!" The scream shattered the air behind Glinda. "No, no, NO!"

Glinda turned to face the angry witch. Her stormy blue eyes matched the amber orbs in intensity. "I beat your giant. I beat your army. The Wizard is mine."

Back at the chariot, Oscar pulled himself to a standing position. The giant body had fallen. The monsters were among the soldiers. The flames died down around him as he grasped the small square green bottle of unguent from the chariot. He breathed deeply as he looked out on the destruction in the battlefield. "It all ends now."

How would he destroy it? The sword? No—it would just bring the blade to life. He did not want a living blade in Oz. That would be almost as bad as the guns Glinda created. If he dumped it on the ground, what foul things would rise up? The flames licked all around his feet. There were enough problems in this magical land without making any more nightmares come to life. He held up the green glass bottle. It glinted in the sunlight. So much power.

"What is he doing?" Kally's eyes grew wide as she saw Oscar lift something from the chariot.

"He is destroying your power." Glinda declared triumphantly.

Kally lifted her skirts and ran toward the Wizard. Striped stockings hugged her legs as she raced, panicked toward Oscar. "NO! Don't!"

Glinda picked up her skirts and ran after the witch. She quickly gained on the older witch. Kally may have appeared young, but she could not compare with the much younger Glinda. With the Silver Slippers on her feet, she could have easily crossed the distance in less than a heartbeat, but, truthfully, she was insanely curious to see just what the Wizard was going to do.

Oscar pulled the cap from the bottle of unguent. He swirled the thick liquid around. He looked up to the sky in exhaustion. This was the end. No more pain. No more tears. Despite his best efforts, tears streaked his cheeks through the dirt.

"No more tears." He sobbed. The hurt echoed from deep in his soul.

Kally flung out her hand to pull the bottle away, but Glinda tackled Kally from behind, dragging her to the ground and interrupting her concentration her for a fraction of a single desperate second.

He threw his head back and quaffed the entire bottle.

"*NO!*" Both Glinda and Kally screamed as one.

"This is what the fighting is over." He swirled the few drops of liquid around in the square bottle. It was very nearly empty. "You two are fighting over this...but not really. *This* isn't really what this fight is about, is it?"

"What do you witches really want? *WHAT DO YOU WANT?*" Oscar screamed at them. Then he hiccupped and looked queerly at them and put his hand on his stomach. "I see...now, here at the end. You wanted *me*. But not me. You wanted what was up here." He tapped on his head. "You have no idea what is up here."

The ground shook beneath them, knocking some of the automaton warriors down off their feet. Oscar swayed unsteadily. The glaze on his eyes thickened and his voice grew slurry.

"What have you done, Oscar?" Glinda took a step toward Oscar, and the ground heaved beneath her feet.

Oscar gasped a choking laugh and stumbled as the world went crazy. "What have *you* done, Glinda? What have *you* done, Kally? I'll tell you. You were naughty. Both of you were very, very naughty. Wicked and naughty. Can a man rule himself? *Can a man rule himself?* I ruled myself!" He shouted. "I kept all of this *inside me!* It was under control until you set it free!"

The Land of Oz shuddered, and the valley quaked as hills sprung up all around them. Strange confectionary trees sprouted up from the ground. Distant mountains roared as they spun to life in the far distance.

"You stole my dreams! You are the monsters here, not your tiger-bears, not your magic pistols. YOU are the monsters! I kept my shadows hidden away inside. You go and drag nightmares out of other people. You stole my dreams. WHY?" His angry voice pleaded for understanding. "Why did you need what was inside me? Why did you need my nightmares?" Oscar fell to his knees as the sky darkened and churned above him. The vortex began.

Then Oscar pulled himself staggeringly upright and pointed a terrified finger of accusation. "They are coming out. Everything that I kept inside, good and bad—it's all coming out. This unguent, Kally—it brings the unliving to life—I think…I think that has killed us all."

"Oscar, we can save you. We can get you help." Glinda rushed toward him, but belching fire from a crack in the ground drove her backward.

"You are not my friends. YOU ARE NOT MY FRIENDS!" Oscar screamed. Then he stared through swimming eyes. "The show is over. The story has been told. There are no more dreams for Oz." He forced a sobbing laugh. "You know what, Glinda? The one question—the one question you never asked—"

Glinda's lower lip trembled. *What question?* Her eyes widened as she watched Oscar sway. Then his eyes lost all focus.

The Wizard collapsed.

As he hit the ground, the entire land erupted in chaos. What little control Oscar had maintained while he was conscious was now lost.

Glinda pulled on the Ruby Spectacles. She screamed in fear. All around Oscar, and spreading through the entire land as far as she could see, the raw dream magic thrust upward in chaotic geysers. The magic churned in raging torrents all over the land as Oscar's dreams and nightmares shattered and reconfigured and erased and rewrote the entire Land of Oz.

End of *Crown of the Dreamer*

To be continued in:

The Hidden History of Oz, Book Three: *Emerald Spectacles*

APPENDIX

TIMELINE

This timeline covers events both mentioned and experienced in **The Hidden History of Oz, Book One: The Witch Queens**, and **Book Two: Crown of the Dreamer**.

Events in this timeline are organized by the rule of the Kings of Oz. The Ozy year notation reflects the reckoning of the years in Oz since the establishment of **Ozma the First** as ruler over the Emerald Lands of Oz. This reckoning was adopted by other cultures as they assimilated into trade and relationships under the royal rule. Count of Oz years (Ozy).

Example: 1 Ozy / 685 AD / 1215 BDG

Where applicable, the years in common reckoning are included. The acronym BDG stands for *Before Dorothy Gale*, or the number of years before Dorothy Gale entered Emerald City in the story, *The Wonderful Wizard of Oz*. For reckoning purposes, the year that Dorothy entered the Emerald City is set at the year 1900, which equates to 1 ADG (After Dorothy Gale) Note that there is no year 0.

This timeline is limited to events mentioned or alluded to in the first two books of the Hidden History of Oz series. In addition, common knowledge of certain events is included. While there are many more additional significant events not yet written, a more complete timeline, including the entire reigns of all of the rulers of Oz can be found on the Hidden History of Oz blog: http://hiddenhistoryofoz.wordpress.com.

The Faerie War / Pre-King era
Sundering of Day and Night (Faerie War)
Arrival of Lurline's band of faeries to the land. Naming of the Land of Oz
Creation of the source of magic (the Emerald Engine) and the Giant Hourglass
Building of the Emerald Fortress. Construction began in 23 Ozy / 708 AD.

Reign of the Kings

King Oz, the First

(Coronation: 78 Ozy / 763 AD)

Founding of Central City in Emerald Valley (87 Ozy / 771 AD)
Construction completed on the Emerald Fortress (121 Ozy / 805 AD)

King Oz, the Third

(Coronation: 244 Ozy / 929 AD)

Creation of the City of Parradime, 294 Ozy / 978 AD. *Parradime* in the fairy tongue, or *Smaragaid Cathair* ("The Emerald City" in Gaelic or Old Ozzian.)

King Oz, the Eighth

(Coronation: 610 Ozy / 1294 AD)

First Witch Wars (616 Ozy - 644 Ozy)
Destruction of the City of Parradime (631 Ozy / 1315 AD)

Queen Ozma, the Fifth

(Coronation: 897 Ozy / 1580 AD)

Second Witch Wars (871 – 895 Ozy)
Witches seek the Queen of Dreams and use her power to slay the seas.
Creation of the Deadly Desert.
Destruction of Gilly city of Rokkamoorah
Gilly-kin Purge by Munch-kin
Great Battle in Valley of Cairn (887 Ozy / 1571 AD)

King Oz, the Thirteenth

(Coronation: 970 Ozy / 1654 AD)

Birth of Gayelette (1000 Ozy / 1685 AD)
Queen of Dreams visits Oz, to seek the heir of the Red Sorcerer

King Oz, the Sixteenth

(Coronation: 1086 Ozy / 1770 AD)

Discovery of Quelala in the South
Gayelette takes Quelala as her apprentice
Creation of the Golden Cap (1146 Ozy / 1830 AD / 70 BDG)
Marriage of Gayelette and Quelala (1147 Ozy / June 14, 1831 AD/69 BDG)
Ondri-baba receives the magic eye, and also the walking hut with the Sapphire Stove
City of Luneska falls into the desert
Birth of Glinda (1152 Ozy / October 19, 1836 AD / 64 BDG)
Mombi becomes a Witch
Kalinya throws her beau into the sky

Gayelette sells half of her kingdom to Kalinya for the price of a single large pearl
Enslavement of the Winged Monkeys

King Oz, the Seventeenth

(Coronation: 1154 Ozy / 1838 AD)

Smith & Tinker present the Hamstrambulator to King Winko

1168 Ozy / 1852 AD / 48 BDG

Events occurring in HH1: *The Witch Queens*.

Abracadabra Bazaar involving Glinda; Kalinya announces that Locasta is her apprentice
Disappearance of the Ruby Palace
Death of King Oz, the 17th

Pastoria, the Proud

(Coronation: 1168 Ozy / August 1, 1852 AD / 48 BDG)

Coronation of Pastoria
Glinda driven from the North
Battle of Winkie Plains; Arrival of the Wizard
Third Witch Wars begin; Discovery of Bloodsand
Destruction of North Village by Ondri-baba
Creation of the Sandy Army
Glinda settles in the South
Destruction of South Castle and the collapse of the Twisted Lighthouse
Disappearance of Quelala
Battle of Emerald Prairie
Kalinya becomes the Witch Queen and protector of the Munchkins; Battle of Munchkin Fields
Construction begins on Emerald City
Conquering of the Winkies by the Winged Monkeys; Ondri-baba "frees" the Winkies and becomes their Witch Queen
Glinda's sixteenth birthday. Banishment of Kalinya on a cloud by Glinda, the Good
Kalinya meets with Nikidik on Mount Munch

1170 Ozy / 1854 AD / 46 BDG

Events occurring in HH2: *Crown of the Dreamer*.

Sky Wizard's Ball
Great Rift in the sky
Creation of the Kalidahs
Creation of the Crown of the Dreamer
Battle of the Thunder Colossus; Wizard's Nightmare that reshaped Oz

1205 Ozy / 1889 AD / 11 BDG

Birth of Ozma Tippetarius, Wednesday, August 21, 1889. Her father is Pastoria.

1214 Ozy / 1898 AD / 2 BDG

Nick Chopper (Tin Woodman) and Captain Fyter (Tin Soldier) both receive their tin bodies.

1216 Ozy / 1900 AD / 1 ADG

Creation of the Scarecrow (May 5, 1900)
Arrival of Dorothy Gale at the Emerald City (May 11, 1900)

THE PLAYERS

Characters in the Story
Note: Most characters are known by their first names only in this story. Full names are given for reference purposes.

Glinda Mahalia Kookaburr—Young sorceress; ruler of the South
Oscar Zoroaster Diggs—The Wonderful Wizard
Wickrie-Kells Dunkle—Captain of the Fighting Girls; Glinda's best friend
"Omby-Amby" Ombrosius Ambrosius Cake—Soldier with Green Whiskers; Captain of the Emerald Guardsmen
Ola Serapenth Griffin—Herald to Glinda; singer
Kalinya / Kally Thistleswitch—Witch of the East
Ondri-baba Thistleswitch—Witch of the West
Mombi—Witch with transformation powers; advisor to King Pastoria; birth name Ozmombina Decheryon Lodoveen Carcose
Promethus—the Guardian of the Gate; former apprentice of Smith & Tinker; birth name Promethus Aronto Teague-Griffin
Ku-Klip Ravensnark—Tinsmith; former apprentice of Smith & Tinker
Professor Pipton Nikidik—Inventor and former apprentice of Smith & Tinker
Margolotte Munch—Wife of Professor Nikidik
Pastoria Mackoo Luneska Tonnason—King of the Emerald Lands; lives in Central City
Leina Le'Mo—Pastoria's Peacock Girl.
Queen of Dreams—Powerful Faerie; real name Ereline
King Klick—King of the Winged Monkeys
Docket—Son of King Klick, heir to the kingship of the Winged Monkeys
Duke Widdershins—Lukasio Markell Widdershins, King Emeritus of the Munchkins
"Boq" Lilboq Malarl Liyonechka—6 year old Munchkin boy.
Big Leebo—tall automaton created by Professor Nikidik
Little Pecan—fat automaton created by Professor Nikidik
"Perilous Eddy" Edvard Soperil Tiddlywink—Winkie, Tower-watcher and Architect-in-training
Toobalott Noone—Emerald City Deputy Guard
Kopp Quaint O'Teig—Young soldier and City Guard in the Emerald City
Rala Purity Sessefress—one of Glinda's Fighting Girls. She finds the Wizard in the forest.

Cornyss Waters—One of Glinda's Fighting Girls. She rescues Oscar's black pearl and gets trapped by the emerald spears.

Toro Plantain Cake—an Emerald Guardsman. Second-in-command and brother to Omby-Amby. He is leading the training mission.

Tjorn Kells Dunkle—Father of Wickrie-Kells

Donya Wickrie Prasen—Mother of Wickrie-Kells

Bartleby O'Brine—Captain of the Emerald Army in Central City

Eyve Munchina Yammersmith—A young teenage girl that wants to join the Fighting Girls. She has exceptional talent.

Characters mentioned in the story

Quelala Kookaburr—Father of Glinda

Gayelette Kronkob—The Ruby Sorceress, mother of Glinda

Locasta Dovina Brenfire—Witch; Guardian of the North; Former apprentice to Kalinya

Lurline—Queen of the Faeries

Red Sorcerer—Garren Kronkob, father of Gayelette

King Oz, the Sixth—Ruler of Central Lands from 421-488 Ozy; birth name Marcus Battlement Ysandrio Cornn (398 Ozy / 1082 AD to 490 Ozy / 1174 AD).

Solomon Sessefress—Poet in the reign of King Oz, the Sixth. Wrote *Song of Smaragaid Cathair*.

Eliyana and Korsovich—mother and father of Kalinya and Ondri-baba. Eliyana Thistleswitch was a powerful Witch. Korsovich Pyotr Munch was an esteemed Keeper of Knowledge.

Fighting Girls in Glinda's army—Corabinth Teague. LeeAnya Fourmiss.

Conroy Methuselah Diggs—one of Oscar's older brothers (not the shadows).

LOCATIONS

Locations mentioned in the story.

South—Quadling Country

Chronometria—Glinda's name for South Castle
Rose gardens
Ballroom
Glinda's Laboratory
Echo Chamber
Glinda's chambers
Scrapyard
Field of Hammer-Heads
Valley of Cairn
Humble cottage

Emerald Lands

Emerald City
Gate of Emerald City
Nebraska Tower—the tallest tower in the Emerald City.
Piper's Bridge—connects to the Nebraska Tower.
Crypt Tower—the second-tallest tower in Emerald City.
Wizard's Chambers
Sorceress Chambers
Ballroom with throne
Pandaemonium Chamber—the throne room of the Wizard.
Hanging Gardens
Guard's Barracks
Stable

Central City
Throne room
Kitchen
Mombi's tower
Honeycomb
Atrium of History
Home of Tjorn and Donya Dunkle

East—Munchkin Country

Mount Munch

The Scar—Chasm created when a powerful weapon was used against the enemies of the Munchkins.
Professor Nikidik's stone garden
Professor Nikidik's Laboratory—Contains veins of ruby and sapphire running through the mountain. There are pools of ruby.
Forest
House of the Witch
Farmer's Fields

West—Winkie Country

Yellow Castle
Throne Room
Stables
Hall of Mirrors
Dark labyrinth—training for soldiers.
Mirror labyrinth—training for kings.
Hearth room
Cylinders of History room—only truth echoes in this room. No lies can be spoken.
Winkie Plains
Mighty Miss Gulch
Borderlands
Forest

Historical locations mentioned in the story

Rokkamoorah—Gilly city that was destroyed
Parradime
Emerald Fortress
Across the desert, the home of the Queen of Dreams

SNEAK PREVIEW

The following is a sneak preview from **The Hidden History of Oz, Book Three: Emerald Spectacles**, due in print at the end of 2014.

All around them the land heaved and groaned as the unconscious nightmares shaped the Land of Oz into the imaginations of an angry wizard.

"He's not dead!" Promethus shouted.

Glinda and Kally glared at each other one last time then rushed to the fallen wizard's side. Promethus held both of his hands gently on Oscar's neck. "His pulse is getting weaker. He is not dead yet, but he is dying."

"We have to save him." Glinda dropped down beside Oscar and laid her head on his chest. "What can we do to save him? I can't let him go. Don't leave me, Oscar." The tears flowed down her cheeks. "I am sorry for all the questions I never asked you. Please don't leave yet. I have so many memories left to make."

Kally snorted and tried unsuccessfully to cover her mocking guffaw.

"So you are the Witch, Kalinya." Promethus said to Kally. "Your face is younger than I have seen it in years. I would not have known you from the pout of your lips. Your eyes, however, bear knowledge a sprig of a girl cannot begin to fathom. Amber eyes have always been the mark of your family."

"All those that mattered. Those that don't, simply don't." Kally curtseyed, displaying her striped stockings and the Silver Slippers.

"What happened to him? A spell?" Promethus asked.

"Unguent. Nikidik brewed it to bring the unliving to life. It has no name."

"No name means no antidote. There was nothing he mentioned at all? His vanity will not allow him to sit silent when he can boast."

Promethus glimpsed the flicker in Kally's eyes before she glanced away.

"Nothing." the Witch said.

"You remember." Promethus accused. "You hide your knowledge, but it is your undoing. If the Wizard dies, this destruction and change continues. Is there magic where he comes from? You had better hope so, because his soul is remaking this land in his image. All that he knows and has seen, or even imagined - nothing is withheld as he floats toward death's threshold. That is the final barrier. Once he is beyond that, our world will be forever changed. And if there is no magic in that world, you, Witch, will simply cease to be. The blood of life has long since fled your veins."

Kally held her hands up and Promethus' hand flew behind him toward the hidden pistol. "All right. Yes, I remember. He asked me something strange that did not mean anything at the time. If you have an answer that will save...all of us," Her eyes lingered on the Wizard longer than they should have. "He said it was the opposite of the Silence the Dreaming Within potion."

"Silence the Dreaming Within. I have not heard of that. Glinda, lassie, have you?"

Glinda shook her head. She brushed Oscar's hair back away from his closed eyes. His face was clammy under her hand. "What can we do?"

Kally lifted her skirts and stepped around the Wizard's body. The Silver Slippers on her feet twinkled in the unnatural firelight.

An idea brightened the Guardian's eyes. "You have the Silver Slippers."

Kally dropped her skirt hem back to the ground, covering the Silver Slippers from view. She warily sighted a spot on the distant horizon. "Yes."

"You can leave at any time. Why have you not?"

Glinda glanced up at Kally's puzzled stare. That was a question worth asking.

"I don't have to justify myself to you. I was concerned. The world is ending all around us."

Glinda stood to face Kally squarely. "You stayed. Whether from spite or love, don't deny it."

"I stayed. It's not like I had any choice. I'm not going to turn tail and let you keep the power."

Promethus smiled tightly. A twinkle shone in his eye. "Glinda, do you still have the Ruby Spectacles? We'll need them where we are going."

The young sorceress felt in her pocket for the magical spectacles. They were safe. "The magic is all around. The land isn't holding it anymore."

"It won't. Whatever control he had over his dreams is gone. That unguent is releasing and bringing to life everything that he dreamed or didn't allow himself to dream. The Land of Oz is reshaping itself into his image. Look around you—this is not normal. The land will destroy itself. His body is the only thing that is keeping the magic from taking on a life of its own. If he dies…"

"I heard what you told her. The Land of Oz dies, too. The magic is too wild. This raw magic was meant to be filtered. The land will tear apart if he dies."

"Yes."

"Do you know how to save him?" Kally asked.

Promethus looked down at the Wizard's pallid face. "No. But I know to keep him from dying."

Promethus removed his jacket and reached inside his shirt, pulling a large ruby amulet from next to his chest. As he removed it from contact with his skin, his soul-stirring gasp of pain startled both the Witch and the Sorceress. Promethus removed the amulet from its chain and placed the ruby amulet on Oscar's throat and pushed it down his shirt. "Live, Wizard, that this magic might calm itself."

Promethus slowly stood. He tucked the chain back into his pocket. Several gray hairs streaked his formerly black hair. His eyes sunk deeper into their sockets. "Look and learn, Witch. Has my face changed so little that you do not see the advancing of years in but a few seconds? If I can learn from the actions of the ancients, perhaps you can learn from me how to keep the Wizard from dying."

"That's impossible. Nobody can stop death. Gaylette is gone. Nobody has that power anymore." Kally scoffed.

"It was not Gaylette that had the power, but the power that she knew how to tap." Promethus said. He coughed, clearing his throat. "What happens every twenty-two years?"

Glinda shrugged.

"Of course you don't know. You're just a sprout." Kally said. "Every twenty-two years? I was not certain that it was so exact. I know only that it happens about every twenty to twenty-five years."

"What happens?"

"The Time of Reckoning." Kally said.

"Oh." Glinda said. "I read that the Kings Oz proved their immortal right to rule. But then with King Oz, the Seventeenth, something happened."

"For a time, death is suspended in Oz." Promethus explained. "During normal times, the Blood of Oz flows, and death is present in the land."

A memory came back to Glinda. "As long as the blood of the land flows, the Queen of Dreams cannot enter."

The older man's face turned pale. "Where did you hear that?" He demanded.

"I am a sorceress. A sorceress does not reveal her secrets."

"So be it." Promethus narrowed his eyes at Glinda. "But what flows? Time flows. Blood flows. The Blood of the Land flows. How is this measured? The Giant Hourglass. Every twenty-two years it turns over and begins anew. While it is turning, the blood is not flowing. Death cannot walk in Oz. In his place, the Queen of Dreams may walk freely, and her power may be exercised."

"An hourglass?"

"A giant hourglass." Promethus confirmed. "We'll have to convince the Guardians of Time to pause the flow."

"I don't think that will be necessary." Glinda said, beginning to see the plan forming. "I can turn over hourglasses. It is one of the spells my mother taught me."

Promethus' eyes brightened. "This may work, after all."

"Where is this Giant Hourglass?" Kally demanded.

"That is for me to know." Promethus said cryptically. "It is far away. That is all you need know." He extended both of his hands to the two girls. "I need both of you. To save the Land of Oz, we three must work together."

"I will not work with her. I don't trust her." Glinda protested.

"We are sworn enemies." Kally agreed.

"Who have gotten along well enough for the love of one Wonderful Wizard." Promethus interjected. To Kally, he said, "You have had ample opportunity to leave. Perhaps the Witch, Kalinya, would have left, but the girl, Kally, has stayed."

Great groanings shook the ground beneath their feet. Kally looked toward the shifting horizon, panicked.

"Do not leave." Promethus commanded. "If you leave, we all die. There is no place to hide. There is no cave deep enough, nor mountain high enough to escape this wild magic. You commissioned the unguent from Nikidik. This is your doing. However, you have the Silver Slippers, which makes you the only person in all of Oz that can get us to the Giant Hourglass before Oscar dies."

Glinda looked up for the first time since Oscar fell. The two armies were still battling. Their purpose was unchanged, though their leaders had reached an uneasy truce.

"I know the Silver Slippers have a charm. I can only hope that you know how the Silver Slippers work." Promethus asked the young Witch.

"Traveling here to there. Line of sight. I can go as far as I can see." Kally said. Promethus crouched down and lifted Oscar up on his shoulders. He grunted at the weight of the smaller man. "My back is not what it was five minutes ago. We need to get him somewhere safe, away from this battle." He pointed northward. "There is a deep forest over those hills. Can you take us to the north side? That should be far enough away from this to protect him."

Glinda picked up the fallen bottle of unguent. There were still several drops of the unguent left. She capped the bottle and put it into her pocket. As she dropped the bottle, she felt the tree seeds that she had received from Perilous Eddy in Emerald City the other day. A thought took hold, and a plan formed in her mind. "I'm ready. I think I know how we can protect him."

Kally reached out and took the hand of her sworn enemy, Glinda, and then took the hand of Promethus carrying the Wizard on his shoulders. They took one, two, three steps together, and they were gone.

The Hidden History of Oz, Book Three: Emerald Spectacles is due in print at the end of 2014. Watch for it on Amazon and wherever eBooks are sold.

GUIDE FOR PARENTS

Overview
This review is based on the format used by Common Sense Media (http://www.commonsensemedia.org). This is not an official Common Sense Media review. The author created this review to give parents an idea of what the book contained, to determine whether or not it would be appropriate for their children to read.

What parents need to know
Parents need to know that this book is part of a prequel series to L. Frank Baum's novel, *The Wonderful Wizard of Oz*. The character names are familiar, but the characters themselves are youthful and inexperienced. They make mistakes, get angry, and do things normal to young people, but very different from their older selves encountered in Baum's books. The story takes place in the year 1854 A.D., forty-six years before Dorothy enters the Emerald City. Oscar is the Wonderful Wizard, and he has established the Emerald City based on the foundations of liberty, freedom, hard work, and responsibility. Many people have come to the Emerald City because they want the freedom to live as they choose, but many have come simply because they want wealthy and feel like they should be in charge of things. They don't do much except follow social trends, attend parties, and congratulate themselves on being important. The author takes a low view of these type of self-congratulatory people.
The story is written at a fifth-grade reading level. The subject matter explores many emotionally heavy topics, such as loyalty, friendship, betrayal, manipulation, isolation, depression, fear, and loss. Young readers may identify with some of these topics as they are growing up. Oscar is the central figure in the story who experiences these things, and the other characters experience the strong emotions and life-changing events as they interact with him.
The characters of Glinda and Oscar were in love, and they still are, but they are very distant from each other. Oscar is building and ruling the Emerald City, and Glinda is building and ruling the land of the South. They don't see each other very often, and their expectations for their relationship lead to problems. In addition, Oscar suffers from sleep deprivation. He is starting to see hallucinations. The magic of Oz brings these hallucinations and dreams to life. Oscar is exhausted and does not think clearly. This makes him an easy target for other people who want to selfishly manipulate his power.
As a character, Glinda acts impulsively and makes many youthful mistakes, causing problems for everyone. This is intended to demonstrate the cause-and-effect consequences of actions. Mistakes made by one person often affect many people. Acting without full information, acting in anger, or acting to

manipulate others may cause problems that might not be immediately apparent. The story is an illustration of the many sides of the story experienced by one person. Only by understanding the different sides can you understand why things happened this way. In many respects, Glinda does not act like a hero. She is accused by another character of being "well on her way to becoming wicked." The characters are not divided into good-guys and bad-guys. Each character has their goals and motivations, and the story comes from the conflict of the characters taking action to accomplish their goals.

This book is the second of many planned stories in The Hidden History of Oz series. The main series is intended for readers age 10 and older.

Educational Value

This story is written at a fifth-grade reading level. For unfamiliar words, readers may want to use a dictionary, or figure the meaning out themselves through context.

Readers may be interested in comparing some parts of the story to L. Frank Baum's original novel, *The Wonderful Wizard of Oz*, to see how everything fits together.

This story is a prequel, or a story that comes before another already-told story. Comparing *The Wonderful Wizard of Oz* to this story gives many answers to questions that L. Frank Baum did not answer in his book.

The story explores emotionally heavy topics, such as loyalty, betrayal, manipulation of others, isolation, and depression. As characters deal properly and improperly with these situations, the reader is shown the results of these actions.

Depression causes (and can be caused by) isolation, fear, sleep deprivation, sadness, loneliness, and despair. As Oscar deals with each of these things, the characters around him at different times in the story try to help him or try to control him. His actions and responses are based on real-world experiences that the author has with these emotions. The hard things that Oscar goes through are intended to demonstrate the right ways and the wrong ways to deal with these conditions and situations.

Positive Messages

Much of this story deals with the consequences of hasty actions. Many of the characters are young, and act without thinking. The story illustrates the consequences of their actions, and how each action affects other people.

Omby-Amby is a good and loyal friend to Oscar. He puts the safety and well-being of his friend above his own. He works to help Oscar get through the darkness of depression and despair.

Oscar wants to help Glinda keep her promise to free the Winged Monkeys. His heart is in the right place in wanting to do good, but he allows himself to be manipulated, causing more problems.

Ola Griffin comforts Glinda when she is having a hard time. She finds ways to do good and be helpful through using her talents of singing and playing a musical instrument.

Positive Role Models
Eyve is a plucky young teen who believes in good. She believes in honesty, fair play, and loyalty. She is quick-thinking and solves problems.
Promethus is an older man who acts as a mentor to Glinda. His is very protective of Ola Griffin, and cares for her after her accident.
Oscar wants to help Glinda keep her promise to free the Winged Monkeys from slavery. If he can get the Golden Cap from the Wicked Witch of the West, he can give it to Glinda. Then she can free the Winged Monkeys. Though Oscar does not succeed in his goal, his intentions were good.
Kally cannot lie to her sister, Ondri-baba. Even though she is there to cause problems, she cannot lie to her.
Winged Monkeys always tell the truth. They are full of mischief, but they do not lie.
Mombi helps Glinda understand why the Wizard is troubled. She gives Glinda advice on how to deal with the Wizard's past.

Violence
A character uses a pistol from a nightmare to shoot automatons (robots) in the real world. Automatons fight with, and are destroyed by, human soldiers in battle. A monster injures several characters in battle. An important non-human character is shot with an arrow and stabbed in the back (to save another character). An inventor character creates a small magical creature out of shadow and then crushes it under his foot. A character falls halfway into a magic portal and receives deep scratches on her legs.
A character is encased in a magical trap like amber.
Monsters fight against human soldiers. Soldiers are injured in battle, and some die, but there is no gore or graphic depictions of violence.

Romance / Sex
Glinda feels jealous when Oscar looks at other girls. Glinda manipulates Oscar to try to make him love her. Oscar sees Glinda in the arms of an older man. He doesn't understand the situation, and he assumes that Glinda loves the man. Oscar asks Kally for a good-night kiss before he falls asleep. An older man and a young woman flirt. Omby-Amby and Wickrie-Kells get engaged to be married. Wickrie-Kells' parents make them sleep in separate bedrooms when they visit because they are not yet married.

Language
A character uses words like "pish-posh" and "fiddlesticks" when she is frustrated. Characters intentionally mislead other characters. Characters argue strongly with other characters, using emotional (but not profane) words.

Consumerism
A character purchases an army of automatons (robots) with pearls. Pearls are the most precious stone in the Land of Oz. Discussion of purchasing land and people with a giant pearl.

Drinking, Drugs, and Smoking
None.

What is the story?
Oscar Diggs, the Wizard, is the central figure in Oz. He has built the Emerald City through his dreams every night for the past two years. The people love him, and they constantly surround him. While he tries to please everyone, Oscar pushes himself too hard and gets exhausted. The magic of Oz brings his dreams to life. With sleep deprivation eroding his sanity, Oscar's dreams start to affect the waking world by bringing shadows to life. He is betrayed by one of his best friends, and rejects her to find companionship next to a new girl, Kally, who is really a Witch in disguise. Glinda searches the land for Oscar, but he is securely under the control of the Witch. After a poorly-planned attack on another Witch's castle, Oscar is recovered by Glinda's soldiers. Kally wants Oscar back, and commissions an inhuman army to battle Glinda's human soldiers to get him back. Oscar cannot think clearly. His delusions turn him against everyone, which leads to a cliffhanger ending.

Is it any good?
The adventures in the story are exciting, and the characters move the story along well. Each character has their own motivations, and each character's actions affect the other characters.

Glinda is the main character in this story. She starts out being self-centered and moody. As she searches for the Wizard, she learns more about his past and comes to understand him better. As the story progresses, she truly wants to help the Wizard and keep him near so that she can help him. Unfortunately, she does not ask him what he wants. Glinda makes decisions for most of the characters in the story, which creates a lot of conflict.

The themes of depression and dealing with the shadows of the past provide several points of view for dealing with these troubles. The characters all have to deal—in one way or another—with the Wizard's troubles.

The cliffhanger ending is abrupt and does not provide closure for the story. This may upset some readers.

Families can talk about

Glinda wants to control Oscar so that he will see just how lucky he is to have her. How does this attitude determine Glinda's actions? Is this an appropriate way for her to deal with other people? How does behavior affect those around Glinda?

Glinda hypnotizes Oscar to discover his deepest secrets. What problems does this create? Should one person manipulate another person when they are not thinking clearly? What problems can this cause?

At the beginning of the story, one character mentions that it has been six months since all of their friends have been together. Why is it important to maintain close contact with your friends? What happened in the story when friends did not stay close? How could things have been different?

Glinda is jealous of any other girls that Oscar looks at. This leads to Glinda punishing both Oscar and the girl (Ola) for the way that she feels. Is this appropriate? How should Glinda have dealt with her feelings of jealousy? What consequences came as a result of Ola's punishment? How could these have been avoided?

Glinda delays taking action on fixing Ola's punishment. What happens next? How could Glinda have acted differently? How do you think that would have affected her friendship with Ola?

Oscar accepts the companionship of Kally, a girl who manipulates him. Even though Oscar knows he is being manipulated, why does he stay with Kally? Why does Oscar work so hard for a person that he barely knows? Have you ever had a friend that manipulated you? How did it feel, and what did you do?

Oscar uses his talents of ventriloquism to navigate through the mazes. Why is it important to recognize our talents and skills? How can you use your talents and skills to solve problems?

Wickrie-Kells gets all of the Fighting Girls to swear that they will not look for love until Glinda and Oscar get together. What is the importance of an oath like this? Was this an appropriate situation in which to swear an oath? Should you take oaths seriously? Why or why not?

When Glinda finds Oscar again, she puts him in shackles (handcuffs). Was this a good solution? Why or why not? How could Glinda have approached the situation differently?

Glinda realizes the terrible power of the pistol. She knows that she is the reason that this weapon is in Oz. She buries the pistol. Is it possible to bury mistakes? How should you deal with mistakes? What could Glinda have done differently?

Book Details

Author	Tarl Telford
Genre	Fantasy / Adventure
Topics	Friendship, Adventure, Loyalty, Betrayal, Depression, Anger, Dreams, Isolation, Sleep Deprivation
Book Type	Fiction
Publisher	Emerald Engine Studios
Publication Date	September 10, 2013
Number of pages	341
Publisher's recommended ages	10 and up
Available on (platforms)	Paperback, Kindle, digital

ON THE WEB

The Hidden History of Oz blog
   http://hiddenhistoryofoz.wordpress.com

Contact the author
   Oz@tarltelford.com

Also available
   The Hidden History of Oz, Book One: The Witch Queens

   Paperback versions available on Amazon.com.
   Digital versions available on Amazon.com and wherever eBooks are sold.

CREDITS

Thanks to the following artists for use of their stock photography to create the cover:

Tiger Head
Animals___Tiger_9_by_MoonsongStock
http://www.deviantart.com/art/Animals-Tiger-9-117022575

Bear body
Stock_393__bear_2_by_AlzirrSwanheartStock
http://www.deviantart.com/art/Stock-393-bear-2-122914401

Tiger legs
strolling_tiger_by_dareisay3-d4n75qj
http://www.deviantart.com/art/Strolling-Tiger-280829899

Special thanks to Glinda for providing the cover image. Without you, The Hidden History of Oz would not be possible.

All images used with permission.

ABOUT THE AUTHOR

Tarl N. Telford (1976-) is a novelist, poet, playwright, screenwriter, and technical writer. Born the eldest of nine children, Tarl quickly found his place on the bookshelf next to the encyclopedias. After devouring the reference books, he moved on to science fiction, fantasy, westerns, weird fiction, and comics. Then he found more reference books on American history, psychology, game theory, ancient history, and many more.

Tarl annotated *The Wonderful Wizard of Oz* novel as part of an interactive app project. His research led to the creation of *The Hidden History of Oz*, a prequel series set in Oz fifty years before Dorothy. He has written multiple screenplays and stories that include magic, mythology, and the power of dreams. All of these elements are explored in the Hidden History novels.

Tarl is the author of 18 screenplays, two novels, several stage plays, and a few short stories. He is working on several additional novels and stories set in *The Hidden History of Oz*. *Crown of the Dreamer* is his second published novel.

He dreams big in a small town in Texas with his red-haired wife.

Made in the USA
Lexington, KY
31 August 2015